Even Exchange

HAILEY DICKERT

First released May 2025.

ISBN: 978-1-960497-09-3

Developmental Editing: Katie W.

Copy Editing: Katie W.

Proofreading: Caitlin Lengerich

Illustrated Cover: Katie Pridige

Published by Hailey Dickert

www.haileydickert.com

CRYSTAL BAY UNIVERSITY
BOOK THREE

Author's Note

In February of 2023, I began writing *Even Exchange*. The first version of it, anyway. Through the years of drafting, editing, and deleting—there was an entirely different story with these same characters—I wondered if I'd ever publish again.

But yet, here it is, finally, in your hands.

Whether I'm a new-to-you author, or you've been along for my entire journey, I'm so grateful you're taking the time to read a story about the girl who feels unlovable and the guy who thinks loving her is easy. Every single one of us is deserving of love—scars and all.

Just as in real life, these characters are flawed. They're not perfect. They make irresponsible choices or say the wrong things in the heat of the moment. As you know from the blurb, one of those choices leads to Charlotte getting pregnant.

While I fully believe discussing safe sex is sexy, it's also realistic these conversations aren't always had. And even more realistic that not having these conversations can lead to, well, an unexpected pregnancy.

Additionally, there are discussions of Charlotte's option for abortion. It is not discussed at length, and while she does ultimately decide to keep the baby, mentioning her freedom of choice was important to me.

Her body. Her choice.

While our reproductive rights are at a devastating risk, I imagined a world for Charlotte where she didn't have to worry about the legalities, but rather the decision was exactly that: hers. As it should be.

Even Exchange is the third book in the Crystal Bay University Series. It is written to be read entirely as a standalone. Because of this, there are certain situations from my previous books that are not mentioned. This is not a continuity error. I wanted to ensure anyone could read this story without spoiling the previous ones, and I hope lovers of my previous books can understand that choice.

Throughout this book, the beautiful Italian language and culture is incorporated. Sensitivity readers were used, and I have done my best to represent that heritage. You can also find an "Italian Glossary" on page 475 which has common phrases along with ones used throughout this book.

There are multiple sexually explicit scenes in this novel. For those of you who'd like to find (or avoid) the smut quickly, please see the "Dicktionary" on page 476.

This book contains serious topics that could be difficult for some readers. For a complete list, please see the "Content Warnings" on page 477.

To anyone who bears scars, whether on your heart or your skin.
May they serve as a reminder you survived.
I'm so happy you're still here.

Playlist

Stranger — Riley Roth
Please Please Please — Sabrina Carpenter
Bitter — Fletcher & Kito
Vanilla — Avery Anne
Cry Pretty — David J
Circles — Post Malone
Red Wine Supernova — Chappell Roan
Dandelions — Ruth B.
Wish on an Eyelash Pt 2. — Mallrat & The Chainsmokers
On Your Way Home — Patrick Droney
Friends Don't — Maddie & Tae
How Do I Do This — Kelsea Ballerini
Greenlight — Tate McRae
Damn — Trey Rose
2 hands — Tate McRae
dandelion — Ariana Grande
back to friends — sombr
Constellations — Jade LeMac
Let's Fall in Love for the Night — Finneas
Capri — Colbie Caillat
Lady — Brett Young
Before You Leave Me — Alex Warren
dead the day ur gone — Matt Hansen

Perfect to Me — Michael Sanzone
If It Weren't For You — Finmar
Like It's His Job — Morgan Johnston
Easy to Love — Kyle Schuesler
Definition — Finmar
Like the Water — Patrick Droney
Yellow — Coldplay
Always Been You — Michael Sanzone
All She Wants Is The Moon — Jordan Brooker
Cosmic Love — Florence & the Machine
For My Daughter — Kane Brown
To The Men That Love Women After Heartbreak — Kelsea
Ballerini
Stargazing (Moonlight Version) — Myles Smith
Slow It Down — Benson Boone
Love Me Back - Max McNown

PROLOGUE

I expected blood, just not *so* much of it.

Although it's hardly a fraction of the amount he's spilled.

My hand trembles, the gun's cool metal a stark contrast to my volcanic veins.

Any remnants of guilt have dissipated.

After all, this was *his* fault.

He came here.

He pressed the pistol to her temple with a vow of vengeance.

He laughed when I begged him to stop.

Regret should be racing through me.

At the very least, remorse.

Instead, all I feel is relief.

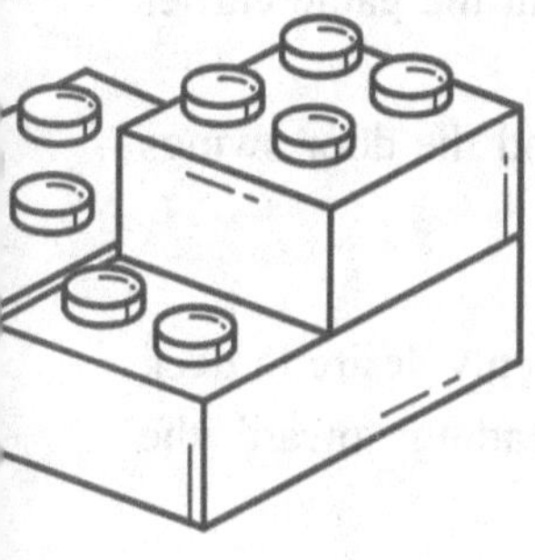

1

NOAH

Halloween

If this sorry excuse of a man opens his mouth one more time, the remaining ounce of my control will break. Scratch that—it'll shatter into eight billion pieces because there's no way Jonathan said the words "Charlie has to learn when she's hit her limit" after forcing fourteen shots of vodka down her throat.

My gaze fixates on the bathroom door Charlotte disappeared through, her disco ball costume scattering light around the room as she went.

Is she okay?

Jonathan mumbles another idiotic, unintelligible comment, the smug look on his face begging to be beat right off. Although, considering I'm a black belt in Taekwondo, they'd probably deem my fists lethal weapons, and I'm really not in the mood to go to jail. Again.

I grit my teeth so hard my jaw aches. Nothing angers me more than a man, or in this case a little bitch boy, who disrespects their partner.

Elijah, my backup quarterback and best friend, nudges me, our eyes connecting as he shakes his head in warning.

He's right. Some bottom-feeding fuck boy won't be the reason I mess up my hand and risk my entire career. *Pretty hard to throw a football with broken knuckles.* Not to mention, I'm still relatively sore from getting the shit knocked out of me in the game earlier tonight.

A few girls exit the bathroom, laughing, and the door swings shut. No sign of Charlotte.

Screw this.

My desperation to check on her overpowers my desire to deck this douchebag, so I drag myself away, heading toward the women's restroom.

What the hell are you doing, Caruso?

Reaching out, I grip the door handle.

She's not your problem.

Slipping inside, I ignore the girls primping, although they certainly notice me, and scan the ground for Charlotte's tall sparkling boots. Scattered geometric light reflects under the handicapped stall, and a bear-like growl paired with a half sob reinforces my suspicions.

The door is partially open, and I peek hesitantly inside. *It's her.* Releasing a breath of relief, I join her, flicking the lock. Crouching down, I place a hand on her back. She sighs, gripping the toilet bowl as I rub soft circles, unsure of what to say.

Hey. Your prick boyfriend wasn't going to come, and I didn't want you to be alone. So here I am.

We sit in silence, nothing but the—*Oh fuck. She's doing it again.*

I gather her brunette hair together, but it's a lost cause. This little disco ball needs a shower. Stat. My eyes drop to the pinkish linoleum stained with dirt, the remnants of spilled cocktails, and who knows what else. A shudder racks through me. On second thought, I need a shower myself. Immediately.

"Jonathan," Charlotte groans, and I freeze. "Take me home."

She thinks I'm her shitbag boyfriend. Of course she does. Because he *should* be the one here making sure she's okay. Not me. Not the guy who's barely spoken to her—*but been obsessed*—since her arrival at Camp Dickson this past summer.

Charlotte was new. I'd never noticed her before. Not around Crystal Bay University, and certainly not around the training camp. I was halfway to asking her name when Mr. Fuck Face came up, scooping her into his arms. It was clear she was taken.

But that was fine. I didn't need the distraction.

"Please?" she adds, and her tone alone makes *me* sick.

I clear my throat. "I'd be happy t—"

Her gaze jerks toward mine, brown eyes wide. "Noah?" Her hands fly to her hair as she brushes through it, peering down at herself. "I'm sorry I—"

"Don't apologize," I interrupt.

"Honestly," she slurs, releasing a slow, shaky exhale, hands dropping to her lap. "I don't care." She scoots back, leaning against the wall beside the toilet. "But I wanna go. Can you get Jonathan?"

Fuck no. "Okay."

Reluctantly, I exit the bathroom in search of him, hands only unclenching when I realize he's nowhere in sight. Elijah and his girlfriend Sophia, who's one of Charlotte's best friends, are near the bar, faces flustered.

"Where's Jonathan?" I ask begrudgingly.

"He left," Sophia supplies with an eye roll.

"Without Charlotte?" I press, not shocked by the news.

"Yep," she snarks, tipping a glass toward me.

Elijah raises his brows with a shrug. "Trash took itself out."

"She okay?" Sophia asks, setting her blue drink down on the bar. "I should go check."

"It's your birthday," I remind Sophia. "I'll make sure she gets home safe."

"You really don't mind?" Sophia presses.

"Not at all."

"Okay." She smiles gratefully. "Thanks."

After pulling out my phone, I order an Uber to Charlotte's place so we can leave as soon as possible.

Estimated arrival: twelve minutes.

"See you," I tell them and head back to the bathroom.

Charlotte's shimmering body remains slumped against the wall, her eyes shut. Crouching down, I place a finger under her nose, verifying proof of life, and conclude she's utterly wasted. After sliding an arm around her back and another under her legs, I lift her off the ground.

Please don't puke on me.

When I nudge the stall door fully open, she awakens slightly, nuzzling her face into my chest. *I've got you.* I ignore the onlookers all the way to the Uber.

Twenty minutes later, we're before Charlotte's door, her body tucked bridal-style in my arms. She slept most of the way, but I did wake her up to obtain a room number and key. The same key I'm awkwardly unlocking the door with while trying not to drop her. *No, Charlotte. I'm not sure how you got that bump on your head.* It clicks open, and I bring us inside, then nudge it quietly shut with my foot. I flick on the light with my elbow, revealing a quaint little space. There's a small kitchen, living area, and three separate bedrooms. Given one of the doors is adorned with a big letter C, I assume it's Charlotte's and head straight for it.

My assumptions are confirmed upon opening the door. Photos of Charlotte and two little kids, presumably her siblings, adorn the nightstand, along with a few others of her and Sir Fuck Face. I choose to ignore those, making my way to her bed and gently setting her atop the pink comforter. The shower will have to wait because she certainly can't stand, and stripping her down and helping her—although I'm not against it—seems like crossing a definite line.

My eyes trail her body—*she's so beautiful*—finally landing on heeled glitter boots that wouldn't be very comfortable to sleep in. Gripping the top of the boot, I slide the zipper down and tug it off. She wiggles her toes, and I chuckle, knowing she'll thank me for this in the morning.

Hopefully… if she remembers.

Her boots land on the floor with a thud, and I grab a small trash bin from next to the desk and place it on her nightstand. My eyes fall to chestnut hair fluttering across the pillow, her chest gently rising and falling in a rhythmic pattern.

Her shoulders jerk, and my heart rate spikes. *Is she having a seizure?* She shoots upright and flies off the bed, sprinting to the bathroom.

It's going to be a long night.

Charlotte takes deep breaths, back flat against her bathroom wall. She's bounced between there and hugging the toilet bowl the entire night. I'm on the opposite side, eyes shut given it's six in the morning and we've barely slept.

"How did I get out of the bar?" Charlotte asks, and my eyes pop open. It's the first time she's spoken in hours, but that question sounds deliberate. Like she's been ruminating a while before surrendering and asking me. Her soft brown eyes meet mine, lips pursed. "I don't remember."

"Yeah, you were pretty out of it," I say gently. "I carried you."

"You *carried* me?" She groans and slowly rests her head back against the wall.

"Yep."

"Why?"

My brows squish together. "Because you were asleep?"

"Sorry you had to do that," she murmurs, eyes dropping to her hands as she picks at her fingernails.

Someone had to. "I didn't mind."

"Jonathan texted me that Sophia kicked him and Seth out. So thanks for coming to my rescue."

I fight the urge to roll my eyes. Yeah, *that's* why he wasn't there.

"No problem," I grumble, trying to keep the bite out of my tone.

She blows a raspberry. "Hopefully no one posted photos of you carrying me out."

My eyes find hers again. I hadn't even considered that.

A headline flashes before my eyes: "Star Quarterback Drugs Cheerleader and Kidnaps Her," paired with a photo of the cute little disco ball passed out in my arms as we left the bar.

Then they'll dig into my past, and while certain files are sealed… if there's a will, there's a way.

"Why?" I ask, rubbing my knuckles against my stubble, heart rate picking up to a gallop.

"Because my mom would have a meltdown."

"Your mom?" I assumed she was worried Jonathan would see and be pissed I was holding his girl.

Maybe he shouldn't have left her.

"Do you know who Georgia Benson is?" she asks, voice scratchy from the night's events.

"The one running for Governor?" My mind races at the realization. Charlotte Benson. Georgia Benson. Of course. "Isn't your family, like…?" I feel like it's a rude question, and my words stumble.

"Mega uber rich?" she supplies, pausing and closing her eyes. She swallows hard, and after what I assume is a wave of nausea passes, she says, "Yeah."

"But you seem so *normal*," I say, despite having no authority to judge. I'm well aware people aren't always what they seem.

"Because I didn't grow up mega uber rich," she says. "My family didn't have access to the Benson wealth until a few years ago."

"I'm surprised no one realizes you're part of that family." *I sure didn't.*

"It's purposeful." She shifts in place. "I want to have a normal college experience like everyone else. If people realized I was *that* Benson, they wouldn't look at me the same."

"I get it." And I do. Because if people knew my family history, they'd certainly stop thinking I'm this perfect pretty boy who gets everything handed to me on a silver platter. But to be honest, I prefer their assumptions over the reality. "That explains why you've never mentioned your mom before."

Her eyes narrow on mine. "I didn't realize you've been paying attention to the things I do or don't mention."

Shit. Be cool, Caruso.

This woman doesn't need to know just *how* much I've paid attention when seeing her around at camp, and practice, and parties, and in line at Crystal Coffee while she chats with her friends about topics I definitely shouldn't be privy to.

"I've seen you around," I say coolly.

"Apparently more than I realized."

A fluttering feeling settles in my gut. I bring a hand to the back of my neck and rub against the tight muscles. "So, back to your mom."

She slumps against the wall. "Do we have to?"

"No, but I'm a pretty good listener."

"Fine." Charlotte sighs. "She tries to control every aspect of my life. And getting shit-faced at some crappy college bar would *not* be on her list of approved extracurriculars."

"You're eighteen. Shouldn't she—"

"Nineteen," she corrects. "Didn't you learn that during your extensive research?"

My cheeks flush, and I glare at her. "Looks like the alcohol's wearing off and your sass is back." She sticks her tongue out at me. "Well, since you're *nineteen,* shouldn't she be okay with you having some normal college experiences?"

Her teasing grin turns to a frown. "She doesn't care about me getting any of those. My job is to graduate, go to law school, play the part of the All-American daughter, and keep my mouth shut so she can win this election."

"That hardly sounds fair."

Charlotte shrugs. "Such is the life of a politician's daughter."

Her nonchalance, like she's already accepted her fate, has a stinging sadness surrounding my chest. "I'm sorry."

"Not your fault." She picks up the water bottle beside her and takes a long pull before setting it back down with a *clunk.*

"Why does she even want to be in politics?" I ask.

"What, are you writing an article?"

"No," I say, holding up a hand. "What I mean is, considering how wealthy your family is, why bother?"

"She was in politics as long as I can remember. But after getting the inheritance, she started making bigger plans. More money, more power, I guess. My grandma had only been dead a month when Mom announced her run for governor."

"Were you and your grandma close?" I ask, absentmindedly touching the gold chain around my neck and toying with the little ring and *cornicello* pendant.

"Not really, but we had some good memories." She smiles softly, her eyes meeting mine. "Enough that I miss her. Not enough that it broke me."

"I get that."

"So, what's your story?" she asks, apparently ready to be out of the hot seat.

"My story?"

"Yeah." She forces a teasing smile. "Who *is* Noah Caruso, team captain and CBU football royalty?"

I huff a laugh, pride filling me at her mention of my captain title. "Is that how you think of me?"

"Me?" she scoffs, placing a hand over her chest. "No. But it is how girls on campus talk about you." Her voice rises an octave. "Did you see Noah's new haircut? He's sooooo hot. I'd choke on his meatballs anytime."

"What?!"

"Pretty sure it was some Italian reference regarding your—"

"Got it." I cut her off, the need for us to discuss my Italian balls highly unnecessary. "Well, football *royalty* seems a bit exaggerated."

"Oh god." She groans. "He's humble too?"

"What can I say?" I flash a grin her way. "I'm a team player."

"Okay then, *Captain* Caruso. What's your story?"

My chest tightens. "I don't have one."

"Bullshit." She narrows her eyes on me, and for a moment, it's as if she can see straight through me. Directly through the perfectly put together, always in control mask I wear so no one will discover the real me. "Everyone has a story."

Sure, but a drunk heart-to-heart at dawn is hardly the time. She doesn't seem to be taking no for an answer, so I do what I always do and default to my comfort topic. "I've been obsessed with football my whole life. Decided one day I'd go pro and wouldn't let anything or anyone get in the way of that."

"Why'd you pick CBU?"

"My mom lives in Tampa." I twist the *cornicello* pendant between my fingers again. "I wanted to be close if she needed me."

"*And* you're a mama's boy?" She huffs a laugh. "I'm not shocked."

"What's that supposed to mean?"

"Just everything about you is Mr. Perfect." *She thinks I'm perfect?* "Of course you'd want to be near her."

If only she knew my need for proximity is vital, not a virtue.

"You have a lot of preconceptions about me, considering we've barely spoken."

"I already told you." A sweet, teasing grin graces her lips. "The cheerleaders *love* talking about Football God, Legend, and *Mama's Boy* Noah Gabriel Caruso."

My mouth falls open. "How do you know my middle name?"

"Don't flatter yourself." She cocks a brow. "It was in a *Sports Illustrated* article last month."

The corners of my lips quirk into the smallest of smiles. I am *definitely* flattered. "You read the article about me?"

She rolls her eyes. "Maybe not so humble after all."

"So I'm Riemann's quarterback?" I ask, referring to the math problem that's never been solved, unable to wipe the satisfied grin off my face. "You admit you're trying to figure me out?"

Her cheeks flush. "That's not what I said."

"Fun fact: you can win a million dollars if you solve an equation with Riemann's hypothesis."

She buries her face in her hands and grumbles, "I will *give* you a million dollars to stop talking about math."

"Keep your money, rich girl," I say, and she glances up, shooting dagger eyes. "We'll circle back in a few days."

"Can't wait." She cracks a smile, gaze holding mine, and sighs. "I suppose I should say thank you."

"For?"

"All of"—she waves a hand at the room—"this."

"It was nothing."

"It may have been unexpected... but it certainly wasn't nothing."

I shift against the hard floor. My ass is so numb at this point, I barely feel it. "Can I ask you something?"

"Sure."

Given her soft expression, I consider changing my question, but the exhaustion and emotions of the night loosen my tongue. "Why are you still with that guy?"

She frowns, eyes hardening. "You wouldn't get it."

"Try me."

"He's just..." She wraps her arms around her legs. "I love him."

"Even though he treats you like shit?"

Her head snaps toward me. "What would you know about how he treats me?"

"He did leave you *wasted* at a bar." Anger thrums through me. She mutters a curse, pushing to stand, and I follow her lead as she rushes out of the bathroom and into the living room. "Not top-tier boyfriend material," I press.

She spins to face me. "Sophia made him leave, remember?"

"Jonathan's an adult, and Sophia's not his boss. If he wanted to take you home, he would have." My jaw clenches. "But he didn't. He left."

"Easy for you to say," she says with an eye roll.

"What's that supposed to mean?"

"I'm sure no one's ever thrown you out of anywhere."

"Yeah," I scoff. "Because I'm not an asshole."

She flings an arm toward the front door. "You should leave."

"I wasn't trying to upset you," I say, lowering my tone, stepping towards her, and she retreats.

Noted.

Rule number one: don't touch Charlotte.

"No, but you are trying to tell me how to live my life," she huffs. "Like *everyone* else does."

"I'm trying to make you realize you deserve better than that shitbag." *So much better.*

Her face flushes, muscles tense. "Jonathan is a good person."

I snort a laugh. "Yeah, if the scale is from asshole to serial killer, sure, he's a good person."

Her mouth falls open. "You know wh—" A pounding at the door cuts off her retort. She stares at it, as frozen as I am.

Another pound is paired with a muffled, "Charlie, it's me."

"*Porca troia,*[1]" I mutter under my breath. The perfect addition to this conversation has arrived.

"Great," Charlotte grumbles, walking to the door and swinging it open.

Jonathan rushes inside. His eyes meet mine, and he halts in place. "What the *fuck* are you doing here?" he snaps.

"Apparently, your job," I reply, arms folded over my chest, trying to suppress the hatred inside me.

"Excuse me?" he asks, coming closer.

"Jonathan!" Charlotte snaps as he stands right before me, seething. "Calm down."

"Calm down?" Jonathan asks, turning his attention to her. "I drove across the state to spend a night with you, only for you to spend it with"—his gaze finds mine again, and he pokes my sternum—"this guy?" He's quick to anger. *Is he worse to Charlotte when no one's around?*

"This guy"—I nudge him away from me—"wasn't going to leave a drunk woman on the bathroom floor of a bar. She needed someone to help her."

"She's not yours to take care of." His face flushes, and he shoves my shoulders. "She's mine."

"That's funny. Because *I* was the one who carried her home last night."

"I bet you were thrilled to swoop right in, weren't you?" Jonathan snaps, starting towards me again, and my body courses with heat.

"I see a fumble, I take possession."

"Stop it!" Charlotte shouts, pulling him back by his shoulder.

"Why?" he barks at her. "So you two cheating motherfuckers can return to whatever the hell you were doing before I showed up?"

He better watch his damn tone.

---

1. IT: *Porca troia* - EN: Holy shit

"Cheating?!" Charlotte shrieks and grabs her head, wincing. "Nothing happened between us," she says quieter, with a sigh.

"Bullshit," Jonathan mutters.

"Think whatever you want," I say, shaking my head. "She was puking all night, and I stayed to make sure she didn't suffocate in her own vomit. You're welcome."

"Well, I'll take it from here," he says with a smug smile, putting an arm around my shoulders and dragging me towards the door. Rage rolls off me in waves, and I shake him off, my attention turning to Charlotte, our eyes meeting.

"Do you want me to leave?" I ask her.

"Get. Out," Jonathan snarls, the door creaking open behind me.

My gaze doesn't leave Charlotte as my pulse pounds in my ears. "Are you okay with him?"

"The fuck's that supposed to mean?" Jonathan demands. "Of course she is." He looks to Charlotte. "Tell him, babe."

She shifts from one foot to the other. "I'll be fine, Noah." My eyes bounce between them, and she softly adds, "You should go."

Bile rises in my throat at the idea of leaving her alone with this guy. I don't know him. What he's capable of. All I know is he's a prick and has a temper. But Charlotte needs to see when she speaks, I listen. Even if I don't agree.

Reluctantly, I slide on my shoes, grab my phone and keys off the counter where I left them last night, and turn to her.

"If you need me, you know where to find me," I say, hoping my eyes express everything I can't. *That conversation wouldn't go very well right now.*

"She won't," Jonathan says as he shoves me out, and slams the door in my face. Within seconds, yelling begins on the other side. I lean my forehead against the door, blowing out a breath.

Is she safe with him?

Would he raise his hand to her?

Would she tell anyone if he did?

I remind myself not everyone is like my father.

And as Jonathan said, she's not mine.
So why do I care this fucking much?

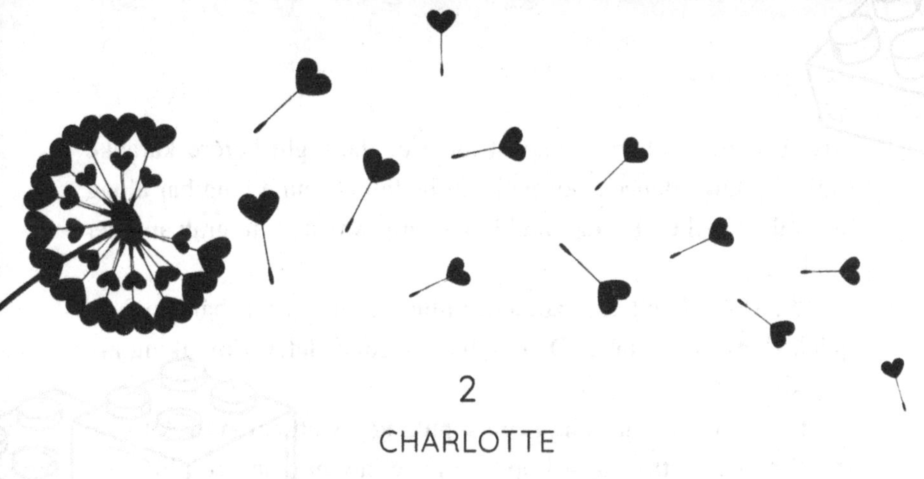

2
CHARLOTTE

Spring Break - Five Months Later

Eleven football players belting boozy karaoke is definitely better than one.

The entire offensive line from Crystal Bay University occupies the spacious stage of the Miami bar. Their screeching voices are drowned out by the crowd singing along from the dance floor, myself included. Because let's be honest, anyone who doesn't know the words to Taylor Swift's "Love Story" is a walking red flag.

And I like to keep mine safely out of sight.

The place is packed, which is no surprise considering spring break is the busiest—*craziest*—time of the year. When we arrived, the line was down the street, and I was skeptical they'd let us all in. Then Theo Schroeder—running back, pretty boy, self-proclaimed sex god, and for lack of better judgment, my friend—made a call. Two minutes later, the velvet rope dropped and we made our way inside.

It's notably nicer than our shitty, sticky bars at home. There's a private lounge where we spent most of the night before karaoke started, a huge dance floor with strobe lights, and a long bar along the wall. My throat is dry, and I make my way over to grab another drink.

"Merlot," I tell the bartender after settling on a bar stool. A quick show of my fake ID, and thirty seconds later, I'm taking my first sip.

The bridge of the song begins, pulling my attention back to the stage to see all the guys drop to a knee, holding an invisible ring box up at Noah Caruso, their team captain and CBU's star quarterback. I can't help the laugh bubbling out of me at the sight of him throwing a hand across his chest, playing along with the "proposal." He is never living this down. I'll make sure of it.

A buzzing in my lap pulls my attention to a new notification.

JONATHAN

Still at Ken's Karaoke?

ME

Yeah, thinking of giving my rendition of "My Heart Will Go On"

JONATHAN

You'll put Celine to shame

ME

Word on the street is she's already looking for a new career path

You sure you won't make it out tonight?

JONATHAN

Yeah, I gotta study for this test

I groan down at my phone. The university my boyfriend goes to already had their spring break, so we couldn't spend it together. Fortunately, my friends wanted to party like it's Coachella within a thirty-minute drive from his apartment, so I've seen him a few times.

> **ME**
>
> Okay :(
>
> See you tomorrow for brunch?

> **JONATHAN**
>
> Definitely

> **ME**
>
> Love you

> **JONATHAN**
>
> Love you too

"No vodka tonight?" Noah asks, pulling my gaze from the phone to his piercing green eyes.

"Never. Again." I glare, and he laughs. After the Halloween shit show, I swore off the clear poison for life. A not-so-fun fact Noah is well aware of considering that poison is the reason we became friends. And when Noah Caruso adds you to his roster, you're set. He's the guy you can call for *anything*. At any time of day.

Not that I ever have.

Asking Noah for help would only perpetuate my boyfriend's unnecessary insecurities, which is why we mainly interact during group activities like parties, games, and events.

Jonathan almost spontaneously combusted when he heard Noah would be on my spring break trip, but our relationship is built on trust, so he agreed I could go.

"Enjoy our performance?" Noah asks.

"I definitely didn't have CBU Offensive Line Eras Tour on my spring break bingo card, that's for sure."

He grins ear to ear. "It was good, right?"

"As if *you* need your ego stroked," I toss back with raised brows.

"Come on," he presses, placing his arm loosely on the back of my bar stool. He's not remotely close to making contact with my skin, yet it tingles with awareness. "Admit you enjoyed it."

"Fine." I smile sweetly, shifting in place. "It was *almost* as good as Elijah's serenade to Sophia." He gave a very drunk, adorable, actually impressive rendition of "Your Man" by Josh Turner, and they disappeared immediately after.

I love the stability of a long-term relationship but can't deny there are times I envy their obsession. Their need for each other no matter where and when.

The most spontaneous Jonathan and I get is when we have sex before date night instead of after.

"Almost?" Noah places his free hand on his chest. "Our choreographed routine totally topped Elijah's solo." Another song begins, and he bends to my ear so our conversation doesn't get lost in the loudness of the room. "Admit it, Charlotte."

Charlotte.

No one calls me Charlotte. Not even my parents. Ever since I can remember, I've been Charlie Benson. My mom even wrote it that way on paperwork, which is why when I was fourteen, I ended up in the boys' cabins at summer camp. They were thrilled, but unfortunately for them, it was short-lived when the cabin counselor walked in and asked why the hell I was there.

"Whatever, Noah *Gabriel*," I counter, sipping my wine, the liquid calming my nerves.

What's with the nerves?

"How'd Nash's Taekwondo competition go last weekend?" he asks, referring to my six-year-old brother.

"It went well," I say, beaming. "He got a participation trophy and everything."

"That's great." Noah lets out a warm laugh. "And Denny's gymnastics meet?" he asks, now referring to my other sibling, and Nash's twin sister.

Damn, does this man pay attention.

"She did good," I tell him. "Got first in beam for her age group."

"That's awesome!" Noah says, removing his arm from my chair to signal the bartender. *Finally, I can breathe again.*

"Yeah, she loves it," I say. "And I'm glad comps keep them busy."

Keeps them *distracted* is what I don't say.

"Well, at least you'll see them this weekend," Noah reminds me, and my mood instantly brightens.

"I can't wait. We're gon—"

"Excuse me," a feminine voice interrupts on the opposite side of Noah.

He turns, and a redhead who looks like she walked off a Miami Swim Week runway comes into view. "Yes?" Noah replies.

"Are you Noah Caruso?" she asks.

A smug smile graces his lips. "I am."

Welp. His ego's officially been stroked.

"Can I buy you a drink?" she offers with a lazy smile, and my lips roll together.

"I appreciate the offer," Noah says. "But no thanks."

My eyes bolt to my hairline, and I force them down.

"No?" she repeats, her smile faltering. Fortunately for her, I'm wingwoman of the week.

"He's kidding!" I tell her, side-eying Noah while leaning on the bar for a better line of sight. "Playing hard to get." I throw a thumb his way. "You know how these cocky little athletes are."

Noah grips the back off my chair, spinning me toward him, and my stomach drops as our eyes meet. "Little?" he scoffs, fighting a smile. *Breathe, girl!*

"Don't get your jock strap in a twist," I choke out, waving him off, returning my attention to the redhead. "He'd love one."

"Thank god." She places a hand on her chest. Her very large, very voluptuous chest. "I'd be mortified telling my friends the hottest guy here turned down a *free* drink from me."

"Come on," Theo says, butting in and throwing an arm around Noah. "He's clearly in second place."

Time to make my exit.

I hop off the bar stool, my body gliding past Noah's to leave.

"Where are you going?" he asks, and our eyes meet. His expression is unreadable. My stomach burns. *Maybe I shouldn't have drank that last merlot.*

"Don't want to be a cockblock," I say with a wink and half-hearted smile, then slip away, his gaze searing my back my entire walk to the lounge.

I spot Sophia and Elijah, along with Sage, another close friend of mine, and her "friend" Julian. I consider joining them but don't want to be a fifth wheel. I also don't want to kill their fun. Every time I hang out with Sophia, it feels off. Which I guess is my fault, considering what happened with her ex-boyfriend, Seth. Part of me does wonder how a good guy like Jonathan could even remotely sympathize with that dirtbag.

I swallow down the unwanted memories. Any desire I had to party has fluttered away like a dandelion in the wind.

"Hey!" There's a tap on my shoulder, and I turn to find Jonathan's roommate, Eric. He scoops me up in a hug, and I feel tiny in his strong linebacker arms. "Thought you left already."

"Tomorrow," I say, pulling away.

"Having fun tonight?"

"Yeah." I force a smile, the truth on the tip of my tongue.

"Bullshit," he says, digging in his pocket and pulling out his room key. Apparently, my frustration is obvious. "Why don't you go surprise Jonathan?"

"You don't think he'll mind?" I ask, hopeful.

"Nah," he says, winking. "I think he might have been expecting you anyways. He had his date night playlist on when I left."

"Okay," I say, adrenaline rushing through me.

See? I can do spontaneous.

He places the key in my hand. "Have Jon text me when it's safe to return."

"Will do." I wave. "See you later."

"There you are!" Sophia says, her cheeks flushed as she stumbles into me for a hug, her blonde hair surrounding me.

"Hey." I give her a squeeze, forcing down the pang of guilt for what I'm about to say. "I'm heading out."

"What?" She pulls back. "Why? We can go dance." Her expression turns apologetic as she looks at Elijah, then back to me. "I'm sorry I—"

"No." I shake my head, smiling. "It's not you. I miss Jonathan. Gonna go see him."

Her positive expression falls. "Char."

"Please, save the lecture," I beg, knowing how much she and Sage—and the rest of our friends, for that matter—can't stand Jonathan. Which is probably the real reason he's not here, since they make him feel so unwelcome.

I'll talk to them about it tomorrow.

"I'm not lecturing," she protests. "I just don't want you to get hurt."

"I appreciate that," I say, squeezing her shoulder. "But I'm going."

"Fine." She presses her lips together. "But be careful, okay?"

"You too." I give her a hug, wave at the others, and make my way out of the club.

Forty minutes and an outrageously expensive Uber later, I'm entering the lobby of Jonathan's apartment building, a Chinese takeout bag swinging from my fingertips. The elevator carries me to the fourth floor, and I bounce anxiously on my heels. A *ding* paired with the opening *whoosh* of the doors, and I'm striding down the empty hallway, mouth watering from the orange chicken aroma. I reach Jonathan's apartment, quietly unlock the door, and make my way inside. It clicks shut, and as I set Eric's key on the kitchen counter, a strangled groan fills my ears.

What the…?

Another breathless whine that definitely doesn't belong to Jonathan reverberates throughout the apartment, and my stomach rolls as my legs propel me towards the sound. As I stop outside his bedroom door, the repetitive creaking of furniture has me second-guessing everything.

"Jonathan!" the feminine voice shrieks.

Please be porn. Please be very specific, AI-generated, loud-as-hell porn. Holding my breath, I nudge open the door.

The dim bedside lamp illuminates a naked girl as she's pounded doggy style by the love of my life. I attempt to speak, but no words come out. My brain can't comprehend the scene before me, let alone my mouth.

"Damn, Kendra," Jonathan mutters, and the words lace the air like poison, seeping into my pores. "You're so tight tonight." A loud slap rings through the room, and she whimpers from his spank. "So good for me, baby."

"What the fuck?" The only three words that leave my shocked mouth as my heart shrivels up like a raisin.

Their heads snap toward me, and Jonathan's eyes go wide. "Charlie."

He pulls out, shoves her to the side, and hops off the bed, his erection swinging through the air like a pool noodle. Societal conventions suggest I should shield my eyes, but why? I've seen him like this hundreds of times. *Including last night, when he left me drained and unsatisfied.*

Kendra scrambles and slips under the blanket, not saying a word. I swear she's fucking smirking, but I choose to ignore it.

My eyes ping-pong between them as my brain fights to catch up.

"Charlie, I—we didn't…" Jonathan stammers while having the sense to pull sweatpants on. "It's not wh—"

"If 'it's not what it looks like' comes out of your mouth, I will cut your dick off and feed it to you," I snap. He reaches toward me, and I slap his hand away, stepping backward.

His eyes wander over me, expression relaxing, a lazy smile spreading across his face. The sight of it causes a nauseating feeling I haven't experienced since Halloween. "I knew you'd show up." He glances at Kendra, and her entire demeanor shifts to mirror his. "We were waiting for you."

"Yeah," she says coyly. "Jonathan thought you might want to experience something different to spice up your *vanilla* sex life." I shake off the sting of her labeling our sex life after a dessert flavor. Although she's not entirely wrong. She sits up, pushing her tits out, attempting seduction, and I surprise the three of us when I throw my head back, laughing.

"Really?" I ask, seething at Jonathan. "*That's* the best you could come up with? That you planned a threeway on the off chance I showed up tonight? Get the hell out." I pause. "Actually" —I spin around—"how about *I* get the hell out?"

He grabs my wrist, and I glance at it, then back to his now hardened eyes. "Please, wait."

"For what? The encore? I'm not going to sit here while you fuck this blonde bitch into next week!" I scream at him.

"Excuse me?" the bitch has the nerve to say.

"You shut the hell up!" I shout, pointing at her, unsure where my brass balls came from. "It's obvious you know who I am, otherwise you'd be having a very different reaction to me walking in on you two fucking, so why don't we cut the shit."

"Charlie," Jonathan snaps, and my eyes flick back to him.

"How long have you been screwing behind my back?" I fold my arms over my chest, feigning confidence.

"Char—"

"How. Fucking. Long?" I ask, snubbing another bullshit excuse.

His silence tells me all I need to know, and my eyes glide back to the bitch on the bed. "How long, *Kendra?* How long have you been fucking my boyfriend?"

"Sweetie, he hasn't been your boyfriend for months." A sardonic smile creeps on her face, worsening my nausea.

"Kendra," Jonathan snaps.

I didn't think it was possible to get angrier once your blood hits boiling, but I've hit molten. My face is on fire, and I blink hard as tears threaten to pour out.

Don't let them see you cry.

Rage surges through me, and my hand takes on a mind of its own, swinging the takeout bag through the air, hitting Jonathan repeatedly. "I can't *believe* you!"

Crushing plastic squeaks and cracks. "Stop!" he pleads as fried rice and orange sauce fly across his room.

"You're insane," Kendra shrieks, an egg roll nailing her in the face.

One point, Benson.

"Fuck!" *Whack.* "You!" *Whack.*

The sack bursts, scattering sticky bits of food over every surface of his room. The ripped plastic floats towards the floor as I make my escape.

"You're blaming me like this is all my fault," he calls out, quick on my heels.

Spinning around, I throw a hand over my heart oozing so much blood it's definitely dripping onto the floor. "Are you suggesting I positioned your dick in front of her pussy?"

"No." He narrows his eyes at me, and if I weren't so devastated, I'd laugh at the sight of egg roll guts stuck all over his hairy chest. *Point two for Benson.* "But did you honestly think we were going to work living so far apart? *You* chose to go to CBU instead of here."

"Because CBU's closer to the twins!" I say, exasperated. "And I try to see you as often as possible."

"Yeah, which is few and far between," he snaps. "And you

rarely want to have sex." *Because you never like anything I do. Last night included.* "A man has needs." My teeth grind, jaw aching. "Not to mention you sure as hell never finished me off without explicit directions."

My open palm flies through the air, delivering a stinging slap to his cheek. "Four years. Four. Fucking. Years," I spit out through tears, unable to contain them any longer. "And this is how you treat me? You could've at least waited twenty-four hours before fucking someone else. If you gave me an STD, I swear to—"

"We're both clear," Jonathan says, as if that should make everything better. As if I should be totally chill with the fact he rawdogged me, then fucked his mistress immediately after.

"If you were so unhappy, why didn't you break up with me?"

He shifts on his heels. "I honestly thought you'd have done it by now."

"Oh, so you're a coward?" He doesn't speak, jaw tight. "Well, you've got your wish. We're done."

"Charlie, wai—"

I rush out the door and pull it shut behind me with a rattle. After sprinting to the elevator, I smash my finger on the down button, praying he doesn't come after me. Hours pass, realistically seconds, but it's too damn long. *He's not coming after me?* My eyes find the door to the stairwell, and I bolt, running down them like I've robbed a New York City penthouse. When I finally make it to the lobby, I'm winded and my veins are overflowing with anger.

How could he do this?

My hands shake as my eyes blur with tears. Four years of my life I've given to him, and this is how he repays me?

My heart aches, the memories of our shared past hitting me like a grenade all at once.

"I love you, Charlie. Forever," he told me for the first time while we were tangled up in the sheets our sophomore year.

"After I go pro, I'm wifing you up," he said, spinning me in

circles on the Longwood High School football field after he'd thrown a game-winning touchdown.

"You'll always have a place here," he told me after my grandmother died. I needed an escape from my home life, and he would whisk me away, keeping me distracted with his smile and pretty words. He was thoughtful and kind and gentle, and god, was it easy to fall in love with him.

What the hell happened?

Stepping outside his building, I'm slammed by a wall of humidity, snapping me back to reality.

For *months* he cheated on me, and I had no clue? Am I really so dumb I didn't see *any* signs?

Guess Sophia was right.

"Maybe you should stop making excuses for him and realize he might actually be the goddamn villain, Char."

Well, fuck me for not believing her.

Jonathan's words about our sex life echo in my mind: *"You sure as hell never finished me off without explicit directions."*

We may not have had the best sex, but was it really all me? I think back to last night and his words to me after another shitty lay. *"It's okay, babe. I'll help fix you."*

I guess I'm still broken.

A rumble surrounds me, vibrating to my bones, and I glance up, small rain droplets hitting my face already damp with tears.

Then the sky splits open, and we cry together.

3

NOAH

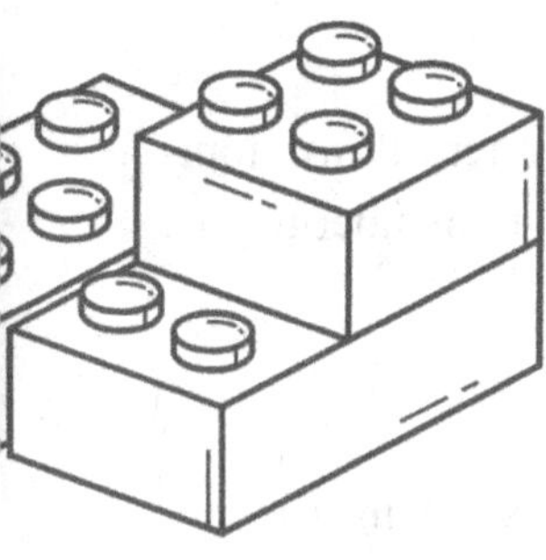

"You're seriously saying no to popping bottles at LIV?" Theo asks, dumbstruck eyes on me as we exit Ken's Karaoke. Our group's heading to one of Miami's most renowned clubs, but after a day at the beach, paired with multiple Grammy-award-worthy performances, my eyes are fighting for life.

"Sorry, bud," I say, the stench of stale beer and cigarettes seeping deeper into my pores with every second. "The hotel shower is calling my name."

"I'd feel less disappointed if the redhead was joining you in it."

"Nah, not my type."

He smirks. "Why, because she's not brunette and in a relationship?"

I glare at him. "Fuck off."

"See you, Cap." He laughs, nudging my shoulder. "Don't wait up." The group waves, heading down the street for the next debauchery of the night.

Thirty minutes later, the scalding water is raining down on me, skin scrubbed new. After turning the metal handle to stop the stream, I step out. Reaching for a towel from the shelf, my hand waves in the air, coming up empty. My eyes fall to the floor, discovering a clumped white mountain. *Thanks, Theo.*

On top of the vanity, a dainty hand towel folded like a bird catches my attention. *Beggars can't be choosers.* I snatch the sacrificial scrap of cloth and rub it against my hair, then continue with the rest of my body.

Knock. Knock. Knock.

I roll my eyes at the door while rubbing the water off my stomach. Maybe if I don't let Theo in, he'll start remembering his damn key.

Do not enable Theo.

Knock. Knock. Knock.

I glance at myself in the mirror and curse, knowing I'm not that guy.

Knock. Knock. Knock.

Knock. Knock. Knock.

Knock. Knock. Knock.

I blow out a breath, heading towards it, hand cloth draped over my dick. Guess Mr. Impatient will have to deal with the indecency.

Hiding my bare body behind the door, I pull it open, craning my head around. "Listen, Theo, we're gon—" The door shoves against me. "What the he—"

Charlotte rushes into the room and spins to face me. Her vacant eyes meet mine, their usual sparkle lacking, arms over her chest as she holds herself tight.

"What's wrong?" Panic sets in, my heart racing. "Did something happen? Sophia said you left the bar. I assumed you came back to the hotel." *I should've walked her myself.* "Did someone hurt you?"

"No," she says quickly, and I breathe a sigh of relief, shutting the door. "Well, yes, technically."

My jaw hardens, worry returning. "Who?"

"It's nothing," she says, attempting to swipe away black

mascara smudges from under her eyes. My Charlotte radar blares. *She's lying.*

"If it's nothing, then why are you here?" I ask, readjusting the tiny towel on my dick. *How can I get clothes without making this awkward?*

"Because—" Her gaze drops down my body, and my skin burns at the attention as her mouth falls open. "Oh my god! Why are you…?" Her eyes are glued to my crotch. "Wow."

And it's awkward.

"First time seeing a naked man?" I ask, trying to cut the tension.

Charlotte squeezes her eyes shut and spins away. "Second time tonight, actually."

A knot forms in my stomach, and I snatch a pair of shorts off the top of my bag and tug them on.

"I'm clothed," I say.

She turns slowly, opening one eye. "Half clothed."

"Charlotte." I blow out a frustrated breath, far too tired and tipsy to play games after she showed up to my room looking like this. I *need* to know what's wrong. Now. "What happened?"

Gnawing on her lower lip, she lies again. "Nothing."

She runs a hand through her hair—her usually beautiful brown hair, which looks almost black in its current state. The same way it did when she emerged from the ocean earlier today. "Why are you soaking wet?" Silence fills the air as she refrains from answering my simplest question yet. "Charlotte." I raise my brows, reaching out to pluck what looks like rice out of her damp hair. *Yep, that's rice.* I flick it into the nearby trash can.

"I had to walk here in the rain after I couldn't find you all at Ken's," she says flatly.

"Everyone went to LIV." My gaze returns to hers. "Why didn't you Uber?"

"My phone died."

"Why didn't you grab a taxi?"

She huffs. "Because I didn't want to be the star of a *CSI: Miami* episode?"

Santo cielo.[1] "Why didn't you call me?"

"Like I said." She looks at me like an idiot, and maybe I am. "My. Phone. Died."

"You could've asked someone to use theirs," I point out, unsure of how I'm trying to help.

"How would I have looked up your number"—she throws her hands in the air—"if. My. Phone. Died!"

"I'm going to tattoo my phone number to your fucking ass, Charlotte," I mumble, dragging a hand over my face.

She rolls her eyes. "What if you change it?"

"Woman." I groan, blowing out a frustrated breath. "I've been sitting up here, oblivious, while you were walking alone, soaked to the bone, looking like someone killed your dog."

Her brown eyes narrow on mine. "No one killed my dog." Her expression softens, a sigh escaping her. "Someone just fucked my boyfriend." My eyebrows shoot to my hairline. "Well..." She pauses, looking down to pick at her fingernails. "Ex-boyfriend."

Maybe I'm not too tipsy or tired after all.

"Wow," I say as the admission hangs heavy in the air between us. Only two ridiculous words finally leave my mouth. "I'm sorry."

"I had the honor of walking in on the whole naked fuck fest," she says, smiling sweetly, but I see straight through her facade. "It was spectacular."

My lips part open, and I have no words. Actually, I have four. "He's a fucking idiot."

And for once, Charlotte doesn't correct me. "You said I could come find you if I needed to."

Nodding, I confirm. "I did."

Her eyes connect with mine before trailing downward. She

---

1. IT: *Santo cielo.* - EN: Holy sky.

sucks her lower lip between her teeth, and if I didn't know any better, I'd say she was checking me out. Her gaze wanders all the way to my cock, and I beg it to stay put so she can't see how much she's affecting me.

My attraction for her has been locked up tight since her boyfriend tossed me out after Halloween like a candy wrapper. For twenty minutes, I listened on the other side of the door before deeming she was safe and dragging myself away.

We were mid-season, and I definitely didn't need the drama or distraction.

My eyes snag on another piece of rice in her hair—or is that egg?—and I'm brought back to how disheveled this poor woman looks tonight. My stomach aches as I determine what the hell to do about it.

"How can I help?" I ask, the words strained.

She steps forward, placing her cool, trembling hands against my bare chest, and I freeze.

Rule number one: don't touch Charlotte.

But she's touching me, so that's a loophole… right?

Her brown eyes lock with mine, and her mouth curves into a smile so wicked it knocks the breath from my lungs. "I need you to fuck me."

My lips part as her words cover every inch of my skin, strangling my dick like a boa constrictor. "What?" I manage to croak out.

"Come on, Noah." She drags a soft fingertip up and down my abs. "We all know about your no-pussy-during-season rule."

"How do you know about that?" I force out, preparing to add whoever broke bro code to my shit list right below Jonathan.

She laughs softly, and it reverberates in my chest like a light echo throughout the universe. "Everyone knows about it."

My mouth opens and closes as I struggle to form a coherent thought.

She drags a thumb beneath the hem of my shorts. Ohhhhh, *fuck*.

Rule number two: don't think about Charlotte.

And definitely don't think about her slipping a hand into your pants and gripping your dick until you—

"Season's over, Noah," she says, feigning confidence, but the quiver of her lip gives her away. She removes her torturous touch from my stomach. I breathe a sigh of relief until her fingers find the hem of her dress, and she pulls it over her head, then tosses it to the floor. Her perfect, perky tits stare at me. Nipples pebbled from the AC hitting her wet, bare skin. *Fuck.* Pretty black satin panties have drool pooling in my mouth.

"I know you're aching for it," Charlotte says, voice sultry but shaky, bringing my gaze back to her eyes. "And I'm aching to make sure I'm not the problem, so for the love of god, will you just *fuck* me?" The desperation in her tone shoots straight to my dick, and it threatens to take over the rest of this conversation.

How could she be the problem?

"Charlotte." I attempt firmness, but it comes out a breathless moan as her pleading eyes bore into mine.

"Please." Her hands find my neck, and I allow myself one breath to enjoy the feeling of her touch before I do the right thing. The noble thing.

An inhale as her thumb glides slowly down my Adam's apple.

An exhale as her fingertips trace my collarbone.

My breath stops as she drags a nail between my pectorals, causing my own nipples to harden.

Being the good guy sucks.

Begrudgingly, I place a hand on hers, halting the torment, and hopeful, pained eyes meet mine.

This can't happen. Not here. Not like this.

"No," I force out, and her lips part open, eyes welling with tears before darting away.

It's official. The hardest thing I've ever done is denying this naked, beautiful, desperate woman sex. Never have I ever hated a two-letter word so much.

Cursing myself, I drop her hands, head to the dresser, and grab a blue CBU hoodie. She doesn't protest as I tug it over head, pulling her arms through the warm material that drops to her upper thighs.

She takes the hem of the hoodie between her fingers, a small smirk gracing her lips that's fiercely feeding the devil on my shoulder, and tucks the material to rest on her waist.

"You're killing me, woman," I groan, retrieving the matching sweatpants, and I bend down, helping her into them. Standing, I'm greeted by her brown eyes glistening to the brim with pain.

"You don't want me?" Her voice cracks, a tear rolling down her cheek. *Fuck.*

"Char, this isn't you," I say, chest aching at her tone. "This isn't us."

She blinks rapidly, more tears escaping, and I reach up to brush them away. My thumb pauses on her jawline, and I know I should keep my distance, but how can I when she stands there looking like a weeping angel fallen from heaven?

"I know," she says, leaning into my touch.

"Get in bed," I instruct, pulling away and pointing towards mine.

She smiles weakly, brows furrowed. "I thought we weren't—"

"We're not," I say firmly, cocking a brow. *And please don't ask me a second time because I am not that strong.* "But you're, like, two degrees away from hypothermia."

"I'm fine." She gestures at the sweatsuit. "All warm."

"Bed." I point, brows raised.

She huffs and pulls back the comforter, then slides under. I sit on top of it and lean against the pillows, fighting the urge to reach out and brush the damp brown strands falling every which way over her face. She beats me to it, tucking them behind her ears, and looks up to catch me staring.

"What?" she asks.

I sigh, worry lines creasing my forehead. "I hate seeing you like this."

"Perfectly content, snuggled in clean sheets?" She cocks a brow, straining to get her armor in place.

I see right through your stained glass window.

"No." I frown. "Sad."

"I'm fine." She nuzzles her head against the pillow, eyes darting away.

Within seconds, I break my own rule and tip her chin to look back at me. "You're not."

"What do you want me to say?" she asks, her tone laced in frustration—in heartbreak. "That I'm so sad I'll never be happy again? That I don't think I can live another day without his dick?"

My lips tug upwards. "Stop making jokes to deflect talking about the real stuff."

"No one ever wants to talk about the real stuff. It's always 'how are you?' and the only acceptable answer is 'fine, and you?' People panic if you say anything else."

"Not me." I rub my thumb selfishly along her jawline. "I want to talk about the real stuff."

She stares at me in disbelief. "Why?"

"Because you're my *friend*," I remind her—and myself—pulling my hand away. "And I care about your well-being. This isn't the first time we've had a heart to heart."

"Yeah." She groans, throwing a hand over her face. "But this time is different."

"Why? Cause you're not puking your brains out in a porcelain bowl?"

She nudges me with her foot under the covers. "We agreed not to talk about that night."

"To *other* people. I'm allowed to bring it up with you. We were both there," I say pointedly.

"Fine." She curls into herself. "Yes, that was different."

"How?" I tilt my head. "What's so different?"

"Last time I was depressingly drunk." Her voice cracks on the last word, along with the rest of my restraint. "Tonight, I'm soberly sad."

"Soberly?" I ask, knowing she had her fair share of wine at the bar.

"Mostly soberly."

"Forget about him. Seriously." My tone is harsher than I intended.

"Easy for you to say. The memory of him moaning that girl's name is seared into my brain." She pauses. "*Kendraaaaa,*" she exaggerates sarcastically.

My thoughts fight for clarity. "I want to tell you it's okay to feel how you feel."

Her eyes flick to mine. "But?"

"You're acting like the perfect man dumped you when you're way too good for him." I shake my head. "I'm talking pee-wee-league-versus-Super-Bowl-status too good for him."

She rolls her eyes at me. "I have flaws, just like everyone else."

"The right person will love your flaws. They'll see them as quirks, not try to make you hide them. And they definitely won't degrade you for your mistakes." She sighs and purses her lips together as heat bubbles under my skin. "Don't you remember how shitty he was to you on Halloween?"

"I know, but maybe I shouldn't have drank so much," she says, picking at her nails.

Typical victim-blaming bullshit.

I shift my body closer. "Look at me." Her head tilts upward, and I instantly realize it was a mistake as her warm breath hits my lips. I swallow hard. "He did you a favor."

"By boning another girl?" she deadpans.

"By proving he doesn't deserve you so you'd finally leave his ass." *Took her long enough.*

She looks away, resting against the headboard. "Shit." She drags a hand over her face. "This really fucks up my five-year plan."

The corners of my mouth twitch upward. "You have a five-year plan?" I ask with a bit too much enthusiasm.

"Apparently not anymore," she grumbles. "The plan was basically to graduate, marry Jonathan, start teaching at the local elementary school, and a few other things. But obviously it's all gone to shit."

"You can still do the teacher thing," I point out.

"Yeah." She sighs. "Until my mom finds out."

"What do you mean?"

"We had to confirm our majors last week to schedule pre-rec classes for sophomore year," she explains. "She expects me to major in pre-law, but I selected early childhood education."

"You don't think she'll be okay with you being a teacher?"

"No chance," Charlotte scoffs. "She's made it clear since I was twelve she expects me to go to law school like she did."

"That's bull," I say, sadness settling in my chest for her. My mom has encouraged me to chase my dreams over stability for as long as I can remember. Constantly saying, *Chi non risica non rosica.*

No risk, no reward.

"Like I said, five-year plan's fucked," Charlotte huffs, and my lips quirk upwards again at the mention. She narrows her eyes, zoning in on my amusement. "What has Noah Gabriel Caruso so giddy right now? Is my life falling apart funny to you?"

"Of course not," I say, the grin not leaving my lips. "I just thought I was the only person who made one in real life."

"*You* have a five-year plan?" she asks, sitting up, a wide grin spreading across her own face, bringing me relief.

"Damn straight."

"Care to share with the class?" Her eyes light up, easing some of my worry.

"Yes, Ms. Benson," I tease, grabbing my phone off the nightstand, pulling the tiny piece of paper out of the case.

She snatches it from my fingers. "You have it written down?"

> **Noah's Five Year Plan**
>
> **Financial:** pay off mom's house + have two rental properties
> **Career:** get drafted to the NFL
> **Family:** don't miss the important stuff
> **Adventure:** travel to five new countries
> **Self:** ?
> **Relationship:**
> **Health:** stay fit as fuck
>
> MORE TITTIES MORE TOUCHDOWNS!

"More titties, more touchdowns?" She holds the paper out. "Really?"

"That was Theo." I snatch the paper back from her, our fingers grazing in the process. *Ignore the electricity, Caruso.*

"Mm-hmm," she hums. "I also noticed the relationship spot is blank. What gives?"

I shrug. "It's not a priority right now."

"So, what? No pussy until the five-year plan is up?" she asks, and my jaw ticks.

"The list didn't say *pussy*, it said *relationship*."

"What would even possess you to make a rule like that?" she asks, ignoring my clarification.

There's an array of reasons that prompted the rule, but I opt for the simplest explanation. "Getting dumped right before the most important game of my high school football career."

Her mouth falls open. "Hold up." She sits up, watching as I place my ironclad plan safely back in my case. "*You* got dumped?" Her eyes are wide, and I'm amused by her surprised reaction. "*Mr. Perfect* got dumped?"

"Shocking, I know," I say with a laugh.

"*Daaaamn*," she says, hitting me with a playful fist. "Mr. Perfect's got secrets." *She has no idea.* "Give me the story. I've earned it for wingwomaning you earlier."

"Fine." I roll my eyes, choosing not to point out the wingwomaning was highly unnecessary. "Senior year of high school, my team made the state championships. It was a huge game for me. Tons of college coaches came to see me play. Even Coach Porter was there." I blow out a breath. "Half the school stayed at a hotel the night before, and my girlfriend asked me to come to her room. I thought we were gonna hook up, but she dumped me instead."

Charlotte cringes. "That's terrible."

"Yep." I huff a laugh. "I wasn't in love with her or anything. We'd only been dating a few months, but it messed with my head so much that the game was almost a disaster. Luckily, I was able to pull my head out of my ass and ended up impressing Coach Porter enough to recruit me."

She eyes me curiously. "Do you miss her?"

"Nah." I shake my head, and it's the truth. "But the situation showed me how much a relationship can affect your focus, and I don't want the distraction. Especially during season."

"Hence the rule," Charlotte says with a small smile.

"Hence the rule."

"I mean, I can understand while you're trying to get drafted, but once you're actually *in* the NFL… would it really be so bad to be in a relationship?"

I shrug. "It's not in the plan."

She laughs, a sweet, infectious sound. "You know that thing isn't written in stone, right?"

"Yes." I pinch her side, and she yelps. "But it's worked for me so far."

"Well, I hope Ms. Perfect comes around and fucks up your plan like Jonathan did to mine." Her shoulders sink, the storm cloud returning overhead. "Well, maybe not the *same* way. Hopefully yours will be for the better."

I slide off the bed, make my way to the mini fridge, pull two pints of ice cream out of the tiny freezer compartment, and grab the plastic spoons from the dresser.

"Look at you, coming in clutch with the Rocky Road." She laughs, making grabby hands as I return to the bed, and I swat her away.

"When I was in high school, my stepdad would take me to get milkshakes after a loss. He'd tell me the sweetest things come after the shittiest moments." I hand her a spoon and pint. "It's not a milkshake, but it's the next best thing." When I play away games, I always go to the closest convenience store and grab a pint. Now the habit's so hard to break, I couldn't stop myself from buying some at the store earlier.

"That's so *sweet*," she teases as I remove the top of the ice cream and pull off the plastic film. I raise my spoon in mock cheers, and she grins, clinking the plastic against mine.

"To fucking up the five-year plan?"

"To fucking up the five-year plan."

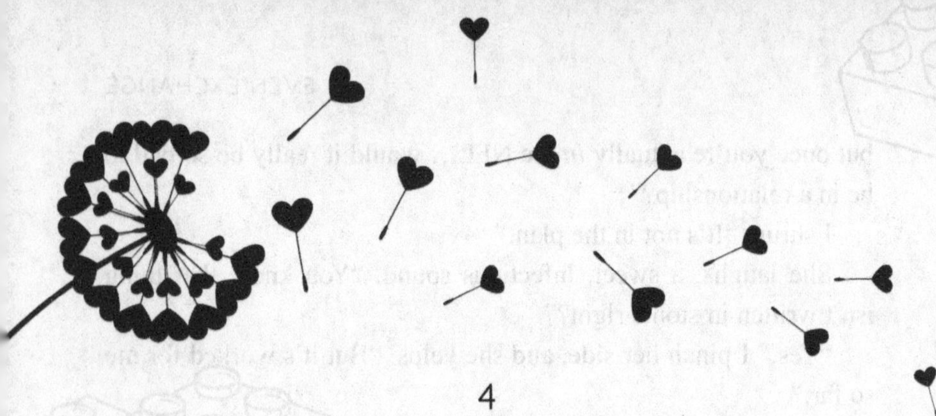

4

CHARLOTTE

Lavish mansions fly by, and familiar clusters of shrubbery line the streets, a stark reminder I'm nearing a place that still doesn't feel like home. As I pull into the lengthy driveway, my eyes wander over the estate's dark brickwork, a fitting representation of its haunting history. Hallways that once held childhood memories now echo ominous whispers from my grandmother who died there. I keep waiting for her ghost to shush me for stepping too loudly down the opulent winding staircase.

"Bensons mustn't stomp. We glide."

As my car rolls to a stop, my mother exits the front door, strolling towards her SUV. She's perfectly put together, like always. A black leather Chanel tote is flung over her shoulder—inherited from my grandmother, like the Benson estate and everything else inside it.

Placing my hand on the gear shift, I put my car in park and swallow down the anxiety that always buzzes through me when she's around.

"Charlie, fix your hair."

"Charlie, why did you get a B on your English test?"

"Charlie, smile, people are watching."

Stepping out, I send a practiced smile her way.

"Hey," she says, her manicured fingers gripping the handle of her Porsche Macan. "I thought you were in Miami?"

"Came home for the weekend," I say, unsurprised she either forgot or simply doesn't care.

"The twins will be thrilled." She dons a politician's smile, opening the car door. "I'm off to a ribbon cutting at the new Longwood Humane Society. See you after."

"I was actually hoping we could get dinner." The words tumble out. There's a conversation I'd like to get over sooner rather than later. In a public place. With witnesses.

"Sorry, but Mayor's duty calls," she says, getting inside the car. "Rain check?" She blows me a kiss and closes her door before I'm able to respond.

I wave as she heads down the driveway. "Sure, rain check."

I shove away the annoyance and remind myself of the main reason I came home in the first place.

After grabbing my cheer duffle from the backseat, I make my way to the house. The ornate front door creaks open, and I'm met with giggles, tiny feet padding through the halls, and background noise of the greatest children's show of all time: *Bluey*. I swear they put some type of crack in it because even as a nineteen-year-old, I can't stop watching it.

"Little pigs, little pigs, let me in!" I shout.

"Lottie!" a high-pitched six-year-old squeals, rounding the corner and flying into my arms.

"Hey, Denny," I say, spinning her in circles until her giggles fill every inch of the foyer.

"Patricia's setting up painting in the playroom," Denny tells me. "Want to join?"

"In a bit. I've got to shower and finish up some schoolwork that's due Monday."

"Who assigns homework over spring break?" Patricia, the live-in nanny, says, coming into view. Her smile is wide, and she pulls me in for a tight hug. *How a mother should.* My parents hired her after inheriting the estate, and I hope she never leaves.

"A monster, that's who," I say with a laugh. "Where's Nash?"

"At Taekwondo," Patricia tells me. "Your dad's picking him up on the way home from the airport."

"Dad's coming home?" I ask, trying to contain my excitement.

"Yes, but he'll be leaving tomorrow night," Patricia says with a sad smile.

Typical.

His visits are usually quick and lacking in quality time. I suppose that's the problem with having a dad who flies 747s for a living.

I thought my parents would slow down after inheriting the estate, but it only made them more distant.

Not only from each other, but from us as well.

Dad spends all his time working, and Mom spends her time, well, anywhere but here.

"Hiiiiiii-*yah*!" A tiny foot connects with my hip, sending me stumbling, and the cup of flour in my hand litters the entire counter.

And me.

"Ow!" I huff a laugh, turning my attention to the little karate kid. "Can we keep the drop kicks to the dojo?"

"Nope," Nash, my younger brother, says while performing what can't possibly be any type of actual Taekwondo move. "Gotta practice."

"I'm not trying to stifle your progress. Just don't want my hip blown out in the process."

He stands straight, puts a fist against his palm, and bows slightly, then runs away.

Six-year-olds are so bizarre.

Turning back to the counter, I examine the mess, then pull the trash can directly under the edge and swipe the wasted flour into it. After a thorough wipe down, I've finally got my workstation clean again, and I continue dumping ingredients into the bowl.

Flour.

Active dry yeast.

Salt.

Baking is my preferred method of stress relief, and Noah once mentioned he makes pizza dough from scratch that is unmatched, so, challenge accepted. My phone buzzes, and I glance at it on the counter.

JONATHAN

I'm sorry.

My blood boils. Two stupid, meaningless words. He can't be that sorry if he did it in the first place. I snatch up the phone and add him to my block list, along with his social media accounts. Shoving the phone in my pocket, I return to the stress relief session.

After thoroughly mixing in the cold water, I pretend the dough is Jonathan's stupid fucking face as I knead it into the counter.

Cheating. *Plop.* Mother. *Plop.* Fucker. *Plop.*

"You alright there?" Dad says, leaning against the door frame.

"Fine," I quip.

"You don't look fine," he presses, tone curious.

My chest squeezes, trying to contain the hurt. "I am."

"You can talk to me." Footsteps grow louder until he's directly next to me. "That's what dads are for."

I slam the dough against the counter once more and side-eye him. He may travel a lot, but the reason I'm upset about it is I miss him when he's gone. He's the only one I'm able to talk to in this family. The only parent who actually cares.

"Jonathan and I broke up," I blurt, eyes stinging as I fight tears that cheating motherfucker definitely does not deserve.

Dad remains quiet for a moment. "And how are we feeling about that?"

I blow out a breath. *Plop.* "Like I'm gonna need more dough."

"Mm-hmm." He taps his fingers against the counter. "Whose idea was it?"

I roll the sticky glob into a large ball. "*Technically*, I guess it was mine."

Although it's not like Jonathan made any effort to reconcile. He didn't even chase after me when I fled the Dangling Pool Noodle Orange Chicken Catastrophe. And one bullshit "I'm sorry" text does not make an apology.

Dad leans against the counter, folding his arms. "And what did Jonathan *do* for you to come to that decision?"

My gaze connects with his. "You can't shoot him."

Dad holds his hands up. "I won't."

"You also can't hit him with your car, have him arrested, or drop a bag of flaming shit from your airplane." I reconsider. "Actually the last one would be pretty cool."

He sighs, a frown present. "He must've really messed up, huh?"

"Big time." I knead my knuckles into the dough, contemplating telling him.

Typically, I keep everything relationship-related bottled up, because if Jonathan and I got in a fight, I always forgave him, but I learned early in our relationship parents don't forgive as easily. And they certainly never forget. Dad still brings up the time Jonathan left me stranded at a party and I had to call him for a ride.

And I damn sure never told Dad about Halloween. I'd dare to say Noah was furious enough for the both of them.

But I don't foresee myself forgiving Jonathan this time, which is why I admit, "He cheated on me."

"Son of a bitch," Dad mumbles under his breath, pushing off the counter. "Is he in town?"

"Dad," I say firmly, stopping him from grabbing his keys. "He's not worth your time. Or mine."

"Not worth my time?" Dad fumes. "He disrespected my daughter! He needs to be reminded of his manners. Linda raised him better than that."

"It's not her fault," I say, referring to Jonathan's mother. "It's his. And I just want to move on."

He releases a heavy breath. "If you change your mind, you'll let me know?"

"I will."

Two beeps from the security alarm sound, paired with the creaking opening and closing of the front door.

"Hi," Mom says, walking into the kitchen with a practiced smile, setting her purse on the counter. My eyes widen at the small patch of flour next to it. Her gaze follows mine, noticing the same. "Charlie," she snaps, snatching up the bag and dusting it off. "How many times do I have to tell you not to get flour all over the house when you bake your little cookies?"

"Sorry, I was jus—"

"It's fine." She waves me off with the flick of her wrist. "I'm glad you're here." Hope blossoms within me. *Is this actually going to be a nice visit?* "We need to discuss the email I received regarding your declaration of major." And the hope shrivels up like a sun-dried tomato.

My mother really needs to be removed from my campus email updates, but she says, *"If I pay the bills, all communications come to me."*

I was hoping I could approach the subject before she got the chance, hence the dinner request. "What is there to talk about?" I ask, buying time to rethink my game plan.

"For starters, you can explain why you're confirmed as majoring in early childhood education." Her jaw is tight, furious eyes holding mine.

My heart races. "Because that's what I chose."

"Oh, really?" she asks, brows shooting to her hairline as she folds her arms over her chest. "Just like that? *You* decided?"

I swallow hard, glancing to Dad for help, but all I get in return is a look saying, *You're on your own, kid.*

Thanks for the backup.

Straightening my shoulders, I attempt to exude confidence. "It's my life. I get to choose what I do with my future. So, yes. *I* decided."

"We agreed you would major in pre-law," Mom grits out. "You want to be a lawyer."

"No, *you* want me to be a lawyer," I remind her.

"Yes, because I want you to obtain a quality education," she says, tone laced with irritation. "Not to study the most up-to-date way to divide numbers by one."

"That's not even what I'll do," I argue, frustration coursing through me. "We're trained to teach up-and-coming generations."

"Let someone else teach them," she snarks.

The hope of a career I'm excited about is crumbling like shortbread. "But it's my passion!"

"Passion is a luxury that families like ours do *not* have."

"Why?" I shriek, rage erupting under the surface. "The only reason you care is so you'll have another thing you can boast about to the media." I raise my tone an octave, impersonating her. "My darling daughter just graduated *summa cum laude* from Harvard."

"Do you even realize what I've had to do to get us where we are?" Mom snaps a manicured finger in my face, and my breath hitches. "You have everything you could possibly want and need. I've paid for cheer camp, the extra tutoring for the SATs, the clothes on your back, and the roof over your head. And this is how you thank me?"

"Stop acting like we have all this because of you," I say, waving around at the residence. "You're a small-town mayor, and Dad makes good money. But not *this* good. We're only here because Grandma died."

Her palm flies through the air, serving a stinging slap against my cheek. My lips part, and my hand finds my tingling face, covering it.

"Georgia!" Dad exclaims.

"Do you know what my mother did when I got pregnant with you at nineteen?" Mom snarls. "She cut me off. Not a damn dime for anything. Yet here I am, trying to be different. To do *better.* And this is how you treat me?" Her eyes dart to mine. "Disrespecting all I've done for you. And not even a conversation before you change your degree?"

"If you weren't so busy with all your political bullshit, you'd realize I've been trying to talk to you about this!" My chest heaves as I struggle for composure.

"I'm *busy* trying to support this family," she fumes. "One day you'll realize you can't pay the bills with papier-mâché hearts." She shakes her head. "You're not majoring in early education. Not while I'm paying for it."

"Then I'll pay for it myself!" *Fuck.*

"Okay," Dad says, finally stepping in. "Everybody calm down."

"With what money?" she asks smugly, folding her arms. "Because you're certainly not using your trust fund." My mother thinks she can dictate everything I do just because she currently controls my inheritance. Well, she can keep the damn money.

"I've got savings," I say nervously, thinking of the tiny bank account I had long before our family inherited the estate.

"Have you forgotten I can see all your accounts?" she asks,

huffing a laugh. *I really need to get her off my stuff.* "How far do you think a little birthday and Christmas money will get you?"

My shoulders tense. "I'll figure it out."

"You're majoring in pre-law," she says firmly.

"No." I grind my teeth, heels digging in. "I'm not."

"Then you're doing it without our support," she says, and panic wraps around me like a tight noose, squeezing the air from my lungs. *Guess I'm really doing this.*

"Fine." My heart pounds against my ribcage, my cheeks blazing.

"And while we're at it, you can go ahead and leave your keys too. Since we're not doing anything for you, you don't need *our* car either."

"Now, hold on," Dad attempts, and she cuts him off with a glare. The room spins as my mind struggles to formulate a solution. No financial support I can deal with, *I think*, but no car?

"How am I supposed to get to school?" I protest.

"Guess your first lesson will be public transportation."

My mother and I don't have much in common, but I sure as hell got her stubbornness.

Guess we'll see who caves first.

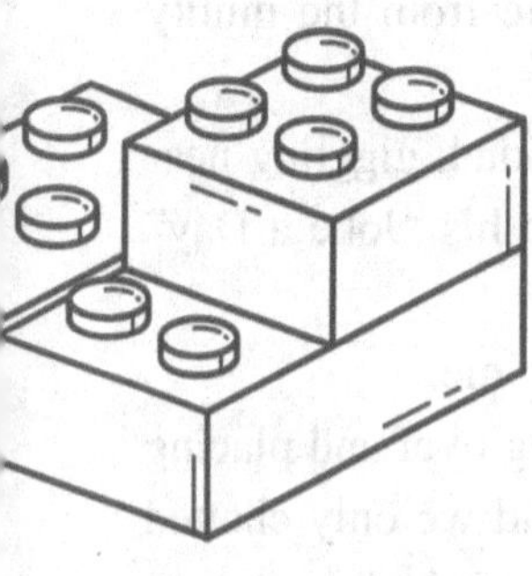

5

NOAH

My frown deepens, arms folded tight as I stare at the bed.

The pillows are crooked.

I re-fluff them, eyes roaming for any other imperfections, but I find none. A satisfied smile spreads across my face.

Clean room, clean mind.

Sharing a hotel with Theo was definitely a test of patience.

Standing in my childhood bedroom, I struggle to pinpoint the emotion it evokes. I've been gone for years, and Mom hasn't changed a thing.

My homecoming king crown sits on the shelf next to the football I threw for the game-winning touchdown during the state championships my senior year of high school. The Lego spaceship I spent an entire summer building—an exact replica of the Millennium Falcon, if I do say so myself—is hung evenly by string from the ceiling above my desk. Mom hasn't even gotten rid of my collection of Rubik's Cubes on my dresser, which serve no other purpose than to remind me of how absolutely awful I am at completing them.

My eyes snag on the dresser's corner, and my lips fall to a frown. The downside of the room being untouched like a mausoleum? Shitty memories reside here too. The chipped wood draws my thumb like a magnet, and I run it over the jagged edge. Habitually, I reach for the back of my head and slide my finger along the mirroring scar. *This stupid hunk of wood was stronger than me.* Not anymore.

"Breakfast is ready," Mom calls, pulling me from the murky memory.

In the kitchen, I find her and Tony, my stepdad, giggling near the coffee pot, probably about whatever was on his "Joke a Day" flip calendar.

"Morning," I say, and their attention slides to me.

"*Buongiorno, sole mio,*"[1] Mom coos, running over and placing a kiss on each cheek. I got in late last night, and we only chatted for a few minutes before I went to my room and crashed.

I chuckle. "*Buongiorno, mamma.*"[2]

She releases me, returning to the coffee pot.

"Morning," Tony says over the brim of his coffee cup with a warm smile. His Italian is limited to the basics, so Mom and I mainly stick to English when he's around for his benefit. Although, given Mom was born and raised Italian, she slips in and out of it more often.

"How long are you here?" Mom asks me.

"Until Sunday."

"Wonderful." She beams, handing me a steaming cappuccino as I sit on a bar stool at the kitchen island. "Nicole's niece is in town. I'm sure she'd love to get together."

Tony snorts a laugh, taking his place next to me.

"I appreciate your enthusiasm," I grumble. "But I'm really not interested in dating the neighbor's niece." Mom plays matchmaker for me like she's an executive of *The Bachelor*. She's also the sole reason I even know what that godforsaken show is. "So how's

---

1. IT: *Buongiorno, sole mio* - EN: Good morning, my sun
2. IT: *Buongiorno, mamma* - EN: Good morning, Mamma

work been?" I ask Tony in an attempt to change the subject off of my dating life.

He smiles. "Just won a big case we've been fighting for months."

"Look at you, out there changing the world, one family at a time." I nudge his shoulder, and he grins into his coffee. He's a family law attorney and never stops advocating for those kids. Every day, he sees the worst of the worst and *helps* instead of being the problem. He sure as hell helped us.

That's why I trust him so much with my mom.

And that trust doesn't come easy.

"Draft's coming up." He arches a brow, and I shift in my seat. "Any top picks?"

Biting my cheek, I look between them. He's the main reason I'm almost comfortable going out of state when drafted. *Almost.*

"You're acting weird," Mom calls over her shoulder. "Spit it out."

I sigh heavily, anxiety consuming me. "I hate having no control over where I end up. What if I'm not close enough anymore?" I ask, eyes finding hers. "What if you need me?"

Mom dons a sympathetic smile. "Oh, *sole mio,* I'll be fine."

"Yeah," Tony says, placing a hand on my shoulder and squeezing gently. "Your mom can handle herself, and if not, you know I'm here." I nod, and with each reassurance, a weight is lifted.

"Please, stop worrying." Mom rounds the island and throws her arms around me. "And no matter where you end up, you need to make a *real* life for yourself. Because if I hear you're going home every night after work to your empty apartment with no friends, or *girl*, that's gonna make my mamma heart really sad."

A tightness squeezes my chest, and I lean my head against hers. "I'll do my best."

"Good." She kisses my hair, then returns to the kitchen.

"Besides, I'm ready for some grandbabies. This big house is too empty and quiet when you're gone."

"*Mamma*!" I groan with a laugh. "One lecture at a time, please."

"Sorry." She throws her hands up, still holding the spatula, and a piece of scrambled egg falls to the floor. "I'll save that one for tomorrow." She bends down to clean up the escaped glob. "So how about Ms. Charlotte? If none of my choices are good enough."

My cheeks warm at the mention. "We're just friends."

What a stupid word.

"Really?" she asks, pinning me with a knowing smile. "I can't recall the names of any of your other female friends." The rest of my body bursts into flames.

"You know what? I actually gotta get back to campus," I joke, standing up.

"That's fine," Tony says. "More tiramisù for me."

My eyes snap to his. "Homemade or store-bought?"

"Has your mother ever bought it at the store?"

A wide smile spreads across my face as I settle back on the stool. "Just had to make sure I wasn't caving for nothing."

It's good to be home.

Flopping on my bed, I settle into the cozy mattress, eyes glued on the ceiling with Mom's and Tony's lecture still present in my head. Of course I have friends, and we do stuff together, but football comes first over everything.

Is that so wrong?

My heart pounds against my rib cage as the anxiety over all these big decisions closes in.

I pull out my phone, and the home screen countdown taunts me.

NFL Draft: 25 days. 22 hours. 1 minute. 12 seconds.

There for no other reason than to remind me of the most important day of my life looming over me.

I really need something, or *someone*, to take my mind off this stuff. My fingers hesitantly find her contact, and I type out a random fun fact.

My thumb hovers over the send button.

Rule number three: don't text Charlotte.

Another guideline I implemented after Halloween, knowing the habit would only cause problems with her shithead boyfriend.

Ex-boyfriend.

I suppose there's nothing wrong about texting a *single* woman…

Images of her tear-stained cheeks flash in my mind, and the urge to know if she's okay overpowers my discipline regarding rules and boundaries.

CHARLOTTE

ME

Fun fact: it's illegal to own only one guinea pig in Switzerland

Her response is immediate, sending a rush through me and leaving no time to second-guess myself.

CHARLOTTE

You're telling me I'd have been arrested at the age of 7?

ME

Yep. You would've had to break your Justin Bieber piggy bank to pay bail

CHARLOTTE
I told you that in confidence

ME
Don't worry, your secret's safe with me

How'd the talk with your mom go?

The bubbles appear and disappear so many times I think one of her siblings may have stolen her phone. Hours pass—okay, five minutes—and her reply pops in.

CHARLOTTE
Fine

ME
It took you five minutes to come up with "fine"?

CHARLOTTE
Looks like it

How about you? Mama Caruso find any poor girls to help fuck up your five year plan yet?

ME
Hey, I told you THAT in confidence. Don't go siding with her

CHARLOTTE
You didn't answer the question

ME
Nah, five year plan is safe

CHARLOTTE
Where should I hide the key to your chastity belt?

My jaw clenches as I fight a smile.

ME
Keep it with your car keys

CHARLOTTE

I would except I don't have a car anymore

ME

What?

Why not?

When we left Miami, I helped put her bags in her car myself. Did she get in an accident and not tell me? More bubbles appear and disappear.

CHARLOTTE

Long story

ME

Are you okay?

CHARLOTTE

Yeah, I'm fine. Just no car

ME

Need me to pick you up on my way back to campus?

CHARLOTTE

lol, no. i'm completely out of your way

Who gives a shit is half typed out when another message pops in.

CHARLOTTE

Sophia will bring me

ME

If your ride falls through let me know

No reply comes, so I lock my phone and set it on the nightstand, fighting off the disappointment. *Buzz buzz.* I snatch it back up like a fumbled football.

CHARLOTTE

Can I ask something and you be honest?

ME

Consider your question truth serum

CHARLOTTE

Did I mess up our friendship in Miami?

My brows pull together. If anything, I'd say Miami made our friendship stronger.

ME

Why would you think that?

CHARLOTTE

Please don't make me say it

My dick hardens as I remember the way she looked at me. Or rather, the way my eyes roamed over her beautiful body like I was a virgin and it was the first naked woman I'd ever seen.

Screw me for being such a gentleman.

I type out a reply, holding my breath, and hit send.

ME

As long as you don't ask me to fuck you again, we'll be fine

CHARLOTTE

Scout's honor

A GIF comes through of a boy scout holding up three fingers, and I chuckle.

CHARLOTTE

I'll buy you a milkshake to make it up to you

ME

Mint chocolate chip or nothing

CHARLOTTE
You got it

I lie against the pillow, smiling till I fall asleep.

The familiar buzz of the athletic building surrounds me as I stroll down the hallway, passing friendly faces. The weekend at home flew by. Mom didn't force me to go on any dead-end dates, and I'm thankful for it. Usually I end up doing at least one to appease her, and then I have to let the girl down easy at the end of the night —*it's not you, it's me.*

I rap my knuckles on a large mahogany door, and James Porter, CBU's head football coach, calls me in.

He stands as the door swings open. "There's my favorite ex-team captain."

I scrunch my nose, sadness surrounding me at the reminder. "That sounds so harsh."

He gestures to the seat in front of his desk, and we both sit. "How was your break?"

"Good. You?"

"Fine, thanks." He clears his throat. "So, I've heard some buzzing around the industry."

I shift in my seat, hands clenched tight. "What's the word, Coach?"

"The Barracudas were pleased with your visit," he says, grinning, referring to the NFL team in Tampa where he also played before ending up at CBU. The team that would allow me to pass my mom's neighborhood every day on the way to work.

"Glad to hear it," I say, relief filling me.

"L.A. was also impressed. And you're heading out to Seattle soon for a top-30 visit?"

"Yeah." My shoulders tense. I'm dreading the distance.

He narrows his eyes on me. "What's wrong?"

"Just getting anxious," I admit, knowing he'll understand. "I hate that I don't really have much control where I end up."

He leans back in his chair, folding his arms. "You won a Heisman as a sophomore, and your record is near perfect. You definitely have some pull if you make your preferences known."

"Part of me thinks staying in Florida would be ideal," I admit. "And the other part thinks going out of state would reduce the distractions so I can really focus."

"I get it," he says, nodding. "As your coach, I'm team No Distractions and going where you can focus."

"But?" I ask, sensing the hesitation in his tone.

"But as a former player, and someone who's been… evolving as of late, remember to have a life outside of football too. Don't forget about the people who are there for you when the stadium lights go out."

I huff a laugh. "You sound like my mom."

"She's a smart woman. Listen," he says, and our eyes meet. "You are a *hell* of a player. You're going to go far. But don't let it strip away who you are. I know you worry for your mom," he says, fully aware of our situation. Some coaches may get a bad rep, and sure he's a hard-ass, but he always makes sure his players can talk to him when they need to. "But getting the opportunity to go pro," he says, pulling me back to the present, "will be the best thing to ever happen to your family."

And I know it will be. Mom and I dealt with a lot of shit in the aftermath of everything that happened with my father. But financial hardship was the worst. She had to take up two jobs to keep us from losing the house until Tony became a permanent part of our lives. I'll never be able to thank him for everything he's done for us. *For her.*

"I appreciate your honesty," I tell Coach Porter. Because I am grateful for it—there aren't many people I can talk to about this without seeing the look in their eyes that tells me they're either pitying me or wondering if I'll end up like *him*.

That's why I can't ever lose my cool. Why I always need to be in control.

"Of course," he says. "And even after you graduate, you have my number. You need something, you call me, okay?"

His offer comforts me. It's hard letting people in, and it's nice knowing he still has my back if I need him. "You got it."

"So, second order of business." He clasps his hands together on the desk. "Who do you suggest for captain next year? I've already talked to Desmond regarding who he wants to turn his co-captain reins over too, but I'd like to hear your thoughts too."

"Elijah should be captain." The words fly effortlessly off my tongue. "He has the full respect of the guys, is dedicated, and no one else wants this more than him."

Coach Porter nods. "Glad to hear you say that. He's my top pick too."

Pride fills me. Elijah's worked damn hard, and it's nice knowing Coach sees that too. "Good."

"And second pick for co-captain?"

That answer takes a little longer because I've been struggling with this decision, but ultimately only one person makes sense. "Theo."

"Really?" His brows pull together. "Why's that?"

"He's loyal, hard-working, and again, all the guys respect him."

"Are you concerned about his lifestyle?"

"Theo likes to have a good time off the field." *A damn good time.* "But he's focused during games. It's never been a problem before, and I don't see it being a problem going forward."

"Hmm. You make a strong case. I'll think about it and make the announcement in a few weeks."

"Great."

We stand, and he rounds the desk, extending his hand to me. "It was an honor to coach you. I look forward to seeing the things you'll accomplish in the NFL."

I return the gesture. "Thank you, Coach."

"Hey, you got a—" The feminine voice stops short, and I turn to find a familiar brunette popping her head in the door. "Oh, hey," Andi, a cheerleader and Charlotte's roommate, says. "I was—"

"I've got the paperwork Coach Landry needed," Coach Porter tells her, returning behind his desk. "And Caruso?"

"Yeah, Coach?" I say, holding the door frame, ready to make my exit.

"If you stay in Florida, Camp Dickson is looking for some mentors this summer, and you'd be a perfect fit. I know you'll be busy, but maybe you could squeeze a few weeks in."

"I'll keep it in mind," I say with a smile, leaving the room for the last time as team captain.

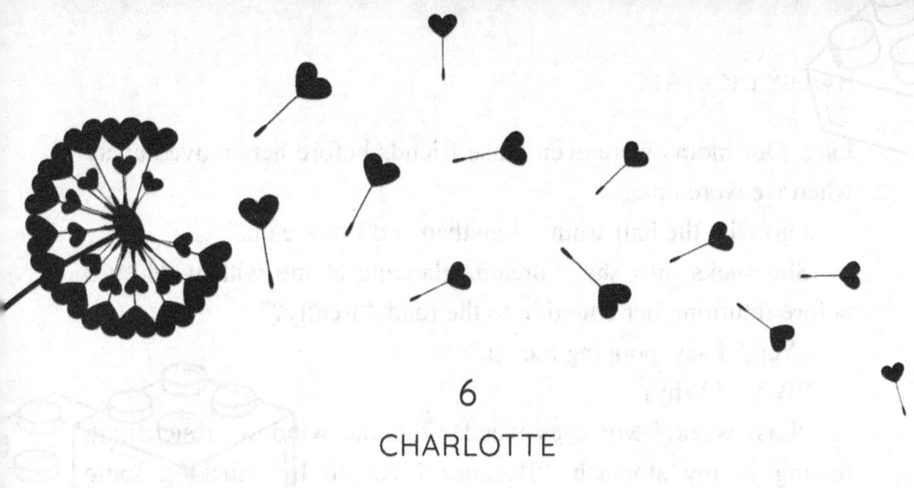

6

CHARLOTTE

Cars zoom past us on a highway that is far too busy for a sunny Sunday afternoon. "Circles" by Post Malone plays low in the background, and I try to keep my mind from wandering back to the chaos ripping apart my life.

"What's up, Charlie?" Sophia asks, glancing over from the driver's seat, worry etched all over her face.

"Huh?" I say, trying to play dumb.

"We've been in the car for thirty minutes, and you've barely spoken a word."

I'm too exhausted to share what's really going on in my head. Too tired from thinking about how the hell I'm going to afford everything next semester. Or how my boyfriend—*ex*-boyfriend—ripped my heart out and threw it in a blender.

Besides, I don't want her pity. I don't deserve it after all the stress I caused her last year.

"It's nothing," I finally reply, picking at my nails.

"Really? We're best friends," she says, adding to the guilt. "I can tell something's bothering you."

This is the hard part about being friends with Sophia. She's known me too long. Like, since doing hopscotch in third grade too long. Our moms were even close friends before hers moved away when we were nine.

I go with the half-truth. "Jonathan and I broke up."

She sucks in a sharp breath, glancing at me with wide eyes before returning her attention to the road. "Really?"

"Yep," I say, popping the "p."

"When? Why?"

"Last week." My eyes wander out the window, a sickening feeling in my stomach. "Because I caught him fucking some blonde bitch."

"What?" she screeches, hand gripping my arm. "Why didn't you tell me?"

"I wasn't ready to talk about it." *I'm still not, yet here we are.*

"So you *caught* him cheating?" she asks, removing her hand.

"Yep. Walked in. He was moaning her name." Bile rises in my throat at the memory. "When they noticed me, he pulled out, and his dick flung around like one of the dancing men in front of a car dealership."

"Lord have *mercy*." She cringes while gripping the steering wheel. "Maybe the girl would be willing to *John Tucker Must Die* his ass."

"Unlikely." Visions of flying food shrapnel come to mind. "She was covered in egg roll guts when I left."

Sophia side-eyes me. "I'm going to need more context."

"I may have brought Jonathan's favorite takeout. And I may have tried to beat the cheater out of him with it after finding them." I press my lips together. "And I may have left the room looking like the trash can outside of Panda Express."

"Charlie!" Sophia howls a laugh. "Wish I was a fly on the wall for that."

Resting my head against the seat, I feel a weight settle in me. "You really don't."

"So what happened next?"

"I told him to go fuck himself." My gaze turns out the window. "And then I left."

Sophia reaches over and pats my head like a child. "Good girl."

"Stop," I groan, dodging away from her. "You read too much smut."

"You can *never* read too much smut." She glares at me in disgust. "And a wise person once told me, 'The best way to get over someone is to get under someone else.'"

"That was before I had my heart stomped all over like grapes at a wine festival!"

Also, tried that, got rejected...

Noah turning down my request as I stood half-naked before him will forever be burned into my brain as the most embarrassing moment of my life.

"Oh, so you're a hypocrite now?" she teases.

"No." I sigh. "But I don't think I'll be ready to put myself out there any time soon."

If ever.

After an exhausting hour-long rant on why Jonathan is a shit-head—*which, okay, fair*—Sophia finally drops me off at my building.

Shaking off the negative thoughts, I open the door to my apartment and am instantly surrounded by laughter and "Red Wine Supernova" by Chappell Roan blaring from a speaker. Andi and Stella, my roommates, belt the lyrics like they're front row at a concert in the living room, their smiles only growing when they notice me. Everything is *easy*. I'm so glad we moved in together after winter break.

"Baby cakes!" Andi runs over and jumps on me so fast I stumble.

I catch my balance and melt into her embrace. "Nice to see you too."

"What about me?" Stella pouts, putting her hands on her hips, and I hug her too.

"Missed you too, Stel." I smile as she squeezes the air out of me. "Jeez, you two are needy little things. It hasn't even been that long."

"I know," Stella says dramatically, releasing me, and I walk toward my room. "I had to watch two seasons of *The Great British Baking Show* all by myself."

I freeze and spin back around. "Excuse me?"

"You heard me." She cocks a brow.

"You continued it without me?" I throw a hand over my heart.

"Sorry, baby cakes." Stella shrugs, giving me a devilish smile. "It's been lonely round this neck of the woods."

I chuckle, already feeling tons lighter than on the car ride here.

"You look tired as hell," Andi says, returning to the living room. "And that only calls for one thing."

"Sushi and shit-talking?"

"Sushi and shit-talking." She winks, and I laugh all the way to my room.

Their presence is a breath of fresh air. I can be someone totally different than who I am back in Longwood. While I ache to spend time with my siblings so they don't feel the gaping hole in their lives where our parents should be, the other part of me savors being in Crystal Bay and actually having my own life.

I'm not weighed down by being Georgia Benson's daughter, the one who has to remain perfectly polished and put together at all times. The one who couldn't possibly be allowed to pursue a career that doesn't fit the predetermined path Mother planned for me.

I'm just... me.

Freshly brewed coffee and blueberry scones awaken my senses as I wait impatiently in line at Crystal Coffee. The on-campus java shop is unsurprisingly packed, given every student is still readjusting to eight a.m. classes after the break.

At least it's Friday and I can finally sleep in tomorrow.

"Morning, Charlotte." My head swivels to find Noah striding toward me in athletic clothes, hair wet, and two to-go cups in hand. "Thought you'd appreciate not having to wait."

He holds one towards me, and a grin spreads across my face as I step out of line, eagerly taking the unexpected offering. "*Ohh, come to Mama.*"

"It's a double shot. I noticed you were struggling to keep your eyes open," he says, with a hint of concern in his tone, and my chest tightens.

"Thank you." The sweet liquid of a vanilla cinnamon latte hits my taste buds, and I side-eye Noah. "How do you know my usual coffee order?"

He holds the door for me while we exit the coffee shop into the warm Florida air. "Lucky guess."

It's the first conversation we've had in person since I asked him to fuck me.

I cringe, my sweet beverage turning bitter.

Is this latte a friend zone elixir?

Is he concerned I'll ask him again?

Is he thinking about that night too?

Tugging my phone out, I check the time, which gives me an escape route from this awkward situation.

"My stats class starts in five," I say, gesturing behind me with my thumb.

"Good thing I rescued you from the coffee line," he says, pleased with himself.

I take another long sip of the warm liquid because without the caffeine boost, there's no point in attending. "Yeah, the probability of me picking coffee over punctuality today would've been certain."

"I'd argue the ends justify the beans," he says, walking past me. "Come on."

I huff a laugh, rushing after him. "Where to?"

"I'm walking you to class," he says as I catch up.

So much for escaping. "Won't you be late to yours?"

"No?" His brows pull together. "I was out for a run. I don't have class on Fridays."

My eyes roam over him: tight, dry wick shirt sticking to his muscular chest. Athletic shorts. Running shoes. No backpack.

"Oh." *Guess we're doing this.* "Lucky you."

"Perks of it being my last semester," he says, reminding me of his impending graduation and the three-year age gap between us. *What the hell was I thinking asking this man to fuck me? Of course he wasn't interested.*

I tip my head back, and the sun hits my face like it's attempting to melt away the humiliation. Memories from last week's beach getaway flash in my mind. "I would *much* rather be walking in the sand than into stats."

Noah chuckles. "You're not the only one feeling that way. The guys and I are heading to the beach tomorrow. Wanna join?"

This awkwardness is killing me, but I'm going to have to get over it sooner or later, so I find myself saying, "Sure."

"Awesome. I'll pick you up at ten?" He halts on the sidewalk.

"Pick me up?" I ask, stumbling to a stop, and he grabs my arm, steadying me.

"Yeah." His gaze drops to his searing hold, and he releases, stepping away. I clear my throat, finding my balance and my breath. "Or were you planning to walk since you don't have a car anymore?"

Right. He's just being nice.

"I'll get a ride from the girls," I assure him. "I'm sure they'll want to come too."

Their presence is mandatory. I need back-up from saying something fucking stupid again.

"They can meet us there." He shuffles backwards, ignoring my offer of an out.

"Or *I* can meet *you* there," I push, fighting a smile.

"See you at ten!" He shoots me a wink, then spins around and jogs away.

My eyes follow him till he rounds the corner of the building and disappears, my cheeks as warm as this latte in my hands.

Maybe he really is Riemann's quarterback... because I definitely can't figure him out.

7

NOAH

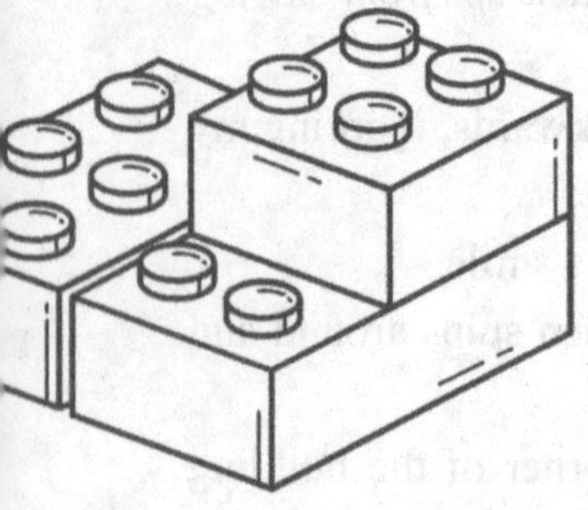

BIG STING ENERGY

ME

Beach day tomorrow, who's in?

ELIJAH ANDERSON

I'll check with Soph

THEO SCHROEDER

I don't need permission, so hell yeah I'll be there

JULIAN LISCERO

I'm down

DESMOND BALL

Can't. I've got a top-30 tour in Vegas this weekend

JULIAN LISCERO

Boooooo

Don't abandon us yet

Alllll byyyyy myyyy selffffff

DESMOND BALL

Save the break up songs.

i'll be back monday

THEO SCHROEDER

put $100 on red for me

ELIJAH ANDERSON

Alright, Soph and I will be there

JULIAN LISCERO

You picking me up, cap?

ME

Can't I'm giving Charlotte a ride

THEO SCHROEDER

Ohhhhhhhhh shit everybody stay calm

DESMOND BALL

it's HAPPENING

JULIAN LISCERO

heavy breathing

ELIJAH ANDERSON

what about sir fuck face?

ME

see you dumbasses tomorrow

My truck rolls to a stop outside Charlotte's building. I glance at the clock. 9:59 a.m. *Right on time.*

I grab my phone from the cupholder, and the damn countdown tortures me again.

NFL Draft: 19 days. 10 hours. 1 minute.

Which teams will make an offer?

Will I stay in Florida?

Will I be okay if I don't?

Shaking away the questions I can't answer, I pull up my thread with Charlotte.

CHARLOTTE

ME

Fun fact: the ocean covers 70% of the earth's surface

CHARLOTTE

I already knew that try harder

ME

Did you also know sometimes sea slugs decapitate themselves so they can grow a new body to be stronger

CHARLOTTE

no one needs to know that

also gross

ME

hah! winner

Btw, your uber is here

CHARLOTTE

The conversation better be excellent or it'll reflect in your tip.

ME

I have the opportunity for a tip? Brb gonna research talking points.

A few minutes later, Charlotte strolls out of her building in a see-through cover-up and bikini so revealing, my eyes practically bulge out of my skull.

She hops in the passenger seat with a wide smile. "Hey," she says, as my eyes wander down her body. Her beautiful, very visible, body. "Problem?"

I rub a hand against the stubble on my jaw while she buckles herself in. "Just wondering if you plan on giving everyone at the beach a fucking heart attack."

"Noah!" Her cheeks flush, and my mouth opens and closes as I struggle for a single coherent thought. "The girls said I look hot," she murmurs, glancing down and adjusting the material, a nipple dangerously close to popping out. A nipple I'm well-versed in the size and shape of as of last week.

Stifling a groan, I reach over, placing my hand on hers. "You do look…" Incredible. Sinful. Fuckable. "Hot." Her skin is warm under my thumb. My eyes trail her body. *So much soft skin.*

"Noah?" she says, and my heated gaze finds hers.

Those brown eyes search my soul, and I clear my throat, pulling my hand back and super-gluing it to the steering wheel. *Rule number one: don't touch Charlotte.* "Let's go."

She takes over the aux cable, and performs "Please Please Please" by Sabrina Carpenter at the top of her lungs. She's just gotten to the second chorus when her phone rings, interrupting the live show.

"It's my brother FaceTiming." She angles the phone screen at me. "Do you mind?"

"Not at all."

"Hey, Nash," she says, her voice happy and light.

"Hey, Lottie," he grumbles.

"What's wrong?" she asks him, shooting me a puzzled look.

He sighs heavily. "Our spring break is this week."

"I'm not getting the problem," Charlotte says. "Don't you love being off school?"

"I love not having homework, but yesterday everyone was

talking about their plans, and we have none at all. Mike is even going to *Disneyland* with his parents. Can you believe it? He gets to go to *California,* and we're staying home."

"I'm sorry, buddy," Charlotte says, dragging a hand through her dark hair. "I wish I could take you and Denny somewhere, but I have school. And you know I don't have a car anymore either."

"Why can't they plan all the spring breaks at the same time? And I still don't understand why Mom took your car."

My eyes swing, gauging her for any reaction since I was curious as well.

"Can Patricia take you two to do something?" she asks. "Or Dad?"

"Dad's flying to New York, but he said he can't take us, and Patricia is sick."

Charlotte sinks in the passenger seat, her sadness stabbing at my chest. "I'm really sorry."

"Can you visit us next weekend?" Nash asks quietly. Desperately.

"I don't ha—"

"Hey, Nash," I say, interrupting Charlotte, and she sends me a sharp look.

"Hi?" he replies.

"I'm Noah," I say. "*Lottie's* friend."

"Oh," he grumbles. "Hey."

"Wanna go camping next weekend?" I ask, and Charlotte's head snaps toward me as I glide my hands around the steering wheel. I probably should have run it by her first.

"Are you serious?!" Nash exclaims, shouting through the phone with a huge smile on his face.

Charlotte whisper-shouts at me. "What are you doing?"

I definitely should have run it by her first.

"You'll have to make sure it's okay with your parents," I continue, a nervous buzz under my skin. "But if th—"

"It'll be fine! Are you serious?" Nash asks again.

"Yeah." I smile, straightening my shoulders. "I'm sure."

Charlotte whispers, "I thought you were going to Daytona with the guys."

"Well, now we're going camping," I whisper back.

"Alright, Nashy," Charlotte says, not taking her confused eyes off me. "I'll call Mom later to talk about the details, okay?"

"Okay!" His energy flows through the screen. "Thanks, Lottie! Thanks, Noah!" His voice fades away. "I can't even believe this. Denny! Guess what? We're go—"

The line goes dead, and I glance over at Charlotte. Her eyes are narrowed on me, brows furrowed, cute little wrinkles on her forehead.

"I don't understand," she says as I return my eyes to the road.

"What's to understand?" I shrug, ignoring the jitters dancing through me at the idea of us spending a weekend together. "They wanted to go somewhere for spring break. I love camping. Win, win."

I *don't* love camping.

But I used to go a lot after Mom and Tony first got together when I wasn't comfortable with him being alone with her. Especially in the middle of nowhere.

So, I know how to camp. And it was the first thing that came to mind given we went for spring break when I was younger.

"I don't have a sleeping bag, a tent, nothing," Charlotte argues. "I don't even know *how* to camp. How the hell to put up a tent."

"Char." I chuckle, interrupting her freak-out. "Calm down. I used to go all the time. My family has everything. Even canoes."

"But what about Daytona?" she asks timidly. *Does she not want to go?*

"Screw Daytona," I reply, waving a hand. "Camping sounds a lot more enjoyable than seeing Theo's bare ass."

She whips her head to me. "What?"

"Story for another time. So what do you say? We taking the kids camping?"

She eyes me, a searing gaze running down my body. "Looks like we are."

Elijah tosses me a beer as I plop on a towel, burying my feet in the warm sand. I crack it open and take a long pull, and he lowers himself next to me.

"Won't be the same without you next year," he says, arms resting on his knees while his eyes remain glued on Sophia, who's taking pictures down by the shore with Charlotte and Sage.

"Thanks." We clank our metal cans. "You're gonna do a hell of a job as captain."

Elijah shakes his head. "I'll never live up to you."

"Stop being such a sappy fuck." I nudge his shoulder, gratitude filling me.

"Sorry." He huffs a laugh. "I think Sophia broke me." A slaphappy grin is glued to his face as he watches her.

"I think she fixed you, man."

His cheeks redden. "You may be right."

"What's up?" Theo asks, joining us with our friend and fellow teammate, Julian, following behind.

"Nothing, just discussing the fact Elijah's man card has been permanently revoked," I joke.

Theo laughs. "Yeah, it's tucked tight in Sophia's little pu—"

"Don't you dare finish that sentence," Elijah warns.

Theo puts his hands up. "I was going to say *purse*." He smirks. "Maybe you should get *your* mind out of the gutter."

"Whatever," Elijah says, nudging Theo's leg. "You'll see someday. Poor girl."

"Hey!" Theo says, hand on his chest. "She'll be *lucky* to have a man like me." Elijah and I share a look and laugh. "Assholes." He waves us off.

"So, I'm not going to Daytona next weekend," I say, deciding to drop the truth bomb on them all at once. Their heads whip to me.

"What?" Theo yells.

"Dude," Julian deadpans.

"Are you kidding? It's our last bro trip before you graduate," Elijah says, guilting me.

"Tequila and tits," Theo says, as if those two words alone should make me change my mind. "Tequila. And. Tits."

"Sorry," I say, fighting a smile.

"Why can't you come?" Julian asks. "You got another top-30 meet?"

"No," I say shifting in place. "I'm taking Charlotte and the twins camping."

"They better be some hot cheerleader twins if you're skipping out on our last guys trip for them," Theo says.

"No, dumbass," Elijah says. "He means Charlie's *little* brother and sister."

"What?" Theo shrieks.

"This dick is trying to say *my* man card's lost." Elijah pokes me. "What the hell do you call this?"

"It's not the same," I argue, rubbing the back of my neck as the tips of my ears burn.

"How the hell not?" Elijah asks.

"We're just friends!" My tone is clearly defensive, and I lower my voice. "Char doesn't have a car, and the twins were sad as shit about their spring break. So I offered to take them camping."

"Don't you *hate* camping?" Elijah reminds me.

"I'm trying to evolve," I say, with a sarcastic smile.

"Doesn't Charlie have a boyfriend?" Julian asks.

"Not anymore," I say, and all three of their heads snap towards me. "But that's irrelevant. We're just friends."

"*Oookay*." Theo huffs a laugh. "And Elijah's never got his dick stuck in someone."

"Let it *gooooo*!" Elijah groans, slapping Theo on the head.

"Listen, you didn't hear the way her brother sounded about having nothing to do for spring break." Another pang hits my chest. "We can go to Daytona anytime. I'd feel like shit knowing I'm there having a good time while he's sitting at home, doing nothing."

"Mm-hmm." Theo narrows his eyes at me. "You're doing this for her *brother*. Sure."

"Fuck off." I flick a bit of sand his way with my foot. "I'll make it up to you guys."

"You better," Theo says, chucking a football at me that I catch with one hand while downing my beer with the other. "You're gonna be a big rich NFL player next year. You can whisk your boys off on a fancy weekend getaway to make it up to us."

"I promise to send you all a dozen roses for your trouble." I stand up, sand trickling off me, football in hand, and the boys follow my lead.

"I'll be waiting," Elijah says, shuffling backwards, and I launch the ball to him.

The second it's out of my possession, my gaze drifts to Charlotte spinning around by the water's edge. Her eyes lock with mine, and she stumbles to a pause. My lips curve up in response, and her jaw drops as my head is pelted with a football.

"Oww?!" I place my hand against it, looking around for the culprit.

Theo is keeled over in laughter with his hands on his knees.

"Dude." Elijah shakes his head. "You are so fucked."

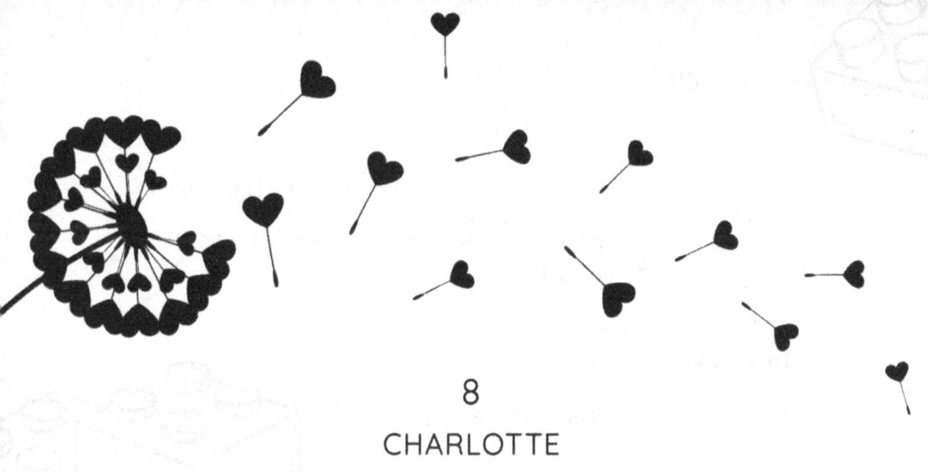

8

CHARLOTTE

I sit in the passenger seat of Noah's truck, an anxious freaking mess, trying my damndest to put on my "I'm totally chill" face.

It's been a week since his offer to take my siblings camping, and I'm still shocked by it. What guy chooses six-year-olds over partying with their friends? *Jonathan certainly never did.*

Not to mention, considering I had a boyfriend until two weeks ago, the times we've spent alone can be counted on a single hand. My phone buzzes in my lap, and I'm thankful for the distraction.

SUSHI & SHIT-TALKING

ANDI

Why are there five types of pie in the kitchen

STELLA

Baby cakes, were you stress baking again?

I grin at the nickname I earned from frequently whipping up some type of sweet treat. *Especially* when I'm stressed.

ME

One of them is a quiche

Mommy couldn't leave without preparing food for the children

ANDI

Thank you, mommy

You make it to the campsite yet?

ME

No, we're on the way to Noah's mom's house & we still have to pick up the twins

STELLA

omg you're meeting his mother

Oh my god, I'm meeting his mother.
Calm. I am the poster child for calm.

ME

So?

STELLA

so noah caruso is not the "bring them home to mama" type of guy

ME

What kind of guy is he?

ANDI

the "bring you home to bone" type of guy

and he is not a repeat offender

this is huge

ME

okay i love you guys. Truly. But noah and i are FRIENDSSSSS.

and jonathan and i JUST broke up

ANDI

I say fuck him

Noah not Jonathan (in case that wasn't clear)

Heat flushes my cheeks.

ME

goodbye!

STELLA

have fun with mama caruso!

ANDI

have more fun with daddy noah

I slap the phone on my lap to avoid combusting with embarrassment just as Noah pulls into a driveway covered with round pool floats, a canoe, coolers, and other supplies that make no logical sense to me.

He puts the truck in park, and my eyes wander over the rest of the two-story, powder-blue house. There's a white wraparound porch and a rocking chair swaying in the wind. Honeysuckle bushes line the walkway on both sides, and a sign that says "LOVE GROWS HERE" sticks out of the grass.

It's quaint and perfect and lovely, and everything my life is not.

"Hey," Noah says softly, looking over at me.

"Yes?"

"Why do you look all stressed?" He narrows his eyes. Guess I wasn't displaying as much "chill" energy as I thought.

"I'm not stressed," I say in a high-pitched voice, completely giving myself away.

"Are you nervous to meet my mom?" he asks, the corner of his lip quirking in a teasing grin. *How the hell?*

"What?" I scoff. "No. I have no reason to be nervous."

Keep telling yourself that, Char.

Noah rests his arm on the back of my seat, and my shoulder tingles. "You're gonna love her."

"Of course I am," I say, trying to shake away the nerves from this bizarre situation.

We hop out of the truck and walk toward the front steps. As we reach them, the door swings open, and a woman with kind eyes steps barefoot on the porch. She's clad in jeans and a white T-shirt, her brown hair twisted up in a bun. A colorful apron dancing with lemons is tied around her with an assumedly Italian saying I can't quite decipher.

Noah was right. I love her.

"Welcome!" the woman says to us, throwing her arms around Noah and kissing him on both cheeks. "*Ciao, sole mio.*"

"*Ciao, mamma,*" he tells her.

She pulls away, turning her attention to me, and tugs me in for a tight hug like she's known me for years. The gesture is unexpected and makes me laugh. "Sorry." She releases me, hands still on my shoulders. "I've just heard so much about you," she says in a beautiful Italian accent, her words wrapping around me. *She has?* "Feels like I know you."

"It's okay," I say, side-eyeing Noah, then returning my gaze to her.

"I'm Noah's mom, Luna."

"Hi, Luna." I wave, a handshake feeling unnecessary after the hug. "I'm Charlie."

"Oh, we know all about you, Ms. *Charlotte*," she replies, and my cheeks warm. "Please." She gestures us inside, and we follow her through the door.

A familiar aroma floods my senses, and my mouth waters. "It smells *heavenly* in here."

"There's cinnamon walnut cookies in the oven." Luna smiles proudly, and I share a look with Noah.

Cinnamon is my favorite baking spice.

We follow Luna to the kitchen, truly the masterpiece of the

house. There's a spacious island, flour sprinkled across it, along with other ingredients set to the side and a used mixing bowl. A massive gas stovetop with a double oven beneath it has my full attention.

"Oh my goodness." I gasp, rushing over to a Smeg Stand Mixer illustrated with the most beautiful floral pattern I've ever seen. "You have the Dolce & Gabbana 50's Retro Mixer!" Upon hearing the words leave my mouth, I realize I'm totally geeking out, but I don't even care. "It's even more stunning in person."

Luna laughs. "My husband got it for me for Christmas. When Smeg came out with the Sicily is My Love collection, he knew it would remind me of my family."

I run my fingers along the intricate colorful pattern. "It's beautiful."

"Thank you," she says proudly.

"You're originally from Sicily?" I ask.

"Yes," she says, retrieving a stick of butter from the fridge. "I moved here in college."

"Is that the NFL's next top rookie quarterback gracing us mere mortals with his presence?" a loud, deep voice says as a man rounds the corner of the hallway.

Noah's smile grows wide as he walks toward the man, who I assume must be his stepdad. "Hey."

The man throws his arms around Noah and hugs him tightly. After releasing him, he wanders toward me and extends his hand. "Tony."

"Charlie." I return the gesture with a smile. "Nice to meet you."

"Can't believe you talked Noah into going camping," Luna says. "We haven't gotten him to go in years."

My eyes flick toward Noah, who's looking at her apologetically. "I've been busy."

Luna holds up a hand. "I'm not saying anything. Just glad you're finally going again."

"Hope you remember how to put up a tent," Tony teases, lightening the mood.

"I think I can manage," Noah grumbles, and I fight a smile. It's nice hearing people talk to Noah like a normal person and not the five-year-plan, perfect-at-everything man he is on campus.

"Well, just in case," Tony tells him. "I'll give you a refresher while we load the stuff in the truck."

He and Noah exit the kitchen, leaving me alone with Luna. *Shit. I'm not prepared for this.* She begins another batch of dough, and I wring my hands together, fingers itching to join in.

"Want to crack the eggs?" she asks, and a smile spreads across my face. I wash my hands, rushing to join her at her workstation. *This is good. Baking is good.*

We fall into comfortable silence, aside from her directions for pouring in the needed ingredients. Although they're hardly necessary. I could whip up a batch of cookies of any variety with my eyes closed.

"Noah mentioned this will be your first time camping?" she asks.

"Yes," I say. "My parents weren't really the camping kind… maybe the *glamping* kind."

Even though I was raised middle class, my mom came from old money. The thought of sleeping in a tent in the middle of the woods repulsed her. She said as much when I called for permission to take the kids, but given her busy campaign schedule and lack of help this week, she was more than happy for the offer.

"We went all the time when Tony and I were first dating," she says.

"How long have you been together now?"

Luna smiles. "About seven years. Married for three."

"He and Noah seem close."

She scoops dough out of the mixing bowl and rolls it into a ball before placing it on the lined baking tray. "Tony was there for us a lot in the wake of my ex-husband." Her admission surprises me, given Noah's avoidance on the subject.

"Noah doesn't really talk about him," I say, rolling dough myself, stomach tightening. "His dad, I mean."

"It's a sore spot," Luna says, and I nod. "Are you missing cheer since season ended?"

"Yes," I say, noting her change of subject. "I'm looking forward to starting training again next month."

"At Camp Dickson, right? Like Noah did?" she asks, and I nod. "Oh, he always loved that place."

"Yeah, it's really fun," I say, thinking of the shenanigans I got into with the girls last year. *And Jonathan.* My stomach sinks at the reminder. The training camp invites a few collegiate football teams, Jonathan's school included, and given he's their quarterback… fuck, I forgot about that.

"Noah mentioned you're majoring in education?" Luna asks, pulling me out of my spiral.

"Yes," I say, shifting on my feet. "Early childhood education."

"That's wonderful." She smiles wide, filling me with a sense of relief. "It truly takes a special kind of person to have the patience to teach. Especially young children."

A special kind of person.

If only my mother felt that way instead of seeing it as a passion profession.

"You gonna give me one of those?" Noah asks as I shove another cinnamon cookie in my mouth during our drive to get my siblings.

"Maybe," I mumble, a cookie crumb falling out, and I catch it, tossing it back in. "If you give me a really good fun fact."

"A good fun fact…" He taps his fingers against the steering

wheel. "Did you know a Roman emperor burned a year's worth of cinnamon at his wife's funeral as a symbol of his grief?"

My face scrunches up, staring at the once delicious treat. "So this is a funeral cookie?"

"Follow-up fun fact," Noah says, ignoring my cookie conundrum. *To eat, or not to eat. That is the question.* "The emperor was actually the one who killed her."

My gaze snaps to Noah. "What kind of fun fact is that? That is the opposite of a fun fact. That is a funless fact." I toss the cookie back in the container and close it. "No cookie for you."

He rolls his eyes, fighting a smile. "But you both worked so hard on them. Can't I have *one*?"

"Later." I wave him off, ignoring his puppy dog pout. "You must be punished for forcing me to lose my appetite."

"Can't you just put me in time-out, Ms. Benson?" he says, eyes lighting up as he grins my way, and I squirm in my seat.

Groaning, I yank open the container, holding it toward him. "Just take your murder cookie."

"Victory!" He snatches one and scarfs it in a few bites, then releases a breathy moan. *"Mmm. Quasi meglio del sesso."*[1]

I ignore the way his impeccable Italian makes me shiver, even though I have no idea what he's saying, and opt to change the subject. "You were right, by the way."

"About?"

"I love your mom. Can we go back next weekend?"

Noah side-eyes me. "This is why I don't bring friends home. They end up liking her more than me."

"Noah's mom has got it going on," I sing to the tune of the catchy 2000s hit.

"Please stop." He cringes. "You're good at so many things, but singing is not one of them."

"Noah, can I come over after schooooool?" I belt off-key.

---

1. IT: *Mmm. Quasi meglio del sesso.* - EN: Mmm. Almost better than sex.

"Stop it!" he begs with a laugh, pinching my side.

I yelp, flinching away. "Hey! Focus on the road."

"My apologies." He places both hands on the wheel. "Ten and two. Ten and two."

"Thank you."

"And besides, I'm in Seattle next weekend for a tour with the Grizzlies," he says, reminding me of his impending move, and my stomach sinks. "I have to leave for the airport Thursday after graduation."

"Right," I say, glancing over, allowing myself to get an extra long look at him. He taps his left hand on his thigh to the beat of the music while his head bobs back and forth. A few days' worth of stubble covers his jaw, and I find myself wondering how it would feel rubbing between my thighs.

Charlotte, it's going to be a long weekend if you allow these thoughts to flood your brain.

Noah grips the steering wheel loosely, his elbow resting on the center console. The veins in his arm tense and release as he moves his hand along the leather. He reaches up to scratch his chiseled chin, and I can't take my eyes off his perfect mouth as he brushes his thumb over his plump lip. The CBU Football hat adorned atop his head is backwards, and that's just not even fair.

It should be illegal for a man to wear a backwards ball cap when you're trying to keep them in the friend zone.

"Something I can help you with?" Noah asks, catching me staring.

My cheeks ignite. Along with the rest of my body. The Roman emperor has burned me along with the cinnamon. "Just trying to figure out why you're doing this for me."

"Your siblings seem awesome, and I'm looking forward to something more low-key."

"Is that really why?" I ask, ruining my illusion of nonchalance.

"I can party with the boys any time," he says, twinkling green eyes meeting mine for a split second before he focuses back on the road.

"Well, I'm super grateful you're giving up tits and tequila for tents and twins."

Theo was very adamant on that fact.

"Stop acting like I'm doing you a favor." Noah shakes his head, a crooked smile spreading across his face. "I'm exactly where I want to be."

A sense of serenity takes hold inside me, and we settle into comfortable conversation all the way to Longwood.

We pull up to the Benson estate, and a rock the weight of a two-ton elephant returns to my stomach. It's cold and callous shell is a total contrast from Noah's cozy white-picket home oozing love and family. He doesn't comment on the lavish building as we get out of the truck, and I'm grateful.

The moment we're inside, Mom's voice pierces my ears. "Kids, are you ready yet?" she calls down the hall.

"Almost!" Nash shouts back.

"I've gotta leave when Charlie gets here," she says as I close the door with a loud thud. *Just like her, always running out.* Her footsteps echo down the hallway, and she comes into view. "Oh, good," she says. "I was worried you'd run late. I have a meeting in"—she looks down at her watch—"well, now, actually."

"We're here," I say.

"Pleasure to meet you, Mrs. Benson," Noah says, extending his hand. "I'm Noah."

"Pleasure's all mine," she says, donning a perfectly poised smile. "Thank you so much for taking them on this trip."

"Of course, happy to." *He's happy to.*

"You're lucky to have such a good friend, Charlie," Mom says, checking her watch again. My eyes find Noah's, and our lips quirk to a matching smile. *It seems I am.* "Kids, you ready?"

Nash rounds the corner, a ginormous backpack hooked on his shoulders, and I'm filled with happiness at the sight of him.

"I'm so excited," he says, grinning ear to ear, one misstep from toppling over.

"Me too," I say, squeezing him tightly.

"I'm *readyyyyy*!" Denny calls out, dragging her equally large bag down the hallway. Noah laughs, the warm, unfamiliar sound echoing in the spacious foyer, and he walks to her.

"Isn't this a little too big for you?" Noah teases.

"Aren't you a little too big for weird mask T-shirts?" Denny sasses back, and Noah glances down.

"This is Darth Vader," Noah scoffs. "It's a classic."

"It's lame," she says with an eye roll.

"Denver," Mom snaps, using her legal name. "Is that any way to speak to a guest?"

"No," Denny mumbles. "Sorry."

"It's fine," Noah assures Mom, grabbing Denny's bag and throwing it over his shoulder.

"Okay, I'm off," Mom says, leaning down to kiss the twins on the head and striding towards the door. *No kiss for me.* "Can you lock up?"

"Sure," I say, giving her a hesitant wave, and she sends me a weak smile. Things are tense, but we're at least on cordial speaking terms.

Noah installs the booster seats into his truck, and we each take a kid. Nash fends me off, climbing up and buckling himself. Denny's giggle pulls my attention as Noah blasts her off the ground, making a whooshing sound like a rocket, then sets her in the seat and buckles her in.

If backwards ball caps are illegal, it should be treason for a man in said friend zone to pair it with effortlessly slipping into the role of *daddy*. My ovaries are exploding.

Down, girl.

Hopping in the passenger seat, I put on Noah's favorite playlist. He drives down the country road toward the highway, and my gaze wanders to him once more. His window is cracked, the breeze blowing the dark hair peeking out from under his hat, the kids are teasing each other in the back seat, and a wide smile spreads across my face at how very normal it all feels.

9

NOAH

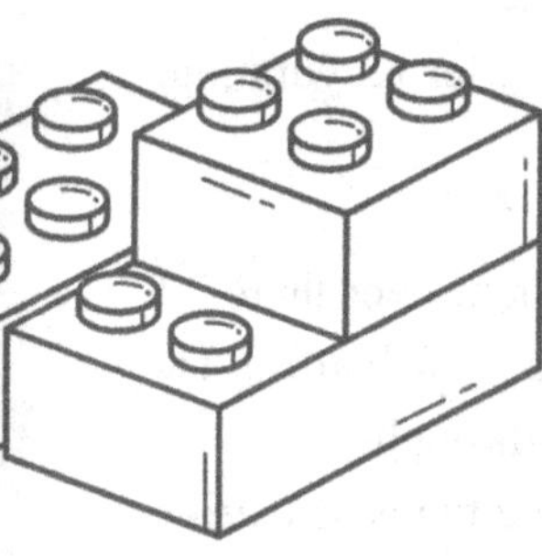

"Come on, Nash!" I shout across the open space. "You've got it." He launches the tiny football through the air, and I catch it easily.

"Yes!" he shouts, jumping with excitement.

"High five, bud!" I raise my hand. "That was awesome." He runs to me and slaps my hand so hard I have to shake out the pain. "Dang, you've got a lot of power for a little guy."

"A little guy?" Nash says with raised brows, then turns to a side stance I'm all too familiar with from my Taekwondo practice. "*Yeop chagi!*" he shouts, and I hop out of the way before he gets a chance to send that little foot flying towards me in a side kick.

"*Kalryeo,*" I beg with a laugh.

He freezes, standing straight. "You know Korean?"

"No," I admit. "Just from Taekwondo."

"What belt are you?" he asks, eyes shining with interest.

"Second dan black belt."

His eyes widen. "Wow."

"You going to shoot a kick my way again?" I ask with a cocked brow.

He shakes his head furiously, and I chuckle. "Come on, let's go grab some water."

My eyes wander to Charlotte, who's coloring with Denny on the picnic table at our camping spot near Ichetucknee Springs. I set up the tents when we arrived, one for Charlotte and her siblings and one for me, with zero issues. Mainly thanks to Tony's twenty-minute camping crash course he gave before allowing us to leave the house, but hey, Charlotte doesn't have to know.

"You wanna do something fun?" I ask Nash after rehydrating, noting the sun's beginning to set.

His eyes light up. "Yes!"

"Go collect some long, thin sticks and put them over there." I point toward the pile of logs I brought to start up our bonfire. He obliges, roping Denny into helping him halfway through.

"Be really careful around this, okay?" I tell the twins as I strike a match and throw it onto the brush I placed for kindling under the logs.

"Yes, Noah," they chime in unison.

In my tent, I grab the supplies for the next item on the list of "Top 5 Things to do While Camping," and when I return, Charlotte grins at me.

"S'mores?" she asks, looking down at the two bags in my hands.

"Yep." I beam. "It's not camping without s'mores." *At least not according to my research.*

I take two thin sticks Nash found and stake marshmallows through them, then hand one to him and the other to Denny. I grab one for myself and demonstrate how to roast them to perfection. *Well, I try.* Only ten are burned before they get the hang of it. I don't mind. That's why I brought extra.

I meticulously stack a graham cracker, toasted marshmallow, piece of chocolate, and another cracker on top. Pressing it together, I grin satisfactorily at my handiwork. *Like riding a bike.* Charlotte sits beside me on a log, a pretty smile on her face, watching her siblings laugh and giggle as they consume their weight in gooey goodness. We might regret this later when they need to go to bed.

Two six-year-olds pumped with sugar? Yikes.

"Here," I say, holding out my perfect creation.

"Thanks." She accepts the offering.

"Have you enjoyed losing your camping virginity?" I ask as she takes a bite, chocolate oozing out and trickling down her chin.

New rule: don't lick the chocolate off Charlotte's face.

She nods, swallowing. "Definitely." She wipes the tasty temptation off with her thumb and sticks it in her mouth, sucking it clean. *Blood, stay out of dick.* Her attention returns to Denny and Nash.

"Maybe we should take them to do stuff like this more often," I find myself saying, the idea of spending time with her appealing. I've got a no relationship rule, sure. But hanging out with a *friend* shouldn't be a distraction… right?

Her curious eyes flick to mine. "Really?"

I shrug, shoving all counter arguments to the who-gives-a-fuck department. "Yeah, why not?"

Charlotte scans my face, her lips dropping to a frown, and she looks away, her knee bouncing.

"Hey," I say softly, and her gaze returns to mine, unreadable. "What was that?"

"What was what?" She smiles, but it doesn't reach her eyes.

"Where did you go there?" I wring my fingers together, fighting the urge to place a hand on her anxious leg. "You were happy, and then…"

"The truth?"

"Always."

"First, I was thinking I'd really enjoy us doing stuff with the twins." My heart swells. "But then I thought how much it would hurt them when you move away later this year."

And just like that, my swelling heart turns to a sinking stomach because, *fuck*. The last thing I ever want to do is hurt the twins, or her.

"Char." I tilt my head to the side, and she looks down at her hands. "We don't even know where I'll end up yet."

Her eyes are glossy in the firelight. "You're graduating next week, then immediately touring Seattle." She pauses. "They're going to love you, by the way," she assures me, gaze meeting mine. "Your life's about to get super hectic. I don't want to put any pressure on you to come see us."

"Seeing you all would be as much for me as it would be for you."

"How so?"

"I'm going to crave this…" Glancing around, I search for the right word. "Normalcy. Spending time with people who see me as more than a vessel for winning football games or for some kind of clout."

"I promise I would never use you for clout." Her lips quirk upward. "You're really not that cool anyways."

"Hey." I throw a hand over my wounded ego.

"Kidding," she says, nudging me with her shoulder. "It was just a… I don't know, stupid thought, I guess."

"It's not stupid." I reach out and rest my palm on her knee. *Guess we're breaking rules tonight.* Her skin is hot under my touch, the heat blazing up my arm like a wildfire. She glances at my hand. *Does she feel the flames too?* Her sparkling eyes connect with mine. "I understand you're afraid for them to get attached," I say, although this seems less of a group concern. "But I promise I'm always gonna come back and see you. *All* of you."

She smiles, nose scrunching. "Sorry I'm such a needy friend. I doubt the guys give you emotional shit like this."

"You'd be surprised," I say, removing my hand. *Smart move.* "Elijah's turned into a big softy."

"I'm well aware. Last week he wore a shirt that said, 'World's

Best Boyfriend.'" She shakes her head, then continues, "'Ask me about my Koalifications.'"

"Oh, I saw it. He's been given the nickname mar-*simp*-ial for that."

Charlotte snorts a laugh. "That's a good one." Her gaze connects with mine. "They've really found something special, huh?"

I memorize the way the flickering fire glistens in her eyes. The curve of her jaw as she trails her fingertips down it, brushing away a stray hair. "Yeah. They have."

The high-pitched sound fills the air. Again.

And again, and again, and again.

All that sugar was *definitely* a bad idea.

Nash bounces around the dark campsite illuminated by the firelight, blowing with all his might into a little toy train whistle. Denny trails him like an energizer bunny, and just *watching* them exhausts me.

"Nash, what *are* you doing?" I ask him, paired with a teasing laugh.

"Scaring off bears!" he shouts, continuing the ear-screeching noise.

"There's no bears out here," I assure him.

"Okay, then the scary things," he argues, and I shake my head as he continues his silly warding-off-evil dance.

"How are we ever going to get them to bed?" I ask Charlotte.

"They'll wear out soon," she promises with a laugh, picking up a candy wrapper and putting it into a trash bag. "Denny's starting to fade. Nash will soon after."

Nash zooms around the tent. Fading seems unlikely, but Charlotte knows them better than I do. *I hope they're enjoying this trip.*

"You think the boys will forgive you for skipping Daytona?" Charlotte asks, gaze meeting mine.

I shrug. "They'll survive."

She suppresses a smile, the firelight dancing in her eyes. "They're probably just heading out, and here we are, cleaning up for the night."

"I'd take this over bar hopping any day."

"Yeah?" She toys with the ends of her loose braid, gaze stuck on mine.

I nod. "Yeah."

My skin flushes hot at the attention. *Or maybe it's the campfire?*

"Lottie," Denny says, interrupting our staring contest. "Will you take me to the bathroom?"

"Sure," Charlotte says, turning to her. "And let's grab your bedtime stuff so you can brush your teeth. You too, Nash." She returns back to me. "Big sister duties await."

"Do your thing," I say, and she backs away with a smile that steals my lungs, then disappears to gather their stuff.

We freshen up in the bathrooms, and Charlotte ushers the kids to their tent, forcing them to bed despite Nash's protests. Taking a seat by the fire, I wait in the hope we can continue talking without little ones interrupting us. Twenty minutes pass, and the low light from their tent fades to darkness.

Guess Charlotte went to sleep too.

I grab a bucket of water near the cooler and dump it on the fire, extinguishing the remaining embers, and my optimism. Entering my tent, I kick off my shoes, tug my shirt overhead, and toss it in the corner. I'm far from tired, so I pull out the *Florida Times* and flip through it. My attention catches on an article from the Opinion section.

GEORGIA BENSON: SOCIALITE OR SAVIOR?
DOES THIS GOVERNOR CANDIDATE HAVE WHAT IT TAKES?

Georgia Benson is the only child of the infamous Benson family, who first grew their fortune through real estate during the early 1800s, making her no stranger to the world of high society. One would assume she'd focus her time on tax breaks for the rich and rezoning to expand her family's real estate empire; however, the impacts of her time in office are intriguing.

Benson has spent the last six years as the mayor of Longwood, a small Florida town. During her time in office, she successfully implemented multiple government-funded programs that benefit the constituents of the town, including Longwood's Rehabilitation House, which assists those who are overcoming drug and alcohol addictions.

Benson's program was inspired by a close friend who almost succumbed to opioid addiction, but thanks to a rehabilitation program in another state, was able to receive help. Benson wanted to develop the same assistance for her local community.

After inheriting the Benson fortune, which is an estimated $350 million, it's clear Benson has set her sights on higher political aspirations. She's even been rumored to have interest in running for president should the opp—

"Knock, knock," Charlotte says, her voice clear given the thin tent. My attention is yanked from the article, and my heart rate skyrockets.

"Password?" I whisper, folding the paper and tossing it to the side so her mood isn't ruined.

"Let me in before I get eaten by a bear!" *She wants to come in?*

I crawl through the tent and unzip it. "Didn't Nash already scare them all away?"

She slides off her shoes and steps inside. "Not taking any chances." She glances around before settling onto my full-sized air mattress. *Charlotte's on my bed. Again.*

"Make yourself at home," I tease, sliding the zipper shut as the mattress squeaks under her while she gets comfortable.

"What are you, a hundred?" she asks, grabbing the paper, and my stomach sinks. "People seriously still read the newspaper?"

"Hey." I snatch it from her fingers, the crinkling sound echoing through the tent. "Some of us need to get our news from more reliable sources than *TMZ.*"

"I'm impressed you even know what that is."

I narrow my eyes, rolling up the newspaper and hitting her hip with it.

"Hey!" she squeals, then quickly lowers her voice. "Shh, I don't want to wake the kids."

"You're the one being loud," I whisper, hitting her softly again, and she releases another quiet giggle.

"Fine." She puts her hands in the air. "I surrender."

I crawl up the bed, and she bounces as I make my way to sit beside her. *Damn air mattresses.* "They both asleep?" I'm assuming so, considering the silence from the tent beside us.

"Yes, they took *forever*," she huffs. "I blame the fourteenth marshmallow."

"Thought it might be an issue." I chuckle. "Is that why you're still up?"

"Yeah," she says, readjusting herself so we sit facing one another. "And I noticed your light was on. Is it okay I came over?"

"Of course. I couldn't sleep either, hence the archaic reading." Rolling away, I drag my backpack closer. "I did bring something in case we got bored."

"Yeah?" She perks up, resting her arms on her knees. "What's that?" After unzipping the front pocket, I pull out the hard card box and hand it to her. "'365 Fun Facts,'" she reads out loud. "'A fact a day keeps the doctor away.' Cute."

"I thought you'd like it." Satisfied, I lie down against my pillow, placing my hands under my head. "Now read them to me so we can pick our favorite ones."

She sorts through the cards, then says, "Fun fact number one: Scotland's national animal is a unicorn."

"How is that even legal? It's not real."

Charlotte cocks a brow. "Do *not* let Denny hear you say that."

"Noted," I say as she grabs another card.

"Fun fact number two: if stored properly, honey lasts forever."

She smiles, biting her lip. *How can one single person be this breathtaking?* Her bright eyes flick up, meeting mine, and warmth spreads across my chest.

I hope we last like honey.

"That's a good one," she says.

"It is," I croak out, and she returns her attention to the cards.

"Fun fact number three: you can hear a blue whale's heartbeat from over two miles away." She glances up at me with puzzled brows. "No way."

I chuckle. "I didn't write the cards."

"Hmm." Her eyes trail my body, and my skin tingles with awareness. She stretches her legs, lying down next to me, and slides down the mattress.

What is she doing?

She pauses near my chest and shifts closer, moving her braid to the other side, the end brushing my ribs and eliciting goosebumps.

What. The. Fuck. Is. She. Doing?

My gaze is glued to the back of her head, unable to conjure up a single coherent sentence.

Is she planning to suck my dick?

She drops her head to my bare chest, pressing her ear against it.

She. Is. Touching. Me.

I stop breathing as the scent of her shampoo wafts into my nose and I'm entirely surrounded by *her*.

What do I do?

My heart pounds.

This is definitely breaking rule number one.

"It's silent out here," she says, bringing a hand up and resting it on my stomach, her touch tortuous. "And still I can't really hear your…" She shifts her head, fingertips dragging gently against my skin, eliciting goosebumps once more. *Does she even realize what she's putting me through?* "Oh, there it is." I release a shaky breath, hoping she doesn't notice, as she uses her ear as a stethoscope. "It's so fast. Aren't athletes supposed to have a low resting heart rate?"

Yeah, except when a beautiful woman is touching him and her mouth is six inches from his dick!

"Uh-oh," I force out, trying to take the topic off my rapidly beating heart. "Is Dr. Benson giving me a bad bill of health?"

"I might have to tell the NFL you're not fit to play." She rolls over, her opposite ear now resting against me as her gaze finds mine. "Then you'll have to stay and take me and the twins camping every weekend."

"How do you suggest I pay for all our camping gear if I don't have a job?"

"OnlyFans." Her tone is serious, but her eyes are teasing.

"I do *not* have the artistic capability to sell my body on the internet. That shit's hard work."

"You don't have to post nudes," she assures me. "You can just sell your bathwater."

I choke a laugh. "Well, I guess I have my backup plan if the draft doesn't go my way."

"It will," she assures me. *And I hope to hell she's right.* A runaway hair frames her face, and I itch to reach out and hook it behind her ear. Within seconds I'm caving and doing just that. She places her hand on mine, stilling it against her face. Her lips quirk into a sweet smile, and I stop breathing. "Thank you again."

I swallow hard. "For?"

"Being my friend." She squeezes my hand. "I really need one right now."

Friend.

"While I'm happy to always be the one you call, are things not good with the girls?"

"No, they're great." Charlotte sighs, and I rub my thumb along her knuckles. "They're fine."

"You can talk to me about anything," I remind her, desperate for a look inside her head.

"I guess I always feel like the odd one out. Never the first choice. Sophia has Sage, Stella has Andi, and who do I have?"

Smiling, I brush my knuckles against her cheek. "You have me."

Her face flushes, and she nuzzles it into my chest. "Okay."

"Wow," I tease, wrapping my arm around her and resting my hand on her back. "Such *enthusiasm.*"

Are we… snuggling?

She takes my chain between her fingertips, the gold ring and *cornicello* pendant clinking. "You rarely take this off."

"Only for practice and games."

"What's its story?" she asks. "And *please* don't say there isn't one."

I huff a laugh. "My mom gave it to me for my sixteenth birthday." Lips falling to a frown, I tap my fingers against her back, unsure how much to share. "The horn-shaped pendant symbolizes protection."

"Is it an Italian thing?" she asks, her hand resting against me while she toys with the necklace.

"Yes, it's called a *cornicello*. It's supposed to ward off bad luck or the evil eye."

"Evil eye?"

"Yeah." A rock settles in my stomach at the thought of who Mom wants to protect me from. "Like people who are jealous of you or wish you harm."

"I need one of those."

"It's actually bad luck to buy one for yourself," I tell her, making a mental note. "The protection comes from it being gifted."

"Well, it's really cool. Thanks for sharing that with me," she says softly, the metal jingling together. "And the ring? What's that symbolize?"

A smile returns to my lips. "That symbolizes my *nonna* being way too invested in my personal life."

"Go on." Her eyes light up.

"When I visited Sicily last summer, *Nonna* kept asking me about my relationship status, or rather, lack thereof." I laugh, recalling the memory of a playful conversation over learning to make her famous *Pesto alla Siciliana*. "I told her I was focusing on football and it would be a while before I had anything to report." I place my hand on Charlotte's, taking the ring between my own two fingers. "Later that day, she gave me this ring to pass on to someone I love when the time is right." Charlotte's gaze lingers on the gold band, mine on her. "And she said, '*Quannu amuri tuppulìa, 'un lu lassari 'nmenzu la via.*'"

She was very adamant about that.

Charlotte's eyes light up at the Italian phrase. "Care to translate?"

I gnaw at the inside of my cheek, her attention stripping away my armor. Making me vulnerable. "It means, 'when love knocks, be sure to answer it.'"

Her thumb grazes my skin. "That's so beautiful."

You're so beautiful.

A rustling outside the tent has me bolting up, Charlotte pressed to my chest, and our eyes lock.

"What was that?" Charlotte whispers, clutching my neck, and my heart pounds.

"Probably a raccoon," I reply, squeezing her hand for reassurance, hoping to ease her fear. "Wait here."

She releases me, and I quietly roll off the mattress, slip on my shoes, and grab a flashlight. Pausing, I listen for signs of movement. Hearing none, I unzip the tent and step out into the darkness.

"Be careful," Charlotte whispers behind me, and her concern for my safety pleases me.

The twins' tent is dark, and I shine the flashlight around the campsite, finding no signs of a furry friend.

Rounding the back of the tent, I direct the light into the trees, scanning. Chirping birds and singing cicadas are the soundtrack to what seems like the start of a horror movie.

A movement in the bushes catches my eye, and I consider getting a closer look but opt against it. It's not as if I'm actually going to catch this vermin. Another loop around the twins' tent and I deem it safe before returning to mine.

"And?" Charlotte asks, her head popped out of the opening.

"Luckily no serial killer, or you'd be pretty silly for showing yourself."

She steps out, slipping on her shoes, breath heavy. "So coast is clear?"

"Yes, it's—" Another loud scuffling in the bushes cuts off my reply. She flies against me, and my arm wraps around her, the other pointing the light toward the clamor and seeing nothing. "It's okay," I assure her, rubbing her back.

She presses her head against my bare chest again. "Your heart's beating even faster now... You should get that checked out."

I wrap both arms around her, resting my chin on top of her head. *You're safe.* "I'll keep that in mind."

Clearing her throat, she pulls away, and my arms fall to my sides. The warm summer breeze dances across my chest, amplifying her absence. "I should get back to the twins," she says. "Don't love the idea of them being alone with all these sketchy noises."

"For sure," I say stupidly as a strand of hair blows across her face, sticking to her lip. I reach out, grazing my thumb along her mouth to brush it away, and tuck it behind her ear. "Goodnight, Charlotte."

"Goodnight, Noah." A devastating smile spreads across her face, and she slowly backs toward the tent, breaking our connection.

Turns out I'm pretty bad at rules.

Who knew?

"It's *soooo* hot," Denny grumbles from her spot on my shoulders as we hike through the campgrounds.

"You're not even walking!" I laugh, gripping her little legs. "Imagine how I feel."

"You're a football person, *Noah*," Denny points out. "You can carry a tiny person for infinite periods of time."

"You sound too old for your age," I say, shaking my head and opting not to mention I'm exhausted from barely sleeping last night. While I'm pretty sure it was nothing more than curious critters around us, I didn't like Charlotte and the twins being unprotected.

Why did I suggest camping again?

"Denny did both our science projects this year," Nash says matter-of-factly, and Charlotte's head snaps to him.

"Excuse me, Mister?" she says with her eyebrows raised to her hairline as she folds her arms over her chest.

"I got an A." Nash skips ahead, and Charlotte chases after him. They both laugh as she scoops him up, tickling his sides.

"That true, Denny?" I ask her.

"Yep." Her little hands grip my forehead. "There were two ideas I wanted to test anyway."

A small clearing filled with weeds appears up ahead.

"Look!" Charlotte shouts, grabbing Nash's hand and running toward it.

Denny wiggles, and I put her down. I've hardly released my grasp before she sprints away, joining Charlotte and Nash as they pluck white fluff ball stems out of the ground.

Charlotte spins around with a huge smile on her face and hands full of dandelions. She skips over, holding one out to me. The unabashed joy is oozing out of her, and it surrounds me like a warm hug.

"What am I supposed to do with this?" I ask, furrowing my brows at it.

"You've never wished on a dandelion?" Charlotte asks, appalled.

"No? Making wishes means you don't think you have any control over your life. I take action to make the things I want happen." And I do *not* like when I'm not in control.

"Seriously?" she deadpans, and I glance at the twins, who are joyfully blowing their way through the field. "You believe jewelry protects you from bad juju but draw the line at wishing on wildflowers?" She holds the dandelion in front of my face, and I realize we're not leaving this field till I cave.

"Fine." I roll my eyes in mock annoyance, snatching the stem, and she jumps with excitement. *Adorable.*

"Yes! Okay, okay." She takes a deep breath. "First, put the dandelion in front of you." She holds one before her face, inches from her mouth. "Close your eyes." Her eyes flutter shut. "Think about your wish." She pauses. "Then blow." Her pretty lips part open, and she blows every petal off the dandelion. Her eyes pop open, and she grins down at the naked little weed as she tosses it to the ground, then looks up at me. "Your turn."

I bring the flower in front of my face, inspecting it. Sensing her excitement in my peripheral, I opt to make a big show of it. Closing my eyes, I think of something I want but *definitely* have no control over, then blow forcefully. As I open my eyes, the flower practically turns to dust, its weightless seeds floating away along with my wish that will likely never happen.

"That was good," Charlotte says, plucking the stem from my fingers. "It will definitely come true."

She skips away, an infectious smile on her face as she spins around in the field, dandelions in her hair.

And if there's one thing I wish more than anything, it's that she's right.

10

NOAH

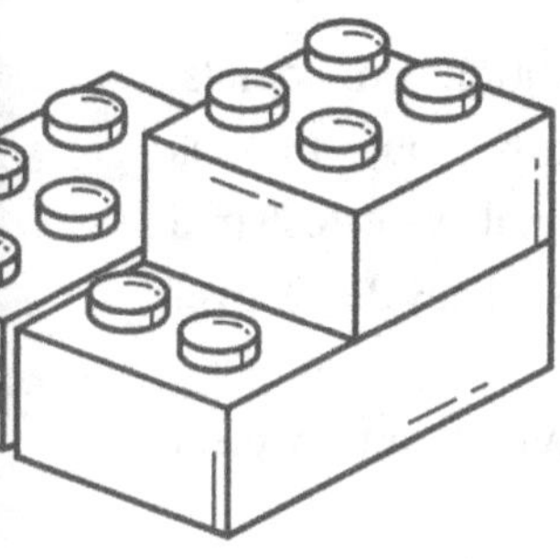

The moon is high, and I have an unobstructed view of the Seattle skyline outside the window of the ritzy hotel room I was put up in for the weekend. The Space Needle's lights glitter in the horizon. They've really gone all-out to not only sell me on the Grizzlies, but on Seattle. Still, even with all their schmoozing, something just feels… wrong.

After pulling out my phone, I take a photo and post it to my socials, along with one of me touring the Grizzlies stadium today, with the caption, *Wake Me Up When Draft Season Ends #dreamsarebecomingreality.* My posts are few and far between, but this seems like a moment to immortalize. The last official meeting with an NFL team before my entire life changes.

I set the phone on the nightstand and head for the walk-in rain shower to wash off the day's festivities.

After I'm done and dressed, I sprawl out on the large king-size bed and grab my phone off the nightstand to catch up on messages.

Damn. My home screen is blowing up. I go to my settings and turn off push notifications for the app responsible, then switch to it.

My Grizzlies post is flooded with comments. Some from guys

excited to see me drafted, but mostly from girls who are using the app as a ballsy Bumble alternative.

I'd rather you wake me up at dawn.

Noah come-fuck-me Caruso is in Seattle? Yes, plz.

Hot hot hot.

Marry me?

It's not the first time I've garnered attention on socials. Comments mostly come from CBU students, but this is unmatched. I discover the Seattle Grizzlies official page reshared my post to their story. *Well, that explains a lot.* They have over three million followers.

With the number of DMs overwhelming me, I opt to clear those next and quickly realize it's a mistake.

Saw you're in Seattle. Lmk if you wanna grab a drink

Hey. Wanna hang with me and a few girlfriends tonight? We don't mind sharing.

FUCK you're hot.

Oop. And there's an unsolicited tit pic.

Auto block.

A text notification pops in.

CHARLOTTE

Fun fact: All Noah Caruso had to do to get famous was sell his soul to Seattle

ME

I haven't sold my soul

CHARLOTTE

The rainy city girls sure seem to think so

My finger hovers over the keyboard. *Is she… jealous?*

ME

Too bad for them

CHARLOTTE
Why didn't you like Seattle?

ME
Never said I didn't like it.

I don't.

ME
There's just some things it's lacking

CHARLOTTE
Like?

A brown-eyed, brown-haired, smartass little cheerleader.

ME
Palm trees & Pub subs

CHARLOTTE
Ohh yeah that's rough

I'm lying about the palm trees. There are surprisingly some around here, but the Publix subs I'm totally serious about.

CHARLOTTE
Anything else Seattle is lacking?

I bite my cheek, unable to gauge if she's baiting a certain answer.

ME
Didn't see any dandelions

CHARLOTTE
Plenty of them in Florida

ME
One is all it takes

CHARLOTTE

Your wish come true yet?

ME

Nah, yours?

CHARLOTTE

Nope.

After the exhausting day I've had, I ache to hear her voice, but as often as we text lately, we never talk on the phone. Guess there's a first time for everything. Ten seconds later, Charlotte's face fills the screen.

"Hey," I say, forcing a relaxed, I'm-totally-not-freaking-out smile.

"Hey," she replies, her voice muffled by her surroundings.

"Where are you?" I assumed she was home by how quickly she was replying.

"Well..." She glances around, and I spot a familiar painting hanging on the wall behind her.

"Are you at *my* place?" I ask, sitting straight up.

"*Maaaaaybe*," she says coyly.

"Without me?" The realization hits me like a three-hundred-pound linebacker.

"*Yeessss.*"

"Are you at Des's graduation party?" I ask, and she doesn't reply, but given the loud noises in the background I can assume. "Seriously? Put Des on."

Charlotte giggles, the video shaky as she makes her way through the house. "It's for you," she says, handing off the phone to Desmond, my roommate, whose grinning face fills the screen.

"What's up?" he says.

"How's the party?" I ask casually to avoid potential ball busting.

He grins. "Good."

"Who showed?" I press.

Charlotte is single now. The guys are going to be all over her.

"Why?" he asks. When I don't reply, he looks away, then grins, returning his gaze to the camera. "Ohhh, I get it. I'll keep an eye on her."

So much for playing it casual.

"Excuse me," Charlotte sasses, snatching her phone back. "Noah Gabriel." She narrows her eyes. *If only she knew my body's reaction to the way she says my name is not one of remorse.* "I do *not* need a chaperone."

"Halloween would beg to differ." Her expression goes flat. "I'm sorry, I just meant—" The camera blurs once more as she shuffles through the house, and when I see her face again, I groan, taking in her surroundings.

She's in *my* room. Sitting on *my* bed while I'm on the opposite side of the country.

The woman is torturing me, and she knows it.

"I'm sorry," I say immediately. "I know that night is a sore spot."

"It is," she says with a searing look.

"You want the truth?" I say, opting for vulnerability to thaw this Elsa act.

"Please."

"I'm frustrated you're in my house and I'm not."

She stares at me, brows furrowed. "Why?"

"Because."

"Because *why?*"

Because the thought of you finding some other guy to be your rebound who's not going to even remotely give a shit about you or your feelings makes me want to vomit.

I drag a hand through my hair. "Because it looks like a good party."

So much for the truth.

"It is," she says, glancing away, then back to the camera. "And I'm actually gonna get back to it if you don't mind."

"Yeah, sure," I say lamely, and she hangs up, killing the call and my mood.

I curse myself, feeling dumb. Why'd I have to bring up a night I know she hates?

When I return to my home screen, the countdown clock stares at me.

NFL Draft: 6 days. 21 hours. 18 minutes. 43 seconds.

By this time next week, I'll finally have the answer to where I'm spending the next chapter of my life, and fuck if that doesn't scare the hell out of me.

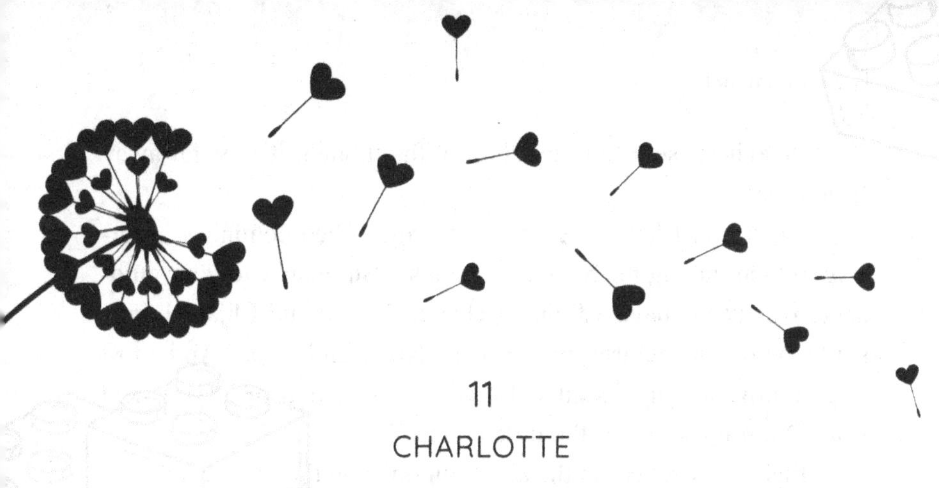

11

CHARLOTTE

"No one could rally a group of idiots the way you two did," Elijah says, tipping a beer towards Noah and Desmond in the crowded kitchen of their off-campus house, aka the Baller Pad.

"Hey!"

"Bro!" players from the CBU team shout, a drink in hand to toast before the start of the NFL draft tonight. Noah and Desmond opted out of traveling to the televised event to spend it here in their home. One last hurrah.

There are easily fifty of us crammed together. A total 180 from the small graduation party Desmond had last week when Noah was gone. They cranked up the music when he called so he'd think it was some big rager, knowing he'd be irritated. *It worked.*

"Simmer down," Elijah says, with a flick of his wrist. "My point is, you're legends. It's been an honor to learn from you. And it's an honor to consider you both friends." Elijah's voice cracks. "Shit." He turns away, wiping his face, and clears his throat.

"Anderson," Noah says, his own voice faltering, trying not to show emotion.

"Whatever happens tonight," Theo says, taking over, "no matter where you end up, we're *so* proud."

A heaviness settles in my chest at the thought it'll be far away from here.

"Elijah and I have huge shoes to fill," Theo continues, referring to them taking the reins of captains. "But thanks to your guidance, I think we have a fighting chance." Theo and Elijah share a smile before he returns his gaze to Noah and Des. "And most importantly, us guys wanted to say we're gonna miss you next year. Don't forget about the little people."

Elijah lifts his beer in the air. "Stingrays on three! One, two—"

"Stingrays!" we all cheer, clinking our drinks.

Desmond throws his arm around Noah's shoulder, and he returns the gesture. They both have wide smiles on their faces as Noah scans the room, bouncing from face to face. He shares a smile with Luna and Tony, and then his eyes connect with mine and his expression softens. Even across the loud, crowded room, his gaze sears me, pins me in place. It's impossible to look away.

"Earth to Charlie," Sage says, paired with a snap in front of my face.

I blink a few times and turn toward her and Sophia. "Sorry, just love seeing all the boys so gushy."

"Mm-hmm," Sophia snarks. "That's what you were watching." I roll my eyes, and they both giggle.

"So did your mom give your car back yet?" Sage asks, running her fingers through her light purple hair.

"No," I say, releasing a sigh. "I haven't even tried."

"Why the hell not?" Sophia asks.

"Because I feel like it'll be a snowball to her trying to make my life choices again," I say as an arm drapes around my shoulders, and I glance up to find Noah.

"Mind if I borrow her for a minute?" he asks the girls, and my stomach swirls.

"Be our guest," Sophia says, gesturing for him to take me away. Noah slips his hand into mine, and my skin tingles with awareness. He pulls me through the loud party, into his bedroom, and closes the door, sealing us off from the noise. My heart rate sputters. All those people here to celebrate him, and he wants to be in here, alone, with *me*?

He releases my hand, and I amble around the space, taking it all in while trying to catch my breath. The only other time I've been in here was when we FaceTimed during the party last weekend, but considering I was trespassing, it didn't really seem like the time to snoop.

A game controller sits on his desk beside a stack of textbooks that look sincerely worn in. Shelves of Lego sets line the walls along with unopened boxes. On his nightstand, photos of him and his mom, and a few with Tony, are placed neatly. A Polaroid taped on a wood frame catches my eye, and I grab it, looking closer.

It's Noah and me at the beach, just the two of us. "I don't remember this photo."

"Sophia took it when we did that beach day last semester," he says. "The one before they all played strip poker."

"Oh, right." I laugh, pulling my brows together. Noah and I weren't even friends yet, but Sophia had gone around with her little camera, making everyone take photos together. She said she was "practicing" for her portfolio. "But how did you end up with it?"

"She gave it to me after you and Jonathan broke up," he admits.

"What?" I spin around. "Why?"

Noah shrugs, sitting on the edge of the bed, rubbing his hands against his jeans, anxiety written all over his face.

"You okay?" I ask, setting the frame back on the nightstand and tabling the conversation for another time.

"I'm freaking the fuck out," he admits, blowing out a heavy breath.

I kick off my shoes and climb on the soft mattress, then sit criss-cross facing him. "Want to talk about it?"

Noah reaches toward me, hand hovering over my knee, then sets it on his own instead.

I wish we were back in the tent.

Reality didn't exist there.

"The draft starts in thirty minutes," he says hesitantly.

As if I need the reminder.

"Is *that* why we're all here?" I tease, hoping to lighten his mood, but when those green eyes flick to mine, a look of pure fear pins me in place.

"What if I don't get picked tonight? What if I'm a second- or third-night pick?" His eyes widen. "What if I don't get selected at all?"

"The guys—hell, every sportscaster in the country—have been saying you're a first-round pick for months." *And it's the truth.* "I don't think you need to worry about that."

"Maybe." He glances down, wringing his hands together. "Which means by the end of the night, my entire life is changing." He looks up at me, uncertainty swimming in his gaze.

I place my hands on his and squeeze. "You have worked your *entire* life for this. All the sacrifices, long practice days, aching muscles, and battered bruises. It's all been for this moment. You've *earned* this." He flips his hands upward, and I entangle my fingers with his, ignoring the memories from our little camping trip fluttering in my mind. Ignoring how nice it feels as he grazes a thumb across my knuckle. "You're one of the youngest quarterbacks to win a Heisman—*ever.* That's a huge deal."

He laughs and shakes his head. "Yeah, but Charlotte, *these* guys are the *real* deal. College ball is child's play compared to the NFL."

"Well, you're not a little kid." A grin spreads across my face. "You're a grown-ass man who plays football like a god."

He fights a smile, squeezing my hands. "Thanks for the ego boost."

"What are friends for?"

"Right," he says, with a gentle smile, setting our hands between us, looking from them to me. "Can you promise me something?"

"Anything," I say, and mean it. Because right now, in this moment, Noah Caruso could ask me to wrangle an alligator, and I'd say, *Where's the rope?*

"No matter where I end up, we can't lose this." His gaze is intense. Steady. And it makes my stomach flip. "You have to promise you're gonna stay in my life."

"Of course I will. You could be on Mars, and I'd still send you Martian mail giving you shit about what you ate for lunch."

He brushes a strand of hair behind my ear. "That's my girl."

My girl.

I allow one selfish moment for my face to rest against his hand. One heartbeat as his thumb trails my lower lip, causing my breath to hitch.

He opens his mouth, words coming out low and breathless. "I never want anything to jeopardize what we have."

I swallow hard. "Me either."

"It's important to me. *You're* important to me."

"You are to me too," I say quietly as the air shifts in the room, the stillness turning into a tornado of emotion I can't decipher. He takes my face in his hands and pulls me toward him. *What is he doing?* My breathing stops, and I close my eyes just before a soft kiss is placed upon my… forehead?

He lets out a heavy breath. "*Mi fai impazzire.*"

I sigh against him. "As much as I love when you speak Italian, I hate not knowing what you're saying."

His gentle eyes capture mine. "It means, 'I'm happy you're my friend.'"

Friend.

That term we keep tossing around. An innocent word that feels more like a curse.

A damnation.

"That's some bull," Elijah drawls.

"Lame!" Theo throws popcorn at the TV as we watch some hotshot quarterback from the University of Minnesota clench the first-round pick from the LA Scorpions, one of Noah's top choices. Noah grabs the ball cap off the table that matches the team mascot and chucks it to Desmond, who promptly stomps on it. The boys are in an uproar for him, but all I feel is relief. Los Angeles is as far away as he could possibly go.

'No matter where I end up, we can't lose this.'

His words echo in my mind. I promised him we wouldn't, but 2,500 miles is a hell of a trek for a *friend*.

Noah's leg brushes mine as he rearranges the remaining hats on the table before settling back on the couch. On his other side, Luna leans over, whispering in his ear, and he nods.

"What excuse do we have to go to the city of babes now?" Theo asks.

"I think you mean the city of *angels*," Andi responds.

"The only angel I need is you," Theo says, winking at her.

"Barf!" Andi replies with a mock gag. "Your game is lacking."

"You love it," Theo tells her.

"Knock it off, Schroeder," Coach Porter says, and Theo throws up his hands.

"*Buzzzzzkilllll*," Andi tells Coach Porter, chucking a pillow at him.

Noah clutches his phone in his hand, his eyes bouncing between it and the TV. The Seattle Grizzlies are currently making their selection, and the Tampa Barracudas are next.

Ring. Ring. Ring.

The room goes silent.

Noah stares down at his screen and blinks. Tony, standing behind the couch, places a hand on his shoulder and says, "Answer it."

Noah takes a deep breath, accepts the call, and holds the phone to his ear as he clutches Luna's hand tightly. "Noah Caruso." All the teasing and talking comes to a halt as we try to overhear what's being said on the other end without success. "Yes sir."

More silence as all fifty of us stare at him, holding our breath.

"Yes sir." Noah smiles up at Tony, who starts grinning too. "Absolutely, it would be an honor." Noah clears his throat and squeezes his mom's hand harder. "Yes sir. See you Monday."

Noah hangs up, brushing his cheek with his hand. He places his phone on the coffee table and stands up, looking around at his old teammates, closest friends, and family. His eyes connect with mine for a moment, and my entire body vibrates with nerves. *Please don't be Seattle.*

Noah shakes his head and laughs. "Looks like you're not getting rid of me that easily." Goosebumps cover my body as he crouches in front of Luna, who beams with pride, and takes her hands. "Guess what, *Mamma*?" His voice trembles as the rest of us hold our breath. "I'm gonna be a Tampa Barracuda."

We jump to our feet, and the room erupts in hoots and hollers. Noah throws an arm around me, pulling me close, relief filling me at his touch as the rest of our friends barrel over. Desmond places a white-and-turquoise Barracudas hat on Noah's head, and Noah glances at me with the brightest smile I've ever seen.

He was so worried about not having control where he ended up. Looks like all that dandelion wishing paid off.

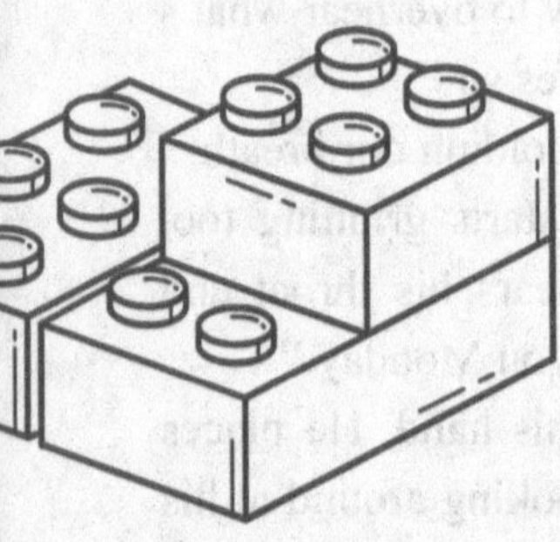

12

NOAH

The aroma of recently cut grass paired with acrylic paint infiltrates my senses. The air lacks the typical musk of a hundred sweaty athletes pushing their bodies to the limit.

The stillness is the most jarring part. Ninety-thousand seats surround me, and not a single one filled. Not a shout, a cheer, a "screw you." Just absolute silence aside from the turf crunching beneath my feet as Sean Bexley, my new head coach, and I walk towards the giant white fish in the center of the field.

Tampa Barracudas' stadium.

My new home.

For as long as they'll have me, anyways.

"What do you think, Caruso?" Coach Bexley asks, raking a hand through his salt-and-pepper hair.

"Hell of a view," I reply, still in awe.

It's not my first time here. But there's something different knowing come fall, I'll be in this stadium—running on this field—in front of ninety *thousand* fans.

Knowing my entire life, every practice, every sacrifice, every painful injury, brought me here.

"That it is," Coach Bexley says as we cross the field toward the locker rooms. "I've seen what you can do, and I'll admit, even I'm impressed. But you still have room to grow."

"Absolutely," I respond, not allowing my ego to be bruised. "There's always room for improvement."

"Training camp starts in July, and I expect you to be physically ready. You'll receive an email this week with a suggested training regimen and diet." *By suggested, he means mandatory.* "Mentally, this will be a big transition. We have team therapists if you need someone to speak to."

"Got it," I say, trying to retain all the information as we pass the field goal posts and enter the tunnel.

"There are a few events over the summer that aren't required, but your presence would definitely be appreciated." *Appreciated also means mandatory.* "You'll get all that information too," he tells me, turning the corner. I follow beside him and a body slams into my chest, eliciting a groan. I reach out my arms, steadying the assaulter, and look into the eyes of a flustered redhead. A *familiar* redhead.

"Watch where you're—" She cuts herself off. "Noah?"

"Hey… you," I say, tone full of surprise, her name not coming to mind. She bought me a drink at Ken's Karaoke, but I headed back to the hotel before anything happened, and we didn't exchange numbers.

"Hannah," she reminds me, a smile creeping on her face.

"Right," I say. "Hannah."

"Mind taking your hands off my daughter?" Coach Bexley says, and I glance from him to my hands and yank them away.

"Sorry, sir."

"You okay, Pumpkin?" he asks her.

"Fine," she says, rolling her eyes and cocking her head at him.

Coach Bexley turns his attention to me. "How do you know one another?"

My eyes bounce between them. "We me—"

"We met when I visited Shannon at CBU a few weeks ago,"

Hannah says, and I try not to display my confusion as she and I certainly know that is *not* true. "Anyways, are you almost ready to go, Dad? I'm starving."

"Sure. I think we're finished here." He pats his pockets. "I've gotta grab my wallet in my office. I'll be right back."

He walks away, and once out of earshot, Hannah snaps her gaze to me. "Sorry, he didn't know I was in Miami for spring break."

"Not my business," I say.

"So you're my father's next victim, I see," she teases.

"Looks that way."

"Good." She smiles, eyes dropping down my body like I might be *her* next victim. *No, thanks.* Coach Bexley turns the corner, and I blow out a sigh of relief.

"Guess I'll see you around?" I say as he nears.

"Hope so," she says, biting her lip.

"Okay, now I'm ready," Coach Bexley says. "See you soon, Caruso."

"Yes sir."

Desmond secures the cover over the pool table as I mount the cue stick holder to the wall of my new house. Staying in the Baller Pad with the boys didn't make sense after graduating, and I have zero interest in getting home from long practice days to a kegger in my living room. I began looking for a new house months ago, and as soon as the signing bonus from the Barracudas dropped in my account, I put in an offer.

Crystal Bay is a quick drive from Tampa, so I opted to stay in the nice little beach town. Since Desmond was drafted to Vegas,

Elijah and Theo are now renting the old house from me. The first of my rental properties—all part of the five-year plan.

"End of an era," Desmond says, eyes glued to the pool table where many, *many* games were played over long conversations about life and football.

"Beginning of a new one," I reply, smiling down at it.

"Still can't believe Vegas drafted me." He was a second-round pick, which is bull considering he's one of the top receivers in college football. But he got drafted nonetheless.

"You're going to crush it," I tell him.

"And we're going to crush you in the fall."

"Bullshit." I shove him.

He smirks. "You don't have your favorite roommate to make you look good anymore."

I laugh, pulling him in for a hug. "We're still gonna kick your ass."

He slaps my back, then releases. "Guess we'll see about that."

"What time are you leaving?"

"I actually gotta head out. Wanna get on the road before rush hour."

"Well, text me when you get there," I tell him.

"You got it," he says, shooting me a wave and walking out the door. *It really is the end of an era.*

Ignoring the pang of sadness, I grab a broom, sweep up the fallen drywall from screwing in the cue stick holder, and head towards the kitchen to dump it in the trash.

Elijah enters carrying a plastic box, Charlotte and Sophia in tow, and I set the broom on the counter to greet them. *She's here.*

"That's the last of it," Elijah tells me.

"This place is sweet," Charlotte says, heading to the kitchen. "Vaulted ceilings, are you kidding me?"

"An outdoor kitchen?" Sophia says, ripping the tape off a small box of dishes. "This is *for sure* the new party house."

"The old house can *keep* the parties," I say firmly, my muscles seizing at the thought of Theo doing a keg stand in my new kitchen.

"Soph, can you help me?" Elijah shouts from the guest room where he's setting up the bed frame.

"Coming," Sophia calls back, walking away.

"Please don't christen the house before I have," I tell Sophia.

She turns around, shooting finger guns and a devilish smirk at me. "No promises."

"God, they are just..."

Charlotte laughs. "I know."

"So you like the place?"

"Hell yes," she says, her response pleasing me as she sets another glass in the cabinet. "Can I sneak in and use your giant bathtub when you're at away games? I'm so sick of only having a shower."

"You don't need to sneak in," I say, reaching in my pocket and glancing down at the shiny piece of metal. *You've got this, Caruso.* Releasing a shaky breath, I say, "Just use your key."

Her head snaps to me. "My what?"

"Your key." I hold up my spare attached to a special keychain.

She walks over slowly and takes it from my hand. "Why are you giving me this?"

"Because you're the person I trust most in Crystal Bay," I say, the admission hanging heavy in the air between us. "And I'm one hundred percent certain Elijah and Theo would throw a rager the first weekend I'm gone, and I'd have to kill them. The backyard is spacious, but not big enough to hide two bodies." She analyzes the little keychain and holds it against her chest. My casual expression breaks into a full toothed smile. "Do you like it?"

She rubs her fingertips over the *cornicello* keychain. "I *love* it."

"To protect you when I'm gone," I tell her, my chest tightening, and she glances up, eyes meeting mine.

"Thank you."

"Welcome." I grin.

She hooks the keychain around her finger, twirling it. "So let's say you were out of town and *I* wanted to use your place."

"Consider it your personal getaway." *Although I'd prefer you use it when I'm here too.*

"And if I want to bring a guy here to use the amenities?"

My veins buzz, and I fold my arms over my chest. "Absolutely not."

She pouts. "Why not?" The corners of her lips curling upward suggest she *must* be messing with me.

She better be.

"If I have to think about you being in my house with some other guy's hands—" I cut off the admission, taking a calming breath. "No."

"Why?" she asks, expression turning serious. "What if he's just a friend?"

I'm "just a friend," and I still think about her naked at least four times a week. But I don't need to mention that.

"No," I repeat, narrowing my eyes at her. "The only guys you're allowed to bring here are Elijah, Julian, and Theo." She cocks a brow at the last name. "Actually, not Theo."

She contemplates me. "You're a possessive friend."

I smirk down at her. "And before you get any ideas, I have a doorbell cam, so I'll know if you show up with any of your suitors."

She presses her lips together and bursts out laughing. "Noah, I'm fucking with you. I wouldn't use your place for that."

"I know." A wicked smile spreads across my face. "Because your possessive best friend would hunt them down and bury them in his new backyard."

She rolls her eyes playfully. "I thought there wasn't enough room?"

"I'd find room."

She shifts in place. "And *best* friend?"

I shrug, heart stuck in my throat. "You got a better option?"

"Andi, Stella, Theo—"

My jaw ticks. "Seriously?"

"Kidding." She grins, picking up a vibrant cappuccino cup with lemons and flowers on it to continue her organization. *One of my favorites.* "This is so pretty."

"I made it in Palermo last summer."

"You *made* this?" she asks, analyzing my handiwork.

"Well, not the cup, but my mom and I took a glaze and sip class to paint them," I tell her as memories of the day come to mind. *Mamma* saw the flyer when we were at a morning market and insisted we go. *Saying no to her is impossible.*

"This is *hand*-painted?" she gasps. "By the famous NFL quarterback Noah Caruso?"

The tips of my ears burn. "Are you really so surprised?"

"No." She side-eyes me teasingly. "I'm sorry, it's just so beautiful."

I take it from her, looking down at the design that took me ages, rubbing my thumb over the little citrus. "Fun fact: Sicily's nickname is the Lemon Riviera because of how important lemons are in the culture and cuisine."

"I can't even imagine the quantity of lemons they go through."

"It's a lot," I tell her, setting the cup down on the counter and leaning against it to enjoy her in my space. "A lot of people have their own trees. My *nonna* does."

"Are they hard to keep alive?" she asks, scrunching her cute nose. "I'm not great with plants."

"It takes time, but with the right care they grow into a strong tree, basically making lemons forever."

"Powerful little things," she says.

"Definitely. My *nonna's* grows so many, we're all but forced to have *something* lemon every day."

"Mmm," she moans, and I can't decide whether to imprint the

sound in my memory or erase it. "The food there must be unmatched."

"It is." My mouth waters at the thought. "We'll have to go sometime."

She smiles at me softly. "Too bad our summer is booked."

"Yeah." I press my lips together, daydreams of tanning on the Mondello beach with Charlotte fading away. "Are you looking forward to Camp Dickson next week?"

Her nose scrunches up. "Kinda."

"I thought you loved it last year?"

She turns to face me with narrowed eyes. "We weren't even friends last year. How would you know?"

"I've always noticed you," I admit, stomach swirling. "You were constantly laughing with the girls."

"Yeah." She smiles sadly. "It was nice to be able to let loose."

"Then why aren't you happy to go this year?"

She blows out a heavy breath. "Noah."

"Charlotte." I raise my brows while keeping my expression neutral. Her concern is, well, concerning.

"I really don't want to talk about it," she says, picking up the lemon cappuccino cup.

I place my hand on the cabinet door and gently close it to steal her focus. "Please?"

Her frustrated gaze slides to mine. "Jonathan's going to be there with his team."

My skin flushes hot. "I forgot about that."

The light in Charlotte's eyes dims, and she turns her attention to the cup in her hand. "I didn't."

She lifts it toward the cabinet and slams it against the closed door, causing it to fall and shatter against the counter. My muscles seize.

"Shit," she says, freezing in place.

"Are you hurt?" My eyes scan every inch of her body, finally landing at her feet, where multicolor ceramic fragments are sprinkled around.

"I don't think so."

"Hey!" Sophia shouts, still in the guest room with Elijah. "You christening the house too?"

"There better not be *any* christening happening today!" I call out, reaching for Charlotte, thankful to have sneakers on.

"Too late!" Elijah replies, and I blow out a breath. *Focus*.

"I'm so sorry," Charlotte says, looking at the mess.

"Put your hands on my shoulders," I tell her, considering it seems like an acceptable time to break rule number one.

"I'm perfectly capab—" Her lips snap shut as my gaze sears into her.

"Hands. Shoulders. Now."

"So bossy," she says, reaching out to grip me.

"Good girl. See?" My teasing eyes meet hers. "I knew you could listen." I place my hands on her hips, holding firmly. "Jump," I instruct, and she pushes off her toes, allowing me to pull her into me. She wraps her legs around my waist, arms looping my neck, and her scent surrounds me. *How does she always smell so good?* Like peaches and torturous temptation. Her warm body is pressed against mine, and I fight a fucking hard-on as I walk over to the counter and set her on the edge.

"Thanks," she says.

"Welcome." I reluctantly remove my hands from her waist as indecent thoughts run rampant. She releases her hold, dropping a leg on each side of me, and I regain the ability to think straight. *Mostly.*

I lift her foot, checking the top and bottom closely for any shards. She doesn't speak as I drop her leg and examine the other foot, only pausing to run my thumb over the softness of her ankle.

Are ankles usually this sexy?

"You sure you didn't step on any?" I ask, slowly sliding my palm up her smooth leg, and resting it on her knee. *So soft.*

"Yes," she croaks out as I step between her legs, and reach around to grab the handle of the broom. Her warm breath fans against my neck. "What are you…" She presses a palm to my chest, and I stop breathing. With my free hand, I brush her hair behind her shoulder and bring my lips to her ear.

"Don't move," I murmur, pausing for one selfish moment in her presence. *Rein it in, Caruso.* Gripping the broom, I pull it around, stepping away.

Charlotte releases a shaky breath. "Yes sir."

She's really not helping the fighting of the hard-on situation.

After the last shards of the cup are tossed, I grab Charlotte's sandals. Taking her foot in my hand, I slide the shoe on, denying myself a pause as I do the same with the other.

"I feel like Cinderella," she teases, and I offer a hand, which she accepts before hopping off the counter.

"Are you okay?" I ask, steadying her.

"Yes." She sighs, releasing me. "I'm so sorry. I feel awful. You must have worked so hard on it."

"I don't care about the cup." *I do, but I'm used to things breaking.* "I want to make sure *you're* okay." A burning feeling settles in my stomach. "You started talking about your ex and immediately spaced out."

"I know." She pauses, eyes on the floor. "I feel ridiculous."

"Don't. You're allowed to feel how you feel."

She heads back to the cabinet, and silence blankets the room. Clinking fills the air as we arrange the remaining coffee mugs. I track her movements, hoping she'll give away anything she may be feeling or thinking.

My curiosity overwhelms me, and I ask, "Do you miss him?"

Her face scrunches up in disgust. "God, no," she says, and I let out a shaky laugh in relief. "I just don't want to see him. Or talk to him. Or think about him."

"I wish you would've told me you were worried about this."

She tilts her head to the side with sad eyes. "I like how I feel around you, and I didn't want to bring him up and ruin that."

'I like how I feel around you.'

"What do you mean?" I ask, heart racing.

"You're annoyed, and now I have to keep thinking about him even though I want to forget he ever existed," she says, exasperated.

I take a step forward, and her eyes find mine. "Charlotte."

She attempts to keep her face passive but one corner of her mouth quirks upward. "Noah."

"Please don't hold anything in with me." I raise my brows at her. "I don't want you bottling things up. You wanna talk about it, we talk about it. You wanna forget it happened, we'll erase it from your memory together. Okay?"

She nods, a smile breaking free. "Okay."

Her agreement fills me with relief. "And promise me something?"

Her expression turns serious. "Anything."

"If that prick tries getting you back, you tell him to go fuck himself and walk away," I say, and she huffs a laugh. "Do I look like I'm kidding?"

She smirks. "No."

"He doesn't deserve you. He never did." My jaw clenches. "Repeat it."

"What?" she scoffs.

"Repeat. It."

She tilts her head. "He doesn't deserve me. He never did."

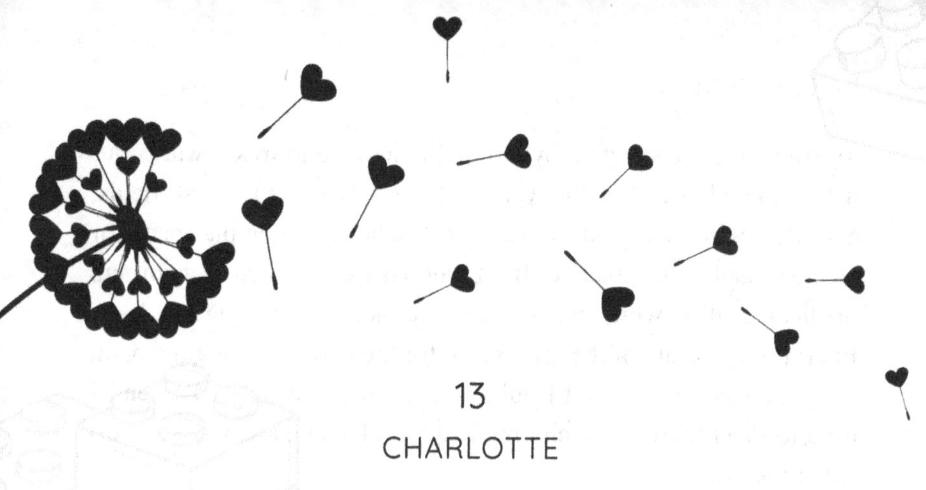

13

CHARLOTTE

A large wooden sign inscribed with "Camp Dickson" passes overhead as Andi pulls through the entrance. We roll our windows down, and shrieks fill the car as a group jumps off a wooden platform, splashing into the lake where we love to cool off in the afternoons. A hot summer breeze blows through, and rocks crunch beneath Andi's tires as she rolls into the camper parking lot to find a spot.

"You ladies ready for this?" she asks, putting the car in park.

"Yes ma'am," Stella says from the back seat.

The familiar scenery brings up a mountain of memories, but I choose to lean into the good ones over the ones with the lying, cheating asshole.

"Yeah," I say, looking over from the passenger seat with a smile. "I'm ready."

We grab our bags and make our way to the auditorium for registration. I haven't seen *him* yet. Maybe he isn't coming after all. Or maybe he got cholera and died. *A girl can dream.*

We check in and receive the keys to our cabins. They're small, with two campers assigned to each one. Andi and I are paired together, and we say goodbye to Stella, leaving to trek towards our new little abode. On the way, we pass two NFL-sized fields, complete with goal posts, a wall of bleachers, and ample space for us cheerleaders to practice. It's bordered by a two-story gym and medical facility, which we all have access to during our stay here. Everything is state of the art, except for the cabins. Along the path, we pass a large tree, and I quickly avert my eyes. Jonathan and I used to meet there between practices, and I shake away the unwelcome memory.

We arrive at the rustic structure made of faux Lincoln Logs, and I unlock the door. Inside, I toss my cheer duffle on one of the wood-framed twin-sized beds as Andi claims the other. It's essentially summer camp… if summer camp were built by football legend and millionaire William Dickson.

"Home sweet home," Andi says, rifling through her bag.

"Six weeks of camp, food, and football boys. Will we survive?" I tease, unzipping mine and pulling out the bed sheets we had to bring.

"They better have peppermint mocha cupcakes or I'll riot," she says, making her own bed in a huff.

"If they don't, I'll sneak into the kitchen and bake you some myself," I promise her.

She pauses, smiling at me. "You're too good to me."

With a wink, I turn to my duffle and keep my hands busy by unpacking my clothes and cheer uniforms. I place the CBU tank top we're required to wear to tonights welcome dinner on the dresser. Once the bag is empty, I lift it off the bed, a rattle garnering my attention. At the bottom of it, I find the tiny toy train whistle Nash had during our camping trip with Noah, and it brings a smile to my face. I must have tossed it in there when cleaning up and forgotten about it. My fingers trail the little object, a twang in my chest at the thought of my three favorite people I won't be seeing anytime soon.

I set it on top of my dresser next to the picture I brought of the twins, then remake the bed and fold my blanket on top of it.

"You okay?" Andi asks, sitting atop her mattress.

A heavy breath escapes me. "I don't know what I'm gonna do when I see Jonathan."

"What do you mean?" Her dark eyebrows pull together. "Do you wanna get back together?"

I shoot her a look of disgust. "I meant if I'm going to punch him, slap him, or portray a mask of indifference."

"I vote the latter. Show Jonathan you don't give a shit about him. You've moved on."

I'd hardly call what Noah and I are doing "moving on." He's been a beautiful distraction, but I'm unsure what will become of our friendship since I'll barely see him this summer.

And I've definitely done my damndest not to think about Jonathan, only allowing the occasional hurtful thought to pop in here and there.

I groan, throwing my head back. "You're right. If I explode, he'll think I still care."

"Exactly." She stands, squeezing my face in her hands. "You can do this. You're a badass bitch."

"Then why do I feel more like a sadass bitch?" I say with a squished pout.

"Because you're letting someone steal your joy who certainly does *not* deserve even an ounce of your brain space," she says, releasing me.

"It's just hard to forget sometimes. Especially when I'm in places with memories of him." I sigh, thinking of our tree rendezvous point. "Of us."

"Girl," she says, not feeding into my pity party. "In the two months you've been free of him, you've been happier, bubblier, and more confident than ever. You're *that* bitch."

I plaster a smile on. There're few things better in the world than true female friendships. They build you up when you feel like nothing more than a sad blob of nothingness. Give you a reality check when you desperately need one, and regardless of if you take their solid advice, are still there to hold your hand in the fall-out. *That's Andi for me.* "Fine."

"Good!" She pulls me for a hug. "You've got this."

I sure hope so.

We continue our tidying, and my phone buzzes. I snatch it up, hoping for distraction by a certain quarterback, and get frustrated by family instead.

THE BENSON FAM

DAD

Have so much fun this summer! Don't forget sunscreen

MOTHER

Make smart choices.

I roll my eyes. It would be physically impossible for her to act like she cares about my happiness or *passions*. Her single concern is if I'll do something stupid to embarrass her. Another message pops in, and I rush to open it.

NOAH

Fun fact: the heart of a shrimp is located in its head

ME

And the heart of a man is located in his dick

Especially if you're Jonathan.

NOAH

I would like to request not to be grouped into this subspecies of man

ME

And what is your argument?

NOAH

My heart is clearly in my stomach

I huff a laugh. This is exactly the distraction I need. Swapping to Google, I do a quick search to up his trivia.

ME

Fun fact: You can't hum if you hold your nose

After a few seconds, bubbles appear and disappear.

NOAH

What the fuck Charlotte

I almost suffocated myself

I burst out laughing.

ME

What can I say, I take your breath away

"What's got you all giddy, baby cakes?" Andi asks, and I meet her curious eyes.

"Oh, nothing," I say, fighting a smile. "Just trying to be *that* bitch."

"Good." She beams, satisfied. "You seem in better spirits. Should we go grab lunch?"

The heavy weight on my chest returns. "Or we could starve instead?"

She raises her brows. "Come on."

I groan. "Fine, let's go."

On our journey through camp, I keep my eyes peeled for any sign of Jonathan. The blue doors of the cafeteria appear before us, and a sigh of relief escapes me. Once I'm inside surrounded by the CBU football players, I'll be safe.

"Charlie." Chills scatter from my neck down my spine. I keep walking. "Charlie!"

The voice is louder, and I glance towards Andi for salvation. "Mask of indifference," she whispers before he reaches us.

"Hey," Jonathan says with a smile, as if the last time we spoke wasn't when I caught him dick-deep in another girl.

"Hi," I clip, folding my arms over my chest.

"How've you been?" he asks. *How have I… Is he for real?*

"Dandy." My skin crawls at the way his eyes wander over my body, and I point behind me. "Well, we're gonna—"

"Wait. Can you give us a minute?" he asks Andi, finally acknowledging her existence. She folds her arms over her chest and smiles, unmoving.

Atta girl.

"What do you want?" I ask, already irritated by his mere presence.

"Come on." He steps toward me, and I back away. "It doesn't need to be like this."

My body flushes with heat. "How about it's like *this*: I pretend you don't exist. And you go fuck yourself."

"Wow." He rolls his eyes. "And here I thought we could be adults about this."

"Adults?" I scoff. "You cheated on me for months, and I'm supposed to what? Act like it never happened? Like *she* never happened?" I ask, voice cracking.

"Indifference," Andi grits through her teeth in my ear.

"It wasn't all my fault," Jonathan says, and my eyes roll to the back of my head. "Just let me explain."

"Keep telling yourself that, buddy." I grit my teeth together, jaw aching. "You can keep your bullshit explanations."

Kendra walks up beside him, snaking her arm around his waist and flattening a hand on his chest. *What the hell is she doing here?* My eyes drop to her Andrews University Cheerleader T-shirt.

He didn't screw some random college girl. He screwed a cheerleader. How stereotypical.

Kendra smiles up at him. "Ready for lunch, *babe*?"

"Sure," he clips. She stands on her tiptoes and angles his face to hers, and he kisses her as if I'm not standing here. As if the girl he made years of promises to marry and build a family with isn't directly in front of him, still recovering from watching that fantasy be demolished firsthand. As if the last time I saw them together wasn't when he was *inside of her!*

Nausea creeps up my throat when he slides his arm around her waist, tugging her close. My eyes fall to his thumb rubbing circles on her hip. *The same way he used to do to me.* The ghosted memory of the sensation dances over my own skin with awareness.

I've spent so much time being angry. Almost so much I forgot to let the hurt in. But seeing him holding her the way he used to hold me, giving her the same affection that used to be mine? It fucking hurts. It's taking everything in me not to shatter like the cup I broke on Noah's floor. But Jonathan doesn't deserve the satisfaction.

Andi coughs loudly and exaggeratedly.

"Oh," Kendra says, turning her attention to me with a condescending smile. "Didn't notice you there."

"Can we not do this whole 'I'm gonna pretend I didn't fuck your boyfriend' thing?" I ask, all traces of sadness gone, replaced by a dragon-sized flaming anger.

She blinks at me. "Well, he's not your boyfriend anymore… so…"

"You're right. Congrats," I say, huffing a laugh. "Got yourself a real prize."

"Don't worry, you'll find someone else," she says, patting Jonathan's chest. "Eventually."

"What part of this conversation makes you think I'm single?" *Fuck. Fuck. Fuck.*

"You're seeing someone?" Jonathan asks, disbelief flickering in his expression.

My hands tremble, anger thrumming my veins. "Not that it's any of your business," I snap, my heart pounding ferociously against my rib cage. "But *yes*, I am."

His jaw clenches. "Who?"

"More like who cares?" Kendra grumbles, tugging him to leave.

Jonathan stands firm. "Who?"

Shit. Shit. Shit.

Folding my arms over my chest, I snap, "I don't have to answer to you."

Good. Vague.

"It's Noah, isn't it?" he asks through gritted teeth, and my muscles freeze.

How did we get here?

"Who. Cares?" Kendra says louder, tugging on him, but she may as well be the invisible woman now.

"I *knew* you slept with Noah on Halloween!" His tone grows louder. Andi takes a step forward, but I put my arm out, holding her back.

"First of all, the only cheater in our relationship was you," I say through gritted teeth, flicking a look towards Kendra. "And yes. I *am* dating him." A mischievous smile spreads across my face as I say the one thing I know will piss him off more than anything. "And he fucks better than you ever did."

I spin around, bolting for the cafeteria before he can respond. Pretty sure he shouts something about me being a stupid slut, but I choose to ignore him, pushing through the double doors and holding my head high all the way to the cafeteria.

"Damn." Andi catches up and falls into stride. "I always knew there was some molten lava inside that chocolate cake."

I let out a shaky laugh. My smile falls. "Holy shit."

"What?"

"Did I tell him I was dating Noah?"

"Yep."

"And implied we've fucked?"

"Implied? Girl, you made it real clear what you've been doing with that Italian sausage."

"Oh my…" Placing a hand on my pounding chest, I suck in a breath. My stomach is heavy, like a dense batch of dough too over-worked to rise. Andi grabs my arm, shoving me through a door. "*Oww!*"

She drops my arm, quickly scans under the stalls in the women's bathroom, and turns, placing her hands on my shoulders. "Get a grip. If you're gonna sell this, you need to be confident."

My eyes widen. "Sell what?"

"That you and Noah are *dating*!"

Thump. Thump. Thump. There goes my heart. "But we're not!"

"Shhh," she says, motioning her hands down. "Damn, baby cakes. Be cool. No one needs to know that."

"Noah's gonna know when one of his friends calls asking when our relationship status changed!" If I thought asking him to fuck me was embarrassing, wait till he finds out I pimped him out as my fake boyfriend because I was too shitty of a lay to keep one. *How mortifying.*

"Then call him first and explain what happened. I *guarantee* he'll have no problem with it." She cocks a brow, and a bit of the bricklike batter dissipates in my stomach. "The only person who hates Jonathan more than you is Noah."

I shift in place, allowing her words to surround me. "That's probably not true."

"Seriously?" she deadpans.

My mind wanders to how concerned Noah was after I destroyed his favorite cappuccino cup post shitty ex talk. He was upset, but maybe it didn't have anything to do with the broken memory.

Gripping the sink, I take in my appearance in the mirror. My makeup is flawless, hair tied back and a pink bow perfectly in place. How can I look so put together when my life is falling apart?

"Char," Andi says, pulling me back to the conversation.

"How do I even bring this up to him?"

"Just try."

"Okay," I find myself saying, when in reality my body is an anxious ball of yarn with no chance of being untangled. "I'll call him after lunch."

We return to the cafeteria and grab food, sitting down with Theo, Elijah, Julian, and some of the other guys. I push the salad around my plate as anxiety threatens to explode me like that poor tiny bird in *Shrek*. I'll be nothing but a fluff of pathetic feathers falling to the ground.

Here lies Charlotte Benson.

A dumb, pathetic little idiot.

RIP me.

NOAH

ME

> Fun Fact: when faced with the possibility of seeing my ex, I will one hundred percent do something absolutely stupid

NOAH

> I do not like that fun fact.

> that is a FUNLESS fact.

ME

> But it is a fact

NOAH

> Did you break our promise?

My chest aches, mind swirling.

ME

I didn't

But I'm not sure you'll like the alternative

NOAH

Call me

ME

I'm eating, can I call you in twenty?

NOAH

Make it fifteen.

Ten minutes and an abandoned Caesar salad later, I excuse myself from the table. Andi mouths "good luck," and my heart pounds against my rib cage. My eyes catch on Jonathan, who's eating with an arm hooked around Kendra, and his fiery gaze burns straight through me. *If he's moved on, why the hell does he care so much?* I shiver at the unwelcome attention and exit the building.

I yank out my phone and find Noah's contact. The cafeteria door slams open behind me, and a breath catches in my throat until a group of guys walks past me, babbling about their first practice.

This definitely isn't the place to talk. If one of Jonathan's teammates overhears this is fake, it'll blow the whole thing before it even starts. Not to mention I'll look pathetic as fuck. I head towards my cabin to have privacy for this conversation.

When I'm less than a minute away, I tap call.

Noah answers immediately. "Charlotte."

"Wow, no hi?" I tease, heart stuck in my throat. "Or how are you?"

"What did you do?" he asks with a sigh, obviously not buying my decoy tactic.

"Give me a sec." I groan. "Want to wait till I'm at my cabin."

"Are you almost here?"

"Yes, I'm around th…" The words evaporate off my tongue as

I spot a dark-haired, handsome man leaning up against my door with a phone to his ear.

"Surprise," Noah says, grinning, and I rush forward, leaping in his arms. He catches me easily as I sigh into his neck, absolutely relieved to see my best friend. Especially after the day I've had. He smells like basil, cedarwood, and home.

"What the hell are you doing here?" I mumble into his neck, holding tightly. "I thought I wasn't gonna see you for at least a month."

He chuckles, setting my feet back on the ground. "I couldn't wait that long."

Me either.

After unlocking the cabin door, I lead us inside and away from prying eyes. "Did you already hear the fuck-up I made and speed here?" I groan, dragging a hand across my face. "Is it really that bad?"

"Char." His tone is unamused. "Please explain before I have a coronary."

My legs take on a mind of their own, pacing the small room. "Basically what happened was I ran into Jonathan, and he was all, 'Let's talk' and I was like, 'No thanks,' and then he was like, 'Why not?' and I was like—"

He grabs my arm and softly tugs me toward him. "The Cliffs-Notes version."

I look into Noah's steady eyes and take a deep breath. "I told Jonathan to go fuck himself."

A smug smile graces his lips. "Good."

"Yes." My jaw clenches. "But then he got all condescending and shit. And that girl he slept with showed up."

"Why's she here?" he asks, as surprised as I was.

"Apparently, she's a cheerleader."

"Oh." His lips press together. "I'm sorry you have to deal with that this summer."

His reminder that it's going to be for the *entire* camp is not comforting. "Me too."

"So I'm not really seeing the fuck-up part?" he presses, rubbing a hand along my back distractingly.

"Well…" I shift on my heels. *Here we go.* "I also told Jonathan you and I are dating."

Noah fights a smile and fails spectacularly. "Oh yeah?"

"Mm-hmm," I hum as he lets go of my hands and they drop to my sides.

"Why'd you do that?" His amused eyes narrow on me, making me squirm.

"That girl." I toy with the hem of my shorts. "They're dating. And it made me feel so inferior." For a moment a flicker of sadness stings my chest, and I douse it with my rage. "And then she said something about something. And I just, I said I wasn't single, and Jonathan asked who. I wanted to piss him off, and I don't know what I was thinking. I'm sorry. Shit. I didn't mean to bring you into this. I just thought—"

"Take a breath," Noah says, lips parting as he sucks air in slowly. I copy his movements, inhaling deeply, chest rising opposite his. He counts down from three as I exhale, the movement calming me. "Charlotte." He shakes his head with a soft laugh. "I will *happily* fake date you to throw a middle finger to your ex."

My eyes snap to his, oxygen stuck in my lungs once more. "Really?"

"Of course."

I stare at him in disbelief. "People are gonna have questions, Noah. It has to be believable or it's pointless."

His eyes dance with amusement. "Then we'll make it believable."

What the hell have I gotten us into?

"You make it seem so easy," I say, exasperated.

"It *is* easy," he says, running a hand down my arm in reassurance. "Char, we're best friends. We talk every day. We spend plenty of time together. What's the difference?"

"The difference?" I scoff, pacing again. "You're going to have to do *boyfriend stuff*. Like, I don't know." I throw my arms in the air. "Hold my hand and shit."

"And shit?"

My muscles freeze. "Or just the hand-holding?" I wave him off, stomach tight. "I don't know."

"Please, relax." He takes a step forward, tugging me into his arms. "It's going to be fine. As far as everyone knows, I'm your boyfriend and you're my girlfriend."

"Oh my god." My heart rate skyrockets. "You have, like, a hundred thousand followers. People are gonna start talking about it, and *fuck*!"

"I don't care about that. Posting you as my girlfriend will hopefully keep the thirsty girls out of my DMs."

My gaze snaps to his. "Is that really a problem you have?"

"I get an unsolicited tit pic a week. At least." He shakes his head in disbelief, and an uncomfortable feeling settles in my stomach. "Yes, it's a problem. So as I said, I get the fangirls out of my DMs, and you get to piss off your ex. It's an even exchange."

"An even exchange?"

"Yes," he says, tucking a hair behind my ear, and I shiver. "An *even* exchange."

"Have you really thought this through?"

"I think everything through." He grins, and it's the truth. Noah Caruso doesn't so much as pick what he's eating for dinner without thinking it through. "It's going to be fine."

Accepting his thought-out reply, I concede, my muscles relaxing for the first time in an hour. "Thank you."

"How many times do I have to tell you not to thank me for doing things I enjoy?"

"You'll *enjoy* fake dating me?" I ask, unable to stop the smile now spreading across *my* face.

"I might," he says, cheeks blushing pink.

"Fine," I say, trying not to read too much into his response. "Then *you're* welcome for evicting the punt bunnies in your DMs."

"Punt bunnies?"

"Yeah, like puck bunnies but for football."

"Well, thanks for rescuing me from the punt bunnies," he says, pulling me in for a hug.

"Any time." I lean into his chest, breathing him in.

Basil. Cedarwood. Home.

14

NOAH

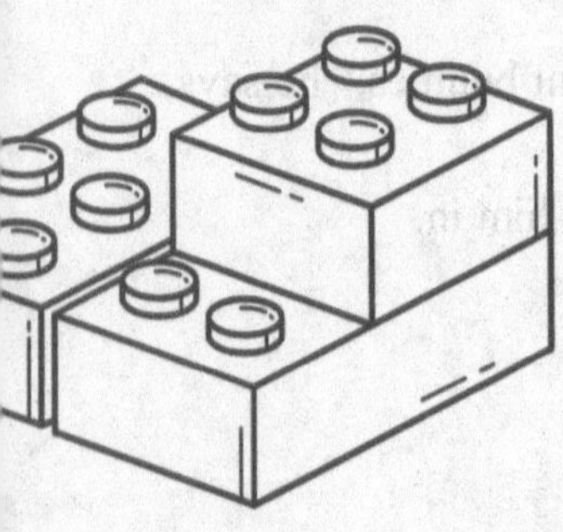

"Wait a second," Charlotte says, pulling away to look up at me. "Why are you even here?"

The corners of my lips quirk upward as I fight a smile. "I'm coaching this summer."

"What?!" she shrieks so loudly it almost blows an eardrum. *Guess I better get used to it since my new girlfriend's a cheerleader.* "You're going to be here the entire camp?"

"Yep." The grin breaks fully free. "Coach Porter was thrilled when I got drafted by Tampa, and he asked me to mentor this year." Since the university's coaches aren't allowed to be here, he wanted to have some eyes on the inside to know how his players are doing.

"How much did you make him beg?" she asks with a brow waggle.

"A decent amount," I lie.

He didn't even need to ask twice before I started packing.

"Somehow I totally fumble the ball, and you're just ready to swipe it up."

"Well, I am excellent at both football *and* being your best friend." My wrist buzzes, and I check the smart watch notification.

"I've gotta go. My first training starts in ten minutes. We'll catch up tonight?"

"Yeah." She grins up at me. "Thank—"

"Don't." I point a finger her way.

"I *appreciate* you." She winks, *terribly*, and I laugh.

"Sure, I'll allow that."

"I still can't believe you're doing this for me." *After all I've done, is she really so shocked?*

"*Mi fai impazzire*," I say, the admission making my stomach swirl even though I know she doesn't understand.

She narrows her eyes. "Again with the Italian."

"Guess you should add it to your curriculum."

"I thought graduating would end your reign of torture," Julian groans, sweat dripping off his face.

"Shut up and run," I tease as they do another fifty-yard side shuffle.

My wrist buzzes, and I glance at it.

UNKNOWN NUMBER

Have a great first day of practice, handsome!
Xox Hannah

Seriously? After running into her at the Barracudas' stadium, she won't leave me alone. I still don't know how she got my number—I'm assuming her dad's phone without his knowledge.

I ignore the notification, as I have the ten before it. Leaving people on read kills me, but she's crossing a line here. I'm also not about to piss off my new boss, or my new *girlfriend*, by making it seem I'm even remotely interested.

A glance at the time, along with the rest of the teams wrapping up, has me blowing my whistle. "Alright, that's enough for today. Hit the showers."

They collapse on the field, and I laugh. I'll admit, I am having fun torturing them instead of being tortured for once. *As if I didn't do a seven-mile run this morning.* The suggested cardio of the day was five miles, but *Mamma* didn't raise no quitter, so I finished the trail near my house before heading to camp.

Charlotte is on the sidelines, hot and flushed, with the CBU cheerleaders. *Mostly hot.* They're drinking water and dripping in sweat as the Florida sun beats down on us. I make my way over, ready to get this dating thing on the road.

"Hey, *soffione*," I say, and Charlotte turns to face me with an amused expression.

"Well, hey to you too." She beams.

Her cheermates eye us curiously, and I glance at Andi, who shoots me a wink. I cock my head, signaling for Charlotte to walk to me. She strolls over in black spandex shorts perfectly hugging her curves and a CBU sports bra that shows a beautiful amount of cleavage. A bead of sweat slips down from her collarbone, disappearing between the valley of her breasts, and I take a shaky breath, forcing my eyes away.

Fake dating, I remind myself.

"Having a good first day?" I ask, relishing in the looks we're getting as the Andrews U team, Jonathan included, walks by us.

"So far so good. You?" she replies.

"Just got better." I throw my arm around her shoulders, and she squirms in an attempt to shrug me off. *She's terrible at this.* I grasp tighter and lean down, whispering, "Jonathan's coming."

She freezes and whispers back, "I'm really sweaty."

"That's fine." My lips graze her ear as I speak, and she shivers. "Pretend I said something funny." She giggles, then looks up at me, our noses touching. "Perfect," I tell her, pulling away as Jonathan passes, giving me a look that says I might end up buried in the woods.

Better share my location with the boys later.

"Doesn't the camp have a no-fraternizing policy?" she asks, glancing around hesitantly.

"We're all consenting adults. They aren't stupid enough to believe a bunch of tightly wound athletes would refrain from sex for a month." *It's the truth. I checked.* "And if anyone asks, we'll say we were dating before camp started, which we could prove with pictures and whatnot."

Easily. It's as if she forgot we've been friends for months and have an arsenal of fun facts to prove it.

She chews on her cheek. "That makes sense."

"Come to my cabin tonight?" I ask, and she furrows her brows. "So we can discuss some *details*."

"Okay, what's your cabin number?"

"Three." I lean down, and whisper, "You did great by the way." I press a kiss on her cheek and walk away, my lips tingling as I fight a smile.

"Noah!"

Turning, I find Elijah and Theo chasing after me.

"Damn," Theo says, clapping me on the back. "I guess you got your own tits and tequila now."

I laugh, shaking him off. "Shut up."

"Only took you what?" Elijah counts on his fingers. "Ten months?"

"She was taken for most of them," I point out, trying to suppress my annoyance at the unwelcome reminder.

"She shouldn't have been." Elijah shakes his head.

"Touché to that." I agree, and we bump fists.

A group of guys passes us, and Jonathan's gaze pierces me. *That's right, McFuck Face.* I shoot him a wink and keep walking. *What was it you said about Charlotte not being mine?*

"Is he gonna be a problem?" Elijah asks.

"Nah, but it would be nice if he'd back off my girl," I say, and damn if that doesn't feel good flying off my tongue.

My. Girl.

FAKE. DATING.

"Say the word. It's done," Theo says. "I mean it. I know people."

"Um…" I give him a sideways glance. "Appreciate the offer, but I don't think that'll be necessary." Elijah and I share a look, then burst out laughing.

"Glad you guys think it's so funny," Theo says with a mocking smile. "Like I said, let me know if you ever want to make someone disappear."

I chuckle, shaking my head. "I'll keep that in mind."

"And that's why we're all here, isn't it?" William Dickson, retired eight-time reigning Super Bowl champion and infamous running back, says while giving his annual speech during the welcome dinner. "I founded this camp to ensure the up-and-coming generations could spend time reconnecting with what they love about their sport. To push boundaries and come out stronger athletes by the end of it. I want you all to learn from your coaches and your peers, keep an open mind, and most importantly, have a damn good time!"

The room erupts in hoots and hollers, but I'm at the "adults" table, as Charlotte would say, where only polite claps are permitted, so I remain composed. My eyes find her across the room, and it kills me not being near, especially with the CBU tank top tight across her chest, pulling all of my attention there.

Unfortunately, I'm not the only one whose gaze she's captured. Jonathan won't stop staring, and I have garlic bread at the ready next time I catch him. I take a deep breath and release it slowly. He is *not* worth wasting precious garlic bread. I bite off a delicious chunk and toss the other half on my plate, throwing dagger eyes instead. He inhales a fork full of salmon, and I gag. Just like the disgusting food, he leaves a bad taste in my mouth.

"Alright," Dickson says, regaining my attention. "Everyone get some sleep. Practice starts nice and early tomorrow."

The campers rush out of the room to do anything *but* sleep, and the commotion causes me to lose sight of Charlotte. I pull out my phone, hoping to catch her before she wanders off, or worse, Mr. Fuck Face finds her.

CHARLOTTE

ME

Where are you?

CHARLOTTE

Where's my fun fact?

ME

Fun fact, I had meatballs for dinner

I exit the building with the flow of the crowd, making it out into the humid summer air. The sun has dipped below the horizon, leaving the sky a dim blue hue.

CHARLOTTE

That's not a fun fact, I was there when you
made your plate

Groaning, I rack my brain, and the perfect idea pops in.

ME

Fun fact: when faced with the possibility of
seeing my girlfriend's ex, I will one hundred
percent make him realize how hard he fumbled

CHARLOTTE

Cute

A tap on my shoulder has me spinning around to see Charlotte's teasing face.

"Your fun fact skills are lacking," she tells me.

"You said it was cute," I say, glancing behind her shoulder and spotting said ex. I reach up, slide a hand into her hair, and tug her toward me.

A giggle slips out of her. "What are you doing?"

"We have an audience," I say, running my fingers through the dark strands. "Just showing him how hard he fumbled."

"*Oookay*," she says, eyes narrowed curiously.

"Fun fact." My gaze roams her body. "You look hot as fuck tonight."

Her eyebrows rise, cheeks reddening. "Well, that is definitely some shit a boyfriend would say."

"It certainly is." *Because it's the truth.* "Do you need to get anything from your cabin before you come over?" I ask, my thumb selfishly grazing her jawline.

"Before I… what?" she says, eyes dazed.

"Before you come over?" I clarify, finger tracing the column of her neck.

"What am I coming over for again?" she asks, and I fight a smile, wondering if my proximity is distracting her.

"To *talk*."

"Right," she says with a nervous laugh. "About the…" She glances around and drops her voice to a whisper. "Rules."

"Exactly," I whisper back. "So, you need anything from your place?"

"Nope."

"Good," I say, throwing an arm around her shoulders and leading the way. "Let's go."

A few minutes later, I'm unlocking the door and gesturing Charlotte inside.

She strides around, taking in my space, and tilts her head at the full-sized bed.

"Do you have this whole place to yourself?" she asks, spinning to face me.

"I'm a coach. I don't have to share like you mere mortals."

She scrunches her nose at me. "I called you the god of football *once.*"

"No take backsies," I tease, booping her on the nose.

She groans, kicking off her shoes and hopping up on the bed, making herself at home like she always does. "Damn, it's soft too." She throws herself back on the mattress. "Lucky bitch."

I glance down at my attire, noting the grass stain on my shirt from the get up and go drill I showed the boys earlier in practice. There wasn't time before dinner to clean up since I had an unexpected coaches meeting, and I definitely don't want to get in my clean sheets in this condition.

"I've gotta take a quick shower," I tell her, and she pops up, resting on her elbows.

"Right now?"

"Do you mind?" I ask, grabbing some clothes from my drawer. "I'll only be a few."

"I suppose I'll manage," she says, throwing herself back onto the bed, then rolling over and unlocking her phone. Her ass peeks out of her little shorts, and I hold in a groan.

"Great," I mumble, heading to the bathroom.

Fifteen minutes and an unavoidable stress relief session later, I'm pulling on fresh sweats and a Tampa Barracudas T-shirt. Feels weird having my new mascot on my chest instead of my usual CBU get-up, but since I'm a coach for *all* the teams, I'm trying not to show I play favorites. *Because I definitely do.*

I find Charlotte in the same position I left her, sprawled across the entire bed, her ass mercilessly torturing me.

"Scoot," I say, shoving her leg. She slides over and props herself up against the pillows, and I do the same, turning to face her.

"Alright, *boyfriend,*" Charlotte says, and I ignore the weird little swirly thing my stomach does. "What did you want to discuss?"

"First," I say, searching my mind for clarity, "I want to make sure we're on the same page with what you're comfortable with."

"What *I'm* comfortable with?" Her brows pull together. "What about you? I don't want to make you uncomfortable."

I narrow my eyes at her. *Is she serious?* "I really doubt that could happen."

She shifts on the mattress. "Then what makes you think *I* would be uncomfortable?"

"Exhibit A," I say pointedly. "When I threw my arm over your shoulder after practice today, you pulled away."

"Because I was sweaty."

"I know that." I give her a reassuring smile. "But if I touch you and you jerk away, it looks suspicious."

"I didn't jerk away after dinner," she says, pleased with herself.

"And you were *such* a good girl for that."

She rolls her eyes, a blush creeping up her cheeks. "Whatever."

"So like I said, I want to know what you're comfortable with so you don't recoil in front of other people."

"Can you give examples?" she asks, toying with her necklace. "Hand-holding?"

"I don't know." She taps a finger to her mouth. "Seems pretty risqué."

"Wouldn't want to cause a scandal," I say, nudging her foot with mine, and she returns the gesture, our legs entangling. "But seriously, Charlotte. This is important. I want us to set boundaries we're both comfortable with."

"Fine." She releases a breath, rubbing her toes against my calf, and I struggle to focus. "Hand-holding *is* allowed."

Permission to hold her hand. Check.

"What about hugging or holding you against me?"

She pauses, nibbling on her lower lip. "Also fine."

I grip her chin and pull her close, dragging my lips along her jaw, and my heart pounds. "Me kissing your forehead or cheek?"

She shivers and clears her throat. "Fine." I angle her face until we're nose to nose, then drag my thumb along her bottom lip. My eyes bounce between hers and her pretty mouth, which reminds me of my very strict set of rules.

One: don't touch Charlotte.

Two: don't think about Charlotte.

Three: don't text Charlotte.

And four: definitely don't, under any circumstance, kiss Charlotte.

One through three are blown to shit, but breaking four? I'll never recover.

"Will you be kissing my lips?" she murmurs, and my lungs cease to function. My palm rests on her neck, her pulse pounding against it. The temperature in the room is hotter than Death Valley, and I lack the basic oxygen to formulate a reply. "Just whenever Jonathan is watching," she clarifies. As if my hesitancy has anything to do with not actually wanting her lips on me. "But we definitely don't have to. I was just ask—"

"Yes."

Fuck.

15

CHARLOTTE

"Want me to wait?" Andi asks as she stands in the doorway of our cabin.

"That's okay," I say, filling my water bottle at the sink. "Noah's walking me to practice."

"Yeah, he is." She waggles her brows, and I roll my eyes. Her attention is pulled outside. "And speaking of, god's gift to women is here."

"You're too nice to me," Noah tells her.

"Stop inflating his ego!" I beg.

"Gotta make sure he doesn't forget about me when he's super famous," Andi says, sending him a teasing wink.

"Didn't you hear?" I say. "He's *already* super famous. The punt bunnies are in his DMs by the hundreds."

Noah shoots me a crooked grin. "Jealous, *soffione*?"

"No." Heat flushes my cheeks, and I'm curious what the nickname means. *I'll ask later.* "Just stating facts."

"Okay, well…" Andi gestures behind herself. "I'm out. See you at practice."

She exits the cabin, shutting the door behind her.

"You ready to do this thing?" I ask Noah, giving him two thumbs up.

He chuckles "Yep. Let's go."

We leave the cabin, joining the path to the football field filled with other players and cheerleaders. Noah slides his hand in mine, my breathing ragged as he entangles our fingers and squeezes gently.

He leans down, his lips brushing against my ear, and goose-bumps scatter down my spine. "Relax. You look constipated."

"Excuse me?!" I drop his hand, shoving him away. "You did not just say that."

He smirks and throws an arm around my shoulders, tugging me to him. "It got you to laugh. You appear much happier now."

"There has to be some kind of rule against saying shit like that to your girlfriend." I cock a brow up at him.

"What would you rather I tell you?" he asks, his familiar scent surrounding me.

"How about, 'Charlotte, relax. You look breathtakingly beautiful but stressed.'"

"Done," he says, shooting me a panty-soaking wink.

Rein it in, Benson.

Who knew fake dating your real best friend would be this damn hard?

"So, Ms. Breathtakingly Beautiful, are you looking forward to your first *full* day as my girl?"

My girl.

Heat flushes my cheeks. There're so many things to unpack from his sentence, I'm not even sure where to start. "Am I looking forward to seeing the look on Jonathan's face every time he sees us? Hell yes." I blow out a breath. "But I'm also nervous about making sure I don't get us caught in the lie."

"Stop thinking about it as a lie," he whispers in my ear. "The current truth is I'm your boyfriend. No one has to know that only officially started yesterday."

His touch surrounds me, along with his reassurance. "I guess you *are* right."

"I know I am," he says smugly.

"Would it kill you to *pretend* to be humble?"

"You know, baby? It just might." He laughs, and my stomach flips at his first use of the pet name. *What's with the flipping?*

"Is that something you'll be doing a lot?" I ask hesitantly.

He looks down with furrowed brows. "What?"

"Calling me sweet nicknames?"

He smiles with pursed lips. "If it's okay with you?"

My lips smash together, stomach begging to do that somersault thing again. "I'll allow it."

"Good." He pulls me closer and plants a kiss on the top of my head as we reach the practice fields. "I'll see you later for lunch, yeah?"

"I'll be waving at you from the kids table."

He chuckles, our mouths inches apart. "You make me feel ancient."

"Didn't you realize we're in an age gap romance?" I tease.

He huffs another laugh, his breath hitting my lips. "We're in a *romance*?"

My mouth opens and closes as I struggle for a reply. My hand grazes my pocket, reminding me of the surprise I have for him. "Close your eyes and open your hand."

"What?"

"Please?" He does as instructed, and I retrieve the tiny red train whistle out of my pocket and place it in his palm. "Okay, open."

He looks down at it and laughs. "Oh god. I can still hear this sound in my sleep."

"I wanted you to have it for good luck on your first full day coaching," I say, chest spreading with warmth. *Man, is the sun beating down on us today...* "It's not a *cornicello*, but it can ward off the scary things."

He grins ear to ear, tapping his forehead to mine. "Cute. Thank you."

"You're welcome, *babe*." I smirk, backing away and spinning around to join practice.

Every girl on my squad is staring as I walk up.

They have no shame.

I toss my cheer duffle on the sideline. "Good morning."

"When did *that* happen?" Cami, one of our captains, quips.

"Does it matter?" I ask with furrowed brows.

She gives me an indecipherable look, then releases a breath in a huff. "I suppose not."

The other girls all busy themselves with tying their shoes or whispering to each other.

"Morning, baby cakes," Stella says, pulling her arm over her chest in a stretch.

Andi just winks at me.

"Alright, girls," Coach Landry, our cheer coach, shouts out. "Let's get to work. Cami, you're in charge of today's practice."

"Great," I mumble under my breath. Well, I'm screwed.

The sun is relentless. Cami has us do a three-mile run and a variety of exercises that would make even the football players gasp for air. The one thing I do admire about Cami: she doesn't treat this like some little performance. She makes sure we are *athletes*.

"You can do better than that, Benson!" Cami shouts as I do my seven-hundredth jumping jack, struggling for oxygen. Today's workout is harder than usual. Maybe due to the lack of sleep from worrying if my little arrangement with Noah will be believable.

"Now spot run. Go!" Cami instructs, pacing the line, inspecting us all as we jog in place.

The humid air has me huffing, and a bit of nausea washes over me. I should have eaten more for breakfast.

"Faster!" she shouts in my face.

My eyes fall past her to Noah. His expression is furious as he blows his coach whistle, the little train one dangling from the same cord. Each time I notice it, the smallest of smiles creeps onto my face, and I push my way through the workout, trying to keep the little food I did eat down.

"Something funny?" Cami snaps.

Her venomous tone has me stopping in place. "What's your"— I pant—"problem today?"

"Maybe if you spent a little less time being a fuck buddy the past few months and more time doing your suggested workouts, you wouldn't be hyperventilating so hard."

"What the hell"—I place my hands on my hips, trying to catch my breath—"are you talking about?"

"She's his *girlfriend*," Andi corrects.

Cami scoffs. "Noah doesn't do *girlfriends*. Don't fool yourself into thinking you're anything more than a summer fling. As if he'd—"

"Cami," Noah's deep voice warns, cutting her off, and her head snaps in his direction. The boys are walking off the field, no doubt heading to the cafeteria for lunch. The other cheer teams are doing the same.

"Noah, I—" she sputters.

"You done with practice?" he asks, unamused, eyes containing a look of annoyance I've never seen.

Cami shifts on her heels. "Yes."

His gaze flicks to me. "Ready for lunch, babe?"

She waves me off, signaling I can leave. I rush to gather my things and head to Noah.

"You okay?" he asks in my ear, throwing an arm around me. He said he doesn't mind the sweat, so I force myself to relax despite my instincts to shrug him off.

"I don't know what her problem is." A heavy exhale escapes me.

"We hooked up my sophomore year."

My muscles tighten. I'm not used to him talking about other girls.

"Great," I grumble. "So your ex is my cheer captain? That would've been useful information before this moment."

"Sleeping with someone once hardly makes them an ex," he says, and a burning sensation settles in my stomach.

"Then I don't know what the big deal is."

He shrugs. "She wanted to hook up again, but I denied her."

"Of course she did," I grumble, wishing I could throw a hand over my mouth and put the words back in.

"Don't worry. None of my other ex-hookups are here."

"Other?!" I balk, the burning sensation crawling throughout my body. "In the duration of our friendship, you've never mentioned a single girl, and suddenly you have *multiple* ex-fuck buddies?"

Noah laughs, removing his arm, and threads our fingers together. "I'm not celibate, *tesoro*," he says, and my cheeks flush at what I assume is an Italian pet name. "I just don't bang and boast like most guys do."

I hum, readjusting my grip in his large palm. "Interesting revelation."

"Sorry to give you the bad news about my virginity," he says, with a teasing shrug.

"Who will I give as an offering to the football gods now?"

"That's okay," he says. "I can't very well be a present to myself."

"Oh my god," I groan as we arrive at the cafeteria with a line out the door.

"I think you meant, 'Oh my *Noah*,'" he says, and I narrow my eyes at him, lips parted. He laughs. "Want to walk by the lake for a few?" He gestures towards it with our interlocked hands. "Give time for the crowd to die down?"

"Sure."

"How are the twins?"

"Good," I say, thinking of the photo Patricia sent me from Denny's gymnastics camp this morning. "Staying busy."

"How are things with your parents?"

I groan. "Going straight off the deep end, huh?"

"Just checking in." He squeezes my hand. "I know it upsets you."

I shrug. "We're talking, but they still won't give me back my car, and I have to pay my own tuition next year."

"How do you plan to do that?"

"I have a partial cheer scholarship and some grants," I tell him. "But they paid for my room and board. So I've been looking into some loan options."

"If you need a private loan, I could—"

"No way." I glare at him. "You *just* got your signing bonus. And also bought a house, which I imagine was not cheap."

"I *really* don't mind."

"I appreciate it, truly," I tell him. "But I won't accept that."

There's no way he can be my fake boyfriend *and* my sugar daddy. Even if it's a loan. That would just be wrong.

"Well, offer stands," he says with a shrug as a few birds swoop down overhead, then disappear into a tree. Water laps at the shore, and I realize we're alone. I glance down at our intertwined fingers, and he follows my gaze.

"Guess we don't have to…"

"Oh." He drops my hand. "Right."

Way to go, loser.

The heat beats down on us, and a shaded bench below the tree catches my eye. I gesture towards it, and Noah nods. We sit, our sides touching as we stare out at the sunshine sparkling on the lake.

"I bet your mom is thrilled about you staying in Florida," I say, trying to break the awkward silence.

"Yeah," Noah says, wringing his hands together. "I'm definitely relieved to be near home."

"You two are really close. I'm guessing it was hard after your dad left?" I ask, knowing it's a sore spot but hoping for some insight.

His eyes dart to mine. "My dad?"

"Never mind." I shake my head. "I'm sorry, I shouldn't have brought him up."

His shoulders drop, distant gaze finding mine. "No, it's okay," he assures me. "I…" He blows out a shaky breath. "I want to talk to you about this stuff, I really do."

A beat of silence passes between us. "But?"

He looks up at the blue sky, then back to the still lake. "It feels unnatural to talk about the darkest parts of my life while I'm surrounded by all the things that bring me joy."

I study his face, taking note of the way he bites his lip. Like he's holding something in. "And what would those things be?"

"Sunshine," he says with a smile. "Football." He gestures towards the fields. "And most importantly"—his gaze connects with mine—"you."

My heart constricts, lips parting. "Me?"

"Yeah," he says, green eyes pinning me in place. "You."

Breathe, girl, breathe.

"That's pretty heavy stuff from a fake boyfriend," I choke out.

"Well, I was your real best friend before I was your fake boyfriend," he reminds me with a gentle smile.

"Right," I say, biting my lower lip. "Well, if you ever want to talk about that stuff, you know, in the dark, on a rainy day, with all the curtains closed…" I release a shaky breath as his sad eyes capture mine. "I'm here."

"I appreciate that." A soft smile graces his face. "I appreciate *you*." I struggle for a response, and he stands, clearly ready for the conversation to be over. "Ready for lunch?" he asks, holding out a hand.

"Yep," I say, placing mine in his, ready to follow wherever he leads.

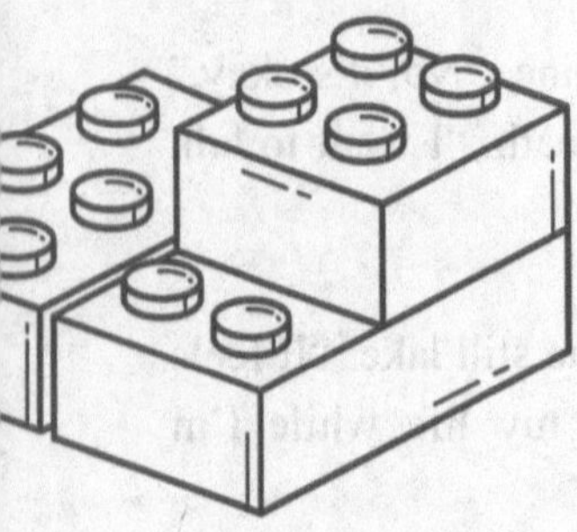

16

NOAH

Blowing the whistle, I suppress my annoyance of having to coach Jonathan and his offensive line. It's Friday, and I survived the entire week barely seeing him. *Happy birthday to me.* They're scrimmaging against CBU, but when I walked to practice, I promised not to favor my alma mater, to ignore the names on the backs of the jerseys and approach it from an analytical perspective.

Jonathan pushes himself off the ground, given a CBU linebacker just blitzed him. *Atta boy.* He rips off his helmet and staggers towards the sidelines with the rest of the Andrews University offensive line. They're actually not half bad, but it seems Jonathan's as distracted by my presence as I am by his.

The players surround me, all awaiting my instruction as I grip a playbook in my hand.

"Your formation is good," I tell them. "But your pass completion rate needs work." Jonathan huffs out a sarcastic breath. "Don't get your panties in a bunch," I tell him, and his face reddens. "In case you forgot, quarterback isn't the only position on the field. This is a *team* game."

"Wow, what a revelation," he says, and I bite my tongue.

Keep it professional.

I may be annoyed at this guy, but his team still deserves my attention and guidance.

"My point is, it doesn't matter how good the quarterback is if the rest of the team isn't in sync. A sloppy offensive line means you're leaving holes open—not protecting your man."

"Or maybe the man is too slow today," one of the guys calls out.

"Even if that's true…" I say, looking at the lineman. And it is. Jonathan's taken about three seconds too long for every play. "It's your job to afford him that time to make a pass or find a route." I turn my attention to the running backs. "It's *your* job to shake the defenders and get open." I speak to the team as a whole. "If there's not an open route, or an open man, it doesn't matter if you've got a D1 quarterback in a peewee football league. He can only do so much. Do you understand?"

"Yes, Coach," they call out.

"Good!" I say, waving my arms. "You're in field goal range, but I want a touchdown. So get back on the field and show me what you've got."

Helmets are pulled on, mouth guards in place, chin straps hooked, and they're jogging back out to the thirty-yard line. The defenders get in place, offensive line sets up, and I walk the edge of the field, watching them.

Jonathan shouts, "Hike!"

Center sends him the ball, and Jonathan shuffles backwards. The guards are holding position, a wide receiver bolting down field, a cornerback quick on his heels.

"Throw!" I shout, hoping Jonathan hears me.

He cocks his arm. The ball soars through the air, lands perfectly in the receiver's arms, and he sprints it into the end zone.

Touchdown.

The Andrews U boys run and high five. A few players dance near the field goal post, and Jonathan holds his head high, walking towards the sideline.

"Thank you!" I shout. "Finally!"

Another twenty minutes of improving their offensive line, and we get to break for lunch. I shove the clipboard in my backpack on the metal bench. My eyes scan for Charlotte, but the cheerleaders had weight training this morning so she must still be at the gym.

"What the hell, Cap?" Theo says, gripping my shoulders and shaking me. "Heard you made our boys look like fools."

"Well, if they can't tighten up, that's not on me," I say with a smirk.

"We'll give you a pass since it's your birthday," Elijah says, joining us.

I throw my backpack over one shoulder and rotate the hat I was wearing backwards. "How kind of you."

"Happy birthday to you!" they sing in unison, Elijah throwing an arm over my shoulder.

"Oh my god, stop," I beg.

"Happy birthday to you!" they screech, others around us joining in as we walk toward the cafeteria. "Happy birthday to Noahhhhhh. Happy birthday to you."

"Thanks, guys," I say, nudging Elijah off me. "I gotta head back to my cabin and drop my bag off. I'll meet you in the cafeteria?"

"Yeah, right," Theo says. "You're probably headed for some *birthday sex.*"

"Dude." I glare at him.

"Later," he says, with a brow waggle.

When I enter the cabin, my phone buzzes. I shut the door and pull it out.

Tri County Correctional Institute.

Rolling my eyes, I ignore the call, shoving the phone back into my pocket.

Every year he tries, and every year I ignore him, hoping it'll be the last time.

Why won't he leave me the fuck alone?

Does he really think I want to talk to him?

It's been eight years, and every single time, the phone rings, my muscles seize up, and I'm fourteen years old, the cold metal in my hand.

I fight the urge to spiral, tossing my backpack on the bed.

Knock. Knock. Knock.

Blowing out a breath, I walk over to the door and throw it open. The weight on my chest is instantly lifted at the sight of Charlotte with a full-toothed smile, holding a hand behind her back.

"Close your eyes," she says, and I eagerly oblige. "Hold out your hands." I do as instructed, and after a minute of shuffling sounds, a small object is placed in my palms. "Okay, you can look."

My eyes pop open to the sight of a plastic container hosting one of my favorite desserts, albeit store-bought, and a lit candle sticking out the top.

"Make a wish," she tells me.

Without a second thought, I blow out the flame.

"It kills me I couldn't bake you a cake from scratch, but I tried to at least find something I know you like," she says, shifting in place. "And you've mentioned a few times how good your mom's tiramisù is. I'm sure this doesn't even come close to live up but—"

"It's perfect," I say, my heart squeezing at the thoughtful gesture. "Thank you."

"Ready for lunch?" Charlotte asks, and I close the plastic lid to protect my little treat.

"Starving," I say, reaching out my hand, and she looks down at it, smile deepening as she takes it.

We stroll down the path, and she says, "Heard you had to coach for Andrews' o-line today?"

"Yep." I huff a breath.

"How was it?"

"Fine." *Annoying.* "Just treated them like any other team."

"What?" she shrieks, and I flinch, eyes snapping to hers. "I was hoping you had them run the bleachers till they puked or made sure Jonathan got his shit rocked."

I chuckle. "As appealing as all that sounds, I was trying to be professional."

"Yeah, yeah," she grumbles. "Can you professionally rock his shit?"

I release my hold on her hand and put my free arm around her shoulder, tiramisù still securely in the other. "Well, you'll have to complain to CBU's defense about that." I place a kiss in her hair, and she grips my waist. "But sure. Next time I'll say, 'Fuck professionalism,' and make him do burpees till he blacks out."

"Is that really too much for a fake girlfriend to ask for?" she says, smiling up at me, her pretty lips inches away. It would be so easy to lean down, claiming them. I wonder how she tastes. The feel of her tongue on mine. What kind of noises she'd make.

"Hey, Caruso!" I'm yanked out of my fantasy, head turning to find one of the other coaches. "You got a minute?"

I glance back to Charlotte with a frown. "I'm sorry."

"It's fine," she says, seemingly unaffected. "You've got big grown-up things to attend to."

"See you at the bonfire later?" I ask.

"It's a date," she says, and I fight a smile. "I just meant—"

I bend down, brushing my lips against her ear. "It's a *date*."

The outside temperature is sweltering, but the bonfire is tradition to end the first completed week of training. So we're all here, roasting both the marshmallows and ourselves. Coaches, staff, and students alike mingle together, eating barbeque and having a good time.

Others splash in the lake, enjoying the cool water to fight off the humid Florida air.

I wander through the crowd in search of a pretty brunette, finally spotting her a few yards away. My lips curve upward as Charlotte lets loose with Andi and Stella, a happy, carefree smile on her face.

"Noah," I hear from behind me and spin around. Hannah, the redhead I can't seem to shake, stands a few yards away. My smile drops, but I quickly recover to avoid looking rude.

"Hey," I say with a curt nod.

"You haven't been answering my messages," she says, a teasing smirk on her face.

"So you showed up to deliver them in person?" I ask, brows furrowing and the word "stalker" on the tip of my tongue.

"Dad's here scouting for players he might want to draft next year," she says, twirling a lock of hair. I glance around, and sure as shit, her dad, aka my new boss, is standing a few yards away, talking to one of the other coaches.

I return my attention to her. "Doesn't explain what *you're* doing here."

"Thought I'd tag along and be an extra set of eyes on the upcoming talent. Any players I should keep my sights on?"

"Not that I can think of," I say, having no interest in prolonging this conversation.

"Hmm…" She twists her mouth. "I find that hard to believe. Maybe I'll attend one of your practices and check it out for myself."

"That seems highly unnecessary."

"We'll see about that," she says, bouncing on her heels. "Well, I gotta run and help Dad with something, but I'll see you around."

"Sure." *No, thank you.*

"Text me if you ever need a late night"—she glances around with a smirk, then returns her attention to me—"distraction." She waves with a wink, walking away before I can reply.

Good lord, that woman can't take a hint.

Turning back around, I find Charlotte in the same place. Her eyes are glued on me, and she quickly looks away. I chuckle under my breath at her attempt at nonchalance and walk to her.

Placing a finger under her chin, I tilt her gaze to meet mine. "Hey, *soffione*," I say, leaning down and kissing her cheek. Pausing, I allow myself one single moment to enjoy the sweet citrus scent of her shampoo, then pull away.

"Hey, birthday boy," she says, jaw tight.

"Andi." I nod. "Stella."

"Noah," they coo in unison.

"We're gonna…" Andi points over her shoulder, and before I can say a word, she and Stella have disappeared.

"Wow!" Charlotte laughs. "Now you're scaring off my friends too. Who knew dating you would be such social suicide?"

"Excuse me?" I scoff, grabbing her hand and tugging her to me. "If anything, I've increased your social status."

Her teasing eyes meet mine. "How do you figure that?"

I cock a brow. "You *are* dating a first-round NFL draft pick for the Tampa Barracudas."

"Am I *really*?" She places a hand over her chest in mock shock. "Well, aren't I the luckiest girl in all the land."

"God, you are just…" I lean down, lips hovering over hers, begging for a taste.

I agreed to kissing for our little arrangement, even knowing what an indisputably idiotic idea it is. But if I avoid it too long, people *will* start asking questions.

"Was that the redhead from Miami?" Charlotte asks, attempting to maintain apathy and pulling my attention back to her eyes.

I fight a smile. "You remember her?"

"Another ex-fuck buddy, right?"

"Absolutely not. We had one drink." *A drink that you basically forced on me.*

Her shoulders relax slightly. "I guess I don't have the right to care anyways."

Neither do I, and I still want to knock your ex out every time he looks at you. "Of course you do. We're dating."

"*Fake* dating," she corrects, adding to the weight in my stomach every time I remember that technicality.

"Right." I clear my throat. "Well, for the *record*, nothing happened between Hannah and me. But she is Coach Bexley's daughter, so I have to be cordial."

Her eyes widen. "She's your boss's *daughter*?"

"Yep."

"And what, she's hoping you wanna sleep your way to the top?"

I note the little green monster in her eyes. "I'm more of a bottom type of guy."

"Noah!" she squeals, slapping me on the chest. "Be serious."

"*Tesoro*," I say, leaning down to her ear. "She's the last woman I'm thinking about in my bed." Her lips smash shut, and I pull away. "Wanna go sit by the bonfire?"

She laughs nervously. "I mean, it's already hot as the hinges of hell, but sure, why not."

I grab her hand, our fingers interlacing, and tug her toward the spot where the CBU boys have taken over. Elijah sits on a bench next to Theo as they laugh like they don't have a care in the world. But, I suppose, why would they? They're two of the top dogs on campus. Football captains. No real responsibilities yet. Life must be good.

There's a free spot next to Elijah, and I sit, patting my leg. Charlotte glances at it, then back to me, and I tug her on my lap before she has a chance to protest.

"Remember," I whisper in her ear. "You have to pretend you're not afraid of me."

She brings her lips to my ear. "I'm not afraid." Her soft breath fans my skin. *PG thoughts, Caruso.* She throws an arm around my neck, and I hook mine around her waist, tugging her against me.

The denim shorts she's wearing give my fingertips direct contact to her smooth skin, and I gently glide my thumb across the top of her leg. Goosebumps appear, pleasing me.

Glancing up, I note Jonathan glaring at us as he takes a seat on the other side of the campfire. *Guess he wants a sideline seat to how bad he fumbled.*

Charlotte shifts uncomfortably, looking toward me. "Why would he come over here if he's just gonna stare?"

"Wanna give him something to stare at?" I ask, the need to claim her overwhelming.

"What did you have in mind?" she asks with a cheeky smile.

My heart pounds hard in my chest. "You still okay with the rules we discussed?"

She nods. "I am."

Gliding my hand in her hair, I tug her to me, our foreheads touching. "Good."

Don't think about, don't touch, and definitely don't kiss Charlotte.

My eyes fall to her lips. Her pretty, plump pink lips. As if sensing my gaze, she darts her tongue out, wetting them.

Fuck.

A man only has so much willpower.

"Pretend it's not the first time," I whisper, more as a reminder for myself, while sliding my hand to her neck. *Don't kiss Charlotte.* My thumb grazes her jawbone before swiping over her soft lip. She smiles, eyes fixed on mine like I'm the only man on earth. Like she never wants to look away. *The feeling is more than mutual.*

"Okay," she says with an exhale, and I pull her closer, our noses touching.

"Don't freak out." *Don't kiss Charlotte.*

"I'm not freaking out," she says, our mouths brushing as she speaks. *How is she not freaking out?*

"Char—" Her lips crash against mine, and my eyes flutter shut. *Cazzo*[1]. Her hand slides into my hair, gripping it tight. My soul exits my body, zips through the universe at the speed of light, and arrives in one where only we exist. Where Charlotte and I are twin suns, held together by the gravity of our kiss.

I graze my tongue against the seam of her lips, and she entangles hers with mine. She tastes like strawberries and peaches and the sweetest temptation I've ever had. Warmth spreads across my chest, as I grip her thigh, desperate to remain in transcendence. She lets out a small whimper, and crackling wood transports me back to Earth. *Bonfire. Audience. Fuck.* Fighting every cell in my body, I break the kiss.

Her heavy breath hits my swollen, wet lips. Unable to speak, my mouth finds her jaw and I plant a soft kiss before forcing myself to pull away. My dick is hard, and I'm praying by some miracle she doesn't notice.

"That was…" She huffs a laugh.

"Wow," I fill in.

She glances across the bonfire, and then her eyes return to mine. "Do you think it was believable?"

Supernova to my heart.

It is for show, after all.

"Yeah." I smile weakly. "It was believable."

"I'm gonna grab us a drink," she says, pushing to stand, and I clutch her firmly to my lap. "What are you doing?" she asks, wiggling in my arms, and I bring my lips to her ear.

"If you get up right now," I rasp out, "everyone here is going to see the effect of the little show we put on."

Her brows furrow, then go upward. "I thought that was your phone digging into my ass."

---

1. IT: *Cazzo* - EN: Fuck

I drop my face into her neck and shake my head. "My phone's in the cabin."

"Oh."

Shifting in place, I try to readjust to Earth's gravity. "Yeah."

"But why?"

"I'm a guy, Char." I bring my lips to her ear, releasing a shaky breath. "Just because this isn't real doesn't mean my cock got the memo. If I kiss a hot girl and she moans into my mouth, things are gonna happen below the belt."

"I did not *moan* into your mouth," she whispers, throwing a hand over her chest.

"Yes." I swallow hard, the heavenly sound still echoing in my mind. "You did."

"Sorry." Even in the low light, I can see the pink creep onto her cheeks. "Guess my vocal cords didn't get the fake dating memo either."

I reach under Charlotte to adjust myself. "I think it's safe for you to leave now."

"Are you sure?"

"It'll be fine." I squeeze her leg. "I'm fine."

She stands up. "Soda okay?"

I consider the Barracudas "suggested" meal plan and the puke-inducing training regimen that goes along with it. "Just water, thanks."

"You got it," she says, heading off towards the drinks table, my eyes trailing her as she goes. Her hips sway, shorts hugging her curves in a way that should be a damn crime. *Take me to jail, Officer Benson.*

Elijah clears his throat beside me, and I turn to him. Theo grins while nodding his head, then says, "I'm glad you finally gave up your no pussy rule."

"That wasn't the rule, and you know it," I say pointedly. But his words are a reminder of the reasoning behind it. Relationships are messy. Distracting. Dangerous. I toy with the gold band on my necklace.

"I still prefer Elijah's," Theo says, nudging him. "More titties…"

Elijah cocks his arm back, throwing an imaginary football that Theo "catches." "More touchdowns!" Elijah says, and they high-five.

"What are you high-fiving for?" I tease Elijah. "You've got the same tits forever."

"Yeah." Elijah smirks. "And they're fucking perfect."

Theo looks between us, face scrunched up. "You guys disgust me. All pussy-whipped and shit."

Elijah throws his arm around Theo. "Wrapped up in a pussy is a perfect place to be."

"Or two, or three," Theo says.

Jonathan's forced laughter pulls my attention across the campfire, and his eyes meet mine in a sarcastic grimace.

"Something funny?" I ask.

"Yeah," he says at the same moment Charlotte returns with our drinks, and I immediately regret involving him in our conversation. She hands me a bottle of water, then slides awkwardly into my lap, glancing between us.

"What's up?" she asks.

"What's up is your little 'boyfriend' here," Jonathan says, using quotation marks that piss me right off, "is making it seem like he's getting some from you when we both know you're a prude."

I open my mouth to speak, but Charlotte silences me with a finger and says, "Maybe *you* should shut the hell up before I tell everyone here about the time you had to go to the hospital because you had an allergic reaction to fucking a grapefruit." Charlotte shrugs. "Oops."

Everyone within hearing distance snorts a laugh, and his eyes go wide.

"In case you forgot, Charlie," he snaps, "the only reason I even tried that was because you couldn't ever finish me off!" My spine straightens, grip tightening on Charlotte. "Noah will be ready to dump your ass once he realizes you're a shitty lay."

Rushing to stand, I pull Charlotte with me and gently nudge her out of the way as my blood boils. I regret not putting a stop to his idiotic comments when they were dating, but I sure as hell will now.

"Why don't you get my girl's name out of your mouth?" I bark.

Jonathan howls a laugh. "She was my girl way before she was yours."

The reminder is unwelcome. "Well, she's not anymore."

"Thank god for that." He rolls his eyes. I glance towards Charlotte, whose arms are wrapped around herself, jaw clenched.

"You should have a little more respect," I say, walking towards him. *Calm down, Caruso.* I scan our surroundings, and it looks like Bexley and some of the other coaches must have left. *Good.*

"I don't need to respect you," he says as we stand nose to nose.

"Not me. Charlotte. *You're*," I say, poking his chest, "the one who fucked up. So maybe shut your mouth, put your tiny dick between your legs, and walk away." I smile in his face as smoke blows out of his ears.

"Or what?" Jonathan asks.

"Trust me," I say, gritting my teeth, fists clenched at my sides. "You really don't want to find out."

Get control of yourself, Caruso.

You're not this guy.

A wide grin spreads across his face. "Maybe I do," he says, shoving my shoulders unexpectedly, and I stumble backwards, the heat of the bonfire throwing up alarms in my head. I leap out of the way just in time, the bystanders gasping as I catch my balance.

"Seriously?" Charlotte shouts at Jonathan, her voice shaky. "You're going to shove my boyfriend in the fire for what?" *My boyfriend.* She's now directly in front of him, and I hurry to her side. If he lays a single finger on her, someone will definitely be headed to the ER tonight, and it won't be me.

Jonathan glances between us, and I can feel the presence of the boys at my back. "Walk away," I tell him.

The wheels spin in his head, but he's at least smart enough to realize he's outnumbered and nudges Charlotte aside as he storms off.

She bumps into my chest and I start after him, but she stops me. I look down at her, unable to ignore the way the orange fire reflects off the moisture welling in her eyes.

"Char."

"I'm fine," she croaks before clearing her throat, and I throw my arm around her shoulders.

"Let's go."

"You just got here," she argues. "And it's your birthday."

"I don't care. We're heading out," I tell the boys, and they wave us off.

I tuck her head into my side, and as we head down the path towards the cabins, her shoulders begin to shake.

"Shh, it's okay," I tell her, squeezing tighter. "We're almost there."

The hike lasts an eternity, but we finally arrive at my cabin. I unlock the door and bring her inside. She pulls away and swipes tears off her face while kicking off her shoes, then crawls into my bed and under the covers. Her pained gaze connects with mine, and my chest caves in on itself.

"Charlotte," I murmur, following her lead and climbing in, then tug her close. She falls against me, resting her hand on my chest, toying with my necklace.

"I feel ridiculous…"

Trailing my fingertips along her arm, I ask, "Why?"

"I swore I wouldn't care what he says anymore. But he talks shit one time, and I'm ready to throw up."

"I'm so sorry."

She scoffs. "What are you sorry for? I'm the one who forced you into all this. I should've asked you before pimping you out to be my fake boyfriend."

Fake.

"You have nothing to be sorry about," I say, and she shakes her head, her pretty brown eyes glistening. "Please, don't cry."

"I don't want to, but I'm so angry." She rubs a tear away. "What if he was right?"

Turning on my side, I face her, and she matches my position so we're lying nose to nose. I tuck a dark strand of hair behind her ear and rest my palm on her neck. "You are perfect *exactly* the way you are." She sucks in a breath. "Don't let your shithead ex, or anyone else for that matter, ever make you believe otherwise." I rub my thumb along her jaw. "There's nothing he said that could be right about you."

"You don't know that." She presses her forehead to my chest. "Not about this."

An uneasy feeling settles in my stomach. "What exactly is 'this'?'" She lets out a heavy breath, and I take her chin between my fingers, tilting it up till her eyes meet mine. "You can tell me anything."

She nibbles on her lower lip. "It's embarrassing."

"And you can still tell me. I won't go anywhere, I promise."

She looks down at her hands, releasing a defeated sigh. "I'm not good at sex."

She's not... what? Anger floods my veins at how much he's screwed up her self-esteem.

"I can't—well, couldn't—get Jonathan off unless he told me exactly what to do," she continues. "And when I'd try my own things, he said it didn't feel good."

"Well, I imagine it's hard to be confident when you're constantly told you're not any good."

She nods. "Yeah, I suppose so."

Their relationship was so much worse than I even realized. "Anything else?"

She twists her mouth. "He always said I was too vanilla."

"There's nothing wrong with not wanting to do more..." I clear my throat. "Erotic things in the bedroom."

"But that's the thing," she says, looking at me. "He only said it when I didn't want to be physical." *So he manipulated her to sleep with him.* "Whenever I brought up anything even remotely kinky, *he's* the one who'd look at me like I had six heads. Or accuse me of needing role play to get off and that I wasn't attracted to him."

The thought of her dressed as a sexy professor slapping my ass with a ruler pops in my head, and I'm immediately hard.

Not the time.

"I'm so sorry he's made you feel this way." *I'm also sorry I didn't knock his ass out when I had the chance.*

She shrugs. "I keep trying to reassure myself I'm not the problem, but I don't really have any other data to go off of. Jonathan is the only person I've been with."

Realization hits me. "Is that why you asked me to fuck you in Miami?" I ask timidly, pushing away the memory of her beautiful naked body begging for my touch. "So you had more... data?"

"Yeah." She cringes. "It was a stupid idea."

I shake my head. It was a lot of things, but—"It wasn't stupid."

"It was," she assures me. "And it was unfair I tried to use you for that. You were right to say no."

"I said no because I didn't want you to do something you'd regret."

"That's why?" She bolts up, and I join suit. "*That's* why you said no?"

My brows pull together. "Yeah."

"You said no because you thought *I'd* regret it?" she presses.

"Yes?" I say, confused by her reaction.

"My only regret is that *he's* the last person I've been..." She swallows hard. "Intimate with." A fire burns in the pit of my stomach. I definitely hate that too. "I keep thinking maybe if I sleep with someone else, I can, I don't know, practice?"

"Practice?" I ask, a brow raised.

A blush creeps up her cheeks. "Yes."

"What exactly are you hoping to *practice*?" I ask, smashing my lips together to suppress a smile.

"All the"—she waves a hand around—"*stuff* I said before."

I rub a palm against my stubble. "So you want to increase your confidence, not be afraid to take charge, and try freaky shit without being judged?"

"Noah!" She slaps me on the arm. "I'm not saying I'm into, like, BDSM or anything."

"You could be." I smirk, tugging her hands forward and holding them in place. "There's nothing wrong with a little light bondage."

She rolls her lips together, a pretty pink blush hitting her cheeks. "I suppose that's also a curriculum I wouldn't mind exploring."

"And you're sure that's what you want?" I ask, releasing her hands, trying to gauge where her head is at. "Someone to help you… practice?"

"Yes, absolutely," she says, and her eyes light up. "Why? Do you know someone?"

My lips part open. "Yeah, *me*?"

"You?" Her eyebrows shoot to her hairline.

"Yes?" My jaw clenches. "Or did you intend on fake dating me while fucking someone else?"

"No." Her eyes widen. "But you told me never to ask you that again."

"Only because if you do, I won't say no," I blurt, muscles freezing.

Why didn't I make a rule for this?

Don't fuck Charlotte definitely seems like it should be rule number one.

"You won't?" she says in shock, the air thick with tension.

"Of course not." I toy with my necklace. *This is a bad idea. A terrible, horrible, no good, very bad idea.* "Like you said, you need to practice so you can get your confidence up and forget *him*. And—"

"You haven't gotten any since spring break?" she fills in.

"Whoa." I throw my hands up. "I didn't sleep with *anyone* on spring break."

"You've been in a dry spell *longer* than spring break? That was months ago!"

"Hey!" My ears turn hot. "This isn't about my sex life. It's about yours."

"It doesn't really sound like you'd be experienced enough to help me anyways," she says with a teasing look of disapproval, and I struggle to form a coherent sentence. I raise my brows, fighting a smirk, and she caves, a wicked smile spreading across her face. "So to be clear, you're offering sex lessons?"

My mouth goes dry. "Call it whatever you want."

"Let's call it that." She sits on her heels, folding her hands in her lap like we're opening a negotiation. But hey, any negotiation that ends with an orgasm is one I want to be a part of. "How are you going to give me lessons if you haven't even got any recently?"

"Charlotte!" My mouth falls open, and she throws her head back, laughing. I release a heavy breath, thankful her sense of humor is back.

"Sorry, sorry." She reins it in. "I know you have your *reputation*." I blink at her, unsure how to respond as she contemplates me. "Okay, I accept your offer."

"Really?" *Is she fucking with me?*

"Yes." She shifts in place. "I don't want to go a single second longer with *him* being the last one to touch me that way."

My body tenses.

You and me both.

"So you… want to start now?" I ask hesitantly.

"I'm game if you are," she says, eyes hopeful.

Stop acting like you're losing your virginity and shake off the damn nerves, Caruso.

I scoot to the side of the bed, sitting on the edge, and place my feet on the floor. "Come here."

She climbs off the mattress and stands before me. I've kept my hands mostly to myself during this conversation because I didn't want her to feel pressured into anything. I didn't want my touch distracting her… or me.

But her intentions are clear.

Charlotte Benson can use me in any way she pleases.

"Are you ready?" I ask, placing my hands on her hips, just below the hem of her shirt.

She nods, releasing a shaky breath as the corners of her mouth quirk. "I'm ready."

"Good," I say, staring up into her pretty brown eyes. With my foot, I kick her legs apart. "Now be a good girl and straddle my lap."

She bites her lower lip and places her hands on my shoulders, gaze not leaving mine as she sends me a wicked grin. *Fuck.*

My dick twitches, and there's no way I'll be able to hide that when she lowers herself onto me.

She grips my shoulders, then throws a leg on each side, straddling my lap as instructed. *Holy shit, this is happening.* Her center brushes against my cock, and even with all these clothes between us, I have to fight a groan.

Her curious eyes search mine.

"Do you trust me?" I ask, holding her hips.

"Of course." She brushes her fingers along the side of my neck. "So tell me, professor, how do we start?"

I stifle another groan. *Don't rush this.*

"If you just want to kiss and get comfortable," I say, dragging my thumb along her lips, "we can do that." I wouldn't mind the opportunity to explore these again without an audience. "If you want to do more"—I slide my hand into her hair, gripping it and angling her mouth upwards—"I'm down for that too." We're a breath apart. "And if at any point *at all* you want to stop, tell me. Okay?"

Nodding, she lets out a whimpered approval. My hands slide down her body, fingertips dipping under her shirt, and she gasps as I nudge the material upwards. "This okay for you?"

She nods again.

"Use your words, *soffione*."

"It's more than okay," she murmurs.

More than okay.

Her response pleases me, and I pull the shirt up and over her head, exposing a blue bra. My eyes zero in on the valley of her breasts. *So soft.* I snake my hand around her back, fingers finding the clasp, and unhook it.

Charlotte giggles. "Maybe you have some experience after all."

This woman.

Pulling away, I narrow my eyes at her. We hold our gaze as I bring my hand to her shoulder, taking the strap between my fingers, and slowly slide it down. Her cheeks flush as we continue our staring contest, and I move to the other shoulder, brushing the strap off. The bra falls, and she shimmies it off, my eyes dropping to her breasts. Her tempting, delicious breasts. *I can't believe this is happening.*

"Fuck, you're so pretty." Sliding my fingers in her hair, I grip it, tilting her head, and my mouth captures the soft skin on the side of her neck, sucking gently. She releases a breathy moan as I pepper kisses on her collarbone, cheek, jaw, everywhere but the one place I'm desperate to. The anticipation of returning to that ethereal plane fires electricity from my every neuron.

"Noah," she whispers, shaking her head as I wrap an arm around her back, holding her to me. "You don't have to do this."

Does she not want to?

Turning, I slowly ease her down to the center of the mattress, my lips tracing her jaw. With every breath her mouth draws closer, my pulse quickening until our lips are centimeters apart. I brush a stray hair out of her face, and her eager gaze finds mine.

"Tell me to stop," I beg.

"I'd rather die."

Our mouths collide, stars dancing in my vision as I'm transported back to our cosmic dream. Slipping my tongue out, I coax her lips open, and she lets out a soft moan that causes the hair on my arms to stand.

"Sorry," she pants, and I pull back, our eyes locking.

"Any normal guy will go crazy if you moan into their mouth. I'm no exception." Nibbling on her lower lip, she gives a small nod and scoots back on the bed. Lying against the pillows, she opens her legs in invitation. *Am I dreaming?* A wicked smile spreads across her face, and her eyes drink me in hungrily. *There she is.* Taking my time, I crawl up the bed, slip between her thighs, and hover over her. "You are breathtakingly beautiful."

"And you are *very* good at this faking it thing."

My jaw ticks. "I have a new rule."

She cocks a brow. "And that is?"

"Whenever we're 'faking it,' whether it's the dating or the…"

"Sex lessons," she finishes, with a teasing smile.

"Right. The dating or the lessons. Can we just live in the moment?"

It's awfully hard to keep it up while being consistently reminded this is all just for practice.

A small smile crosses her lips. "I can do that."

"Good." I slide my palm up her leg, and she giggles, squirming beneath me. I sit up, straddling her, and remove my shirt, then toss it to the ground. She places her hands on my stomach, dangerously close to my dick, and I savor the attention. "Fuck," I say breathlessly, looking down as her perfect, perky tits beg for me to taste them. Our eyes connect as I run my hands along her soft sides, pausing on her ribcage, inches from her breasts. Her chest rises and falls heavily.

Lowering my head, I trail kisses from her jaw, down the column of her neck, and toward her collar bone. She squirms beneath me while I drag a calloused hand up her leg.

"Relax," I remind her gently. "You don't have to hold back with me. Be yourself. Let loose. You want something? Tell me."

Her breathy sigh fills the air as she throws her head against the pillow and pushes her chest toward me in invitation. Anticipation races through me. *Does she want this as bad as I do?* I dart out my tongue, gliding it over the swell of her breast, and suck her hard nipple into my hungry mouth, flicking against it. Bringing my hand to her other breast, I caress it gently, then rub my thumb over the hardened peak.

I grin, fully satisfied, continuing to taste every inch of her skin as my throbbing cock begs for more. *This isn't real.* I glide further down her body, kissing her soft stomach, and our eyes connect as I hover above the hem of her shorts. *This isn't real.*

I drag the denim downwards, and she lifts her hips, allowing me to tug them off her perfect body. *This isn't real.* She lies spread out before me, only a pair of forest-green panties separating us, and I rub my hand against my hard dick. "*Cazzo.*"

This isn't real.

Then why does she feel like mine?

17

CHARLOTTE

Noah's eyes swim with lust, instilling a sense of pride in me I didn't think possible. His mouth hovers above my panties, and I know I'm soaked for him. Hopefully he doesn't mind.

Come on. Be confident.

He sits on his heels, eyes stuck on me as he drags his hands along my sides, resting them on the hem. He dips one hand below the side of the material and grips my thigh with the other. Butterflies swarm in my stomach. His eyes flicker with indecision, and as he's encouraging confidence, I reach my hand down, dipping below the fabric. Hopefully he likes this.

Noah's eyes darken as I swipe between my thighs. "Don't stop touching yourself," he growls, grabbing the lace and tugging it off my body. *This seems like a good sign.* Cool air dances across my skin, a reminder of just how much Noah Caruso is seeing of me tonight.

He crawls back between my legs, face hovering over my center, and his hungry gaze connects with mine. *He's so damn hot.* Shivering at the attention, I graze my clit with my thumb and whimper. "Fuck, Charlotte." His eyes drop down to my hand, and he lets out a low growl. "Shit."

My muscles tense, and I pause my movements. *Did I already do something wrong?* "What?"

"You're soaked," he pants, eyes glued between my legs. "Can't wait to taste you." I release a sigh of relief as he nudges my hand to the side and lowers his head directly above my aching center. His eyes connect with mine. "Can I?"

My lip curls upwards at his consistent concern for my consent. "Noah," I say gently. "You don't need to keep asking if I'm okay with this. I am *so* okay with everything happening here." *More than.*

He chuckles, eyes darkening. "Message received."

Without breaking our gaze, he darts out his tongue, swiping across my clit.

A moan escapes me as I grip his hair. "Oh my." He flicks his tongue against a sensitive spot, and I buck off the bed, unable to relax my anxious body. "Sorry," I mumble. But how can I relax when Noah Caruso is buried face-deep between my thighs?

"Don't apologize," he murmurs. "Be wild for me, baby."
Baby.

There go those damn butterflies again. I try to put them back in their cage—remind them this is fake—but it's a lost cause as they whirl around my stomach, making it their permanent home.

Noah continues his torment, and his stubbled jaw rubs against my thighs, my body trembling. *Is this really happening?* My heart pounds so rapidly I worry I'll go into cardiac arrest. But honestly, death by orgasm seems like the way to go.

A flick of his tongue over my sweet spot, and another wave of pleasure racks through me.

I've been missing out.

Jonathan certainly wasn't afraid to ask for oral, but he rarely went down on me.

Another swipe from Noah's tongue brings me back to the present as he drags a finger between me. "You taste like heaven,

Charlotte." I squirm beneath him as he slides one finger inside. "Please, don't ever make me stop."

His pleading tone heats my arousal up to eleven. *Such pretty words.* He adds a second finger, and I moan, "Noah."

He grins lazily with hooded eyes. "That's it, baby. Say my name."

"*Noah*," I whine.

"How do you want me to finish you?"

"What?" *I've never been asked that before.*

"Do you want me to eat this needy little cunt while I finger fuck you?" His smirk is wicked. The perfect golden boy has been replaced by a dirty-talking sex professor, and I am *here* for it. "Maybe you want me to slide my hard cock deep inside and fuck the word 'fake' from your vocabulary?" I squirm beneath his darkened stare as he rubs his thumb over my clit. "Or do you want to be on top, using my body to prove who's really in charge?"

He's letting me choose? My mind swirls with indecision. "I like all those options."

He grips my thigh. "I thought you would."

"I don't know how to choose." He arches his fingers inside of me, and I gasp.

"Pick one and we can do the others later."

A thrill overtakes me at the promise of this continuing through the night. "Later?"

"Was this supposed to be a one-time lesson?" he teases. "I'm good, but I'm not *that* good." *He wants to do this again?* My hips rotate absentmindedly, grinding against his hand, the friction distracting me. "So what do you want?"

All of Noah's options are appealing, especially the idea of him edging me till I pass out. But knowing I'm the reason *he* falls apart would be indisputable evidence that maybe I'm not the problem after all. "I want to be in charge."

"That's my sexy girl," he says, and my face flushes as he

removes his fingers. Rolling to his back, he pulls me on top of him in one fell swoop. *Hot.*

I shimmy my shoulders, shaking off the nerves. *You can do this.*

Dragging my finger along the hem of his athletic shorts and briefs, I say, "The only problem is these." Pouting, I force myself into the role of an assertive, not damaged, dom.

He rests his hands under his head. "You're in charge."

I crawl off of him, pointing to the floor. "Strip."

"Yes ma'am," he says, rolling off the bed without hesitation.

He turns to me, our eyes connecting as I sit on my heels. *Confidence* rings through my mind, being the word of the day, and I pull my shoulders back, puffing out my tits.

His appreciative eyes wander my body, leaving goosebumps in their wake as he drops his shorts to the floor and kicks them off. My eyes fall to his blue boxer briefs emphasizing his well-endowed package.

"Fuck," I blurt, unable to formulate a single other thought.

He rubs his palm against his dick, and I fight a satisfied hum, squirming in place. The wetness between my legs intensifies, and I'm dying to see what's underneath.

"Those too," I instruct, pointing to his boxers.

Good. I'm doing good.

Noah fights a smile, toying with the waistband, then drops them to the floor, his erection springing free.

My mouth opens and closes as I stare at his delicious dick. It's long and thick. It's also extremely hard. His eyes roam my body greedily. *He's* hard for *me.*

He's turned on by *me.*

I, Charlotte Benson, got Noah Gabriel Caruso hard and naked.

And now... I'm going to make him come.

"On the bed," I instruct, and he laughs, following directions.

"What's so funny?" I ask hesitantly as he returns to his position on his back, hands under his head.

"I love how eager you are for me," he admits, and I release a sigh of relief. *This man is clearly into you. Stop being nervous.*

"Well, you know I love a lesson plan," I tease, reaching toward his hard length and wrapping my fingers around it.

His relaxed expression turns to surprise as I stroke him lightly. His breath staggers, and I bring my mouth inches from his cock, our gaze holding steady. The obvious lust in his eyes encourages a wicked smile across my face. I tighten my grip on his shaft and dart my tongue out, licking the pre-cum off his tip. The sweet taste has my eyes rolling to the back of my head. "*Mmmm.*"

"Charlotte," Noah says breathlessly, a hand sliding into my hair and gripping tightly. "If you make that noise again, there's a ninety percent chance I'll come on your face."

Ignoring his warning, I take his cock in my mouth and suck softly, panting and groaning while he fists my hair. "Char," he moans, but it sounds more like a plea. *Is he really so turned on by me?* As good as he tastes, and as much as I love torturing him, I'd really rather he came somewhere other than my face. I release him with a *pop* and crawl up his body slowly, taking note of every rigid, delicious muscle on the way. I place a leg on each side, allowing my center to rest against his rippled stomach. He grabs my hip with one hand, his thumb finds my clit with the other, and my head drops back.

"You're better than every fantasy I've imagined," he says, and my gaze snaps to his face for any hint of sincerity. Surely he's in a lust trance and this is all part of his dirty talk, but damn, does it sound convincing.

He continues rubbing my most sensitive spot, and I whimper, my eyes connecting with his as I grind against his rippled stomach for added friction.

"You've thought about me?" I ask, his searing gaze fueling a newfound courage within me.

"I'm always thinking about you," he says matter-of-factly.

I swallow hard as my chest tightens. "Have you thought about me when you touch yourself?"

"*Soffione.*" He chuckles. I struggle for air. "You're the only one I think about."

The only one. My lungs collapse. "Tell me."

"Tell you what?"

"About the last time. Every detail." He increases his pace, pleasure coursing through me, but I don't dare look away. Whether it's dirty talk or a lust-fueled admission, I want to experience every second of this with his eyes on me.

"I was in the shower," he says so quickly, I almost believe him.

"Where?"

He lets out a shaky breath. "Here."

Is he serious? "Keep going."

"It was earlier this week," he murmurs, the low, sexy tone dancing over my skin. "While you were waiting in my bed for me after the welcome dinner." My lips part at his confession, all the air squeezed from my lungs. "You looked so hot in those little shorts." I take rapid breaths, the thrill overwhelming me. *This doesn't sound like fiction.* "And I knew if I didn't relieve myself, I wouldn't be able to concentrate during our talk." My lips curve upwards, and I grind against him, greedily chasing release.

"Keep going," I encourage while panting. *Turns out I like dirty talk. Who knew?*

"I fisted myself as I imagined sliding into you bare. Your tight little pussy getting me off." He groans, rolling his hips, and his hard cock presses against my ass. "I fantasized about my name falling off your pretty lips as I fucked you from behind." My inner walls throb, and I slide downward till my center is directly over his cock.

"I thought about waking you up in the middle of the night with my face buried between your pretty thighs." *Please do.* I reach down and swipe his dick over my soaked sex. His fiery gaze sears me, and he wraps my hair around his hand. "I imagined making you beg for me." He tugs my head backwards, and I whimper. My legs spread apart, and I sink onto the tip of his cock. "*Porca troia*." He lets out a heavy breath. "I thought about how when I fuck you, I'm going to make you come so hard, I'll ruin you for anyone else. I'll be the only one who gets you to that perfect place with your taste on my tongue and my name on your lips." His tip stretches my entrance, but I need more. I need him. All of him. Immediately.

Spreading my legs, I sink down, moaning loudly when his tip touches that glorious spot inside me. "*Fuck*!"

"That's it," he praises. "So good for me." I move my hips as he continues swiping his thumb against my clit. I lean downward, resting my hands on his tense shoulders, and he keeps his rhythm.

"*Oh my*." I gasp at how incredible he feels. How all of this feels. It's been a long time since I've actually felt desired during sex. He thrusts, and I whine, "*Yes*!"

He pulls me to him, our mouths crashing in a searing kiss. Our tongues tangle as my soul leaves my fucking body. He removes his hand from my clit and snakes it around me, pressing against my lower back as he thrusts deeper.

If he thought living in the moment was going to be a problem, he was wrong. Because holy fuck, I'm drowning in this kiss, and I never want to come up for air.

"Char…" His voice comes out a plea.

"Yeah?" I pant into his mouth, hips rotating greedily to find that perfect place.

"We should…" He struggles to breathe as I tremble with need. "I'm gonna…" Another breath hits my lips. "*Cazzo*." Another shaky exhale. "Condom."

My lust-filled mind sobers slightly. Jonathan and I dated so long, we rarely used protection by the end. We banked on the pull-out method, and while most people wouldn't condone it, it was effective for us. "Right," I say, and he thrusts again, knocking the air from my lungs. "Do you have any?" I freeze, wide eyes boring into his. "Please tell me you have one."

He laughs breathlessly. *Thrust.* "Don't worry, baby." He grips my hip, reaching to the bedside table, and grabs a condom out of the drawer. Relief floods through me. He rolls me on my back, locks eyes, and thrusts again. Heat flushes my body, heartbeat pounding. He brushes a hair behind my ear. "You're doing great, by the way." My face lights on fire as he pulls out of me, and I weep at the loss. Within seconds the condom is on, wrapper on the floor, and he's realigned with my entrance.

"You ready, *tesoro*?" he asks, voice low and sinful.

"Please, yes," I beg, my entire body trembling with need, and he slides back in, stretching until he's filled me completely. His hands wander every inch of me as he delivers slow, deep thrusts. He reaches between us, and when his thumb touches that sensitive spot, my back arches reflexively. I force it back to the bed.

Jonathan hated when I moved too much. *'I can't find my spot if you keep fucking moving.'*

I shake away the unwelcome memory.

"Let go," Noah instructs, bringing me back to the present.

"What?" I ask with furrowed brows.

He thrusts harder, and I dig my fingernails into his shoulder. Soft moans escape me. The orgasm is building, just within reach. So close. But it's not my turn yet, so I force it down.

"Let. Go." His voice is commanding yet soft.

"But you haven't finished yet."

"Come for me, *soffione*. Let me hear exactly what I do to you, and I promise I'll be right behind." *Thrust.* A loud moan escapes me as my head falls against the pillow, and I arch my back. "Such a good girl." He rotates his hips, and I soar higher, white spots blurring my vision. "Fuck, you're so hot," he praises, and the pleasure hits me in waves so strong my entire body shudders, toes curling as I grip the bed sheets, my inner walls convulsing around him.

A whine escapes my lips as his cock twitches inside me, and we're engulfed in the inferno. He drops his head in the crook of my neck, heavy breath fanning over my skin. All the energy in my body flutters away with the orgasm, and I sink into the bed, struggling for air.

"Wow," he pants, having the same issue.

After a minute of labored breathing, I reply, "Double wow."

He pulls out of me, climbs off the bed, and disappears into the bathroom. I lie there like a puddle of jelly, the sound of the shower starting the only noise louder than my shaky breaths. Noah returns, a satisfied smile on his face. Pride fills my chest. *I caused that smile.*

"What?" I ask as he walks to me and scoops me into his arms. I squeal, my naked body flush against his. "What are you doing?"

He rests his forehead on mine. "Cleaning you up." My lips part, body shaking with nerves. *This is new.* He walks us into the steamy bathroom and sets my feet carefully on the shower floor. After I've got my balance, he closes the curtain, towering over me in the small space. The warm water streams down my skin, and I attempt to ignore his proximity. *And fail.* Every inch of my body is acutely aware that the man who gave me the best orgasm of my life is standing six inches away.

"You did a great job," he tells me, fingertips grazing my skin, continuing to fuel my recently discovered praise kink.

"Thank you," I choke out.

"Did you come, or did you fake it?"

My lips part open, mortification washing over me. "I can assure you I didn't *fake* it!" A worse realization hits me. "Did *you*?"

He grips my hips, eyes narrowing. "Much harder for a guy to fake it."

Holy shit.

I did it.

I made Noah Caruso come.

He slides his hands into my hair, and while the sex was hot and fun, this feels awfully intimate for being fake.

I shake the thought from my head.

Noah said we can't think about that stuff during the lessons. And I'm pretty sure he just fucked the word from my vocabulary.

He pulls me towards him, planting a gentle kiss on my lips, and my knees threaten to buckle beneath me, still wobbly from the mind-altering climax.

Damn, does this man know how to kiss.

"See, you were right," he says. "You just needed to practice your confidence."

Another rush at his appraisal.

"I think I'm going to need lots and lots of practice," I say, lips grazing his.

"I can arrange that." He presses a kiss against my lips, then releases me, grabbing the bottle of soap and squirting some in his hand. He lathers up and has me switch places with him, rubbing his hands along my body. *What does this all mean?* I force my muscles to relax and enjoy the attention. He takes his time washing every part of me, and I have to stop my knees from buckling as he holds eye contact, gently gliding his hand against the sensitive spot between my legs. He smirks when I shiver and ends my torment by turning me around to wash my hair. He rinses out the shampoo, then brushes through my locks with his fingers, and I let out a soft moan.

He chuckles, squirting soap in his hand and washing himself. "I'm learning all the ways to make you moan tonight, *soffione*."

My heart catches in my throat, and I'm unable to conjure up a single reply as my eyes trail his wet, soaped-up body hungrily. He rinses off and has me switch so I'm back under the warm water.

"Wait in here," he instructs, getting out and drying off. He reaches in and turns off the water, then opens the curtain and holds a towel open for me.

"I can do this myself," I tease, secretly enjoying the princess treatment.

"I know," he says, the corner of his mouth quirking. "But I want to."

"Okay." I grin, stepping out of the shower and onto the towel he placed on the ground, allowing him to wrap the other around my body.

He positions me away from him in front of the mirror, and I wipe it clean so I can see him. He pulls a brush out of the drawer and gently tugs all the knots out of my hair.

"You're spoiling me," I say.

"You wanted to practice having good sex," Noah says, the corner of his mouth quirking. "That means aftercare is required in the lesson plan."

"Will it be on the final exam, Professor?"

His eyes find mine in the mirror, and he sets the brush on the counter with a tap. "If you keep calling me that, class will run *very* late tonight, Ms. Benson." Noah yanks off my towel, and I squeal as he scoops me up cradle style, walking us back into the dimly lit room.

He tosses me onto the bed, his eyes drinking me in as he climbs after me. He lies beside me, and I hook my leg over him, our naked bodies entangling like those little Lego pieces he loves so much.

He tugs the covers over us and runs his hand along my back. Snuggling into him, I allow my body to *fully* relax for the first time in months.

It's perfect.

Too perfect.

"Noah?"

"Yeah?"

"When should we remember this isn't real?" His touch pauses, fingertips tapping on my skin.

"When the sun comes up?" he suggests.

"When the sun comes up," I agree.

And his hands are back in my hair, his lips on my skin.

"Stop!"

My eyes pop open, darkness surrounding me.

"Don't do this," Noah pleads quietly, and I jump, flicking on the bedside lamp.

Turning back to the bed, I find him, eyes squeezed shut, clutching the comforter.

"Noah," I say, nudging him, but no response. His grip tightens on the blanket, his breathing heavy.

Is he having a nightmare?

"Noah," I say louder, and his head moves slightly, eyelids fluttering.

What do I do?

Throw water on him?

Slap him?

Shake him?

I don't want to startle him or make it worse.

"Please," Noah begs, his shoulders shaking. "Please stop."

My pulse pounds. I've never seen this side of him. Never seen him be anything other than Superman.

It's almost a relief.

Guilt settles in my stomach.

Wishing night terrors on someone to prove they have flaws is fucked up.

"Noah," I say gently, nudging his arm. "Please, wake up."

His head switches sides. *I think we're getting somewhere.* "You're okay," I assure him, rubbing his hair. "I'm here." His shoulders tighten. "It's just a dream."

He gasps, bolting up, and I flinch, heart racing in surprise. He takes loud, ragged breaths, eyes finding mine as I do the same.

"Charlotte?" he says, voice trembling, gaze distant.

"Yeah, it's me. I'm here." I rub his back, releasing a sigh of relief. *He's awake.* "You're okay. Everything's okay."

His eyes are filled with sadness as he flattens a palm over his chest, blowing out a shaky exhale. "I'm so sorry you had to see that."

I attempt to return my heart rate to a safe level. *That scared the shit out of me.* "Does it happen often?"

"No." He rolls onto his back, staring up at the ceiling.

"I didn't know how to wake you." My lips roll together. *I felt so helpless.* "I just kept talking to you till you woke up. I was worried I'd scare you worse."

"You did perfect," he assures me.

I place a palm on his shoulder. He rolls his head to face me, our eyes locking, his expression tormented. "What were you dreaming about?"

He sighs. "*Soffione*, I don't want to pull you into this."

"Remember what we talked about by the lake? I said if you wanted to talk about anything in the dark with the windows closed, I'm here." I take his hand and squeeze it. "There's no sunshine or football."

"But there is you," he says with a weak smile.

"Well, yeah, because I'm always here." My heart constricts at the admission, aching for him to be vulnerable. "Do you *want* to talk about it?" He nods, a single tear rolling down his cheek.

"I've wanted to tell you," he promises me. "I just never knew the right time. And it's not exactly something I go around broadcasting. You never know who you can trust."

Swallowing hard, I ask, "And you trust me?"

Noah smiles weakly. "Yeah, baby. I trust you."

He trusts me.

Relief settles in my chest, and I return a gentle smile, rubbing my thumb against his hand in reassurance. "What was your night-mare about?"

His eyes bore into mine, indecision flickering over his features. "The night I shot my father."

My eyes widen, and I suck in a breath. *That is not what I was expecting.* "What?" I sit up, turning to face him, and he does the same. "You... *what?*"

He looks away, leaning against the headboard. "I shot my father." His expression is blank as he stares ahead. *Noah is capable of shooting someone? His own father?*

"You shot your father?" I repeat. "With... a gun?"

"Yes."

My brain is running on overdrive. "On purpose?"

Should I be afraid of him?

The thought crushes my heart with guilt. I *know* this man. If he shot his own father, he must have had a good reason... right?

"Yes." He swallows hard. "On purpose."

Did Noah want to kill him?

Did he?

"Is he... dead?" I ask.

"No." He laughs humorlessly. "Unfortunately not."

What the fuck is happening right now?

We sit in silence as he formulates his thoughts, and I doubt if I even know the man beside me. Can *I* trust *him?*

"My father was abusive," Noah finally says, wringing his hands together, and relief swarms me that it was justified. "I got my first scar from him when I was six." He lifts his arm, showing me a small burn mark on his inner bicep. *Horrendous.* The relief is quickly replaced by guilt, and a gut-wrenching ache settles inside.

"Your dad did that to you?" I whisper, reaching out and drag-ging a finger along it. "When you were *six?*" My voice cracks, in tandem with my heart, as I remove my hand. *How could a father do that?* Images of the twins' smiling faces come to mind, and I want to hurl at the thought of someone hurting them.

"Yes." He shifts on the bed. "I had forgotten to clean my room, and he thought I should be branded with a permanent reminder." I place a hand over my mouth. Heart aching. "By the time I was ten, I'd had enough visits to the E.R. it was getting suspicious, so he'd hurt Mom when I misbehaved instead."

"That's terrible," I whisper, blinking back tears.

Of everything I know about Noah, it's devastating to me he's been harboring all this under the surface. Alone. Portraying this sunshine persona when inside, his heart must feel black as night.

"He had always hurt her," he says. "But it got worse after that." *Worse?* "When I was fourteen, my parents were arguing in the kitchen. I don't even remember what it was about. Something inconsequential. He was screaming at her." His hands tremble, and I attempt to hold them steady although my own are shaking. "I couldn't take it anymore, so I got between them. We struggled, and he dragged me to my room and threw me against my dresser." I gasp, waves of anger crashing through me. "When I came to, I ran back out to him holding her by the throat, a gun to her head." I suck in a breath at the thought of Luna in danger, and Noah swallows hard. "He was going to kill her." Another tear rolls down his cheek, and I reach up, wiping it away. Moisture wells in my own eyes, and he turns to face me. "Is this too much?"

Shaking my head, I assure him, "I can handle it."

I have to. For him.

"Are you sure?" He uses his thumb to wipe away my own escaped tear. "Because I know it's a lot."

I nod, squeezing his hand. *Please, let me in.* "Keep going."

Noah releases a heavy sigh. "Mom knocked the gun out of his hand. I grabbed it in the shuffle, and by the time he'd shaken her off, I had it pointed his way." I reach out, resting my hand against his face, and he leans into it. "Then I pulled the trigger."

And he had a good reason. A terrible reason, but a valid one nonetheless.

I understand why he didn't tell me this before. Why he keeps it locked up tight. Because if someone found this out before knowing *him*, before really fully knowing who Noah Caruso is to his soul, they might not believe him. Or even worse, be afraid of him.

"I'm so sorry you went through that," I say, and he nods, placing his hand on mine.

"I only clipped his arm, so there was a lot of blood, but he didn't die. The cops arrested me, and I was questioned at the station."

"You were *arrested?*"

"Protocol." He shrugs. "Thankfully, they agreed it was self-defense and released me. After my father recovered, he went to jail. Mom divorced him, and that's how she met Tony. He was our lawyer. Helped us get restraining orders and all that too." He rolls his lips together. "I started focusing on football. Mom and I took martial arts classes, and last year we got our concealed weapons permits so no one can ever hurt us like that again." He drags a hand down his face. "Watching her get hurt and not being able to do anything about it was the hardest part."

A sharp pang of sadness grips my soul. "I can't even imagine," I say, resting a hand on his face.

"My father called me yesterday," Noah admits, and my brows rise in surprise. "I didn't answer. But he always tries on my birthday... Maybe that triggered the nightmare." I wrap my arms around him, holding tight.

"Thank you for trusting me."

"I wanted to tell you." He looks towards me. "So many times. But I didn't—"

"Noah, I'm a politician's daughter. I get being careful with a story like that. Some people would use it as a rising from the ashes story—"

"And others would say I have a violent background, paired with a career in an aggressive sport. Then spend pages analyzing what kind of man that makes me." He sighs, wringing his hands together, and looks at me. "I'll understand if you don't wanna do the whole lessons or fake dating thing anymore."

"What?" I sit up. "Why wouldn't I want to continue?"

"Like you said, you're a politician's daughter." He shifts in place. "And if we were dating—or fake dating—and that got out, I guess it wouldn't look good."

"You think any of that matters to me?" I ask, tilting my head, and his lips press together. "Well, it doesn't. *You* matter. And I am not afraid of you *or* this information."

His eyes hold mine, and he reaches out, cupping my neck. "Are you sure?"

"One hundred percent."

"Thank you."

"For what?"

"Joining me in the dark for a little while."

"What are friends for?" I say stupidly.

"Right." He rubs his thumb across my cheek. "What are friends for?"

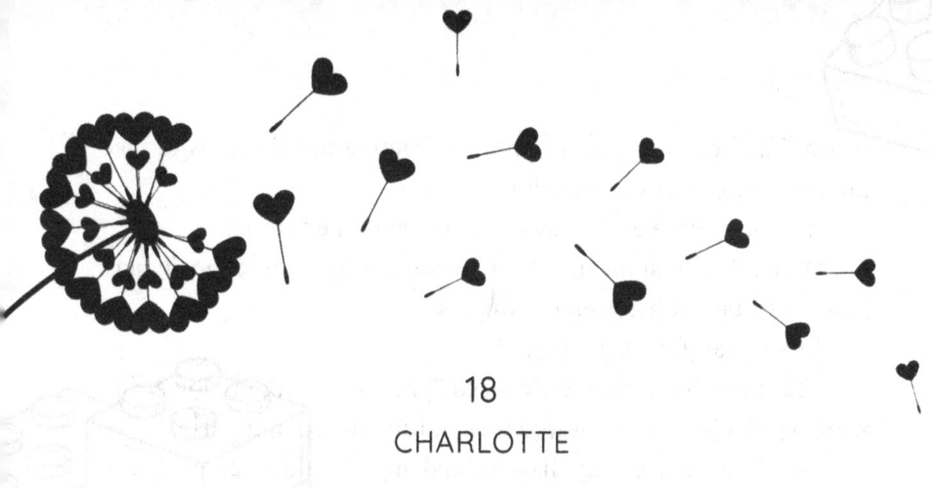

18

CHARLOTTE

"Can we *please* go eat something?" I beg on the third mile of our run as trees pass by in a blur. Nausea rises, and I force it down.

Damn Noah for making me do cardio before breakfast.

It's been a week since his nightmare, and I've slept over since. The fear in his eyes is embedded into my memory, and I never want him to experience that alone again. He's always there for everyone else. Now he needs someone to support him. He needs *me* to support him.

"We're almost there," Noah says, not even slightly out of breath.

I huff loudly, keeping in stride, so focused on trying to stay awake, I can barely keep my eyes open. "Fine." We run a few more minutes, and just as I think I'll have to take a break, Noah stops abruptly.

"What are you doing?" I ask.

He grabs my shoulders, spinning me around to a sea of a million wildflowers. A beautiful blend of green, pink, orange, purple, and white is before me. In the distance, a few cabins and a goal post border the rolling field. *Breathtaking.* Noah walks forward and reaches down to pick something up. He spins to face me, holding out a tiny dandelion.

"For my *soffione*," he says with an unabashed smile.

"What does that mean?" I ask, unable to fight my curiosity any longer as I take it between my fingers.

"It's Italian for 'dandelion.'"

"Because I'm a weak little weed?" I tease, biting my lower lip, knowing that's how he viewed them during the camping trip.

"No." He pushes my hair behind my shoulder, cupping my neck. "Because you're incredibly resilient."

My cheeks flush pink. "I'm not."

"You are," he says, dragging his thumb along my jaw. "Whatever life throws at you, you just keep going. You don't lose hope." He presses a kiss on my lips. "You keep wishing on dandelions."

I place my hand on his. "I'd argue *you're* the *soffione*," I say in a terrible Italian accent.

Noah grins. "Sorry, the nickname has already been assigned." He holds up his dandelion with a cocked brow. "Make a wish," says the man who doesn't believe in wishing, and my chest warms.

Closing my eyes, I take a deep breath, then blow on the little flower. When my eyes pop open, I see he's done the same, his gaze following the petals drifting in the wind.

"Look at you becoming a serial dandelion wisher," I say.

"There's a lot out of my control these days," he replies, and we continue down the path.

Guilt surrounds me for being one of those unexpected things. "Like when your best friend volunteers you to be her fake boyfriend?"

"No," he says quickly, relieving my anxiety. "You're helping me too, remember?"

"How have I helped you so far?"

"The orgasms have been *excellent*," he says, and my jaw drops open. Given our new sleeping situation, we've been having some morning lessons. Which have, in fact, been *excellent*.

"Noah!" I push his shoulder. "Be serious."

"I am," he says, grabbing my wrist and pulling me to a stop, eyes holding mine. "I promise you this little arrangement is one of the only things *not* stressing me."

"And what is?" I press. "Stressing you?"

Is he still worried about the nightmare?

"It's not important." He brushes a strand of hair behind my ear.

"That's literally the point of this, remember? An *even* exchange?"

He rolls his eyes with a huff. "I'm fine."

"And how are the punt bunnies doing?" I ask.

"Well, I haven't posted anything with you yet," he says as if I'm not acutely aware of this fact. "So… still pretty crazy."

"Then post something?" I suggest, stomach in my throat. As if the thought of us officially hard-launching our relationship so publicly doesn't scare the hell out of me. But we did agree to an even exchange.

"I don't have any good pictures of us alone."

"Then let's take one," I suggest, forcing my nerves to relax.

"You sure?" he asks, eyes hopeful.

"Absolutely." *Not at all.*

"Great," he says, pulling out his phone and holding the camera up for a selfie.

"Hey!"

I turn to find Andi running up to us, trailed by a shirtless Kensington Knox, defensive cornerback for the Tampa Barracudas. His muscles are huge, dark skin covered in tattoos, and he's dripping in sweat.

Hot.

"Hey," Noah says, waving to Andi and his new teammate who came to coach for a day of training.

"What's up, rookie?" Knox asks.

"Just working on our cardio, old timer," Noah replies, then

turns his attention to Andi, holding his phone toward her. "Mind taking a picture of us?"

"Do I?!" she says, snatching it out of his hand.

Noah and I stand before the field. He puts his arm around me, and we smile towards the camera.

"Seriously?" Andi frowns. "You look like two dorks taking a yearbook photo. Kiss her."

"Andi!" I squeal, risking a glance at Noah, and our eyes connect. They're so damn green. Flashbacks of this morning's lesson—Noah's gaze locked on mine, pounding in and out of me—flicker in my mind.

Andi snaps her fingers, breaking my connection with Noah. "Earth to baby cakes?"

I blink back to reality. "Yeah?"

"What was that?" she asks, pointing between us with narrowed eyes.

"What do you mean?"

"That look… that 'I've seen you naked' look."

"Whaaat?" I say a high-pitched voice.

She gasps, turning to Knox. "See, I told you they wouldn't last a month."

"You told him?" I squeak, skin flushing hot, and Noah squeezes my hip with a laugh.

"Relax." She waves me off. "Knox is good at keeping secrets."

"And apparently *you're* not!"

"I mean, I figured it anyway since you've been sleeping over, but this totally confirms it," she says, wagging a finger between me and Noah. "Nice."

"It's not what you think," I assure her, while Noah remains suspiciously quiet. "Right?" I say to him for backup.

"Right," he agrees.

An awkward silence surrounds us.

"He's giving me sex lessons," I blurt.

Knox fights a smile, and Andi laughs. She *actually* laughs out loud.

"Now that's a class I'd take," Andi tells me. "I think I could use a bit of *coaching*. Don't you?" she asks Knox, who grins. I can't say I'm surprised. Photos of the two of them were all over the news after Christmas, and she basically admitted to sleeping with him—although she was cagey on the details.

"That could be arranged," Knox replies, and my eyes bounce between them.

"Okay," Andi says, holding the phone back up. "But this is good. Now take a picture like two people who actually are into each other."

Noah turns me to face him, slides a hand into my hair, and yanks it down, angling my mouth to his. Our lips are a breath apart.

"You certainly were into me this morning," Noah murmurs teasingly, for our ears only, and we both fight a smile.

"I'd dare to say *you* were into *me*."

"Good, got it," Andi says, and Noah waits a beat, presses a kiss to my mouth that steals all my oxygen, then releases me.

"Thanks," he says, taking the phone from Andi.

"Will we see you two at the gala next week?" Knox asks.

My brows furrow, and I look up to Noah. "Gala?"

"It's this fancy thing for work," Noah says, glancing at Knox, then back at me. "I hadn't gotten the chance to invite you yet."

"But you wanted to?" I ask, holding his eye contact.

"Of course. Wouldn't it make sense for my *girlfriend* to be there?"

"Right." I nod. That would make sense.

"Come on," Andi chimes in. "It'll be fun!"

Noah grins at me, eyes hopeful.

"I don't have anything to wear here," I say. "My cheer uniform is about the fanciest thing I brought."

"Don't worry." Noah smirks, eyes lit with mischief. "I'll take care of it."

"I do look *great* in pink," I tell him.

"Yes!" Andi says, throwing an arm around my shoulders and dragging me away. "Then let's talk details."

"I said I'll take care of the wardrobe," Noah shouts from behind me.

Glancing over my shoulder, I give him a wink. "Then we've got to take care of what's underneath."

"This selection is garbage," I tell Andi as we sift through racks of lingerie at a discount shopping center. Camp Dickson is in the middle of nowhere, so our options are limited. And I've found nothing, which is very bad news considering the gala is tomorrow.

There's a nightgown that definitely won't work, but I rub the silk between my fingertips anyways, imagining Noah's hands sliding it up and off my body. When I flip over the price tag, my eyes bulge. $39.99.

And that's a discount?

I groan internally.

This is the problem. Lingerie costs an arm and a leg, just for it to get ripped off after thirty seconds anyways. Total waste.

Especially since my parents have frozen my cards and I'm using the money from my very limited savings for this. My mind wanders back to the daydream of Noah's gaze searing into me as he takes in the little nightgown, undressing me with his eyes.

Fine. Worth it.

"Oh my gosh," Andi says, pulling me back to the present. She holds out a black lacy set. "Noah would die if you wore this."

"I don't want to kill the poor man," I say with a smirk.

She shoves it towards me, and I peek at the price tag. $19.99 for the tiny bra and panties. That I could definitely swing.

"Fine," I concede, grabbing the same set in a lighter color since I don't know what dress Noah's getting me yet.

"Yes, girl!" Andi says as we head towards the register. "Make that man drool."

"Did you find anything?" I ask her.

"A few little sets," she says, arms full.

"Knox is going to *love* those."

"Yep." She nods.

We check out, get in Andi's car, and head back to camp.

"So how are you feeling, all things Noah considered?" she asks.

I rest my head against the seat, memories of our sex lessons fresh. My body is light. Weightless. Pleasantly sore.

"Good," I say with a satisfied smile.

"Are you two still pretending it's all fake?"

"Andi!" I snap my gaze to her. "We are not pretending."

"So you're not faking that you're faking it?"

"We're not…" My brows pull together. "Huh?"

She rolls her eyes with a laugh. "And this, my friend, is what they call idiots to lovers."

"Idiots to what?"

She waves me off. "You'll realize what I mean soon enough."

We roll under the wooden sign for Camp Dickson and quickly find a spot. I glance at my phone.

NOAH

I've gotta leave in twenty, you back yet?

ME

Yes, where are you?

NOAH

Heading to my cabin

"Would you mind taking my stuff?" I ask Andi as we get out of the car. "I want to catch Noah before he leaves for a meeting in Tampa."

"No problem," she says, and I hand her the small bag.

The sun shines on my face, and I can't help but smile.

Sure, my boyfriend's fake and the sex is just lessons.

But if this is an illusion, I hope we stay in it forever.

19

NOAH

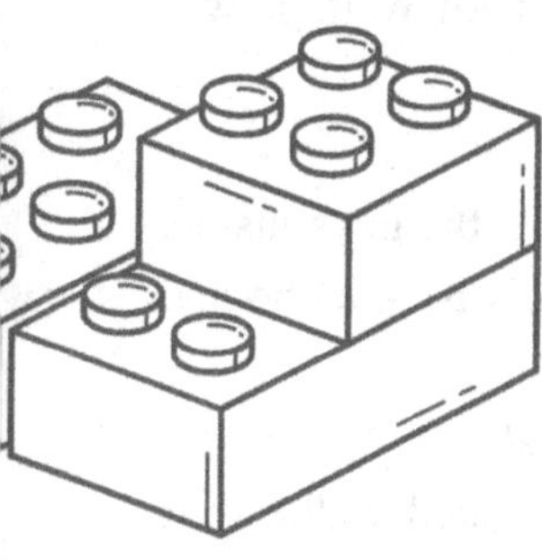

"You should take me as your date instead," Theo says, scrolling through pages of gowns on an iPad as we walk towards my cabin.

"What about me?" Elijah asks, batting his eyelashes and throwing an arm around my shoulder. "Come on, darlin', you know you want some arm candy."

"I'm the one who grew up going to these fancy things," Theo scoffs. "Why do you think I've been appointed to find Char the perfect dress?"

"Because you vetoed all Noah's choices till he threw the iPad in your face?"

Theo waves him off. "She'll thank me for it. Noah's style is game day chic."

"Hey," I say, shoving him. "I have style."

"Yeah, but Charlie goes to these things all the time because of her mom," Theo points out.

My stomach sinks. "I hadn't considered that."

"Exactly, so it needs to be better than anything she has in her closet," Theo says. "Let me take care of this, and you focus on you."

"I want it to be a gift from *me*," I say, brow cocked.

"How about you let this be *my* gift to *you*," Theo says. "I promise you'll thank me."

"Well, pick something that can be overnighted," I remind him. "The gala is tomorrow."

I curse myself for being so indecisive, but I wanted to make sure it was something she'd love, and before I knew it, it was Thursday.

"You got it, Cap."

We arrive at my cabin, and I open the door, let the guys inside, and shut it behind me. I walk directly into Theo's back as he and Elijah stand, unmoving.

"Nope." Elijah spins around, staring at the wall.

My eyes dart past him to where a very naked redhead is sprawled out on my bed, smiling at us.

I divert my eyes and open my mouth to speak, but nothing comes out.

"Should we… go?" Theo asks hesitantly.

"No," I say at the same time Hannah says, "Or you could stay."

There's no way I'm being left alone with this woman.

"Why are you in my room?" I ask, my question directed at Hannah while my gaze burns a hole into the wall, ensuring I look anywhere but at her.

"I saw you at practice earlier, and you looked like you could use a little stress relief," she replies, unmoving from my bed.

The same bed Charlotte and I sleep in.

The same bed where she moans my name, over and over and over.

The same bed where I have to remind myself that none of this is real with her taste on my tongue and my name on her lips.

"You need to leave," I tell her.

"Come on." The bed squeaks beneath her as I continue my staring contest with the wall. "Your friends can join. I don't mind being shared."

"I don—"

"What the *fuck*?" Charlotte's voice has me whipping around to find her standing at the door. Jaw slack. Eyes bulging out of her skull. Her gaze finds mine, a question behind them. A plea. They jump past me to Hannah and finally settle on Elijah. Charlotte's lips open and close. She shakes her head then flies out of the cabin, and my stomach drops. *Shit.*

"Get that woman out of my bed," I tell them, not awaiting a response.

Charlotte's already half a football field away, and I sprint after her. "Wait," I call out, chasing her down the path as curious campers glance our way. "Please!"

"No!" she shouts, not looking towards me. "I can't believe this," she huffs as I catch up, jogging behind her.

"It's not wh—"

She spins to me, her eyes full of fury, and I stop dead in my tracks, mouth zipped shut. I've seen her upset, but never have those molten eyes ever been directed at me. My throat constricts at her glistening eyes. "I *knew* the sex was just lessons. But as my *friend,* you could've at least told me you were fucking someone else!"

"I'm not!" I assure her pleadingly.

"Right." Her jaw ticks, and she looks at the ground.

Panic courses through me as Charlotte slips through my fingers.

"Look at me." I reach towards her and lift her chin. "Please." Her eyes slowly find mine. "I asked you before if you trusted me." A silence falls between us. "And you said yes."

"That was before I found a naked girl in your bed."

"Was *I* in the bed?"

"Well, no, but—"

"Was *I* naked?"

Her eyes slowly drop down, as if to confirm I'm fully clothed. "No."

"Ask Theo and Elijah. Please. We walked in, and she was there."

Please believe me, baby.

"But why would she think she can do that?" she asks, tone aching.

"Insanity, Char." I shake my head. "That's my *only* explanation."

Her eyes bore into mine, and I don't dare look away. Don't dare give her any possible reason to think I'm telling anything other than the truth.

"I promise I haven't, didn't, and wouldn't ever sleep with her."

She blinks up at me. "I want to believe you."

"Please believe me, *soffione*?" She blinks, and I brush a strand of hair behind her ear. "Have I ever lied to you?"

"Not that I know of."

My chest aches. "Never." I rub my thumb across the pad of her lip. "She's another reason I wanted to fake date in the first place. So she'd back off."

"Well, that worked well," she says, brow cocked.

I take her hands in mine. "Maybe she'll get the point when you come to the gala with me."

"She'll be there?" Charlotte says, a worry crease on her forehead.

"She's my boss's daughter. Remember?"

"So that's why you wanted me to come," she says, dropping my hands and stepping away.

"No," I say firmly. "I *want* you there."

So badly.

"Is this going to affect your play time? Is your coach going to bench you because you won't date his daughter?" *Is this really what she's thinking about?*

"I'm pretty sure he'd kill me if I did."

"So is that why you're pushing her away? Because your boss wouldn't like it?"

The thoughts going through her mind are giving me whiplash.

"No," I say, blowing out a frustrated breath. "I'm not interested in her."

Charlotte narrows her eyes. "You seemed interested in Miami."

"*You* were the one who practically forced me to get a drink with her." I grip Charlotte's chin, angling her mouth to mine. "And then you left me to go see your *boyfriend*. In case you forgot."

Her eyes narrow on mine. "*Ex*-boyfriend."

"Right," I say, corner of my lip quirking up at the pleasant reminder. "And then you showed up at my hotel, where I was *alone*."

She gnaws on her lower lip. "So you don't plan on sleeping with anyone else while we do the fake dating thing?"

"Of course not." I scoff. "I definitely don't." The thought of even looking at another woman while Charlotte's in my bed is laughable. She folds her arms over her chest. "What?"

"Aren't you going to ask me?"

I bite my lower lip, holding in a smile. "Are you going to sleep with anyone else?"

"I might," she says playfully, and even knowing she's kidding, my veins still flush with heat.

"Then I might have to punish you after the gala," I tease. "If you're still coming?"

She looks down at her hands, picking at her nail, and then her gaze returns to mine. "Yeah. I'm still coming."

"Good," I say, relief flooding me, and I glance at my watch. "I have to leave for my meeting, but a car will pick you girls up tomorrow and drop you off at our hotel."

"Hotel?" she says, brows raised, a curious smile on her face.

"Yeah, it'll end late, and I didn't think we'd want to drive back to camp the same night." I realize now I maybe should have asked first. "Is that okay?"

She sways back and forth on her heels, and I swallow hard. "Yes."

Another wave of relief barrels through me. "Okay, good." I pull out my keys and hand her the one to my cabin. "In case you still want to sleep there tonight."

"You wouldn't mind?" she says, eyes hesitant.

"Not at all. I know you prefer sprawling out on the bigger bed."

"I do not *sprawl*," she scoffs, and I raise a brow. "Fine." She snatches the key from me. "Thank you."

I lean down, nuzzling her nose, and press a kiss to her lips. "See you tomorrow, *soffione*."

My stomach twists as I head back to my cabin, and I tug out my phone. I've been distracted this past week by long legs and soft skin, but I don't want another moment to go by with people not realizing I'm taken. Don't want another bullshit situation like today to happen and give any fuel to further her trust issues.

After pulling up the photo of me and Charlotte by the wild-flower field, I post it with the caption, *That's amore,* hoping people get the hint.

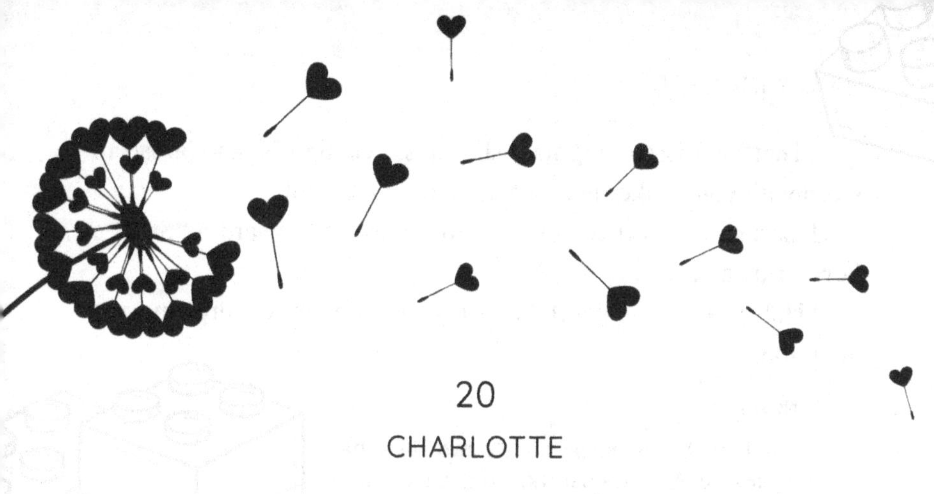

20

CHARLOTTE

"If Theo doesn't show soon, we'll be going in our cheer uniforms," Andi says, braiding the sides of her hair and tying them together in the back.

"Have faith," I say, glancing at the options of lingerie on the bed. Black or baby pink, depending on the dress Theo brings.

"You still mad at Noah?" Andi asks. I didn't make it two feet in the door yesterday before blurting it all out. *Talk about triggering your trust issues.*

"Do I even have the right to be mad? What he and I are doing is pretend." The word is bitter on my tongue.

"Sure." She nods her head. "I'm sure all those orgasms feel sooo fake."

"It's only been a few times," I say, biting my lower lip.

"That's a few more than anyone else has gotten from him," Andi points out. "He's usually a one and done type of guy. No repeats. No strings."

A strange feeling settles in my stomach. "I'm sure that's not true."

It's totally true.

"That man is an enigma," she says. "Getting Noah Caruso to sleep with you is like finding a unicorn in the wild."

I shrug, the corners of my lips quirking upwards. "Save a horse, ride a unicorn."

"Hell yeah." She snorts, and my phone vibrates, drawing my attention.

NOAH

Fun Fact: Some galaxies have two stars that orbit so close together they're destined to connect in a cosmic kiss

ME

That's hot

Will I be getting one of those later?

NOAH

Absolutely.

The car will be there in an hour

I release a shaky breath, excitement coursing through me.

ME

I'll be coming naked if Theo's not here soon

NOAH

That's an option?

brb, telling Theo to return your dress

"Holy shit," Andi says, and my eyes pull to her. "Did you see this?"

She holds out her phone, and the photo of me and Noah in front of the wildflower field shows on the screen. He must have finally posted, and it has—what the fuck.

"Thirty *thousand* likes?" I gawk.

"Yep," Andi says. "And three thousand comments."

I click on the responses, immediately regretting it.

Who does this bitch think she is?

Noah baby you're cheating on me??

Excuse me, he speaks italian?

Another rookie focused on pussy instead of playing.

Andi plucks the phone from my hand.

"Hey!" I protest.

"Nope." She shakes her head. "We are not doing this tonight."

"Doing what?"

"The social media sabotage."

"Why are people so mean on the internet?" I say, sighing and sitting on the bed.

"Because they're salty."

"There should be a rule that if you wouldn't say it to someone's face, don't type it."

Andi sits beside me, throwing an arm around my shoulder. "But then how would the haters get their hate-orade fix?"

"I'm used to attention from the press." I rest my head on her shoulder. "But this feels different."

"Yeah," she says, rubbing my arm. "Because people aren't focused on your mom like usual. They're focused on you. They're *jealous* of you."

My mouth twists. "Little old me?"

"Girl, you are a smoke show, come on," she says, standing and dragging me with her.

Releasing a heavy breath, I look in the mirror, frowning. Tiny baby hairs stick out of my scalp, and I pat them down. Turning side to side, even in my comfy clothes, I note my bloated stomach and suck it in. I shouldn't have eaten the extra portion of rice at lunch today.

Visions of Noah's appreciative gaze on my naked body come to mind. He said I should never view myself as anything less than perfect.

I shove the insecurities away in a tiny box as a knock comes on the cabin door.

"Finally!" Andi says, hopping off the bed, and a handsome, familiar face walks in with a bouquet in one hand and two garment bags in the other.

"Special delivery," Theo says, beaming proudly.

Andi grabs the vase of wildflowers with dandelions sticking out of the top. "I think these are for you," she tells me, and I take them, placing them on my dresser.

Noah is so thoughtful.

"First of all, you ladies already look *hot*," Theo says. "But wait till you see what I've brought you."

Andi extends grabby hands. "Show us the goods."

My palms rub against the silk of the fitted baby pink gown as I stand outside the door to Noah's hotel room. It's tight around my core—was almost too tight to zip, but I won't be telling him that—and flares slightly at the knees to the floor.

Hopefully he likes it. My arm wraps around my tummy, as the snug fit of the dress doesn't hide that little insecurity like I hoped.

'You just needed to practice your confidence.'

Noah's words echo in my mind, and I blow out a shaky breath. I can't change what I look like, but I can show him how much the practice is helping.

Bringing up a hand, I rap my knuckles against the door.

Within seconds, it flies open, Noah's smiling face falling to a dropped jaw in a millisecond. He's clad in a black suit with a bow tie matching the color of my dress, and I have to stop my own jaw from unhinging because it should be illegal to look that good.

"Wow," he says, green eyes dragging along my body, lighting a fire trail. "You look…" He rakes a hand over his face. "Wow."

I sway on my heels. My very high, uncomfortable, totally worth it heels. "You look pretty 'wow' yourself."

He gestures an arm for me to come inside our hotel room, which is also… wow. There's a long teal couch, a small kitchenette, a cozy king-sized bed I'd love to dive into, and a gorgeous view of the Bay. The gala is for the conservation of Tampa Bay's aquatic life, so I suppose they decided a hotel by it would be appropriate. The sun is setting, and the orange light dances across the water, the colors blending as if they were always meant to meet.

My attention returns to Noah, and I wonder if all the theories of kismet and invisible strings are true. Is it possible that maybe, just maybe, everything in my life has brought me here, to him?

Noah stands before a gold-framed, floor-length mirror, adjusting his bow tie.

"First time?" I ask, desperate for a distraction from the over-thinking.

His eyes slide to mine in a glare. "No." He continues fiddling in the mirror before blowing a breath of defeat. "I just can't get it to be symmetrical. Every time it's a little lopsided."

Noting the slight shaking of his fingers, I walk over, resting a hand on them. They still instantly.

"Allow me?" I ask.

"You know how?"

"I always watched my dad put one on before events," I say with a smile, chest aching. *I should call him.* "He taught me how once I was older. Said it was an important life skill." *I'm definitely grateful for the lesson now.*

"Can't be worse than I'm doing." He removes his hands and sits on the arm of the couch, bringing us eye to eye.

"Raging endorsement," I tease, sliding between his legs, untying his lopsided bow and pulling the sides evenly. My eyes fall to his pulse, the memory of his skin under my lips imprinted in my memory.

Noah taps his fingers against his thighs. *Is he itching to touch me like I am to touch him?* My gaze wanders back to his, and I grip the bow tie strings, tugging him forward until our lips are inches apart.

"You are breathtakingly beautiful," he says against my lips.

"I would hope so. This dress is clearly couture."

"Not the dress." He places a hand on my hip, gaze locked on mine. "You."

A blush creeps up my cheeks. With one word, he's vanquished every negative self-sabotaging thought. My eyes fall to the bow tie, opting to focus on the task at hand. My fingers work on the silk material, and in a few quick moves, I'm done. "There. All better."

He places a hand on mine. "Thank you."

"It's just a bow tie."

"How ever will I repay you for ensuring I don't look entirely out of place?"

His musky cologne overtakes my senses. Making me weak. Making me brave. "I could think of a few things."

His fingertips find my thigh, trailing upwards and nudging the material with it. "You have fun choosing what to wear under this dress?"

"I decided it was better to go with nothing."

His fingers pause. "*Soffione.*" He grips my thigh tight, and my center throbs, aching for him.

His warm, raspy voice echoes in my mind. *'Be confident, Charlotte.'*

I hook my hands around his neck and tug him towards me, our lips inches apart. "How did you sleep last night without me?" I ask. It was the first we'd been apart since the bonfire, and after tossing and turning in my cabin, I took his offer of sleeping at his place. Once I was wrapped in his sheets, his scent surrounding me—*basil, cedarwood, home*—I drifted right to dreamland.

"Terrible."

"Did you have a nightmare?" I ask, chest heavy with concern, and he shakes his head. Relief floods me. "Good."

"How did *you* sleep?"

"Fine." I shrug, remembering the ache, looking at his empty side of the bed this morning. "Was pretty lonely when I woke up though."

"Yeah?" he says, pleased, grip tightening.

"Mm-hmm." The need between my thighs intensifies. "And giving *myself* a morning orgasm was way less fun. It took me *forever*."

His lips part, and he leans to my ear. "Did you think of me when you were taking care of that needy cunt, *soffione mio*?"

Goosebumps scatter down my spine. "Well, I was spread naked on *your* bed."

He drags his calloused fingers up my arms, causing me to shiver. "Now it's your turn to tell me what you fantasized."

My stomach tightens as his hungry gaze urges me on. "I imagined making you sit and watch."

"*Hmm*." His hands find my neck, angling my mouth to his. "And were you able to take care of yourself in this little fantasy? Or did you cave and imagine me taking over?"

My clit throbs. "I imagined you stroking your cock and getting off from me pleasuring myself," I admit. The idea of him coming without even touching me makes me insane.

He stands to his full height and nudges me backwards, caging me against a wall. Groaning, he grips my neck gently and angles my mouth towards his.

"Fuck the gala," he says, warm breath hitting my lips. "Let's stay here."

My breath shudders. "That is a very appealing option."

His lips crash against mine, hand slipping in the slit of my dress, pushing it upwards. My body molds to him, bright light surrounding me, body weightless. He rolls his hips, and I whimper, hooking my leg around his waist, tongue slipping into his mouth, that gravitational pull making it impossible to stop.

A horny motherfucker in motion must stay in motion.

Knock. Knock.

Unless a cock-blocking force gets in the way.

He squeezes my leg, and grips my hair with his free hand, deepening our connection. I'm lost in him. Drowning. He sighs into my mouth, and if he weren't holding me, I'd collapse with need.

Knock! Knock! Knock!

"*Helloooo,*" Andi's familiar voice calls out, muffled by the door. "Can you two save the shenanigans for after the gala?"

Noah curses, pulling away. His eyes meet mine, our breathing heavy. "We are finishing this later," he says, tone firm.

"It better be cosmic."

21

NOAH

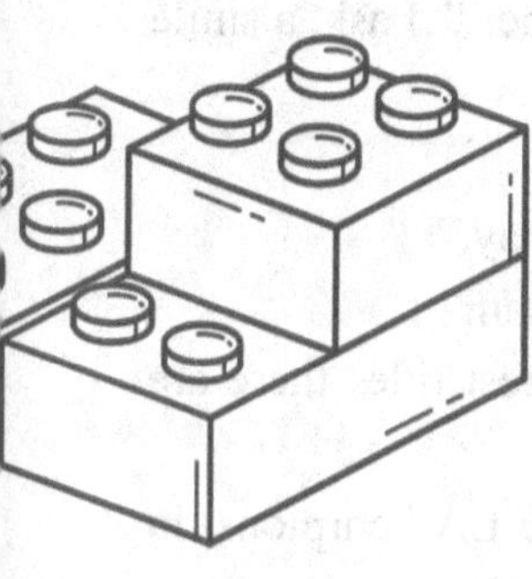

"Stop fidgeting," Charlotte says as I run a hand through my hair for the tenth time. Every person important to the sport of football is here. From newscasters to Super Bowl champions and everyone in between.

Charlotte told Andi we'd meet them downstairs, and after getting my boner under control—which was not easy, because my god, does she look hot—we finally made it to the lobby.

"I'm sorry," I whisper down to her. "I'm not used to these types of things."

"You've done plenty of fancy events for CBU."

"Yeah," I say as we walk through the rows and rows of round tables anointed with gold cutlery and enormous bouquet centerpieces. The only word I can use to describe it: lavish. "But at CBU I knew everyone."

"It'll take time for this team to feel like family too." She hooks her arm in mine. "Take my word for it. By next year, everyone will know you."

I swallow hard, anxiety buzzing in my bones. "Maybe."

"Can I give you a few tips?" she asks, her soft smile bringing me comfort.

"Sure."

"For one." She squeezes my side, and I yelp.

"Charlotte!" I glance around as my cheeks turn red from the high-pitched sound she forced out of me.

"You need to loosen up. You look constipated."

"I thought that wasn't anything to tell a partner?" I ask, a smile creeping on my face.

"Well, if it's the truth, it's the truth. Relax."

Rolling my shoulders, I release a breath. "Okay."

"These are just *people*. They're literally human."

"Yeah, super humans who've won the greatest titles there are to win in football."

I spot Derek James, the running back of the LA Scorpions, in the far corner toasting a drink with another man. Every nerve fires off in rapid succession. Is this how people feel meeting Taylor Swift? Because if so, I get it now. I want to kick my feet and give him a friendship bracelet with my damn phone number on it.

Charlotte follows my eyeline. "Do you think Derek James woke up one day with a Super Bowl ring on his finger?"

"*Six* Super Bowl rings," I correct, and she narrows her eyes at me.

"My point is, he lives, breathes, and sleeps football—just like you. Just like everyone else here. So bond over that. These are your peers. You have nothing to be nervous about."

I clench and release my hands, hoping to expel some of the tension. "And if I still am?"

"Then you need my final piece of advice," she says, accepting two glasses of champagne from a passing waiter. "Always have a drink in your hand."

"I don't think drinking is a good idea." Not trying to embarrass myself or Charlotte.

"I didn't say you had to drink it." She rolls her eyes, passing me my glass. "But holding it keeps you from fidgeting or awkwardly finding something to do with your hands."

I tip the flute at hers. "That's all good advice."

"You're not the only teacher in this relationship," she says, clinking my glass. My eyes fall to her lips. So soft.

"Well, hello, gorgeous people," Andi says with Knox trailing behind her, along with another familiar face.

Cockblocked. Again.

"Hey, Coach," I say, reaching out a hand.

"Caruso," Coach Porter says, returning a firm shake.

"Surprised to see you here."

"I used to play for the Barracudas," he reminds me. "So they rope me into every event they can since I'm still living in Tampa."

"As fun as this is," Andi says, clapping her hands together, "can we find our table? I'm starved."

"Two glasses, please," I tell the bartender before shoving money in an already overfilled tip jar. We've enjoyed a four-course meal, and now it's the "fun" small talk, mingling part of the evening.

"One of those for me?" a familiar voice says, and I turn to find the same unwelcome redhead who's going to be the death of me. Seriously. If Charlotte finds us together again, that's the end. And that in itself would kill me.

"No," I say, unamused.

"Oh." She pouts. "Thought it might be an apology."

My eyes fly to her. "For what?"

"For pawning me off on your little friends," she says with a smirk.

She's relentless.

"How about *you* give *me* an apology for almost ruining my relationship?" I say, tone low.

"Your relationship," she scoffs, and my veins run hot. "You didn't seem to care when she threw you at me in Miami."

"That's funny," I say, taking a calming breath. "Because as far as I remember, *she* was the one who ended up in my bed that night."

"Yeah, okay." Hannah huffs, signaling the bartender for a drink. "Just another guy blowing me off because of my dad." *She is delusional.* "Can't a girl have a little fun?"

"Fun?" I scoff, then lower my voice to a whisper. "Fun is not showing up naked in someone's bed unsolicited."

"It's called the Naked Man. Ever heard of it?"

I blow out a breath. "*How I Met Your Mother* is one of the best sitcoms, so yeah. I've heard of it."

"Okay, well, I was trying the Naked Man."

"You're supposed to do that after a *date*," I remind her.

"So I skipped ahead a little. Sue me." She swirls her drink with a thin straw. "I'm sick of being around all these ten-out-of-ten men and them not giving me the time of day because of who I'm related to. They're all terrified of my dad, and I thought since I met you *before* you were his bitch, I might have a chance."

I ignore her comment about me being her dad's bitch because, well, to be honest, as long as he determines my playing time, I am. And that's fine by me.

"Want my advice?" I say.

"Be my guest." She takes a sip of her drink.

"Stop trying so hard. No guy wants a girl who stalks them."

"I didn't *stalk* you," she squeaks, mildly offended, and I raise my brows. "Fine. Maybe a little."

Our defensive line coach, Mateo Cruz, walks up, towering behind her. "Everything okay here?"

My stomach sinks. I hope he doesn't have the wrong idea. Not trying to run side steps till I vomit. Hannah rolls her eyes. "Yes, Matty. Everything is fine."

Two glasses of champagne are placed in front of me, and I retrieve them with haste. "Have a nice night."

I make my way towards Charlotte, and her eyes—or rather, laser beams—are glued to mine. Setting the flutes down on the table, I take note of the fullness of it and the lack of privacy. The question in Charlotte's eyes has me tugging her to stand and towards the dance floor. A string quartet is playing, and I twirl her to face me. Her one hand grips mine, the other around my neck. Our eyes meet, and I glide my opposite hand slowly down the soft silk of her dress to land on her lower back. *She's so beautiful.*

"Speak your mind," I tell her as the full dance floor surrounds us like a privacy wall.

"Hannah looks"—her mouth twists—"nice."

"She looks fine."

"Fine?" Charlotte scoffs. "She looks perfect."

"*You* look perfect," I say, tugging her body against mine. "She looks fine."

"Don't stroke my ego," Charlotte sasses with furrowed brows. "She looked hot. Admit it."

I fight a smile, noting the wrinkle line on her forehead. "If I didn't know any better, I'd say you're jealous."

"Jealous? Of the model with legs for days, perfect tits, and a siren smile?" she says sarcastically. "Now, why would I ever be jealous?"

I chuckle as we sway to the music. "Can I add my own rule for the night?"

"I didn't give you rules. I gave you tips."

"Okay, well, I'm adding one."

Her grip tightens in my hand before loosening again. "What is it?"

"No more talking about other women."

"Coach Porter looks *very* handsome tonight," she says with a brow waggle, gesturing to him and Andi, who are dancing near us. *Is she serious right now?*

I narrow my eyes. "Or men. We're on a date."

"A fake date."

Annoyance thrums through me. "Right." I tug her closer and tap my forehead to hers. "No using that word either."

Her deep brown eyes bore into mine. "You're bossy tonight."

"No worrying about other people. No jealousy. No talking about this being fake or anything like that." My hand cradles her waist, the shape of her hip perfectly molded to my palm. "Let's be on this *date*, enjoy each other's company." I lean down to her ear, whispering, "And maybe, if you're a good girl, you'll get another lesson later."

She trails a thumb along my neck, eliciting goosebumps. "What if I don't wanna be a good girl?"

My jaw clenches, fighting a shit-eating grin. "I'd be okay with that too." A wicked smile spreads across her face. "I was trying to take my time undressing you earlier and ended up screwing myself." I rub my hand over the swell of her ass, squeezing a handful. "Because I've been dying to find out what's underneath this dress."

"I already told you," she says coyly as I return my hold to her lower back. "Nothing."

"I don't believe you."

"Guess you'll have to check for yourself then," she says, and all the blood rushes south.

"Fuck, Charlotte." I drop my head into the crook of her neck, the room around us entirely forgotten.

It's just me, the hottest woman alive, and a raging boner.

"What?"

"I'm pretty sure walking around this gala with a hard-on would be against the rules."

She nudges me away so we're eye to eye, our lips nearly touching. "Don't worry, *baby*," she says with an exhale. "I'll take care of that later too."

If I thought she was irresistible before, confident Charlotte is an undeniable temptation. She's the first warmth of sunshine after a cold, dark winter, and I will never get enough.

"*Soffione*."

"Noah."

"*Mi piaci da impazzire*."[1] If she only knew how much.

The song ends, and Andi and Coach Porter come our way.

"Hey, love birds," Andi says.

I attempt to steady my breathing. "Hey."

"Char, I've got to go to the bathroom. Join me?" Andi asks.

"Sure," Charlotte says, giving my arm a squeeze before stepping away. "I could use a little freshening up myself."

The girls walk off, turning heads as they make their way toward the exit. That dress was worth every damn penny.

"Wanna grab a drink?" Coach Porter asks, turning my attention back to him and gesturing towards the bar.

"Definitely," I say, and this time, I intend to actually drink it.

"How are you handling everything?" he asks.

"Everything?" I repeat, Charlotte stuck in my mind.

"Yeah. The transition to pro?"

"It's been a lot," I admit, considering the rigorous training regimen and meetings on top of helping at Camp Dickson.

"Well, keep being the Noah Caruso I know, and you'll be fine."

Pride fills me. "Thanks, Coach."

"Can we stop with the 'coach' thing?" he says with a laugh. "Just call me Porter."

"Okay… Porter," I say awkwardly. "I'm sorry, it feels wrong."

"We're peers now," he reminds me. "I was honored to coach you, and now I look forward to watching you play for the Barracudas next year."

"Hey," Coach Bexley says, coming up to greet the two of us, and we return the gesture. "Nice to see you, Porter."

---

1. IT: *Mi piaci da impazzire* - EN - I like you like crazy.

"Bex," he says with a nod.

"Ready to take me up on my offer yet?" he asks Porter.

"Get the approval for the additional benefits I requested?" Porter replies.

"You know they'll never go for it," Coach Bexley tells him. I glance between them, wondering if I should excuse myself from this conversation that clearly doesn't involve me.

"Then they'll never have me," Porter says smugly.

"Bastard," Bexley says, turning his attention to me. "Anyways, Caruso, I want to invite you to a pre-training camp starting next week. It'll run till the end of June, and then you'll have a few days off over the Fourth before official training starts."

"Oh," I say, surprised. "End of June?"

"Yeah?" His brows pull together. "That gonna be a problem?"

I think about the time I'd be missing with Charlotte before life really gets crazy. The time she'd have to be at camp with McFuck Face without me.

"I'm actually training at Camp Di—"

"He'll be there," Porter says for me, and my eyes dart to his face. His expression tells me to shut the fuck up if I want to live.

I return my attention to Coach Bexley, and say, "I'll be there."

"Wonderful," he says. "You'll get an email with the details. See you Monday."

And he's gone.

"What the hell?" I say to Porter.

"What the hell, me?" He slaps me on the back of the head. "What the hell, you? You're going to give up a *private* extra training for the NFL team you *just* signed with? Why? You need to get your priorities straight."

"They are," I tell him weakly. *Aren't they?*

"They better be," he tells me firmly. "If you want this, if you want to be the best, you have to practice like the best. You have to play like the best. And you sure as hell will not be giving up any opportunities or extra attention."

A stadium-sized weight presses on my shoulders. I've been so focused on Charlotte, I haven't prioritized football. She's not even my real girlfriend, *yet,* and it's already affecting my job. *This is why I avoid relationships.* The thought leaves a bitter taste in my mouth. Charlotte is the one thing keeping me sane right now. She is *not* a distraction... is she?

"I vouched for you," Porter continues. "And you are not going to make me look like an idiot. Especially not this year."

"Why exactly *is* this year different?" I ask, ready to be out of the hot seat.

"It's on a need-to-know basis," he says, returning to nurse his drink.

"Will I *need* to call you Coach Porter again sometime soon?" I press, fighting a smile.

"Not likely. They can't afford me."

"Are we done here?" Knox asks, throwing an arm around Porter.

"Yes," Porter says before downing the rest of his drink. "Please."

"We're going to Ploutos," Knox tells me. "Care to join?"

"I'll ask Charlotte if she's up for it," I say, thinking about the hotel room awaiting us upstairs and all the things I'm planning to do to her in it. We walk out to the hallway and meet the girls.

Charlotte saddles up next to me, and I throw an arm around her shoulder, tugging her close. "They're going to Ploutos, a club near here. Do you want to go?"

She contemplates me, biting her lip. "No, I don't think so."

I grin, looking towards our friends. "We're going to call it a night."

"Have fun," Andi says with a teasing wave as the three of them walk away.

"You sure you're fine with not going out?" I ask, turning to face Charlotte.

"Definitely," she says with a mischievous grin. "I'm not really in the mood for clubbing tonight."

"What *are* you in the mood for?"

"Isn't preparing the lesson plan your job, Professor?" she says, low and sultry, gripping my suit jacket and tugging me with her as she retreats towards the wall, her back hitting a wooden door with a rattle.

"If I didn't know better"—I flatten my hand behind her, caging her in—"I'd say you're asking for trouble."

"What makes you assume you know me so well?"

The click of a door followed by a flood of chatter fills the hallway. One voice in particular stands out that I would definitely not like interrupting this moment. My eyes snag on the door behind Charlotte, and I reach around her, tugging it open. Gripping her waist, I pull us inside the room and shut the door with a quiet click. The space is dark, an exit sign illuminating it enough to indicate it's some kind of supply closet.

"What are you doing?" Charlotte giggles as her hands clutch my suit jacket, tugging me close.

"Taking a private minute with my beautiful date where I don't have to make small talk." *Or deal with unwanted advances from my boss's daughter.* My hands hold her waist, the delicate material begging to be rumpled.

"So you'd rather be in the closet?"

"I'd rather be anywhere you are," I admit, the urge for her overwhelming.

"Well, I am great company."

Our breaths are heavy in the small space. Even with the limited visibility, her curious gaze sears me.

"I think the lessons are working," I tell her.

"Why do you say that?"

"You're confident tonight." *And fuck, is it hot.*

She slides a hand under my suit jacket, pushing it off to rub my torso. "I feel sexy."

"You are." A beat passes between us. I drag my hand down her leg to the slit of her dress and slide under, gripping her bare thigh. "Care for an extra credit opportunity on public fornication?"

She snorts. "Well, I definitely am hot for teacher."

"Hmm," I say, my fingers inching up her thigh. *I am finding out what's underneath this dress.*

"Noah." She giggles, placing a hand on mine and pausing it in place. "What if we get caught?"

"That possibility makes it all the more fun." I bend down, placing a kiss on her neck.

"I don't know..."

"Are you uncomfortable right now?" I ask, gripping her thigh.

"Maybe."

"Because we're in a closet or because you want me to stop?"

"Oh, god no. Don't stop," she tells me in a desperate plea. "I've just... never done something like this before."

"Well, let me help you relax a bit." I drop to my knees, and she grips my shoulders. I drag my hands down to her ankles, thumb brushing against the soft skin as I take off her heels. "Better?"

"Loads," she says with a satisfied moan.

"That wasn't the relaxing part." Sliding my hands up her calves and past her knees, I inch the silk material to her thighs. "It's a tragedy I can't see you right now. You're so beautiful."

"How would you know if you can't see me?"

"Because you always are."

"Noah," she says with a breath.

I push the material upwards, determined for an answer, and—

"Fuck."

"What?" she asks, tone panicked. My fingers trace the skin of her hips. The *bare* skin.

"You're not wearing any underwear," I croak out, my mouth dry.

"I told you I wasn't," she reminds me, sounding pleased with herself.

My grip tightens on her hips in an attempt to ground myself. To stop myself from going too fast. To remind myself to *enjoy* her. To take my time.

"You've been walking around like this all night?" The room is quiet. "Charlotte?"

"I may have taken them off in the bathroom at Andi's encouragement."

I chuckle. "Well, thank her for me."

"Is this the relaxing part?" she asks. "You massaging my ass?"

My hands seem to have wandered, squeezing tighter than intended. "I…" My mouth opens and closes, her sweet smell drawing me closer to that spot between her legs, the throbbing of my cock growing painful. "Fuck, I want you."

"Then take me," she begs.

"I want to touch every inch of your skin."

"Please do."

"I want to taste you."

"Then shut up and do it already," she pleads desperately, and the dress is shoved up, my mouth on her cunt.

Gripping her waist, I hook her legs over my shoulders, slamming her back against the door, which rattles once more. Soft moans escape her as I flick my tongue on her clit, drowning myself in her pretty pussy. A supernova of sweetness. Even better than last time.

I hum against her, unable to stop myself as my hard dick makes my suit pants even tighter. She grips my hair, whimpering, and I place soft kisses along her inner thighs. "This dress needs to go, *soffione.*"

She unzips it, tugs it off and over her head, and tosses it behind me. Something falls with a crash but I'm too preoccupied with her to care.

"Non fermarmi mai," I mumble against her. *"Per favore, non mi stoppare mai."* [2]

She whimpers. "If you keep speaking Italian, I'm going to come in seconds."

"Ah sì?" A thrill rushes through me. *"Ti piace quando ti parlo in italiano?"* [3]

"Noah," she pleads as I thrash my tongue against her, only coming up for air to torture her again.

"Vorrei essere dentro di te," I groan, gripping her thigh tightly.

"Tell me that in English or we stop."

No fucking chance. "I wish I was inside of you."

She gasps, taking a pause. "Then what are you waiting for?"

I freeze. "I don't have a condom."

Why the fuck didn't I bring a condom?

"Just pull out when you're close," she says breathlessly. "I've done it plenty of times."

I shove away the jealousy, remembering *he's* been inside of her. Bare. But I haven't, other than a quick teasing session. *Yeah, that pisses me right the fuck off.*

The need to claim her is overwhelming.

I drop her to the ground and pin her naked body against the door, bringing my lips to her ear. "Are you sure?"

"Remember what you said to me the first night? That you fantasized sliding into me bare? Feeling my 'tight little pussy' get you off?" Her fingers dance along my neck, clouding my mind.

"As if I could forget my favorite fantasy," I say with a quick breath, my cock throbbing.

"Let's bring it to life so you don't have to wonder anymore."

"Are you drunk?" I ask, struggling for my own sobriety. Not from alcohol, but from her. She fucking intoxicates me. Keeping

---

2. IT: *Non fermarmi mai. Per favore, non mi stoppare mai.* - EN: Never stop me.

3. IT: *"Ah sì? Ti piace quando ti parlo in italiano?"* - EN: Oh yes? Do you like it when I speak to you in Italian?

my thoughts straight is impossible. Especially when she undoes my belt buckle and pants, nudging them down, along with my boxer briefs, and they drop to the floor.

"Only on you," she says, wrapping her fingers around my cock, and I groan as she slides her hand up and down the shaft. "Fuck, you're so hard."

"Of course I am," I growl. "Have you seen yourself? It's a miracle we made it out of the hotel room."

She tugs me towards her and places her hands on my shoulders. I grip her hips, lifting her so our centers are aligned, and she swipes my dick between her until I'm drenched, pressing against her entrance. Her warm breath ghosts my mouth. "Kiss me, Noah."

Our lips collide. Hungry. Desperate. As my need for her intensifies, she moans, and I grip her ass, tugging her towards me. My tip slips inside, and I gasp for air.

So. Damn. Warm. "Fuck."

"Yes. Fuck me." She kisses my neck, nibbling against my collarbone, hands tight in my hair.

I hold her body close, trying to steady myself. Flashes of every fantasy I've ever had about this exact moment go through my mind. Except they were nothing compared to the perfection that is this reality.

"Please," she begs. "Please, baby."

Baby.

I slam in to the hilt, silencing her cries with my mouth, our tongues tangling. Frantic. Like if we stop, we might die. I know I would.

I thrust slowly, that euphoric feeling building. "This good for you?" I ask.

"Yes," she pants out.

I slide my fingers into her hair. "You're so beautiful."

She laughs breathlessly. "Again, you can't even see me."

"I don't need to." I slow my movements. "I have you memorized."

"How do I look now then?"

I bring a finger to her mouth, dragging it along her lower lip. "Your smile is relaxed. Comfortable." My knuckles brush her cheek bone. "Your eyes, the most perfect shade of brown I've ever seen. Like dark honey." I run my fingers through her curls, brushing out a few knots. *Thrust.* "Your hair is flawless." I tighten my grip on it, and she gasps as I sink deeper. "Begging to be tousled." I run my hands along her shoulders. *Thrust.* "Your skin is soft and perfect." My fingers trace her sides down to her hip bones, landing on her perfect bare ass, and I squeeze. *Thrust.* "And don't even get me started how pretty your pussy is."

"Noah," she whines, rotating her hips.

"*Sì, soffione mio?*" I chuckle, her impatience growing.

"I need more."

"I'm trying to savor you."

"You have all night to savor me," she promises. "But right now, I want you to give me what I need."

I slide a hand into her hair, the other gripping her thigh. "And what exactly is that?"

"Faster." She pants. "Deeper." She drops her mouth to my neck and bites. Hard. I gasp at the delicious pain, increasing my rhythm. The clap of our bodies echoing in the space. "And don't you dare fucking stop."

Tingles dance down my body. "I wouldn't dream of it."

She gasps against me. "I'm close."

Shit. "Me too."

My mind blurs, and I'm lost in her. Lost in us. She pulses around me, throwing herself over the edge. Her body sags slightly, and I pull out, my warm release landing between her thighs and on my hand. Once again, the small room is filled with purely the sound of our labored breaths blending together in a beautiful harmony.

Charlotte laughs. "You made a fucking mess of me."

Pride fills my chest. "Hell yeah, I did."

"I have tissues in my wristlet," she says. "Can you look for my dress while I clean myself up?"

"Sure," I reply, pulling out my phone and turning on the flashlight. Shining it on the floor where I heard the crash earlier, I locate a pile of crumpled satin. "Found it." I pick it up, my fingers wet on contact. "Uh-oh."

"What's wrong?" she asks urgently, grabbing my arm to spin me around. The low light on her naked body has me wishing for another go. "Noah, focus!" she chastises, noting my distraction.

I drag my eyes from her beautiful body and shine the light on the material. "Your dress is covered in… paint."

She gasps, snatching it out of my hands, voice cracking. "I'm so sorry."

"What are you sorry for?"

"You got me this gorgeous dress, and it's ruined," she says, tone laced with sadness.

"Taking it off you was worth *way* more than having it on," I say, smiling at her. *Way. More.*

"Noah." She slaps my chest. "I can't go out there like this! With this tie-dye fail?"

"Just put it on, and we'll head straight for our room to clean you up," I offer with images of her in the walk-in shower, my hands in her hair—and other places—flashing in my mind.

"And how will I explain this?" she asks, gesturing towards the sticky black liquid.

I set my phone down, the low light still illuminating the room, and shrug my suit jacket off my shoulders. "You can put this over it."

"Then *your* suit will get ruined too."

"But you won't feel self-conscious the entire way upstairs."

"It's fine." She sighs, stepping into the stained satin. "It'll be fine."

When she has the dress secure, I place the jacket on her shoulders and she shrugs it off. *This woman.* "Just wear it, baby. Please?"

"I already ruined what I imagine is a very expensive dress, and your suit is Armani."

"I couldn't care less about the suit."

She concedes, surely knowing she's not winning this fight. I help put her arms through and tug the sides of the jacket, pulling her towards me. Our lips are inches apart, and I smile down at her.

"What?" she asks, her own smile breaking through.

"You look…" I slide my fingers into her hair, angling her mouth towards my own.

"A mess? Ridiculous? So embarrassing you want to leave me in this closet and never come back?"

Like mine.

"Perfect." I press my lips to hers, slipping my tongue into her mouth to deepen the kiss. Pulling away, I release the dress, and it drops to her ankles. "Let's go." I listen at the door before popping my head outside. "Coast is clear."

We hurry out of the room, shutting the door behind us, and rush down the hallway. I slide my arm around her waist, pulling her close. "What should the next lesson be tonight? Safe shower sex techniques? The multi uses for a detachable shower head? How many orgasms are possible until you pass out?"

"You're insatiable." Charlotte giggles as we round the corner to the elevators. I place a kiss in her hair, my hand gripping her waist.

"Well, I take my professor in Sexology role very seriously," I tell her, eliciting another giggle as we near the elevators.

"Caruso," I hear and fight the urge to groan.

"Coach Bexley," I say, turning to him with a smile as he appears to be on his way out the door.

His eyes wander over Charlotte and me, and if he minds our disheveled appearance, he certainly doesn't let on.

"Hope you both had a nice evening," he says.

"You too."

"See you at training Monday," he says to me, and my stomach sinks. *I wanted to break the news to Charlotte myself.* I know how much she hated sleeping alone last night. But Porter was right. It's important to take this job seriously. "I'm glad you'll be joining us."

"Looking forward to the extra practice," I tell him, the picture of poise, while inside I'm reeling. I've never dated anyone—or fake dated—while having to worry about football. I have no clue what that's going to look like or how I'll balance it. And I definitely can't risk fucking up my rookie year.

Coach Bexley walks away, and the wait for the elevator feels like hours as Charlotte remains quiet, tugging my jacket tight around her.

"I was going to tell you," I say.

"It's fine." She waves me off.

"He asked me about this extra training, and Coach Porter insisted, and—"

"Noah," she says, cutting me off with a smile. "I'm not mad. I get it, you have a job you have to get back to. I didn't think we could play hot teacher forever."

The elevator dings, and we step inside. When the doors close, securing us in privacy, I nudge her against the wall, towering over her.

"But Ms. Benson, I have a very long lesson plan, and participation is a significant part of your grade."

"What's next on the syllabus?" she asks, staring up at me with a teasing smile.

"Showing me how good you are on your knees."

She nudges me forward and drops to the floor, staring up at me with beautiful doe eyes. "Yes, Professor."

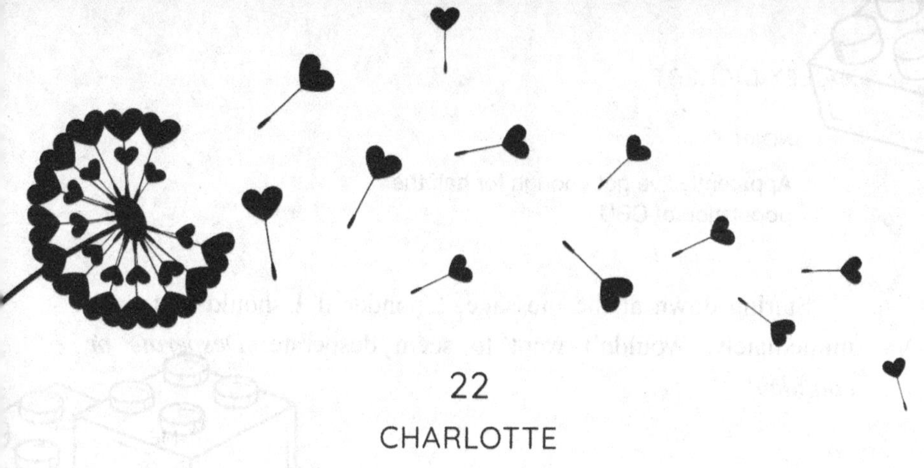

22

CHARLOTTE

NOAH

ME

Fun Fact: There are around 80 Lego bricks for every person on earth

I sigh, staring at the phone as I'm snuggled in my tiny bed. Noah had to clear his cabin since he wasn't returning, so no more sprawling for me.

The room is dark and quiet. Andi's been asleep for hours, so it's just me, my thoughts, and this unanswered message. I sent it around lunch time, and I know Noah's busy, but I thought he'd at least text me before bed. Especially because of his cute obsession with Legos.

Maybe this really was all for show.

At the gala, I thought we were starting to have something real, but maybe he's a professor of Faking It too. Tossing my phone next to me, I force my eyes shut, opting to dream about him instead.

I awake in the morning to a text.

NOAH

Apparently I've got enough for half the
population of CBU

Staring down at the message, I ponder if I should text back immediately. Wouldn't want to seem desperate. *Desperate or confident?*

ME

Thought you'd like it

NOAH

Have a good day, soffione

ME

You too quarterback

A week has passed since Noah left camp, and our routine is the same. Minimal surface-level texting, and both of us too exhausted to hold a conversation at night. I knew our arrangement wasn't going to last forever. I just didn't expect it to end so abruptly.

He doesn't owe me anything. He's not my boyfriend.

And yet, I still try

ME

How was training today?

NOAH

Hot and exhausting

Kinda like you

ME

I'm not sure if I should take that as a
compliment

NOAH

You should

I bite my cheek, opting to be brave, and click call. The phone rings once, then goes to voicemail.

NOAH

Sorry, I'm heading into dinner with some of the guys. Rain check?

It's official. I'm no longer a priority.

ME

Sure. Rain check

Another week passes with the same routine. Today I got a good morning text, but besides that I haven't heard from him.

"You okay over there?" Andi asks, concerned eyes on me as we change into comfy clothes after dinner.

"Yes," I tell her, taking the big blue bow out of my hair. "Are *you?*" I ask with a cocked brow. "You've been acting strange ever since we got back from the gala."

"Same with you," she challenges, and I roll my eyes. She grabs a swimsuit out of her drawer. "I'm going to meet Theo and a few girls for a lake swim. Wanna join?"

I glance at my bed. My little lonely bed. "Nah, I'm good."

"Seriously? You need to get out."

"I'm exhausted," I say, and while that technically is true, it's not why I want to stay in.

"We'll be by the dock if you change your mind." She shoots me a wave and is out the door.

Blowing a breath, I jump into bed, picking up my phone. My lips quirk into a smile at the message on the screen.

NOAH

Did you know giraffe tongues can be up to 20 inches long?

I consider how to reply. We've been doing this boring little check-in texting banter for weeks, but every time my mind wanders to those sex lessons, I'm aching for release.

ME

No, but now I'm a little turned on

NOAH

Great, and now I'm thinking about other tongues in certain places

Good. This is good.

ME

You're the one who mentioned the tongue thing

NOAH

It was the fun fact of the day

ME

Well the fact is, I could really use some fun

NOAH

Not a good day?

Char?

My phone buzzes in my hand, the red button begging to be touched. Just like me. I roll my eyes at myself. *Stop being so desperate.* Or am I flirting? The temptation of hearing Noah's voice is too much to resist, and I tap green instead.

"Hi," I say to his smiling face popping up on FaceTime.

"Hi," he replies. "What are you up to?"

I roll on my side, the cabin bed squeaking. "Just chilling."

"Chilling." He nods his head. "Are you alone?"

"Yeah, Andi went swimming."

"You didn't want to go?"

"Not really."

"Why?"

Because I had a terrible day. Fell on my ass twice. Threw up in

the bushes. All but cried when I found your T-shirt in my drawer because it's been two weeks since I got to kiss your stupid face even though I know we were faking it. Oh, and all I can think of every time I close my eyes is your hands on my skin and you whispering my name like a prayer. "Just tired."

"Charlotte," he says, tone accusatory.

"Noahhh."

"What's wrong?"

I shake my head, fighting tears. *Why are there tears?* "Everything's fine."

"Is that what we're doing now? Lying to each other?"

"I'm not—" My voice cracks, and I clear my throat. "I'm not lying."

"Please, talk to me."

Thoughts of all the hard days of work he's been putting in and the opportunity of a lifetime he has right now in Tampa fill my mind. He doesn't need distractions. He doesn't need *me*. "Nothing."

Another message pops in and I groan.

THE BENSON FAM

MOTHER

Will you make it for the twins' birthday party
Saturday?

"What's wrong?" Noah asks.

I opt to use this as the out for my unexplained shitty attitude. "Just Mom trying to rub it in that I can't go to the twins' birthday party this weekend."

"Why can't you go? Doesn't camp end Friday?"

"Yeah," I say. "And Andi is heading straight back to campus after our physicals, so I don't have a ride."

"I always hated those things," Noah says, shuddering. "The needles and weighing and prodding."

"I know," I say with a laugh, remembering the judgy nurse from last year who told me I needed to lose a few pounds if I want to keep being a flyer. Unfortunately the school requires it for us to be cleared for the team.

"Do you know anyone else at camp from Longwood who could bring you?" Noah asks.

"Well…" I shift on the bed, remembering how I got home last year. "Jonathan."

He laughs sarcastically. "No."

"No?" I say with a cocked brow. *Not that I had even a minuscule intention of considering the option.*

"Yeah." He smiles. "No. I'll take you."

"Doesn't one of your new teammates have some big Fourth of July party thing this weekend?"

"So?" His brows pull together. "I'd rather see you."

He would?

"You don't have to—"

"Yes, I do," he says. "And besides, I *want* to go. In fact, I'm a little offended I wasn't invited."

I fight a smile. "Yeah, because birthday parties with screaming children are sooo your vibe."

"If you're there, it's my vibe," he says, and a blush creeps on my cheeks, all negative thoughts shoved into the "you're such an overthinker, girly" category.

"Okay, then thanks," I say. "So you'll pick me up Saturday morning from camp?"

"It's a date."

It's a date.

"Thank god," I say, folding a shirt and putting it in my duffle. "Only one more day of camp food and low water pressure."

"Why do you think I'm leaving tonight?" Andi says, pulling the sheet off her bed.

"Because you're cruel," I say, grabbing another shirt out of the drawer. I want to make sure I'm ready when Noah arrives tomorrow.

"What time is your physical?" Andi asks.

"Eleven thirty, you?"

"Eleven. Wanna walk together?"

I check the time on my phone. "Sure, but we should get going."

A quick walk later, and we're striding into the gymnasium housing the medical facility. The roof is high, and even on the last day, the weight floor is packed full of cheerleaders and football players getting in one final workout.

We arrive at the medical station and check in. A short question-naire later, and we're sitting in the waiting area.

"Andrea Lyons," a nurse calls, and Andi shoots me a wave, disappearing into the back.

Twenty minutes pass, the time ticking like molasses in an hourglass. I check my phone but haven't gotten any new notifica-tions besides a good morning fun fact from Noah.

"Charlie." The hair on the back of my neck stands, and I glance up to find Jonathan standing before me.

"What are you doing here?" I ask stupidly.

"Just finished my exam," he says, pointing back towards the doors Andi disappeared through.

"Right," I say, standing. Because somehow sitting makes me feel inferior to him, and I won't allow that. "What do you want?"

"I'm heading out today," he says.

"Okay… and?"

He blows out a breath. "I wanted to apologize."

I fold my arms over my chest. "Whatever for?"

He looks down then back into my eyes. My skin crawls from his direct attention. The last time he stared into my eyes like this, he was sliding into me and whispering how much he loved me.

What a crock of shit.

Jonathan swallows hard. "Just for everything that happened."

Generic and meaningless. I'm so ready to be done with this conversation.

"Great," I say, jaw grinding. "You're forgiven."

"Really?" he asks, ignoring the bite in my tone. "We good then?"

"Yep," I say, forcing a smile. *Walk away, fuck boy.* "We're good."

"Bye, Charlie."

He leaves the room, and I turn around to find Andi glaring at me. "What the hell was that?"

I release a heavy breath, sinking back in the waiting room chair, and Andi sits beside me. "Can we not do this?"

"That guy blew up your life, and you're, what, giving him a free pass?"

"God, no," I say. "But I didn't want to even entertain the conversation. And honestly, if Jonathan didn't do what he did, we would still be together, and I wouldn't have Noah. Or be faking it with Noah. Or whatever we're doing. Because I'm the loyal one. The 'never gives up' one. And I never would've given up on him."

Andi stares at the door Jonathan walked out of, then turns to face me. "We should be egging his car, leaving flaming shit bags at his doorstep, putting permanent blue dye in his shampoo, *Big-*

Fat-Liar-style, *not* forgiving him! What kinda bullshit logic is that?"

I shrug.

"Charlotte Benson," the nurse calls, and I pop up, glad to be done with this conversation too.

I want to move on.

Hate is a poison that spreads slowly, killing you from the inside out. Forgiveness is the antidote. I did it for me.

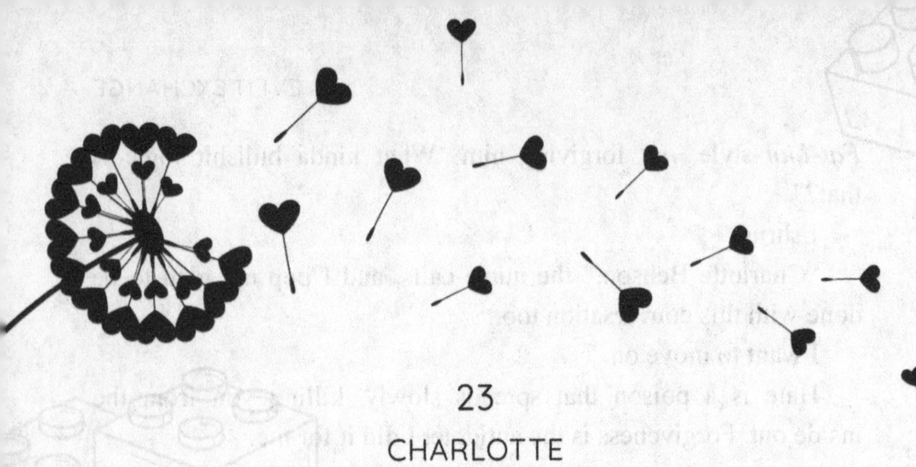

23

CHARLOTTE

"Again!" Denny tells Noah, and he does yet another backflip in my parents' backyard garden. A bounce house is set up in the corner, and rows of catered food line the perimeter. The best way to describe it is White House Fourth of July BBQ Chic. Hot dogs and baked beans have been traded for filet mignon and smoked-salmon canapés.

It's all very *posh,* but I can't deny I'm obsessed with the apple rose puffs adorning the dessert table. They're beautiful *and* delicious.

The twins love being born on the Fourth because they think all the fireworks and hoopla is for them, but I fear as they get older, they'll realize this party is really for Mother's donor friends to schmooze and booze them.

Noah does another flip, then stands in place, glaring at me. "Why did you tell her I could do this?"

I shrug, keeping my deal with Denny to myself.

"You feeling queasy yet?" Denny asks, and I pin her with a look.

"What?" Noah says, eyes narrowed. Denny fights a smile, looking at me, then back to Noah. "What are you two up to?"

"Nothing," we both say too quickly.

Noah's eyes lock on Denny. "Spill."

No! She's too weak.

"Lottie-said-she'd-pay-me-ten-bucks-if-I-got-you-to-backflip-till-you-puked," Denny says in a rushed admission, then inhales loudly. *Like I said, weak.*

"Really?" Noah's eyes swing to mine, and he folds his arms across his chest. My eyes drag along the flexed muscles. His long fingers that know how to edge me to the brink of release. "And why might you force that kind of torture upon me?"

My gaze returns to his. "Call it payback."

"For what?"

For blowing me off the last two weeks while you've been away. It's been nothing but small talk and surface-level conversation since he picked me up from camp earlier. We were running late because he'd hit traffic, and we rushed to make it before the party started. The kids and my parents have had us preoccupied ever since.

"For the little mermaid impersonator I found in your cabin a few weeks ago," I lie, since tiny ears are around.

"I love that movie!" Denny says, running off belting "Under the Sea."

"I have been told I look like Prince Eric," he says once we're alone.

"With that inflated ego, you're more like the hot air balloon in *Up*."

"Cute." His eyes narrow, then he reaches out and brushes my hair behind my shoulder. "If you wanted to punish me, I could think of much better ways."

"The point is that you *don't* enjoy it." I step closer, lowering my voice. "Pretty sure if I tied you up and whipped you for being such a bad, bad boy, you'd like it a little too much."

Noah's eyes blaze. "*Porca troia, soffione.*" His gaze says he's ready to rip these clothes off my body. "Please don't make my mind go there right now."

I'd actually love his mind to go there. Would love to join him there, in fact. "How about I show you around the house?" I ask, biting my lower lip to exude sex appeal.

His eyes drop to them. "I'd like that."

Good. This is good.

We head toward the back door, and I take deep breaths to shove down the absolute ridiculous need I feel for this man. My mind runs through where we can go for some one-on-one time I've so desperately missed.

My bedroom? *Too easy.*

The garage? *Too hot.*

The study? *Mom would kill me.*

I glance around, eyes connecting with my mother's.

"Charlie," she calls, waving us over with a smile.

"Shit," I mumble, and Noah reaches out, interlacing our fingers.

"It'll be fine," he says as we head towards her.

"This is Tabitha White," she says, gesturing to a woman who looks to be in her early forties. "She's a criminal defense attorney in Tampa and offered to host you for an internship next year, should you come to your senses." Mom's smile is mocking. Noah's hand grips mine hard, and I side-eye him, his expression unreadable.

"Thank you for the offer," I tell Tabitha, using my free, not squished hand for a polite shake, biting back any arguments. I just want to get through this conversation, slip away, and let my boyfriend fuck me six ways to Sunday. Fine, *fake* boyfriend, but the orgasm will be 100 percent real.

"It's my pleasure," Tabitha says. "Anything for a Benson."

"And this is Noah Caruso," Mom says, gesturing towards my date, and Tabitha reaches out a hand. "Charlotte's *friend*."

Friend?

I introduced Noah as my boyfriend when we arrived, and the intentional omission pisses me off. He looks down at Tabitha's hand, and I nudge him, letting go of his.

"Have we met?" Tabitha asks Noah as they exchange a polite shake.

"I don't think so," he says quickly, placing his palm on my lower back.

"Are you sure?" Tabitha cocks her head. "You look so familiar."

"He's a quarterback for the Barracudas," I say, providing an explanation.

"Hmm," Tabitha hums. "Maybe, but I don't really watch football."

"Georgia," Patricia calls over. "Someone's on the phone for you."

"Excuse me," Mom says, smile tight, and walks away.

Tabitha studies Noah with a laugh. "I'm sorry, you look so familiar. It's driving me crazy."

"I have one of those faces," Noah answers curtly, fingertips gripping my back. *What has gotten into him?*

"And thanks for the internship offer," I tell her. "But I'm no longer pre-law."

Tabitha nods. "Well, it's standing should you change your mind."

"Thank you." *I won't.*

She excuses herself, and I glance around. Mom's near the food, engaged in a heated conversation with Patricia. Dad is by the bounce house, playing with Nash.

Perfect.

I make a beeline for the back door, Noah quick on my heels. We are *not* getting interrupted this time. I'm also dying to ask about his bizarre reaction to Tabitha, but that can wait till *after.* We make our way into the house, dodging caterers and cocktail waitresses. Some guests are chattering in the foyer, but they don't even glance our way as we turn down the hall towards Mom's office. Any hesitation of using it vanished the second she tried to undermine my career choice. Again.

Glancing behind us, I ensure we're alone, then grab Noah's hand, tugging him along.

He chuckles, interlacing his fingers with mine as we jog down the hall, and the closed office door appears up ahead. I check for witnesses one last time, then tug Noah inside, close it quickly behind us, and flick the lock. My breath is heavy as my back presses against the door, and Noah towers over me, an inquisitive look on his face.

I'm thankful my mother removed all the cameras when we moved in—my grandma was obsessed with her security.

"So I'm assuming you didn't really want to show me the house?" Noah asks, brushing a strand of hair behind my ear and gripping the side of my neck. His green eyes bore into mine. Oh, how I've missed those eyes. I have questions for him, but those can wait.

"Noah," I say, his attention filling me with the courage to tell him exactly what I want. What I crave. "I need you to fuck me."

His lips part open. "That's the second time you've asked me that."

"I'm not asking," I say, the lust glimmering in his eyes. "Are you gonna miss your opportunity again?"

"Not a chance," he says, hooking a hand behind my head and pulling my mouth to his. Our lips crash, tongues tangling. I loop my arms around his neck, and he nudges me toward an empty wall on the back side of the room.

Noah scoops me up, and my legs wrap around his waist. His hands wander up my sundress, my back slamming against the wall, and all the breath expels from my lungs.

"I've missed this," he murmurs in my ear and plants soft kisses down my neck.

I rub my fingernails under his shirt, up and down his bare torso. "Me too."

"Being away from you was torture," he says, sliding my thin strap off my shoulder and nibbling on the soft skin.

"Why do you think I was punishing you?" I admit.

He pulls away with narrowed eyes. "*That's* why Denny was training me for the Olympics?"

"A girl has needs," I say. "I even had to resort to your strategy of shower masturbation for a bit of relief."

He groans, dropping his head into my neck, hands gripping my thighs. "If you really wanted to torture me, you just needed to say stuff like that." I giggle. "Why didn't you tell me you missed me?"

"You were busy." I shrug, heart twisting. "You have to be able to focus on your job. Fake dating comes secondary."

"What did I say about using the f word when I'm inside of you?" Noah says, gaze searing, causing goosebumps down my spine.

"You're *not* inside me," I remind him, and he pulls me tight against his body.

With his free hand, he reaches between us to unbutton his shorts and pushes them down.

His eyes hold mine, a smirk forming upon his lips as he nudges my soaked panties to the side. I'm already dripping for him, and after a few swipes of his tip against me, he's easing inside. *Yes, please.*

"Now, as I was saying"—his grin is wicked—"lose the word 'fake' from your vocabulary when I'm fucking you, *soffione mio.*"

My head drops against the wall, and his lips fall to my neck as my needy cunt pulses around him.

"Do you understand?" he asks, filling me completely, and I gasp.

"Yes." *Thrust.* "I understand."

"Good," he says with a satisfied smile, increasing his rhythm. "Now, can you come for me please? As much as I'm enjoying this, I really don't want your family to walk in on all the things I want to do to you."

"And what are those?" I pant as he continues his torture.

He grips my hips, nails digging in. "I was thinking about bending you over that couch over there. Fucking you from behind, then stopping to devour your needy pussy every time you get close."

"What else?" I ask, closing my eyes to allow myself to join his daydream.

"I'd lay you down on the desk, sprawled out, so I can eat you and finger fuck you till you come on my tongue." *Thrust.* "You always taste so good." *Thrust.* "*Cazzo.*" He walks us over to the desk, his dick still inside me, and sets me on it.

"What are you—"

He slips out, knees hitting the floor before me. Gripping my calves, he tugs me to the edge of the desk and glances up with a satisfied smile on his face. "Why should we have to imagine when I can show you everything I want to do to you?"

"You're no longer concerned about being caught?" I ask, brow cocked.

"Do you trust the lock on that door?" he asks.

"Absolutely," I say, and he grins, gripping my thighs. My head falls back, his warm breath fanning against my center, causing me to shudder.

His tongue swipes through me, and I struggle to hold in the wide array of sounds I'd love to be making right now. He flicks my clit, and a tiny moan escapes. His hand slaps over my mouth and I nod, getting the message. He removes his hand, fingers inching up my inner thigh. Seconds later he slips them inside me, curling them to hit that glorious spot. It's too much. His mouth, his fingers, his addictive fucking scent. It's embarrassing how quickly he could get me off right now.

"I'm so close," I whine, and he pulls out abruptly, standing. "Noah!"

He positions himself at my entrance. "I changed my mind," he says, smile wicked. "I want you to come on my cock. I'll pull out after you're done."

I nod ferociously, and he slides inside, gripping my ass while holding me against him.

"You're doing such a good job," he tells me, the tension building.

I bite my lip, stifling a smile, opting to try for a bit of dirty talk myself. "I love how you fuck me, baby," I say, feeling awkward, but only for a moment as I notice the way his eyes flare. Note to self: Noah loves pet names in the bedroom.

He quickens his pace, the table rattling, but I'm too lost in it to care. Lost in *him*.

"Come for me," he says, and with another thrust, I'm seeing fireworks. Red, white, and royal fucking blue. *Happy Fourth of July to me.* My back arches, breathing labored while I ride out the entire explosive rush until I'm nothing but a puddle of Jello.

He slips out, gripping his shaft and pumping hard.

I use my remaining energy to nudge him away, hop off the desk, and drop to my knees.

"You don't have t—" His protest is cut off by my lips circling his tip, and within seconds, his hands are in my hair, directing me exactly where he wants me to go. I lap and suck and taste, and it doesn't take long till his cock jerks, filling my mouth to the brim.

"Don't swallow," he commands with labored breaths. "Show me."

I glance up, our eyes connecting, and open, presenting his release.

"Fuck," he says with a shaky exhale. "Look at your pretty mouth filled with my cum." My stomach swirls, and he tugs me by my hair to stand. "Swallow," he instructs, and I oblige, licking my lips for any excess. "Such a good fucking girl."

I giggle. "I think it's safe to say the lessons are working."

He shakes his head. "Baby, that was all you."

The door rattles, and our heads jerk towards it.

My mother's voice is muffled. "I must have locked it before the guests arrived. Wait here. I'll grab the key."

My wide eyes meet Noah's.

We are so fucked.

24

NOAH

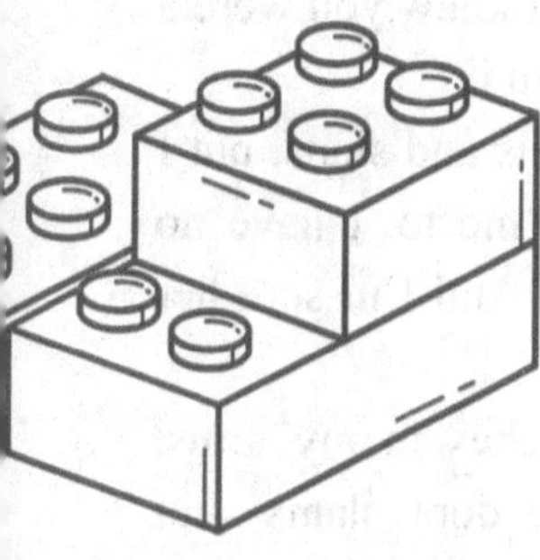

"What are we gonna do?" I ask, veins pumping with adrenaline as we secure our clothes back in place.

Charlotte's eyes dart around the office, and she grabs my hand, dragging me toward a door. She opens it, presenting a small closet, then tugs me inside and closes it quietly.

Our hushed, rapid breaths fill the small space as our bodies press together.

"What is it with us and closets?" I tease.

"*Shhh!*" she says as the office door creaks open, and she grips my shirt. I snake my arms around, holding her to me.

Muffled voices fill the room.

"You shouldn't have come here," Georgia snaps.

An unfamiliar male voice speaks. "You didn't take my call."

"That was purposeful."

"People are asking questions."

"Well, tell them to fuck off," Georgia spits out.

"I'd be more inclined to tell them that if I were compensated."

The room is quiet. "You have been *more* than compensated."

"Need I remind you what's at stake here?" the voice says, and although we can't see them, the thick tension in the air is obvious.

"Need I remind *you* of your involvement?" There are muffling sounds. The opening and closing of drawers. "This," she says, slapping something on the desk. "This is all I have to show to hide my name while indicting yours."

"How did you get this?"

"It's not a matter of how, but why? Because I knew you were a snake. Now slither out before I do something with it."

Whispered curses fade out and the door opens and shuts, but I don't dare move a muscle until Charlotte tells me to. I have no clue what we heard. If it even means anything. And I'm sure her head is spinning even worse than mine.

"Shit!" Georgia shouts, and Charlotte flinches in my arms. More drawers open and close, then the office door slams shut again. After a few minutes of silence, she deems it safe and we leave the closet.

"What the hell was that about?" I ask.

"No clue," Charlotte says. "But let's get out of here."

We sneak out of the office and rejoin the party, no one the wiser, and I release a breath of relief. Tabitha walks by us, and my eyes trail her till she's out of sight, my stomach churning. Charlotte was a beautiful distraction, but I can't deny the emotions swirling back up, seeing her again.

"How do you know Tabitha?" Charlotte asks, and I return my gaze to her, dropping my voice to a whisper.

"She was my father's lawyer." A shudder racks through me, remembering how she tried every trick in the book to get his sentence reduced.

Charlotte's jaw hardens. "She helped an abuser?"

My teeth grind. "I mean, it is her job."

"I'm surprised she didn't recognize your name," Charlotte says. "Although I guess lawyers deal with tons of cases."

I gnaw on my lower lip, choosing to be vulnerable. "Mom and I reverted back to her maiden name when they got divorced." I swallow hard. "My father's last name, my old last name, is Lewis."

"Oh." She takes my hands in hers. "Thank you for sharing that with me." I nod, unable to conjure up any other words. "Do you think my mom knows? About you, I mean?"

I shrug, stomach sinking. "I don't know."

Charlotte glances around. "Do you wanna leave?"

My eyes wander to the twins playing in the yard, and I know how much Charlotte's missed them. I shake my head. "Nah. I'll be fine." I take her chin between my fingers. "As long as you're by my side."

"Consider me your personal bodyguard," she says, shoulders pulled back, wide grin on her face.

Leaning down, I press a quick kiss to her lips. "I've never felt safer."

The rest of the day goes by in a blur, no more awkward run-ins with ghosts from my past, and before we know it, we're finally in my truck, heading to Crystal Bay. Camp's over, and Charlotte's stuff is secure in my back seat. *Where will we go from here?*

"Do you wanna talk about what happened in the study with your mom?" I ask hesitantly, remembering how she flinched in my arms.

"Nah." She stares out the dark window, watching fireworks bursting in the distance. "She's been deep in political shit my whole life. And to be honest, I've stopped trying to figure it out."

It didn't sound like normal political stuff, but the last thing I want to do is upset her. I'm hoping she'll stay at my place tonight and we can talk about what we're doing now that the dating doesn't really feel fake anymore. I tried to keep my head down and focus on football the past two weeks, but that clearly made Charlotte feel overlooked, and I am *not* okay with that.

"Do you remember where I put my phone?" Charlotte asks as I pull onto the dark highway. "I told Andi I'd text her when we were heading to CBU."

"I think it's in your tote behind my seat."

She digs it out and brings the phone to her ear. A muffled message comes through, and Charlotte gasps, my eyes pulling to her.

"No," she says, her voice firm.

"What's wrong?" I ask when she puts the phone back in her lap.

She doesn't speak.

"Char, what's wrong?" I ask again, and she clears her throat.

"Nothing."

My brows furrow. "Are you sure?"

"Yeah." She smiles, but it doesn't quite reach her eyes. "Noah, could you focus on the road?" Her tone is teasing, but my Charlotte radar tells me she's hiding something.

She turns up the radio, face buried in her phone, and when we finally get into Crystal Bay, I ask, "Wanna come to my place tonight?"

She stares out the window. "I can't. Andi and I have plans."

"It's midnight," I say, brows pulled tight.

"Yeah, she…" Her voice trails off. "She needs some girl time."

"Okay," I say, trying to mask my disappointment. "Can I see you tomorrow?" I readjust my grip on the steering wheel. "Was hoping we could hang out before my official training starts Monday."

"Sorry, tomorrow I have plans with Sophia and Sage," she says.

"Isn't Sophia leaving for Georgia with Elijah?"

"Oh, right." She waves me off. "Just Sage then."

Why's she being so squirrely?

I abide by her wishes, and a few minutes later, I'm pulling in front of her apartment building, putting the truck in park, and turning it off. *I don't like this.*

"What are you doing?" she asks.

"Helping you bring your stuff up," I say, gesturing to my packed back seat. *What the hell is going on with her?*

"Oh." She smiles, but it feels forced. "Thanks."

We grab her bags and take the elevator to her floor in silence.

Was it the phone call?

Was it the thing with her mom?

Was it something I did?

We arrive at her door, and she unlocks it, bringing us inside. Andi and Stella are sitting on the couch, and their eyes widen.

"Hey!" they exclaim, jumping up to greet us.

"Hi…" I say, following Charlotte to her room, and set down her things.

She rushes back out, and I trail her towards the front door.

"Thanks so much for helping me up here," she says, opening it and gesturing outside for me to leave.

What the hell is going on?

The girls stare at me with creepy smiles on their faces, and I take the out, heading towards the door. When I pause in front of Charlotte, our eyes meet. I can't for the life of me figure out what's going on in that head of hers, but I can make sure she knows exactly where I stand. I slide my hand into her hair, and she releases a little sigh. Tugging her to me, I plant a firm kiss on her lips.

"Good night, *soffione*," I mumble against her lips.

"Night, quarterback," she murmurs.

I walk out the door, and it slams shut behind me.

For the second time, I've been thrown out of Charlotte Benson's apartment.

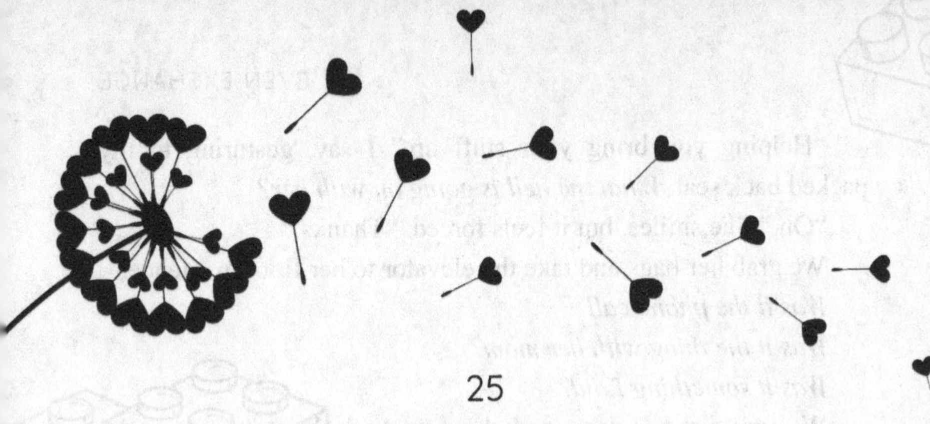

25

CHARLOTTE

My back falls against the front door.

"What am I gonna do?" I say, and the girls rush to me. "Did you get what I asked for?"

"Yes," Andi says, swallowing hard. "We got it."

"Play us the voicemail," Stella says as we walk to the couch, and I sit between them.

They put their arms around me as I pull out my phone, release a shaky breath, and hit play.

"Hey, Charlotte. It's Coach Landry. I'm really sorry to do this over voicemail, but I'm heading on a trip for a few days without service, and I thought you'd want to know as soon as possible." She sighs. "Your physical yesterday came back with a result I don't think either of us were expecting. But, according to your urine test, you're pregnant."

The voicemail continues another minute about resources and reaching out to her for support, but the rest of it was drowned out by the sounds of Andi and Stella having a full-blown meltdown.

"How did this happen?"

"How far along are you?"

"Have you told Noah?" Andi asks.

"Clearly not," Stella points out. "Given the way you threw him out of our apartment."

"I did not *throw* him out," I say, placing a hand over my chest, then suck in a breath. "I totally did." My heart aches, and I jump to my feet. "He probably thinks he did something wrong."

"I mean, he got you pregnant," Stella points out.

"Allegedly," Andi says, standing. "Let's not freak out until you pee on a stick."

Twenty minutes later, I stare down at the results on the counter. Stella was smart enough to suggest I pee in a cup so we can take multiple tests for accuracy.

"Can I freak out yet?" I ask, tears welling in my eyes, looking at the four very clear, very *positive* pregnancy tests.

"Yeah." They put their arms around me. "You can."

And I break down in their arms and cry.

I awake in my soft bed with puffy eyes and a pounding headache. I wish I could say I don't know how I got here, but it looks like joke's on me. The pull-out method is *not*, in fact, an effective birth control.

Who knew?

"Charlie?" I hear, paired with a knock.

"Yeah," I groan, covers pulled over my head.

The door creaks open and the bed dips at my feet. I peek out from the blanket, shooting straight up when I see who's sitting there. "Sophia?"

"Yeah," she says as Sage, Stella, and Andi stroll in after her, all joining her on the bed.

"What are you doing here?" I ask Sophia, and she and Andi

share a look. "I thought you were in Georgia." I glare at Andi. "You told them?"

"No," Andi says, taking my hand. "I said you *needed* them." She smiles, looking at them and back to me. "I didn't expect they'd show up here first thing, banging on the door."

"That's what friends are for," Sophia says.

"I thought you left for Georgia today?" I ask her.

"We were supposed to, but plans changed," she says with a soft smile, squeezing my hand.

I throw an arm over my head. "So now I'm affecting everyone's lives?"

"Char," Sophia says, taking my arm off my head. "What's going on?"

"I got kicked off the cheer squad," I say, thinking of the second half of the message that pulled the rug out from under me. Not only am I pregnant, but I also lose a huge part of my identity.

"What?" Sophia squeaks. "Why?"

I drag a hand down my face as they all look at me expectantly. "Because I'm pregnant."

Sophia's and Sage's mouths fall open. "No."

"Yes," I say.

"It's Noah's?" Sophia asks.

"Obviously?" I say, brows furrowed.

"So you two were just raw dogging it all summer?" Sage asks.

I roll my eyes. "It seems that way."

"When was your last period?" she asks.

"I don't know? It's super irregular, so I never track it."

"Are you not on the pill?" Sophia asks.

"No," I say, cursing myself. *How could I be so reckless?* "It always fucked up my hormones."

"Being pregnant *also* fucks with your hormones," Sage reminds me.

"You're not helping," Andi tells her.

"Sorry." Sage throws up her hands.

"So what are you gonna do?" Sophia asks.

I rest my chin on my knees. "I don't know."

"Well, whatever you decide, we're here for you," Andi says, squeezing my hand.

I glance around, all my girls by my side, and while I might have been upset with Andi at first, I'm relieved to not be dealing with this freak-out alone.

Now I won't have to do a huge "surprise, I'm pregnant" tour.

Although that tour should probably start with Noah.

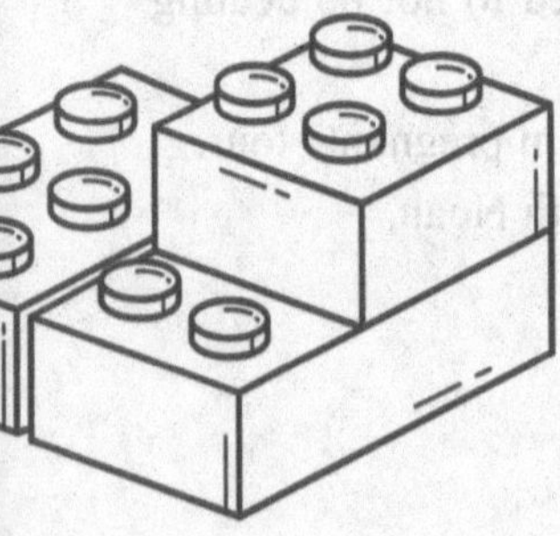

26

NOAH

CHARLOTTE

ME

You have fun with the girls today?

Forty-five minutes and still no response. Tossing my phone on the kitchen counter, I turn my attention back to what's in front of me, picking up parmesan and a cheese grater.

"You want some?" I ask Theo, hovering over our plates of pasta.

Since Charlotte wouldn't hang out with me today, I opted for a guys' night to at least try and get my mind off it. I considered ordering pizza, but since my training formally starts tomorrow, I want to stick to the diet plan. So pesto pasta and grilled chicken it is.

"Sure," he says.

The front door opens, and my eyes fly to it as Elijah walks in. *It's not her.*

"What are you doing here?" I ask, brushing away the disappointment as he shuts the door behind him, kicking his shoes off.

"Theo texted me," he says with furrowed brows, taking a seat beside him on the kitchen island. "Should I leave?"

"No," I say with a laugh, grabbing another plate. "But I thought you left for Georgia today."

"We're leaving tomorrow now," he says. "Sophia wanted to hang out with Charlie and the girls."

"Oh," I say. Maybe she really did have plans.

Monday

CHARLOTTE

ME

> Fun Fact: the only thing that smells worse than a skunk is a men's locker room

My first official day of practice is finished, and I pick up my phone from my locker with no new notifications. None that I care about at least. I shower and dress quickly, then head for the parking lot. It's been less than forty-eight hours since we've spoken, but it's driving me crazy. Even if we don't talk *much*, we usually talk every day. I open the door to my truck, shut myself inside, and tap the call button.

No answer.

I drive home, prepare dinner, spend three hours putting together an Imperial Star Destroyer Lego set, and still nothing. Not a text. Not a call. Not a fucking carrier pigeon.

Picking up the phone, I call again. It goes to voicemail after two rings.

Great. She's avoiding me.

Tuesday

CHARLOTTE

ME

Am I going to have to send out a search party?

I'm on my way to practice, listening to an audiobook Porter suggested about work/life balance to get my mind off things. My phone dings with a notification, and I almost crash the truck, checking if it's her.

CHARLOTTE

Sorry, been busy. You free tonight?

At a red light, I type out a resounding:

ME

Yes

Rubbing a towel against my head, I walk towards the kitchen for water. Practice today had me so dehydrated I threw up—twice. The Florida sun is *brutal* in July. Not to mention it's been impossible to focus since Charlotte's avoiding me.

Maybe she's still upset about how distant I was after starting the Barracudas' pre-training camp? This is my first time playing football while being in a relationship, which I'm hoping this is, and I definitely need to learn how to balance that. The last thing I want is her feeling second-best.

The ring of the doorbell has me tossing the towel on the kitchen chair and rushing towards it.

I throw it open, my body immediately relaxing at the sight of her.

"Hi," Charlotte says, her weak, defeated expression reigniting my anxieties.

"Hi," I say, hand gripping the door.

"May I?" She gestures inside, and I snap back to reality.

"Yeah, please." The conversation is formal. Awkward. And I hate it. "Why didn't you use your key?"

She wrings her hands together. "I forgot it."

Is she dumping me?

Can you even be dumped if you aren't actually dating?

"You thirsty?" I ask, and she follows me towards the kitchen as I try to shove down the anxiety threatening to overwhelm me.

"Sure," she says, setting down her purse on the kitchen counter. "Noah, I—"

"How was your—" We chuckle awkwardly. "Sorry, you first."

I grab two water bottles out of the fridge, hand her one, and turn the cap of the other.

"We need to talk," she says, and I stop mid-twist.

"That sounds serious," I say, and she bites her cheek, all the color draining from her face. "Char?"

I set the water bottle on the counter, heart rate skyrocketing.

"I'm not sure how to start," she says, hopping up on the countertop, and I walk over, standing directly before her.

"Just start."

"Okay." Her eyes dart around the room, landing on everything but me. "Here it goes." She swallows hard, and I'm certain I'll stop breathing if she doesn't spit it out soon. "Noah..." Her caramel eyes meet mine. "I wasn't sure how I was going to tell you this. Or what it all means, or what to do—"

"You know you can tell me anything," I say, brushing her hair behind her ear.

"Noah." She releases a deep breath. "I'm pregnant."

27

NOAH

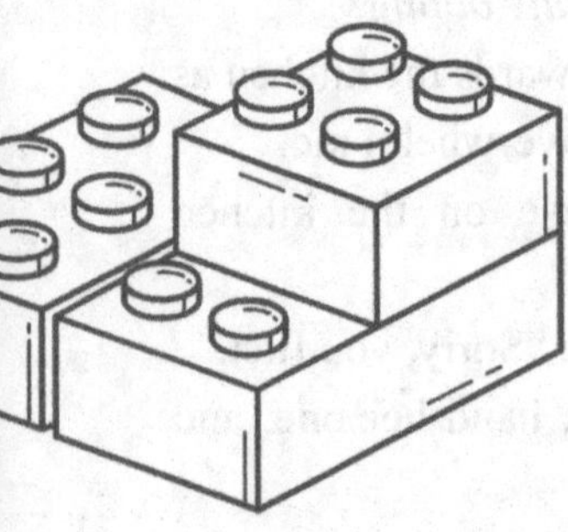

"You're pregnant?" My heart is in my throat, hand resting on Charlotte's cheek.

Her hesitant eyes bore into my soul, and she nods. "I am."

"But we—"

"Used the very ineffective pull-out method because we were stupid and horny? Yeah."

We were so reckless.

I haven't even figured out how to be a boyfriend and play football. How am I going to be a dad and put in the work to succeed as a pro player? I thought it would be years before I had the chance. Definitely after I settled into the NFL.

"You don't…" She trails off. "You don't have to…" She clears her throat, eyes dropping to her hands as she picks at her fingernails. "I mean, if you don't want to, you don't."

My hand falls to hers. "What?"

"You don't have to be involved," she murmurs, and my chest tightens.

She thinks I'm going to abandon her in this?

Sure, I may be having the biggest inner freak-out of my life, but I can save that for later.

"Charlotte." I take her face in my hands, and her gaze meets mine. "I'm not going anywhere."

She gnaws on her lower lip. "But what about your five-year plan?"

"We already agreed to fucking it up months ago. Remember?"

"The clink of plastic spoons and a forced *fake* relationship shouldn't ruin your life."

My muscles tighten, every nerve ending in my body igniting. "*Fake*?" I grit out, and her eyes widen briefly. "That's bullshit, and you know it."

"W-what do you mean?"

"You're *pregnant* with *my baby*, and you're going to look me in the eyes and tell me you still believe we're faking it?" I place my hands on her thighs, and she sucks in a breath as I slide them up to rest on her waist under the hem of her T-shirt. "Does this feel fake to you?" I tug her against me.

"Noah." She gasps, her center pressed to my stomach. "What are you doing?"

Cupping the back of her neck, I brush my mouth over hers. "I said, does this feel *fake* to you, *soffione*?"

"I'm gonna need you to be more specific," she rasps.

"Have the past few months not felt real? Falling asleep tangled in one another? Our dates? Late nights FaceTiming?"

"Yes, but—"

"How about the things I've shared with you that I haven't told anyone else? Ever." Memories of how absolutely understanding she was flood my mind. "Does it feel fake when I hold you like this?" My grip on her hips tightens. "Does it feel like I'm faking it?" She shakes her head again. "How about when I make you moan my name until you collapse in my arms? Does *that* feel fake?" Another head shake. "Say it out loud."

"No."

"No, what?"

She sucks in a breath. "It doesn't feel fake."

"Because it's not. You and I are the real deal, and I can't pretend any longer. Especially not when you are walking around growing *our* child." I bring my lips to her ear. "I'm a strong man, but hell, Charlotte, I'm not that strong."

"Are you sure you want me?" She places a hand on her stomach. "Want us?"

I pause millimeters from her ear, releasing a low, breathy chuckle. "Charlotte, I've told you so many times. *Mi fai impazzire.*"

She goes rigid. "You're happy we're friends?" The false translation I told her.

I drop my head in the crook of her neck. "It means you drive me crazy," I mumble against her skin.

"Well, that's wonderful," she mutters.

"*Soffione.*" I pull away, looking into her shocked eyes. "I'm crazy *for* you. I thought about tasting every inch of your skin for months before we started things. *Months.* I'm not *just* attracted to you." I hook a strand of hair behind her ear, rubbing her cheek with the pad of my thumb. "I'm *weak* for you. I *crave* you. I think about you from the moment I wake up to the second I fall asleep."

She studies me. "You do?"

"Of course I do."

"I appreciate that… But just because your feelings for me are real, doesn't mean *this*"—she places a hand on her stomach—"has to be real to you."

"It's real for you, isn't it?" I ask, and she nods. "Which means it's real for me too." Her eyes swim with uncertainty, and I tap my forehead to hers. "I'm right here. And I'm *always* going to be here. For you *and* our baby." Placing my palm over her stomach, I remind myself that as much as I want to be a father, I also can't force this decision for her. "Or whatever you decide to do, I support you."

Her brows furrow as she rests her hand on mine. "What do you mean?"

I clear my throat. "Your body, your choice."

She looks down at her stomach. "I'm keeping the baby, Noah."

"*We* are keeping the baby." Taking her chin between my fingers, I tip her gaze to meet mine. "No more 'I.' It's you and me. For real this time."

Her lips quirk with a smile. "Okay, then what comes next? I don't think you covered this in the syllabus."

"Move in with me," I say, placing my hand back on her stomach.

She huffs a laugh. "That's not necessary."

"You already have a key," I say, knowing damn well I gave her one hoping she'd make it her second home. "And I'm pretty sure there's no room for a nursery in your apartment."

She tilts her head back and forth. "I don't know."

"If you don't, I'll be worried about you *all* the time. Wondering how you're feeling or how baby is." I worry enough as it is. Add our baby in the mix, and I'll be an anxious fucking mess.

"Phones do exist," she says, but her tone is teasing.

"*Please* move in with me?"

"I don't want to intrude." *Is that her concern?*

"Let me ask a better question. And, for a moment, I need you to expel any worries that you're intruding or not welcome or whatever that pretty little head of yours is thinking." She fights a smile, her eyes meeting mine. "Would it make you happy to live here?"

"Yes," she says without hesitation.

"Then welcome to Casa Caruso."

Charlotte rolls a suitcase up the driveway, and I trail behind her, a heavy box in my arms. It took her a few days to pack, but we retrieved her things today, and she's finally, officially, moving in.

I've been fighting to suppress my inner anxieties, my hyperfixation on ensuring our home is a safe space, not a house of horrors like my childhood was.

Right now, my job is to support her, and there's no time to let my toxic past get in the way. No time to curse myself for being so stupid. For knowing better than to keep hooking up without some kind of safe sex talk.

But as we get to the front door and she stands up the suitcase to dig in her purse, I'm reminded of why she's here. Filled with pride knowing even though this was definitely not in the five-year plan, this woman is growing my baby. Our baby.

She retrieves the key, her *cornicello* pendant dangling off it. I hope it protects her and baby when I'm away. The thought of leaving them puts a pit in my stomach, but it's part of the job. *And I love my job.* After pushing the door open, she grabs the suitcase, rolling it inside.

In the foyer, she pauses, looking from my room toward the other side of the house.

"What's wrong?" I ask, setting the box on the floor by the front door and shutting it.

"I can keep my stuff in the guest room?" she suggests. *This woman.*

Walking over, I take the suitcase handle in my hand with a wide grin and pull it to my bedroom. *Our* bedroom.

"Wait!" she calls after me. "I don't want to take up all your space."

I hoist it onto the mattress so she doesn't have to bend down when unpacking.

"Noah." She puts an arm on mine, tugging me away from the luggage.

"You are sleeping in my—our—bed," I tell her. "Your things will be in *our* room." I point to the empty dresser I cleared for her. "That's yours. But if you need more room, you can have mine too." I take her face in my hands, and her gaze meets mine. "I *want* you taking up every inch of my space." Bending down, I kiss her softly on the mouth, then push up her shirt, splaying my fingers over her stomach. "Both of you."

"I don't want you to feel trapped."

"Charlotte. I have spent so much time in my life feeling like I don't have a choice." I brush my fingers against her belly. "But this? I want this." *Even if I'm freaking out, I can't deny how much I want this.* I tap my forehead to hers. "And I want *you*." *So. Damn. Much.* She smiles, and I nuzzle her nose. "So please stop fighting me and unpack your things in *our* room, yeah?"

She nods.

"I'll bring the rest of your stuff in, but let me show you a few things first," I say, walking toward my nightstand.

"Okay."

She may not like this, but it's important. "Remember how I told you Mom and I got our concealed weapons permits?"

"Yes?" she says, tone curious.

Sliding open the drawer, I grab the pistol I keep there. "This is for emergencies," I say, showing it to her, and her eyes widen. In case the *cornicello* doesn't do its job. "Do you know how to use one?"

She nods. "My parents made me take a self-defense class in high school, and gun knowledge was one of the lessons."

"Good."

After ensuring the safety is on, I return it to the drawer, making a mental note to buy a safe before the baby comes. My phone rings, and I tug it out. *Mamma* is displayed on the screen, and I blow out a shaky breath, shoving it back in my pocket. *I'm not ready.*

I head to the bathroom, and Charlotte follows me. "You can take whatever drawer, vanity, cabinet you want."

"Noah."

"Charlotte." I pin her with a look. "This is *our* home. I could not care less if you allot me a single drawer."

"How much stuff do you think I have?" she asks with a laugh.

"I'm just trying to make a point," I tell her and point to the tub. "I bought you some salt and bubble stuff. You'll have to keep the water warm instead of scalding because of the baby, obviously, but it can help if you get any back pain."

"Noah Caruso, have you been doing *Daddy* research?" she asks, grabbing my arm and pulling me to her, looping her hands around my waist.

"Gotta make sure *Mommy's* taken care of too," I tell her. She reaches up and rests a hand against my face.

"I adore you." She presses her soft lips to mine, and a warm feeling spreads across my chest. "Now show me the rest of *our* house."

28
NOAH

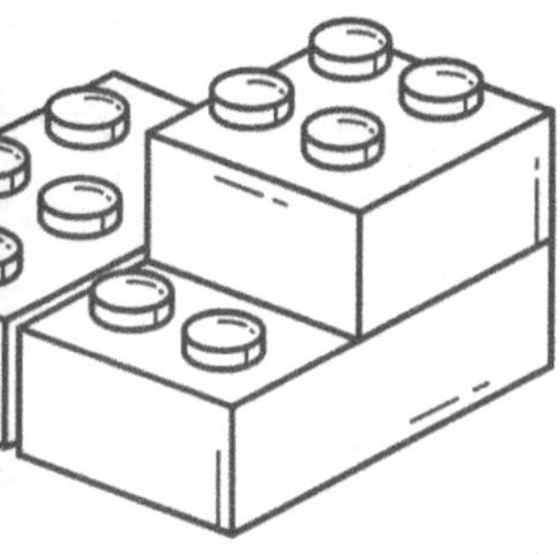

BIG STING ENERGY

THEO SCHRODER

I can't believe we lost our Founding Father to fatherhood

JULIAN LISCERO

Who are you talking about??

DESMOND BALL

Definitely not me

ELIJAH ANDERSON

Really Theo? In the group chat?

JULIAN LISCERO

oh my god, the honey bee has pollinated the sunflower??

THIS IS NOT A DRILL

ELIJAH ANDERSON

Relax. My sunflower has not been pollinated (yet) gimme a few years damn

THEO SCHRODER

The sooner we talk about it the sooner he
doesn't have to deal with it alone

JULIAN LISCERO

WHO IS 'HE'

DESMOND BALL

I'm trying to do my morning savasana and you
guys are stressing me the fuck out

JULIAN LISCERO

Yeah, you interrupted my morning wank

wtf is going on

ME

Thanks, Theo

Guess the news is out.

You guys won't be the only ones calling me
Daddy

DESMOND BALL

WTF CALL ME IMMEDIATELY

JULIAN LISCERO

Who's the baby mama??

THEO SCHROEDER

Charlie OBVIOUSLY

JULIAN LISCERO

if you were gonna give up your no pussy rule
you could've at least wrapped your dick bro

THEO SCHROEDER

Guess you switched bros and beers for babies
and bottles now

ME

This is all really helpful. Thank you.

THEO SCHROEDER

We're messing with you. You know we're here
for you.

DESMOND BALL

Anything you need.

JULIAN LISCERO

What they said (unless it's diapers. I don't do
those.)

ELIJAH ANDERSON

Nah man. ANYTHING you need. Or Charlie.
Call us.

ME

Thanks guys. Headed to training but we'll catch
up later

Today's practice was brutal.

Fortunately, it had nothing to do with my skills, but two of my linemen were dragging and I got blitzed five times.

Wincing, I readjust my grip on the steering wheel, and my eyes snag on a road sign up ahead. The same road sign I pass every day to and from work, yet lately I've been pretending it doesn't exist.

Hibiscus Pines.

3 Miles.

Blowing out a breath, I ignore the reminder of my proximity to Mom's neighborhood. It's been a week since I found out about the baby, and I've avoided her calls since. How can I pretend everything is normal when my entire life changed with two words?

Mom reads me too well.

She'd know something is up.

There's no way I can hide the absolute inner panic I feel. I already have to do that around Charlotte so she doesn't get spooked and bolt under some ridiculous act of self-sacrifice, thinking it's what's best for me.

Turn arrows appear in the empty lane to my right, and my skin crawls with awareness.

"Screw it." I swerve and take the exit.

Ten minutes later I pull in the driveway, my veins buzzing, and park beside Mom's car. Tony must be working since his truck isn't here. That's fine. She'll tell him later.

Hopping out of the truck, I force myself toward the house before I lose my nerve.

As I walk by the garage door, my eyes snag on the dented bottom corner, the damage courtesy of my father throwing me against it after I broke the side mirror of his car with a football when I was twelve.

My fingers go to my scalp by reflex, tracing the eight stitches hidden by hair. Even if they aren't visible, I still know they're there.

At the front door, I let myself in because though I've been gone for years, this is still home. Scars and all.

"Hello?" Mom calls from the kitchen, her face lighting up when I turn the corner. "Oh, *sole mio*!" She rushes over, throwing her arms around me, placing a kiss on each cheek, then pulls back, brow furrowed. "*Perché non mi hai richiamata?*" She takes my face in her hands, moving it in all directions. "*Sei malato?*"[1]

I chuckle nervously, swatting her away. "*No, non sono malato.*"[2]

"*Allora perché non mi hai richiamata? Mi richiami sempre. Ero preoccupata.*"[3]

"*Mamma, sto bene.*"[4]

---

1. IT: *Perché non mi hai richiamata? Sei malato?* - EN: Why didn't you call me back? Are you sick?

2. IT: *No, non sono malato.* - EN: No, I'm not sick.

3. IT: *Allora perché non mi hai richiamata? Mi richiami sempre. Ero preoccupata.* - EN: Then why didn't you call me back? You always call me back. I was worried.

4. IT: *Mamma, sto bene.* - EN: Mamma, I'm fine.

"You're lying," she says, swapping to English and squinting at me. "Come." She walks towards the kitchen island and grabs the floral Lego set I bought her for Mother's Day on the way.

"You haven't built it yet?" I ask.

"I was waiting so we could do it together," she says with a soft smile, and guilt racks me that I didn't make time for it sooner.

We sit side by side, and she rips the little plastic bags, dumping small pieces on the counter. After a few minutes, all the parts are organized by color and shape.

"So," she says. "Want to tell me why my son is ignoring my calls and looks like he hasn't slept in a month?"

I bite my lip, placing two green Lego pieces of the stem together. "I don't really know where to start."

The front door opens and Tony walks in, briefcase in hand.

"Hey!" he says, a big smile on his face when he sees me.

"Hi," I reply.

"Are you okay?" he asks, setting his briefcase on the counter. "You look sick."

"See?" Mom says, waving a hand at me.

I blow out a breath. "Want to join us?" I ask Tony.

Mom's going to end up telling him anyways, and I can honestly use all the moral support I can get right now.

We spend a few minutes in silence, clicking pieces together. The floral arrangement is almost done. I suppose it's a lot quicker when you build as a team.

"Charlotte's pregnant," I blurt, unable to keep it in any longer.

"*Oh, sole mio,*" Mom says, her pieces clinking against the counter, and she turns to face me, her eyes welling with moisture. She pulls me into her arms, squeezing me tight. The dam breaks, and my own tears flow. All the anxiety, confusion, and frustration pours out of me. Here I don't have to be strong. I can just… feel. My chest heaves, and she rubs small circles on my back. A few minutes pass, and I compose myself, pulling away. "Is she keeping it?" I nod. "And how are *you* feeling?"

My eyes meet hers. "Scared."

"Of?"

I lean back against the seat between them, releasing a sigh. "How can I balance it all?"

"What do you mean?" Mom asks, and I look to her.

"You know how I am during season. I'm obsessive. And I can't risk this job. I've worked my whole life for it." My stomach sinks. "God, I sound like a self-centered asshole." Pushing the chair back with a screech, I stand and pace the room. "Charlotte's growing our child, and I'm sitting here worried about football."

"You've worked hard for your career," Mom says. "It's okay to think about it."

"But shouldn't I be focusing on Charlotte?" I say, exasperated. "Be worried about her and her well-being over a stupid football game?"

"The *football* is your job," she reminds me. "It will bring in the money to pay…" With a soft voice she adds, *"Per il tuo bambino."*[5]

"And it's okay to still think about yourself," Tony says. "To be worried about what it all means."

"But I can't." I drag my hands through my hair, taking quick breaths. "I don't know what will happen. I don't know how this will play out." My head spins. "What if she needs me and I'm gone at an away game or something? What if—" I gasp for air. "I don't—maybe she—"

"Noah *Gabriel*," Mom commands, her hand on my back. I've stopped in the middle of the room, gripping my knees. *"Inspira… due… tre… espira… due… tre…"*[6]

We continue for a few minutes until my breathing has returned

---

5. IT: *Per il tuo bambino.* - EN: For your baby.
6. IT: *Inspira… due… tre… espira… due… tre…* - EN: Inhale…two…three… exhale…two…three…

to normal. She takes my face in her hands. "*É normale avere paura*," she says, eyes holding mine.

It's okay to be afraid.

I blink at her, face damp with tears. "I can't control this."

Her eyes are soft. "I know."

"What if I'm like *him*?"

She wipes a tear off my cheek. "You will never, *ever* be like your father."

"But what—"

"He's a terrible man," she interrupts. "Full of darkness and hate. But you, *sole mio?*" She places a hand on my cheek. "My *sun*. You are light. To everyone around you. You are light."

"*Grazie, mamma*,"[7] I whisper and clear my throat.

"Now can I be excited?" she asks, a smile spreading across her face as a tear drips down her cheek. "*Diventerò nonna!*"[8]

I push down the anxiety. "You're excited?"

"Of course?" she says, brows pulled together.

My eyes bounce between her and Tony, whose expression is unreadable. "You don't think I'm an idiot? That I ruined my life?"

She takes my hands in hers and squeezes. "Do you think you're ruining your life?" I shake my head. "And you want this baby, no?"

"Of course," I say without hesitation.

"Then do you expect us to do anything besides support you completely?" Mom asks, placing a hand on my face.

I shift on my heels. "No."

"Good," she says, tapping my cheek and pulling away. "How is Ms. Charlotte doing?"

"She's okay," I say, thinking of her current manic obsession of reading every parenting book ever written. "I'm hoping she'll feel more relaxed after the first appointment."

---

7. IT: *Grazie, mamma.* - EN: Thank you, Mamma.

8. IT: *Diventerò nonna!* - EN: I'm going to be a grandma!

"Well, we're here for you," Mom says, rubbing my back. "Both of you."

"*Grazie, mamma.*"

"*Ma figurati, sole mio.*"[9]

Unlocking the front door, I'm greeted by the overwhelming scent of citrus and sounds of banging and clanking. As I close it behind me, a smile spreads across my face.

"Hey, *soffione,*" I say, walking toward the kitchen to the sight of Charlotte over the stove. Bare feet, hair clipped back with a bow, and cute little sundress on. A plate of homemade cannoli resides on the kitchen island, and my mouth waters. A soft feeling warms my chest. *I could get used to this.* "Elijah and Sophia on the way yet?"

She looks up, smiling wide as she stirs something in a pot. "They'll be here in twenty."

Charlotte suggested we invite them over for dinner, and I wasn't going to say no to the moral support. At first I was pissed Theo bombed the news in the group chat, but I'm honestly glad everything's out in the open.

She looks at me, lips puckered, and I hurry to her, planting a firm kiss. *I could definitely get used to this.* "Smells incredible in here," I say, turning back to the stove, noting a cream sauce in a large pan. A massive bag of lemons sits beside her, yellow wedges scattered on a cutting board.

"Thanks." She beams, grabbing a tiny spoon. "I hope you'll like it."

She dips it in the sauce and blows on it before presenting it to

---

9. IT: *Ma figurati, sole mio.* - EN: You're welcome, my sun.

me. Grinning, I open my mouth and lick the spoon clean. My taste buds dance with enjoyment, and I groan in approval. "Delicious."

"Thank you." She sets down the spoon and turns on another burner with a pot of water atop it. "And I have a surprise for you."

"Really?"

"Mhm." She walks to the drying rack, dishes clinking as she retrieves something, and she turns to me, hiding it behind her back. "I still feel *so* awful about destroying your favorite cup," she says, and my heart twists.

"It was a nice memory. But it was *just* a cup."

"A very cute cup," she pouts, and I fight the urge to tug her to my chest as she continues her surprise. She brings her arms around, handing me a blue mug inscribed with #1 Dad.

My eyes well with tears. *Fuck.*

Bringing a hand to my face, I rub my fingers against my eyes.

"You don't like it?" she asks hesitantly.

Removing my hand, I look down at her, setting the cup on the counter. Finally, I give into the urge and tug her to me. I blink a few times to clear the moisture and take a deep breath. "It's perfect. Thank you so much."

"It's not hand-painted lemons," she says, nuzzling her head to me. "But I thought you'd like this one."

Pulling away, I take her face in my hands and tilt her gaze to mine. "I *love* it."

Charlotte kisses me softly and steps away, returning to the stove. She removes spaghetti from a package, and I lean against the counter, admiring her in *our* kitchen. Collecting the noodles together, she—*Italia, perdonala.*

Italy, forgive her.

The air is frozen in my lungs at the sight of the broken pasta in her hands.

"What's wrong with you?" she asks, my jaw hanging open as she places the evidence in the water.

"You did *not* break spaghetti." I balk.

"It's too big for the pot," she says, brows furrowed.

I grab a tea towel, twisting it, and gently flick it towards her. "Out of the kitchen."

"What are you doing?" She giggles, backing away.

"*Soffione*," I say, with a teasing grin. "You cannot break pasta in an Italian household. Or *any* household. It is against the law!"

"Uh-oh," she says, moonwalking backwards away from me. "Am I going to have to relocate my Justin Bieber piggy bank again?"

I chase after, scooping her in my arms, and she hugs my neck. Squeezing tightly, I press a kiss into her hair. "Or you could pay in other ways."

She giggles, nudging me off, and sways back to the stove. "The sauce is going to burn."

We haven't been physical since the twins' party, and I don't want to pressure her. But it definitely sucks when all I want is to hold her in my arms and she pushes me away.

"I'm serious, Charlotte," I tease. "That was your first and only warning."

"Oops." She pouts. "Wouldn't want you to have a reason to whip me with the tea towel again."

Why are women so confusing?

"So how was your day?" I ask, changing the subject.

"Good, yours?" she says, picking up some plain salt and aiming for the boiling pasta. I cringe, quickly plucking it out of her hand, and give her the sea salt. She narrows her eyes, turning to crank it over the pot.

"Actually, I stopped by my mom's," I say, and her gaze snaps to mine. "Told her about the baby."

"Was she furious?"

"No." I shake my head, grin breaking free as tension leaves my body. "She was excited. Supportive."

"Really?" Her brows pull together.

"Yep."

"That's great," she says softly.

"Have you thought about telling yours?" I ask as she sets down the salt, picking up a spoon to stir the sauce.

"I'm waiting till I'm further along, just in case."

"In case what?"

She tilts her head. "Well, there's no reason to get them up in a tizzy if there's no heartbeat."

My own heart stops. That possibility didn't even cross my mind.

"When will we know?" I ask, panic rushing through me.

"I was able to make an appointment for the last week of July. They said it's best if I'm eight weeks or later, so we have to wait."

"Let me know when so I can make sure I'm there."

"Really?" Her dark brows draw together. "You don't have to come."

"You think I'm letting you go alone?" I ask. *Not a chance.*

She shrugs. "I don't want you getting in trouble for missing practice. I can ask one of the girls."

The thought of her needing to rely on rides from friends throughout the duration of her pregnancy puts a pit in my stomach. *What if she needs something and I'm not around?*

I place my hand on her lower back. "Like I said before, we're doing this together, okay? It's *our* baby, and I *want* to be there with you."

She blushes. "Okay."

The motion sensor for the front door cam chimes, and a few seconds later, it swings open, Elijah and Sophia letting themselves inside. I sincerely love having a place that feels like home to everyone. My eyes wander back to Charlotte. I hope it feels that way for her too.

"Hey, Mom and Dad," Sophia says, pulling my attention to her, a photo frame settled in her arms.

"Thanks for inviting us to dinner," Elijah says, trailing behind.

"Sorry Theo spilled the beans," Elijah says to me. "He overheard me and Soph talking."

"It's okay," I say and mean it.

"We're here for y'all," Elijah says, looking between us. "Seriously."

"We also brought a little congratulatory gift," Sophia adds, setting the frame on the counter and spinning it to face us. A hand-sketched drawing of two koalas holding a baby koala is perfectly centered in the frame. Charlotte's face brightens, and she hugs Sophia tight. "It's beautiful, Soph."

"Thank you," I say, a grateful smile on my face. "It'll look perfect in Gabriella's room."

"Gabriella?" Sophia repeats. "You already picked a name?"

"No," Charlotte says, staring me down. "We most certainly did not."

"Okay, but you have to admit it's a cute name," I say to Charlotte, tugging her to me.

"Fine." Charlotte playfully rolls her eyes. "I suppose it wouldn't be terrible to have her named after her father. Noah *Gabriel.*" She stands on her tiptoes, pressing a soft kiss to my lips, and everything just feels right.

"Smells good in here," Elijah says, glancing around the kitchen.

"Thanks." Charlotte grins proudly as a timer goes off. She heads to the oven, pulls out a tray, and turns around with a pan of —shit. It's salmon. The vilest fish to exist. Eating it should be a crime.

The mother of your child worked hard on this meal. Don't be a dick.

She sets it on a potholder on the counter, and I put my hand on her back. "Looks great, baby."

"What are you eating?" Elijah asks me, and I shoot him a glare. He's well-aware of my hatred for the fish. The guys were banned from cooking it in the Baller Pad.

"The salmon, obviously," Charlotte says, eyes bouncing between us. "It was on his meal plan."

I glance to the fridge where it's pinned with a magnet. Guess I should've blacked out the ones I didn't like. "Yeah, I'm loo—"

"Noah hates salmon," Elijah cuts me off.

"Anderson," I snap in full captain tone, and his eyes widen.

Charlotte's confused gaze connects with mine. "You do?" My mouth opens and closes. Say something, Caruso. Anything.

"Oh my god, you hate it!" She throws her head back, groaning. "Noah, I'm the mother of your child, for god's sake! I should know if you hate something as basic as salmon."

"Really, it's fine," I say.

Elijah's eyes connect with mine in a silent apology, and I flick him off.

"What else don't you like?" Charlotte folds her arms across her chest.

"Just salmon."

"Noah Gabriel," she says my name like a curse. *Why am I so turned on right now?*

"He *hates* Chef Boyardee," Elijah says, smirking like a smug bastard. *Asshole.*

Charlotte's mouth falls open. "You let me buy ten cans for when my siblings visit."

"You were so excited they had the kind Denny likes," I say with a sheepish smile. *Although I was planning to make it for the kids from scratch.*

"Ugh," she groans. "I'm trying not to have my feelings hurt that your *boyfriend* knows you better than I do." She scowls at Elijah, who laughs and helps himself to water from the fridge.

I throw my arm around her shoulders. "Don't worry. We've got all the time in the world."

29

CHARLOTTE

My fingers ache from an afternoon of rapid-fire googling.

What size is a baby at 7 weeks?

When do you feel the first kicks?

What is a suggested diet when pregnant?

What are pregnancy symptoms?

Is sex safe when pregnant?

Is it normal not to have pregnancy symptoms?

Noah Caruso Barracudas Quarterback.

Okay, the last one was more out of sheer curiosity of how famous my best friend turned fake boyfriend turned baby daddy is, all things considered.

Answer: Super Mega Fucking Famous.

There were pages and pages and pages of articles on "Noah Caruso: Tampa Bay's Newest Shining Star," "Heisman Winner Paving His Path in Tampa," and my personal least favorite, "Noah Caruso: Tampa Bay's Most Eligible Bachelor."

Like, excuse me, bitches, he is not eligible. Did the photos of us on his Instagram not award our relationship the respect of "off the market"? Not to mention the fact this man's baby resides in my womb. Although that's not public knowledge for obvious reasons…

Actually, Noah may not want anyone to know. The headlines "Heisman Winner Got Horny: Baby On The Way" or "NFL Quarterback and Daddy at 23: What Will This Mean For His Career?" ring in my head, and suddenly I'm glad I'm way further off their radar than I originally hoped.

Groaning, I throw my head against the back of the couch. *Stop torturing yourself.* Tossing the phone on the cushion, I get up to grab a drink. According to my thorough research, pregnant women need to drink water. Lots and lots of water. Like, almost *one hundred* ounces per day. And people wonder why we have to pee so much.

After hydrating and a quick bathroom break, I settle back into the couch, tugging a soft cozy blanket over my legs. I pull my shirt up and stare at my stomach, poking it with a finger. *Maybe it's a little firmer than usual?* Although I exercise pretty regularly, so I'm used to having a harder stomach.

I tap on it. "How you doing in there, little blueberry?" I pause, as if actually waiting for a reply, then have vivid *Finding Nemo* flashbacks. "Oh, shit. I probably shouldn't tap on your fish bowl, baby." I rub soft circles around it. "Mommy's sorry."

The word feels foreign, but that's what I am now. A mom. And I knew it from the second the first test turned positive on the bathroom counter. And especially after the second, third, and fourth.

The motion-censored doorbell sounds, alerting me someone pulled into the driveway, and yanks me out of my pity fest. I jump off the couch and pad over to the window, attempting to hide myself as Noah's not home.

We need a dog.

A gorgeous powder-blue, four door Bronco Heritage is in the driveway, and I wait for the person to leave, but instead, my brows draw together at the sight of Noah stepping out of the SUV.

"What the…" I say to myself, rushing outside.

He smiles wide. "Hey, *soffione*."

"Don't you 'hey, soffi-whatever' me. What is this?" I walk around the brand-new Bronco that has a Tampa Barracudas sticker on the back windshield directly next to another that says Baby On Board. "Did you trade your truck in?"

"Nah," he says casually. "I'll pick it up later. This is yours."

My mouth falls to the floor. No, scratch that. It falls to the center of the actual earth because what in the ever flabbergasting fuck is he talking about?

"Noah, you can't buy me a car."

"It's not a car. It's an SUV."

"Okay," I say, narrowing my eyes at him. "Then you can't buy me an SUV."

"Fine, then I bought a second vehicle, and I'm letting my girl use it."

I sigh heavily, staring at his grinning face. It's so hard to stand firm when he looks at me like this. Like all the answers to the universe reside behind my eyes.

"Why?" I ask.

He takes a few long strides, quickly eating up the space between us. "We're gonna need something to drive the kids around in, Charlotte."

"*Kids*?"

"Sorry." He beams, cheeks flushed. "Kid."

"Are you already planning our football team?" I ask, my own smile widening.

"Semantics," he says, waving a hand, brushing off the subject. "Can't we use your truck?"

He blows out a frustrated breath. "I need it to get to and from the stadium. How did you plan to get to school or appointments?"

I gnaw on my cheek. "I don't know, the bus?"

"As if I'm going to let you rely on the bus. We live in Florida, not a big city. In case you forgot, public transportation isn't exactly in abundance here. You *need* a vehicle."

"Even *if* so, it didn't have to be brand freaking new."

"It's safe, kid friendly, and you'll look sexy in the driver's seat." Noah grins, and I roll my eyes, stomach flipping.

My gaze trails the beautiful blue paint, and I sigh. I'm trying to hold my ground, but damn is it pretty.

"Noah, this is too much," I say, guilt settling in my chest. This particular problem is one I could solve if I put my passions aside. "Maybe I should change my major back to pre-law and my parents will give me my old car back."

"Hell no," he says. "No way. You are meant to be a teacher. And the paperwork has already been finalized for the Bronco. No returns, no refunds, Charlotte."

"You've already done so much for me." I place a hand on my stomach. "For us."

"And I'm gonna keep doing it," he says, smiling wide. "We're family."

Family.

My heart soars to the moon.

Never when we started this did I think it would end with Noah Caruso calling me his family.

I love the sound of that.

The paper crinkles beneath me as I shift in place. Any attempt to steady my breathing only makes me hyperventilate more. The thin sheet over my legs does nothing to alleviate the chill from the room's cool temperature, and I shiver. Noah sits beside me, his warm hand on mine, giving me a soft smile.

"Whatever happens," Noah murmurs, placing a soft kiss on my knuckles, "I've got you."

Nodding, I squeeze his hand tight.

"How have you been feeling?" Doctor Rigou asks, grabbing latex gloves and pulling them on with a slap.

"Besides a little weight gain, I haven't had any symptoms at all. Is that bad?" I ask, panic setting in. Of all the things I read during my Google extravaganza, the lack of symptoms is what has me most concerned. "Could that mean something is wrong with the baby?"

"Not necessarily. All women experience pregnancy differently. My best friend was five months pregnant before she realized it."

"And there were really no signs?"

"Besides her hangovers being worse than usual, no." Her round rolling stool squeals as she slides towards the monitor.

"Probably because there were two people drunk instead of one," I say, huffing a laugh, and the expression on Doctor Rigou's face tells me it wasn't a funny joke. Noah and I share a look, and he fights a smile, telling me it was, in fact, a good joke. I clear my throat. "But surely there would've been *some* signs," I argue, hoping for clarity.

"Cryptic pregnancy is more common than you'd think," she says.

"Cryptic pregnancy?"

"Yes," Doctor Rigou says, grabbing a large wand-looking thing. "Some people have really minimized symptoms, and some have none at all."

"Weird," I say, glancing at Noah, who gives me a tense smile.

When I look back at the doctor, she's holding a large lightsaber in her hand. "Could you please bend your knees and spread your legs apart?" *Excuse me, what?*

"I thought this was a stomach ultrasound?" I ask, clenching my thighs together.

"Before twelve weeks we do a transvaginal ultrasound, as it's the most accurate."

"Okay." I gulp.

"You may feel a slight pressure, but this shouldn't hurt,"

Doctor Rigou assures me, rolling a condom onto the vagina wand and squirting a gel-like substance all over it, which relieves me a bit that it will slide right in.

Although sliding it in is what got us into this mess in the first place.

I take a deep breath and tug up the sheet, spreading my legs.

Pull yourself together.

Doctor Rigou slides the wand in, and as she mentioned, I do feel a slight pressure, but it doesn't hurt. She angles the monitor so Noah and I can watch as she probes me like an alien. Noah takes my hand again, giving me a light squeeze.

A little sack comes on the screen, and I gasp. "Is that their tiny head?"

"Yep," Doctor Rigou says.

This is for real.

"Baby Caruso is pretty cute," Noah says to me, and we share a teary smile.

We're family.

"How can you tell?" I ask Noah teasingly. "I'm only eight weeks."

"I'm going to switch to an abdominal ultrasound," Doctor Rigou says, removing the big wand, and my vagina is grateful.

"Because it's ours," Noah says as I cover my legs with the sheet and push up my shirt, exposing my stomach. "It'll have your eyes and my great sense of humor."

"Oh god, this baby is in trouble," I say with a laugh as Doctor Rigou squirts the cool gel on my stomach, rubbing it around with the much smaller, much less invasive probe and pulling our attention back to the cute baby blob on the screen.

This is the best day of my life.

"So..." She taps around on a computer, her tone making me nervous. "You actually look to be around fifteen weeks."

Every single bit of oxygen leaves my lungs at once. My eyes

bounce from the screen to Doctor Rigou to Noah, then back to the screen.

"I'm sorry," Noah says, hand squeezing mine. "Did you say *fifteen* weeks?"

"Yes," she says, gliding the probe over my stomach. "I can even tell you the gender right now if you'd like?"

"Really?" I ask, my voice a whisper, glancing at Noah, whose face is white as a ghost, eyes glued to the screen.

"Yes," she says, gaze meeting mine. "Would you like that?"

I nod, body trembling. Has it gotten colder in here?

"See these three little lines?" She points a finger on the screen and smiles. "Congratulations. It's a girl."

Tears blur my vision, my brain running on overdrive while she finishes answering rapid-fire questions from Noah. About what? I have no clue. A printed ultrasound is placed in my hand as we leave the room.

Noah guides me to the parking lot and helps me in his truck, buckling me in without a word.

My eyes fall to my hands containing the first photo I'll ever have of my daughter.

The photo that confirms how real this all is.

My finger traces her little body. She's so perfect.

The gestation stamp pulls me back to reality.

15 weeks. 3 days.

Noah climbs in the truck, and our eyes connect. The agony behind his slices through me.

He doesn't deserve this.

Looks like we're not family after all.

30

NOAH

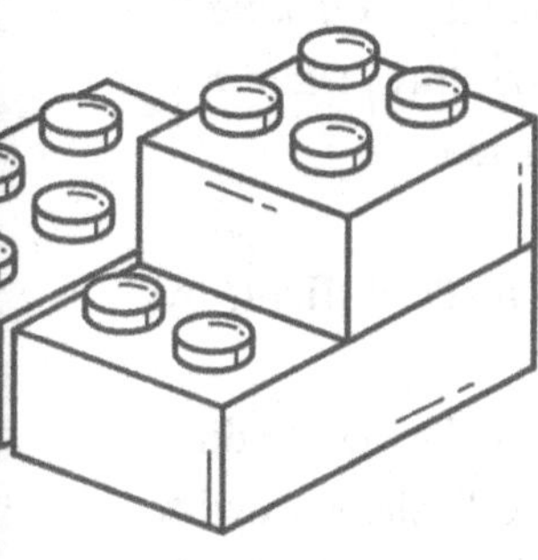

Fifteen weeks.

I don't need to be a mathematician or have a PhD in Gynecology to know Charlotte's not carrying my baby.

I don't need to wonder if she'll have my eyes or if she'll inherit the Caruso charm.

I don't need to worry if she'll be allergic to nuts like my father or have a sun sensitivity like Mom.

I don't need to bring my family history to every doctor's appointment.

And the worst part of all, I don't *get* to.

My eyes are fixed on the truck key in my hand, a Barracudas training bag heavy on my shoulder, reminding me where I *should* be. Coach Bexley gave me a late pass, and I'm already cutting it close, but how can I leave?

The rattling of tiny wheels draws my attention to Charlotte dragging her suitcase from the garage to our bedroom, and my body stiffens.

"What are you doing?"

"Packing," she says, disappearing into the bedroom.

"What?" I drop everything to the floor with a thump, chasing after her. She yanks open her dresser drawer and scoops clothes by the handful, then tosses them in the suitcase like she's trying to flee the country.

Is she?

"*What* are you doing?" I repeat, hoping for a clearer response.

"Like I said." She tosses a pair of shorts in the bag. "*Packing*."

"To go where?" My eyes bounce between the drawer and her suitcase as more items get haphazardly thrown inside.

"I don't know," she says, exasperated.

"Then *why* are you packing?" I ask, words made difficult by my full-blown inner fucking panic.

"Didn't you hear the doctor? I'm *fifteen* weeks. Ding ding ding! Congratulations, Noah, you are *not* the father!" she says with a sarcastic laugh, but her attempt at humor only rotates the knife deeper in my chest.

"Charlotte," I say, softly, blinking back tears so she can't see how affected I am by this. "Please, stop."

"Why?" She shrieks, throwing her arms in the air, a bra in each hand. "You should be relieved! Mr. Perfect still has his scot-free record, and you aren't gonna be a daddy at twenty-three! You can go focus on football and your career, and we are not your problem anymore." My chest aches, lungs constricting as she rushes off to the bathroom, clattering and banging away. Sure, I worry about my career, but I would have never wished for this.

Muffled rings from my phone by the door attempt to pull my attention, but I ignore it, following after her.

"Is that what you think I want?" I ask, entering to the sight of her throwing more shit in a small bag.

She stays silent and shrugs.

"You think I wanted this baby *not* to be mine?" I ask, heart bleeding, eyes stinging.

Stay strong, Noah.

Charlotte can't see how devastated you are.

"I mean…" She glances up, catching my gaze in the mirror. "Isn't it better this way?"

"For who?" I snap, tone harsher than intended. "For Jonathan? Is that where you're going? Straight to your *actual* baby daddy?"

"What?" She fumes. "No."

"Then *where* are you going?"

"I. Don't. Know!" she shouts, shoving more stuff in the bag. "Somewhere I'm not a burden."

"Char." My voice cracks. I reach for her, but she steps away. "You are *not* a burden here."

"How could I not be? It's not your baby, Noah!" She throws her hands in the air. "You can stop faking it now." She turns back to the vanity, and every item thrown in the bag jabs the wound more.

"You think I'm pretending?" My voice is calm, but inside there's a black hole looming, ready to swallow me alive.

She laughs, but there's no humor in it. "I think everything got real so fast, and the baby made you believe the feelings were real too. And it's fine, I understand. I really appreciated the fake boyfriend act." Her eyes meet mine. "But fake baby daddy? That's insanity."

Anger thrums through me. "Seriously?"

"I'm giving you an out," she says, exasperated. "Take it."

"An out?" I step towards her. "I don't want an out."

"Then what do you want?" she cries, spinning to face me, tears pouring down her face.

"I want you!" I plead, and her glistening eyes widen. "I want you. And I *want* this baby."

She analyzes me, stunned. "But why?"

"I told you I would be with you through all of this."

"When you thought the baby was yours," she points out.

"I still stand by my words."

"Because you're honorable."

"No," I say, shaking my head. Heart aching.

"Then why?"

"Because!" *Not like this*.

"Because why? Why would you possibly want me? This?" She sobs, tears streaming down her face. "Why would you agree to stay with me when I'm carrying someone else's baby?"

My phone rings for the hundredth time. *"Che stress, "*[1] I groan, shooting a death glare towards the noise. If I don't leave for practice right at this second, I might not only be benched but fired, and then where does that leave Charlotte and the baby? I have to provide for them. "Fuck," I say, dragging a hand down my face.

"What's wrong?"

"My coach gave me a late pass, but I can't—I don't—"

"Go," she says, with a weak smile.

"No. This is important."

"So is your job."

A year ago, I'd have already been at practice, saving the personal stuff for after the stadium lights went out. Funny how two words can change everything.

Even your priorities.

And yet...

"Please, don't leave," I beg. "We'll continue this when I'm home tonight, okay?" She stays silent. "Okay, *soffione*?" I press, my voice cracking.

She nods. "Okay."

I lean down, inhaling her, memorizing her, sending up a silent prayer for her, then press a light kiss on her cheek and drag myself out the front door. It clicks shut, the sound a bullet to my heart.

Then I get in my truck and cry.

---

1. IT: *Che stress*. EN: How stressful.

Did she leave?

Does she not want me involved?

Will she push me away?

Should I let her?

A few days ago, I was cursing myself, wondering how the hell I got in this situation. And now? I'd wish on every dandelion in the world it won't be ripped from my hands. *They* won't be ripped from my hands.

"Caruso!" The shout penetrates my self-pity wallow fest, and my head snaps up to discover Coach Bexley with defined wrinkles on his forehead, eyes blazing. "What the hell's going on out there?"

I blink the field into focus. The guys are staring at me, ball in my hand, and it all comes rushing back. The center hiked, offense started the play, and I froze—completely lost in my thoughts. Luckily, we were practicing a play with no defense, otherwise I would've been blitzed.

"It won't happen again!" I promise. *It can't happen again.*

I have to stay focused.

For Charlotte, and for the little baby girl growing inside of her. Even if it's not biologically mine.

"It better not. We don't pay you to daydream. If I wanted that, Knox would be out there!"

"Hey!" Knox says from the sidelines, and I crack a smile.

Inspira… due… tre… espira… due… tre.

"Down, set, hike!"

I'm ten houses from ours and already suffocating. Charlotte's Bronco is in the driveway, which is a good sign, but the house is dark. Too dark. When I'm not home, she keeps every damn light on. That drove me crazy when the guys did it, but it makes her feel safer, so I won't argue with that.

"Please be home, *soffione*," I mutter to myself, pulling in the driveway.

I barely have time to turn off the ignition before jumping out and running towards the house.

Releasing a shaky breath, I unlock the front door and head inside. "Charlotte?" I call out, dropping my duffle and flickering lights on as I walk through the house.

Silence.

"Charlotte?" I call out again, checking our bedroom. *Empty.* Bathroom. *Empty.* With each room I check, I grow more panicked. "Fuck!"

Pausing in the kitchen, I white-knuckle the counter in an attempt to steady my breathing, but it's no use. Every muscle in my body aches. Including my heart.

Snatching my keys from the counter, I make a beeline for the front door. Where could she be?

The Baller Pad?

Andi & Stella's?

Swallowing hard, I think of a third place I wouldn't even know how to check.

Jonathan's?

Settling back in the driver's seat of my truck, I pull out my phone. My last three messages to Charlotte are unread and unanswered. I attempt to call, but it goes straight to voicemail. Did she *block* me? *Oh, hell no.* My fingers hover over the keyboard. *I'm so going to regret this.* Unfortunately, desperation overtakes giving a damn.

BIG STING ENERGY

ME

Does anyone know where Charlotte is?

THEO SCHROEDER

You lost your baby mama already?

ELIJAH ANDERSON

I'm gonna get y'all one of those toddler leashes for the baby shower so you don't lose Gabriella too

JULIAN LISCERO

Now I know why you have your no pussy rule

You can get it but you can't keep it

DESMOND BALL

guys there's no point in busting his balls

wherever charlie is she has those with her
I'm sure

I blow out a heavy breath. There're too many emotions running through me to deal with this right now. And if one more comment gets made about her being *my* baby, I'll implode.

ME

I'm calling immunity necklace.

The rule is simple. When you call it, no one can judge whatever ridiculous shit comes out of your mouth.

THEO SCHROEDER

You have to call that BEFORE saying the thing.
That's the rule.

ME

Do you know where she is or not?

JULIAN LISCERO

Nah, sorry cap

DESMOND BALL

She's not in sin city

After a few minutes of no response from Elijah and Theo, I say fuck it and make the quick drive to their place. Technically *my* place.

The driveway is full, so I park on the grass near the mailbox, fly out of my truck, rush to the door, and throw it open. Glancing around, I find Elijah and Theo sitting at the island. They jump to their feet when they see me, eyes wide.

"Okay, okay," Theo shrieks, hands in the air. "I'll allow your immunity necklace. Calm Down."

"I can't," I say, teeth gritted, heading his way.

"I'm sure wherever your baby mama is, she is *just* fine," Theo says.

"Please *stop*!" I beg, my body buzzing with annoyance.

"What the hell's gotten into you?" Theo asks, brows furrowed.

Gripping the edge of the counter, I blow out a shaky breath. "It's not mine."

"What's not yours?" Elijah asks, concern etched all over his face.

I grip the edge harder, knuckles turning white. "The baby."

"What?" Theo shrieks, and he and Elijah share a look.

"It's not my baby," I choke out, shaking my head, eyes stinging in disbelief. "It's Jonathan's."

"Oh shit," Elijah says.

"Isn't this good news?" Theo asks, and my muscles tense.

"No, it's not good news!" I snap, pulse pounding in my ears. "It's the worst news I've ever heard in my fucking life."

"Most guys our age would be happy to find out they're not the father," Theo says.

"Well, I'm not."

"Maybe she went to see a friend," Elijah suggests.

"Well, *maybe* she did!" I say, throwing my arms in the air, unable to suppress my frustration.

"So relax then," Theo says, gesturing down with his hands.

"Relax?" I shriek. "You want me to relax? Charlotte's out there convinced she should leave me because… because why?!"

Theo places a hand on my shoulder, our eyes meeting. "Because she knows this baby is not your problem."

"This *baby,*" I seethe, pushing Theo's hand away. "This perfect little girl Charlotte is growing"—I blink hard, shoving down the overwhelming emotions—"is *not* and never will be a *problem.* And neither is she."

"Noah," Charlotte's voice fills my ears, and I freeze, every hair standing up.

Theo flashes a smug grin. *He knew she was here.*

Turning, I find Charlotte standing near the island with her arms crossed. I move toward her slowly on unsteady legs. Her eyes meet mine, and I place my hands on her face, analyzing every inch of it, as if to make sure she's real. "*Stai bene.*"[2] I throw my arms around her, tugging her against my chest. She loops her arms around my waist, nuzzling into me. *She's here.*

Dropping my face in the crook of her neck, I inhale deeply, her sweet scent flooding me with a cosmic wave of relief. The surge is so strong, tears escape my eyes as I hold her tight. Afraid if I let her go for even one moment, she'll vanish.

"You left," I mumble into her hair, attempting firmness, but the words come out broken. Just like I am.

------

2. IT: *Stai bene.* - EN: You're okay.

"No, I didn't," she says, the shakiness in her tone showing she's just as distraught. Pulling away, I hold her face in my hands, lips pursed. "I just needed a little friend time," she adds, fingers gently wrapping around my wrists, the physical contact reducing my anxiety.

"Did it help?"

"A little," she admits.

"I couldn't get a hold of you."

"My phone's dead," she explains, and I release a frustrated breath.

"You're lucky you're pregnant, because you're oh for two, and that tattoo of my phone number would be on your ass *today*." She rolls her lips together. "When I got home, you were gone, and I…" *Lost my ever-loving mind.* "Panicked."

She fights a smile, and someone clears their throat, pulling me back to reality, reminding me of our audience.

"*Soffione*, go get in the truck," I tell her. Because there're a few things I need to tell my asshole best friends that I don't want her here for. She cocks a brow, unmoving, and I grip her chin, our eyes connecting. "Please?"

She nods and I pull her to me, pressing a kiss to her forehead, then hand her my truck key. A minute later, she's out the door with Sophia on her heels.

Grinding my teeth, I spin to face Theo and Elijah.

"Bro," Theo says, that smug smile still plastered on his face. "You are so fucking gone for her."

"Read the damn room," Elijah tells him.

"You should've told me she was here," I grit out, and they share a look. "Did you already know the baby wasn't mine?"

"No," Elijah says quickly. "I swear."

"She showed up about an hour ago," Theo says. "She and Soph have been locked in the room ever since."

"Why didn't you tell me she was here?" I press, searching for clarity.

"Probably because I'm an asshole?" Theo says.

"Well, that checks out," I mutter, turning my attention to Elijah. "What's your excuse?"

"I was kinda hoping you'd make some big love confession she'd overhear."

Is he for real? "I could've also said something idiotic because I'm freaking the fuck out!"

"I hadn't considered that…" he responds, eyes darting to the floor.

"*Did* I say something dumb?" I ask, trying to recall the conversation, anxiety coursing through me.

"Nah, you're good," Theo assures me. "Go take care of your girl."

Don't have to tell me twice.

I hurry to the truck.

When I open the door, my eyes find Charlotte's. I'm unable to conjure up a single word as I pull onto the road. Itching to touch her, I extend my hand, and she laces her fingers with mine, tethering us. I grip it tight the entire silent ride home.

When we finally make it through the front door, she trails me to the living room, and I throw a pillow on the ground by the coffee table, gesturing toward it.

She stares at the pillow. "What are we doing?"

"Sit."

"Should I *stay* too?" she asks teasingly, lowering herself to the cushion, and her attempt at humor lessens more of that anxiety.

"Only if you're a good girl." I wink, playing along, and grab a small box from the sideboard under the TV. I return to her, dumping a hundred little bricks onto the table.

"We're playing with Legos?" She picks one up, analyzing it. "Like, right now?"

"Yep," I say, grabbing a pillow and situating myself on the floor across from her. "Because we're about to have a serious conversation," I say, sorting the pieces for an orchid set I bought to make Charlotte for her bedside table.

She laughs. "And that equals Legos?"

I pause my organization and look up at her. "Mom and I always do this when we have something serious to talk about."

"Why?"

"Because no one is allowed to get up and walk away until either the Lego build is finished or the conversation is."

She smiles softly. "That's actually kind of beautiful."

"And highly effective," I say, continuing to sort the pieces.

"Where should we start?" Charlotte asks, joining me timidly.

I swallow hard. "Do you want this baby?"

"Would it hurt you if I said yes?"

"Hurt me?" I repeat, holding her gaze. "Why would it hurt me?"

"Because it's Jonathan's."

"I don't care about that. I care about you and what you want."

I definitely do care.

"He might want to be involved," she reminds me.

"Do *you* want that?"

"I don't know," she says, placing a hand on her stomach. "I feel like I have to at least tell him. Give him the choice, you know?" *I'm trying hard to understand, but involving him will only cause her pain.* She sighs. "It's weird. I spent a large part of my life dreaming about having his children, and now that it's happening, all I want to do is make it go away."

A sickening feeling creeps up my throat at her mention of her former planned future. Her current future.

"Is that what you want?" I ask, my chest constricting. "To make it go away?"

"No," she says quickly. "I meant—I didn't—"

"You don't have to filter yourself with me," I say, connecting two more blocks. "We have to be open and honest, or this conversation is pointless."

A few minutes pass as we put pieces together, pausing to check directions, and she finally says, "I don't want an abortion."

I nod. "Okay."

"The second I saw that screen"—she smiles softly—"I had this overwhelming sense of joy. Like there was so much of it, it may come bursting out of me." She glances away and huffs out a laugh. "Well, I suppose it will come bursting out at some point."

I scrunch my nose. "Yeah, I'm going to have to do some reading up on that part."

She releases a heavy breath. "You really don't have to do this."

Abandoning the little brick, I place my hand on hers and stare into her caramel eyes. "I want to."

"I appreciate all this," she says, waving at the house. "Truly. But you just made the NFL. You have everything in life you've ever wanted. Why not let me handle this and forego all the inevitable drama?"

"Because I wouldn't have you," I say, rubbing circles on her palm, and her eyes drop to our hands.

"I'm not that special," she says, shaking her head.

"Yes." I tip her chin up, and our eyes connect. "You are."

"Noah," she says, her gaze not leaving mine.

"Yes, *soffione*?"

"*Mi fai impazzire tu anche.*"

The second that broken Italian leaves her lips, I know I'm well and truly fucked.

Because I am, without a doubt, devastatingly in love with her.

SKITTLE BABES

SOPHIA

We're having a get together around 6 tonight to welcome Abbs to the Baller Pad

SAGE

I'm still mad at you for moving

So I'm not coming

SOPHIA

It'll be funnnnn

Besides, living with Julian can't be all bad

SAGE

It's definitely not all good

SOPHIA

how can having a live in friend with benefits be bad

you can get dick 24/7

SAGE

Because we're just friends now. NO BENEFITS.

SOPHIA

what

that sounds terrible

SAGE

it is

SOPHIA

please come, Elijah is so excited for his sister to be starting CBU

he wants to make sure we give her the big stingray welcome

i bet she'll let you ride her motorcycle

SAGE

fine i'll come

SOPHIA

YAY. Charlie? You and Noah coming?

ME

You sure you don't mind the preggo girl ruining your fun?

SAGE

someone has to be the designated sober friend. I designate you

ME

awh so kind

but Noah has a late practice

SAGE

So? He's not your keeper

Let him meet you there

Don't stay home all sad and boring while we're having FUNNNNN

ME

Fine, see you guys in a bit!

SOPHIA

DOUBLE YAY

The front door opens, Sage and Abbs strolling in.

It's not Noah.

Since I can't fall into his arms, I guess I'll fall into these cushions. Groaning, I throw myself on the corner of the couch, sinking in, and it accepts me like a warm hug. It's no comparison to Noah's, but I guess it'll do for now.

Great, I'm resorting to objectophilia.

It's been a week since we found out about the paternity, and while I'm grateful Noah is accepting me—us—I still never want to be a burden or a distraction. This baby isn't even his, after all… and as much as he's shown he cares, it's still hard for me to believe a man would want to raise a baby that's not his own. That's a hell of an ask.

I want to believe his pretty words. But after having my heart ripped out and stomped on by someone I fully relied on, I can't ignore that tiny little carry-on of trust issues screaming at me to watch out for the next plane crash.

It also doesn't help that Noah's been having late nights this week preparing for their first preseason game, and we've barely seen each other. I *miss* him.

"That was sick," Sage tells Abbs, a motorcycle helmet hanging from her fingertips.

"Anytime you wanna ride," Abbs says, fingers unknotting her dirty blonde helmet hair, "just let me know."

"I really wish you'd get a different mode of transportation," Elijah says, brows raised.

"Why?" She rolls her blue eyes. "Finding parking's easy. Gas is cheap."

"And it's *sexy*!" Sage points out.

Abbs sends her an approving wink. "Exactly."

"It's also *dangerous,*" Elijah says, brows raised. "And you know it rains in Florida. Like, a lot."

"Okay?" Abbs shrugs. "Then I'll borrow the truck."

Elijah narrows his eyes. "Did you move here just to stress me out?"

Abbs strides over and wraps her arms around his waist. "I missed you too, Eli."

Laughter erupts in the kitchen, and I glance over to the sight of Julian and Theo keeled over while Sophia flicks them off.

The front door opens, and my eyes dart to it, finding Noah clad in a Tampa Barracudas T-shirt, sweats, and a backwards ball cap. Relief floods through me. My lips quirk into a smile, and his gentle eyes find mine as my chest flutters. *He's finally here.*

"Hey, you made it!" Elijah says to Noah.

"Hey," Noah says, shutting the door. "Sorry, we have our first preseason game this week and practice took forever."

"No worries," Elijah says. "Pro ball trumps party."

The others go back to their conversations, and Noah beelines my way. His gaze connects with mine as he plops onto the couch, throwing an arm behind me. "Hey, *soffione,*" he says, leaning in without hesitation. Our lips meet, and all the heaviness on my shoulders melts like butter.

"Hey, quarterback," I say, and he scoots closer, putting a hand on my stomach. It flutters, and I can't tell if it's from butterflies or tiny toes.

"How's baby girl?" he asks, rubbing gently, and I don't ignore the way he leaves out the word "our."

Another flutter. *It's definitely him.* Placing my hand on his, I say, "She's good."

He grins at me. "And how's Mommy?"

I bite my lower lip, clenching my thighs. "Better now that you're here." He leans in again, placing a firm kiss on my cheek.

Julian and Sage walk over, splitting to sit at opposite sides of the couch.

"Are you guys in a fight?" Theo asks, trailing after, looking between Sage and Julian.

"No, why?" Sage replies.

"You just made an active effort to *not* sit next to each other," Theo points out, and I bite my lip, holding in the information.

"Why are you so obsessed with me?" Julian asks. "Worry about yourself."

"Yeah, and we don't have to be attached at the hip," Sage says.

"We literally got kicked out of a bar cause you fucked in a closet," Elijah reminds them.

"What can I say?" Julian grins. "I love Halloween."

Memories flash in my mind of the night Noah had to carry me home from the bar. My eyes find his, and he rubs a hand along my arm knowingly. If only I'd listened to him that night, maybe I wouldn't be in this situation.

Guilt sinks deep in my stomach, and I place a hand over it. *Hopefully she didn't feel it.* Never would I wish to change the miracle growing inside me. But I can't deny I wish it was from the man beside me.

"I don't know," Theo says, tugging me out of my head. "Still seems sus."

"They made a vow to stop screwing since they moved in together," Sophia says as she and Abbs walk in and take a seat on the couch beside Sage. *Apparently, so did Noah and I.* We haven't slept together since the twins' birthday party. I didn't know how to bring it up after I found out I was pregnant. Wasn't sure if it was even safe. It is. But now I'm embarrassingly desperate for connection.

"Joey!" Sage snaps at her, using the nickname she gave her when we were kids because of Sophia's koala obsession. Noah places a hand on my thigh, and I fight the urge to squeeze my legs together. *It's going to be a long night if he keeps touching me like this.*

"Sorry not sorry," Sophia says, taking a sip of wine. "We were all gonna know eventually."

"What kind of idiotic vow is that?" Theo says, taking a seat next to Abbs. "Living with a fuck buddy would be a blessing."

"Yeah, it works pretty well for us," Elijah says, winking at Sophia, and we all groan, throwing pillows at him.

Noah continues his torment on my arm, and our gazes connect. *Maybe we should test that theory.*

Twenty minutes later, Noah and I are in the kitchen, grabbing drinks. He boiled us water and is pouring it over tea bags.

"Do you guys have any honey?" I ask as Elijah strolls in.

"Do we have honey?" he scoffs, walking over to a cabinet and opening the door.

My mouth falls open at the filled shelves. There must be at least fifteen jars.

"Listen, your honey bee nickname is cute," I say. "But this seems over the top."

"Funny," he says, narrowing his eyes. "Abbs had a beekeeping phase, and we're *still* trying to get through the sweet stuff. She brought an entire suitcase full of these."

"You're welcome!" Abbs shouts from the living room.

Elijah hands me a jar, and I set it on the counter.

"Use the entire thing, please," Theo says. "Don't want that shit expiring in the pantry."

"That's not necessary," Noah says. "Honey lasts forever."

The memories of snuggling up in his tent under the stars dance into my mind. *Fun fact number two.* I think about my wish the next day when we found the field of dandelions: *I hope Noah ends up exactly where he's supposed to be.*

It was more so because he was so stressed about the draft, but I wonder if some small part of me wished—hoped—he'd end up with me.

Noah tugs me to him, soft smile on his lips, and our eyes meet. "I'm surprised you remembered that," I say.

"Well, it was my favorite fact from our camping trip," he admits, hooking a strand of hair behind my ear, adoring eyes capturing mine.

"Really?" I ask, my chest filling with warmth.

He nods. "I hope *we* last like honey."

"And I hope we grow like lemons."

"Three. Hundred. Dollars?" I balk. "For a single textbook?"

"This is a hate crime to my bank account," Andi says, grabbing her own and adding it to the stack of required reading for the upcoming school year. Classes start next week, and since Noah is in New York for a pre-season game, I'm using school prep as a distraction from being in his big empty house. "Can we petition for e-books? It's the 21st century. If I can read about a man with an octopus schlong fucking a mermaid, certainly we should be able to read about the Byzantine empire without being robbed."

"Sure." A laugh bubbles out of me. "Why don't you put exactly those words in your letter to the school president?"

"What an excellent idea." She smiles proudly.

We check out, and I only *almost* throw up at the grand total of $1023 for textbooks and assisting materials. Thankfully, my student loans dropped, but since I lost my cheer scholarship, it's definitely going to be tough this year. Living with Noah saves the room and board money, so it won't be *as* bad as anticipated. *I hope.*

"Wanna grab dinner?" Andi asks.

Pulling out my phone, I check the time. 5:14 pm.

"Noah and I are supposed to FaceTime at six," I tell her. "He's so busy, we literally have to preplan a simple phone call."

"Ohhh, yes girl," she says. "Phone sex is the best."

"We are not phone sex'ing!" I squeal. "We're just phoning. Only phoning."

Her face scrunches up. "Why?"

"Uh, because I miss him?"

"And you don't miss his dick?"

Heat creeps up on my cheeks. "I do…"

She narrows her eyes. "Why are you being weird?"

"I'm not."

"When's the last time you got some?" she asks, and I side-eye her. "Come on. You can tell me!"

"Fine," I grumble. "Fourth of July."

"Oh, girl." She throws an arm around my shoulders.

"I suppose I shouldn't be surprised carrying another man's child puts a damper on the love-making department."

"First of all, let's not put Jonathan in the category of 'man.'" She pinches her fingers together, and I huff a laugh. "But yeah, I get what you mean… Now I know why you've been so uptight lately."

"Hey!" I reply, slightly offended.

"You need to get dicked down." She nods. "Dicked down good."

My eyes bulge as I glance around us. "You are so—"

"Cool? Awesome? Edgy?"

"I was going to say *embarrassing*."

"No, baby cakes. Your sex life is embarrassing."

My cheeks burn. "Well, thank you."

"You are living with 'Tampa's Most Eligible Bachelor,'" she says, and I groan. "Please put him to good use."

"Things have just been awkward since we found out about the whole 'who's the daddy' thing…"

"You know what would solve that?" she asks, and I glance her way. "Fuck him. Literally. Fuck the poor man."

"But how do I even bring it up?" I blow a raspberry. "I don't know where his head's at."

"Here's an idea." Andi raises her brows at me. "*Ask* him."

"He's the quarterback. Shouldn't he call the play?"

"Yes, but quarterbacks can't throw a pass if they're not given the ball. And right now"—she drops her eyes to my belly— "you've got the ball."

"Ugh, fine," I groan. "Maybe I'll talk to him tonight."

"Good," she says as we reach our cars. "See you tomorrow?"

"Yeah, wanna get lunch?"

"I can't," she says, lips rolled together. "I have cheer practice."

"Right," I say at the reminder of yet another thing that's been taken away from me. I knew my life would change when I got that message. I just didn't realize it would happen so fast.

"We could do dinner?" she asks, eyes hopeful. "Sushi and shit-talking?" Her eyes widen. "Wait, fuck. Can you even have sushi?"

"Oh my god! Goodbye."

"See you tomorrow," she says as I turn toward the Bronco. "And you better have some good details to report. My sex diary awaits!"

I get in the driver's seat, setting my bag of textbooks with a Louis Vuitton price tag on the passenger floorboard. The engine roars to life, and I glide my hands around the steering wheel. *I can't believe Noah bought me this car.* I should've never accepted it. He surely wouldn't have done it if he knew whose baby I was really carrying.

'*I hope we last like honey.*'

A smile graces my lips. I need to stop making assumptions about what he would want and do. Actions speak louder than words, and Noah's actions are resonant.

I make it in the house with twenty minutes to spare, Andi's pep talk fresh in my mind. My phone's at fifteen percent, typical, so I put it on the charger by the night stand. Rushing to the bathroom, I take in my appearance. My attention hones in on the sloppy bun atop of my head. Groaning, I quickly unravel it and untangle the hair with my fingers. Once deemed acceptable, I make a beeline for the closet. A celestial light beams down on Noah's old CBU jersey with the number thirteen, and I throw it on, knowing he'll go crazy.

I pick my phone back up from the nightstand, unplugging it.

17:44: Missed Call. Noah.

Shit.

A text notification is also on the screen, and I click on it.

NOAH

I tried to call early. Coach is making us go to a press conference tonight

Time stamped ten minutes ago. I didn't notice it because I was getting ready for our "not" date. The disappointment rips me apart like a supernova tearing through the fabric of space.

So much for some long-distance love-making.

32

CHARLOTTE

I'm officially doom scrolling.

Noah's on his way home from practice and I'm curled up on the couch, phone in my hand, jittering with nerves. He's been gone so much the past few weeks, including the away game last weekend, and I'm desperate for connection. *Girl, you are thirsty.*

As I tap through stories, a sickening feeling sits in my stomach at a post from a high school friend that includes Jonathan's smiling face at the Longwood Springs.

Jonathan.

My cheating ex-boyfriend, and by unfortunate circumstance, father to this child.

You need to tell him.

I've struggled with this decision. It would be so easy to pretend the baby is Noah's, although given how far along I am, most people could piece it together, and I'm really not trying to hide anything. I am *not* ashamed of her.

I want to tell him and get it over with. Rip the final band-aid off the gaping wound of our relationship and see how it heals.

A text pops through.

> MOTHER
>
> I have a campaign fundraiser in Longwood tomorrow evening. Would appreciate it if you'd come.

What she means is she'd appreciate it if she can show the porcelain persona of a perfect family while people are watching. *You need to tell them too.*

Groaning, I throw my head against the pillow. Might as well make it a double band-aid rip.

I toss my phone on the other end of the couch and pick up a book. Sophia suggested I try reading to get my mind off things, but I can barely keep my eyes on the page. I'm exhausted from the nights waiting up for Noah, and my mind is a tangled mess pulling me in every direction.

The front door opens, and I perk up to the sight of Noah walking through. He drops his practice duffle and strides my way, a handsome smile on his face.

"Well, hey, *honey,*" I say, and his smile deepens.

"Hi, *soffione.*" He beams, leaning down to plant a soft kiss on my lips. "You have a good first week of classes?" he asks, sinking on the other end of the couch and taking my feet in his lap.

"Yeah." I fold my book with a clap. "It was nice having something to do."

"I'm sorry I've been gone so much," Noah says, squeezing my foot.

"It's fine." *It's not fine.*

"I don't want you feeling lonely," he says, eyes concerned, thumb stroking my ankle, making it impossible to concentrate. Even when I try to hide my emotions, he reads me like this damn book.

"I've always got my fictional boyfriends," I say, waving the paperback at him.

He grabs my calves, and I yelp as he drags me across the couch, pulling me into his lap. He wraps his arms around me, tugging me against his chest, and I melt into him. It's the most physical we've been in ages and very much needed. He plucks the book from my fingers, tossing it to the other end of the couch. "And what about your *real* boyfriend?"

"Have you seen him?" I ask, glancing around, a teasing grin on my face. "He hasn't been here much lately."

"I know." He sighs, splaying his fingers over my stomach. "I hate being away from you so much."

A sting pangs my chest. "Baby, I'm kidding," I say, putting a hand on his face, hoping the pet name will show him how sincere I am. "I know you're busy." And I definitely do. "I just miss you when you're gone."

I'm trying my best not to be the needy girlfriend who's carrying another man's baby, but *fuck*, it's hard to be the supportive one when my world is crumbling around me.

"Let's go out tomorrow night when I'm home from practice," he says. "A proper date with your *real-life* boyfriend."

"As much as I'd love that…" A weight settles inside me. *Rip off the band-aid.* "Mom is having a fundraiser in Longwood for her campaign, and I thought I'd use it as an excuse to tell them about the baby." The heartbeat was confirmed, we know it's a sweet baby girl, and I'm definitely far enough along now to share the news. "I don't really want to wait any longer even though I know she's going to rip my joy away from me."

"Maybe not," Noah says optimistically.

"Trust me. Georgia Benson is a politician at her core. All she'll see are the headlines this could make."

"Well, whatever happens, we'll figure it out together." He squeezes my thigh, his reassurance calming.

I bite my cheek, anxiety creeping up my spine. *Double band-aid rip.* "I'm also thinking of stopping by Jonathan's."

"What?" Noah says, pulling away to look at me.

"He's in Longwood, and I kinda wanna get it over with."

"I'll come with you," he says quickly.

"You have practice," I remind him.

"But I don't like the idea of you going alone." His voice is firm.

"Noah, I just want to get it over with. I'll be fine," I assure him. "Jonathan and I dated for years. I can handle him."

My voice is calm and collected, but a whirlwind of doubt spirals inside me. I have no idea what to think. What to expect. I definitely don't want to get back together, but part of me hopes he'll still want something to do with this baby's life. Not for me, but for his child.

Noah pulls his phone out.

"What are you doing?" I ask.

"Calling Elijah." He places his free hand on my thigh. "I won't say you can't go. But you *can't* go alone."

I press my lips together, heart soaring at his overprotectiveness. "That's really not necessary."

Noah's concerned eyes hold mine. "I do not trust Jonathan." He moves his hand to my stomach. "You are not alone in any of this. Elijah said to call him if we need him." He drops his forehead to mine. "We do."

I release a sigh. "Okay."

Five minutes later, Elijah has more than agreed to be my bodyguard. With shaky hands, I grab my phone up off the couch.

MOTHER

ME

I'll be there.

Elijah pulls in the driveway, parking next to Jonathan's car. It's the only one here, which suggests he's alone. *Definitely don't want his parents around for this conversation.*

"Thanks for coming with me," I tell Sophia before turning my attention to Elijah in the driver's seat. "And thanks for driving."

"Any time," he says, with a weak smile, unbuckling his seatbelt. "Besides, you really think Noah would let you come face this prick alone?"

"I can handle him." Tilting my head, I cock a brow. "And you should wait in the truck. I think your presence would piss him off, all things considered."

Elijah's lips press together, and he rolls down his window. "Holler if you need me."

I open the door of his truck and hop out, Sophia following suit. "I really can do this on my own," I tell her.

"Of course you can, but"—she takes my hand—"you don't need to."

I take a deep breath, holding her gaze. "Please wait here."

"Char—"

"I appreciate it, I really do. But I *need* to do this alone."

"Okay," she concedes reluctantly, pursing her lips. "You've got this."

Swallowing hard, I stroll up the path, passing the rose bush that supplied all the flowers Jonathan would bring me. *He insisted buying them was a waste of money.* As I walk up the stairs, my eyes pause on the spot where he asked me to be his girlfriend.

The wooden porch creaks beneath me as I walk slowly to the front door I've stepped through hundreds, if not thousands of times. Often greeted with make-up kisses from the time we'd spent apart.

I place a hand over my stomach. Four years of my life. Four years that a young, naive girl, who had no clue about life, or love, or anything, really, wanted nothing more than to spend her life with this person.

I've suppressed Jonathan from my mind, but being here, surrounded by all things *him*—or rather, *us*—has those memories flooding back.

Sucking in a breath, I knock three times, then fold my arms over my chest, hoping the pressure will hold me together.

Reality? I'm seconds from blowing away like a dandelion in the wind.

There's no response, and I jam my finger into the doorbell.

Ring. Ring. Ring. Ring. Ring.

Another moment of impatience and I'm pounding again, psychotically. I did not come all this way to lose my nerve at the last second. Muffled noises draw closer behind the door, and it swings open.

"Jesus, give me a—" Jonathan freezes, lips parted open. "Charlie."

"Hey," I say, shifting on my heels.

"What…" He eyes me up and down, and I'm suddenly grateful I went for a loose sundress hiding any hint of the breaking news I'm about to share with him. "What are you doing here?"

"Can we talk?"

"Uh, sure." He gestures inside, and my eyes fall past his shoulders to the living room. The couch where two teenagers shared a sloppy first kiss. The kitchen where I baked so many cookies trying to perfect my snickerdoodle recipe that Jonathan threw up at football practice. The spot on the floor where we spent hours playing Uno on a rainy Saturday, a day that ended with us tangled in the sheets in his room. My eyes sting, and I blink back tears.

This house is a living memorial of all the times we shared. Memories where we were very much in love from a time we'll never get back. Just because I've moved on doesn't mean I don't remember.

"Let's talk here," I suggest, motioning to the front porch, and he steps out, eyes darting past me.

"What is *he* doing here?" Jonathan asks, tone sharp.

"He gave me a ride."

"What do you want, Charlie?"

I take a deep breath, feeling queasy for more reasons than one. "I'm not sure how to tell you this." Instinctively, I put a hand on my stomach, and Jonathan's eyes drop.

"No," he says firmly.

"Jonathan." My tone is gentle.

"Nope." He shakes his head. "No way."

"You haven't even let me talk."

"Are you gonna say anything other than, 'I'm pregnant?'" My lips smash together, and he laughs maniacally. "Why are you telling me this? Just to hurt me?"

My brows pull together. "To *hurt* you?"

"It's Noah's, isn't it?" he asks, and I stay silent. His tone softens. "Isn't it?"

"No," I say, and his lips part open. "It's yours."

He blinks at me. "No."

"Yes."

"How?"

"I don't..." Shaking my head, I try to gather my thoughts. "From spring break, I guess."

His eyes analyze me, brain clearly on overdrive. "You're *five* months pregnant?"

"Yes."

"And you're *just* now telling me?" His tone is accusatory.

"I only found out like a month ago," I argue.

"A *month* ago?" he snaps. "Why didn't you tell me sooner?"

"Because..." The words fall off my tongue.

"Because you *thought* it was Noah's," he says with a sarcastic laugh.

I look down at my feet, unable to conjure up any words. Am I ashamed? Am I sad? Am I angry? Why should he care? "Yeah."

"So why are you telling me now?"

"Because I thought you'd want to know about a child that is literally *half* of you?"

"Well, if you wouldn't have blocked me, you could have saved yourself a trip."

My mouth falls open. Okay, I've decided. I'm angry. No, I'm furious. "In case you forgot, the only reason I blocked you is because you *cheated* on me."

He releases a heavy breath. "Can we not start this again?"

"Start this?" I laugh humorously.

"I don't…" His eyes drop to my stomach. "I just—I can't deal with this." He turns towards the house, and I grab his shoulder.

"Where are you going?"

"Like I said." He wiggles out of my grasp. "I don't need this."

"So, what? You're walking away?" I don't know what I expected from him, but as the memories of our past pounded into my mind, I guess I thought he'd at least want to be involved.

"Charlie, I'm a sophomore and already getting calls from prospective NFL teams," he says as if that's even remotely relevant.

"And?"

"And do you think they're going to want some guy who has a fucking baby at twenty?"

"Okay, let me get this straight," I say calmly. "You don't want to be involved at all in your child's life because you *might* have a shot at the NFL?"

"Let me make this easy for you," he says, pulling out his wallet and shoving something in my hand.

"What the fuck is this?" I ask, glancing down at a few crumpled hundred-dollar bills.

"That should cover an abortion."

I gasp. "An *abortion*? I'm *five* months pregnant!"

"Okay?" he says with a puzzled expression. "Are they more expensive when you're that far along?" He digs in his wallet again.

"No," I seethe, swatting it out of his hand. "I don't need *more* money. I'm *not* getting an abortion!"

"Well, I'm *not* being involved, so consider this my only child support."

"I don't want your money!" I scream at the top of my lungs, throwing the cash at him, unable to shove down the anger exploding out of me.

"If anyone asks if that's my baby, I'll deny it," he says, bending down to collect the bills and his wallet. *If only I'd done the same.* "I don't want anything to do with it," he spits out, standing to his full height, and our eyes connect. "Or you."

And just like that, the roses are wilted, there are cracks in the stairs, and the front door is only an exit.

His eyes dart behind me, becoming murderous as Elijah appears at my side.

"Go to the truck, Char," Elijah says, gaze glued to Jonathan's.

"It's okay, I'm—"

"I let you deal with this like you asked," Elijah says, gaze connecting with mine, leaving no room for argument. "He's done disrespecting you. Please, get in the truck."

"Come on," Sophia says, grabbing my arm gently, tugging me away, and my eyes meet Jonathan's.

"I never want to see your face again," I shout as Sophia drags me away from the house.

"Too bad you'll be looking at it for the rest of your life," Jonathan says, and I rear back as if he slapped me.

"Fuck you!" Tears sting my eyes as I fight the urge to throw up.

A sickening smirk spreads across his face, and he places his hand on the door frame. "Well, *babe*, that's what got you into this mess in the first place, isn't it?"

Elijah snatches Jonathan, shoving him up against the wall of the house. "You're a real piece of work, you know that?"

"Get off me," Jonathan says, pushing Elijah away. Sophia holds me back and I try to shake her, but she won't let me go.

"Men take responsibility," Elijah continues.

"The only thing I'll take responsibility for is fucking that cunt without a condom," Jonathan snarls, and Sophia gasps.

Elijah cocks his fist and slams it directly into Jonathan's nose. *One point, Anderson.* My body trembles with rage.

"*Oww!*" Jonathan cries out like a little bitch, back against the wall, then turns to Elijah, eyes full of fury. I can't even pretend I'm upset Elijah did it.

"You deserved that," Elijah tells him, backing away. *He totally deserved that.*

"I'm calling the cops," Jonathan says, spitting blood on the front porch.

"Go ahead!" Sophia shouts, gripping my arm. "Elijah, give him your dad's number."

"That's bullshit." Jonathan slips inside, his eyes connecting with mine. He shakes his head and slams the door. A final nail in the coffin.

In a haze, I walk to the truck. Sophia helps me inside, pulls the buckle over me, clicks it in, and I'm on autopilot the entire drive to my parents' house.

My stomach flutters. I place my hand over it, and a little kick responds to my touch. I gasp. *This is new.*

"You okay?" Sophia asks.

"Yeah," I say, a smile spreading across my face, heart swelling. "My little girl was just reminding me she's here."

I'm so happy you're here.

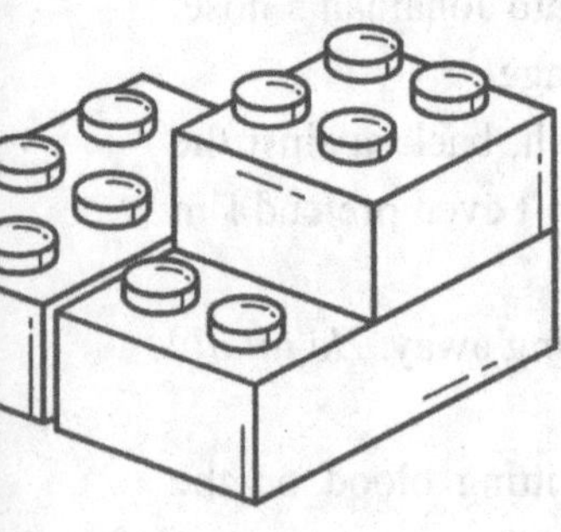

33

NOAH

Knowing Charlotte's in Longwood without me, talking to that shit bag probably at this very moment, makes me want to vomit. To top it off, Bexley let us go early so we can rest up for the first regular season game tomorrow, and given my extra time, I'm once again in the driveway of Mom's house to deliver unexpected news. She's been begging for an ultrasound photo, and I know the second she gets one there will be questions.

Questions I don't have the energy to answer.

It's not my baby, *technically*, and it feels weird to make some big "I'm not the father" announcement when they still both feel like mine.

But if Charlotte is brave enough to tell her parents tonight, so can I.

Ten minutes later, Mom, Tony, and I are situated on the living room couch, drinking espresso.

After downing the caffeine boost, I finally pull out my wallet and retrieve the little image from Charlotte's last appointment. "I've got an ultrasound photo for you." *But I'm unfortunately not the father.*

"Why didn't you start with that?" Mom gasps, setting her cup on the living room table with a clink, and she snatches the paper. *"Oh, che meraviglia!"*[1] She runs her fingers over it, then pauses. *"Noah Gabriel?"*

Her tone heightens my anxiety. *"Mamma?"*

"I thought Charlotte's three months pregnant now?" she says, gaze glued to the tiny paper.

"She's further along than we expected," I say, tone trembling.

Her eyes find mine. *"Quindi, non è tua figlia?"*[2]

"No," I say, voice cracking. *"Non è mia figlia."*[3]

"What's going on?" Tony asks, unable to translate.

"Noah's not the father." Her eyes hold mine. "This changes things, no?"

"No." I shake my head. "It changes nothing."

"If you're not the biological father," Tony says, releasing a heavy breath, "it does change things."

"Why?" I snap.

"Because *legally* this baby is not yours."

I stand, anger rolling through me.

"Tony," Mom says gently.

"He needs to hear this," Tony tells her.

"They're still my family," I say, chest panging.

"Not in the eyes of the law," he reminds me.

"Fuck the law!" My tone is laced with frustration.

"Noah," Mom says sharply. "Do I need to get the Legos?"

"No, I'm sorry, I just… I don't care if they're not 'legally' my family. Family is made up of more than signed papers and blood relations." My eyes meet Tony's. "You taught me that."

"Of course I know that," Tony says, his eyes full of concern. "But legally, you have no ties to her or this baby. She can leave

---

1. IT: *Oh, che meraviglia!* - EN: Oh, how gorgeous!
2. IT: *Quindi, non è tua figlia?* - EN: Is this not your baby?
3. IT: *No. Non è mia figlia.* - EN: No. It's not my baby.

anytime she wants, and there's not a damn thing you can do about it."

A needle has pierced the happy bubble I've been living in. I'm plummeting towards earth. No contingency plan. No audible.

"You're wrong," I say, walking towards the kitchen for my keys. "Charlotte wouldn't do that." Would she? I've been telling her I'm not going anywhere. I never even considered the fact she could. That she might want to. Maybe that's why she hasn't tried to be physical lately either. Or why she insisted on seeing Jonathan alone.

I shake away the thought the second it enters my brain. She wouldn't do that.

"I've been practicing family law for twenty years," Tony reminds me. "I've seen tons of cases like this one. You won't win."

"I don't need to win anything." Panic sets in. "I just want Charlotte. And I want this baby."

"I know your heart is in the right place, but I don't wanna see you blind-sided." He grips my shoulder and looks into my eyes. "I'm trying to prepare you for if sh——"

"I don't need you to 'prepare me,'" I spout, the words venom on my tongue, and shake him off. "I need you to be there for me. For us."

"We're always here for you," he says with a defeated sigh.

I blink back tears at the thought of this life being taken away from me and straighten my shoulders, locking eyes with him. "You can tell me I'm crazy, because I know this happened fast. And I know they aren't my blood. But Charlotte and this baby, they're my family. And I'll do whatever it takes to make sure they're safe and cared for."

"I know you will, but I ju——"

"Whatever it takes."

My phone buzzes in my pocket and I pull it out, hoping to finally hear from Charlotte.

ELIJAH ANDERSON

Just dropped Char off

ME

How'd it go?

ELIJAH ANDERSON

I think i broke his nose

"I have to go," I tell them. "See you at the game tomorrow."
And I'm out the door before they can say another word.

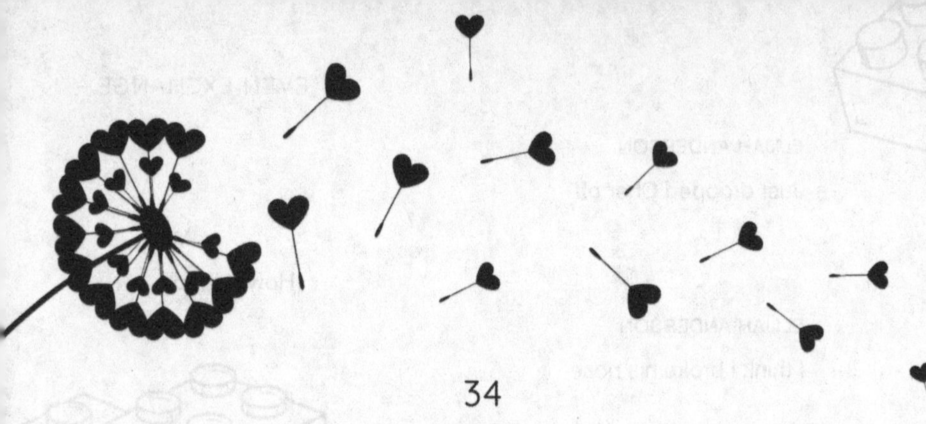

34

CHARLOTTE

An intense battle continues. Me vs. the zipper on this gorgeous, albeit very small, gown. Dresses are sprawled over every surface of my room in piles.

Too small.

Too bump-revealing.

Too ugly.

Although, the too ugly ones are about to make a comeback if I can't get this stupid damn dress—the fastener slides up, forcing out a breath—*zipped.*

This is progress.

Turning in the mirror, I note it hides my bump, which is also a plus. However, breathing is problematic, which must be terrible for baby. *Damn it.* Back to the drawing board.

My bump is small, but it's definitely noticeable in a form-fitting dress. Especially since my entire life was spent ensuring I stayed in perfect shape.

My mother saw to that.

The reflection in the mirror reminds me of the day's events. Dark circles and puffiness from crying—or rather, sobbing—earlier hidden behind concealer and eyeshadow.

I didn't know what to expect from Jonathan, but I never expected *that*.

Knock. Knock. Knock.

"Come in," I say.

The door opens, then clicks shut. "Hey, *soffione*." I spin to face Noah, almost tripping over my dress as I bolt to him. He drops something, catching me easily, and I melt into a puddle of relief in his arms. Tears sting my eyes at the overwhelming emotions of the day.

I blink them back, no desire to reapply my makeup. *Again.*

"What are you doing here?" I ask, pulling away and taking in his attire of a fitted black suit and bow tie already perfectly in place. *I like where this is heading.*

"I got out of practice early," he tells me. "Thought you could use a little backup tonight, of the handsome date variety."

"How did you know exactly what I needed?" I ask, smiling softly.

He presses his lips together. "Elijah called."

"Of course he did," I say, uncurling from his hold and returning to the mirror.

"Do you want to talk about it?" Noah asks as I pat down the satin material of my dress.

"Can we wait till later?"

"Sure." His eyes find mine in our reflection, sparkling with adoration. "You are breathtakingly beautiful."

"I appreciate that, but I can't breathe," I grumble.

"Well, that's a problem," he says, leaving me to scoop up the bag he abandoned when he arrived.

"What's that?"

Noah smiles weakly. "Sophia may have mentioned you'd ripped through half your closet by the time they left." He unzips a garment bag and pulls out a black strappy maxi dress with a flowing skirt that has a slit up the leg, and spins it around, showing me the corset details on the back. "So you can make it as loose or tight as you need to for baby girl," he says, and my heart squeezes. "The flare of the skirt should hide your bump until you're ready to tell your parents."

I rub the material between my fingers. "After the gala."

"Do you want help?" Noah asks, eyes dropping down my body, and I certainly will never deny this saint of a man the opportunity to undress me. Especially since he hasn't done it in months.

"I would *love* help."

In front of the mirror, I pull my hair to one side, exposing the zipper on the back of my dress. Noah places his hand on my bare shoulder, finding my eyes in the mirror, and takes the metal fastener between his fingers with the other.

My breathing shudders as he slowly drags the zipper down, holding the material, and tugs it all the way open.

The dress falls to my ankles, and I stand naked but for a pair of black panties. Instinct has me itching to cover myself, but I don't want to hide. Not when Noah looks at me like a man starved. *And I suppose he has been.*

"You're perfect," Noah whispers, snaking an arm around my waist and splaying his fingers on my stomach. *I wish she was yours too.* He slides his other hand around my neck, tilting it to the side, and brings his mouth to the exposed skin. "You should go like this," he mumbles against me, tone low and gravely, planting soft kisses towards my collar bone, and I shiver.

"My mother definitely would not approve," I say, leaning against him, savoring his touch. His warmth. His arousal.

"True." Noah nips at my neck, eliciting a giggle. "And this beautiful body is for my eyes only." His gaze holds mine as he bends, palm dragging slowly down my leg to my ankle. *His hands feel so good on me. Where they're meant to be.* He grabs the dress off the floor, tosses it on my bed, and returns with the new one.

Holding his shoulder for balance, I step into it and pull it up to my chest. I situate the corset top, trying not to be disappointed he didn't cop a true feel or throw me on the bed and ravish me before I redressed. *Damn him for being such a gentleman.*

He brushes my hair to the side, leaning down to drag his lips against my bare skin. I tilt my head back, and he continues peppering my neck with kisses, his fingers fumbling with the laces of the dress, pulling slowly. My heart rate skyrockets. *I've missed this.* He tugs the corset, and a heavy breath is expelled from my lungs.

"Too tight?" he asks.

"Just a bit."

He loosens it. "Better?"

I release a shaky breath. "Yes."

A few more quick movements, and he's running his hand down the material on my back. "You're stunning."

Spinning back to the mirror, I take in the beautiful dress he put the extra effort in to bring me, on top of the fact he showed up here when he didn't have to. I'm sure he's exhausted from a long week of practice, but instead of doing a Lego build to calm his nerves, eating an exorbitant amount of protein, and ensuring he gets exactly nine hours of sleep, he's here. With me. For me. Tears burst free.

"Baby?" he says, turning me to face him. "Why are you crying?"

"I don't know," I scoff, looking at him, blinking them back. *Think of the makeup!* "Pregnant women cry, okay?"

"Okay." He laughs, cupping my face in his hands, and places a gentle kiss on my lips, calming me instantly.

"Thank you for coming."

"You needed me," he says, hands on my shoulders.

"I know, but you must be so tired."

"It's fine." He waves me off. "I'm free tonight, and I wanted to spend it with you. I'm glad Elijah called."

"Me too."

"But it should've been you," he says, tucking a strand of hair behind my ear.

My stomach tightens. "I know."

"You can always call me." His voice is pleading.

"But what if—"

"*Always.*"

"I know, but—"

"Always, *soffione.*"

"Well, this brings back memories," Noah says as we walk in the country club ballroom arm in arm.

I lean up to his ear and whisper, "Maybe we should find a closet for old times' sake."

"Don't tempt me."

A throbbing between my thighs gives me hope we haven't lost our physical spark. "Noah." I smile at a couple as they pass us, then return my attention to him. "If you keep talking to me like that, it's going to be a long night."

He laughs softly as we arrive at my family's table. My mother, speaking to someone off to the side, turns, noting my date.

"Hello," she says, eyes bouncing between us. "Charlie didn't mention you were coming."

"It was a last-minute addition," Noah says with a courteous expression.

"Well," Mom says with a tight-lipped smile, "lucky for you, my husband isn't going to make it, so we have an extra seat."

"Dad's not coming?" I ask, panic setting in. There's no way I can tell her about the baby without Dad to back me up. I don't even know if he will back me up, but he's usually the more reasonable one.

"He got called for a last-minute flight."

"Oh," I say, when what I really want to say is, *Fuck*.

"Anyways, enjoy the event." She leans in to whisper in my ear, "And *please* don't embarrass me."

She strolls away, leaving a stinging feeling in my chest. Why did I even come? I should've excused my way out of it like I have every other invite since I found out I was pregnant.

But Noah's right. I have to tell them. This is real, and it's happening, and I can't show up one day like, *Hello, here's your first grandchild!*

"Want to dance?" Noah asks, hand on my waist, pulling me back to reality.

Our eyes connect, and I force a smile. The day has been emotionally exhausting, and honestly, all I want is my hot-as-sin boyfriend. "Thought you'd never ask."

"I'm going to grab us another drink," Noah tells me, standing from the table.

"I can come," I say, rising from my chair.

"No, stay. You've been dancing for an hour." Noah leans down to my ear. "I'm sure you could use a few minutes off your feet."

"Fine," I concede, settling back in the chair, a hand on my stomach. "I'll have water."

"You've got it." He kisses me on the cheek and leaves, my eyes trailing him as he makes his way to the bar. *That suit does wonders for his ass. Damn.*

"Charlie," Mom says, sitting next to me and begrudgingly yanking me out of my drool spiral.

I turn towards her, moving my hand to my lap. "Mother."

"How are your classes going?" she asks.

"Good," I say, not bothering to mention how it's actually been really difficult to concentrate. But unless I change my major back, I doubt she cares anyways.

"Here." She offers me a glass of champagne, a matching one sitting in her hand.

"What are we celebrating?" I ask, accepting it so I'm not too obvious.

She smiles, but her eyes are empty and lack emotion. "You tell me."

I stare down at the liquid. "I don't drink during cheer season."

"Good thing you aren't cheering anymore," Mom says, and my muscles freeze.

"How did you know that?"

She scoffs. "I know everything."

Well, not everything.

"Then, I guess…" I shakily pick up the glass. "To your campaign."

I tip the champagne flute towards hers, and they clink. Bringing the glass to my lips, I keep them pursed to avoid the alcohol and set it back down. My tongue darts out, clearing the moisture by reflex, and a sweet taste dances across it.

"Ginger ale?" I ask, brows pulled together.

She leans in, snarling in a low voice, "Well, I wasn't about to give my *pregnant* daughter champagne, now was I?"

My gaze snaps to hers. "How'd you know?"

Her eyes go wide. "I didn't for sure, but I do now." She stands, pulling me with her, and drags me through the room and out a side door.

"What are you doing?" I say, snatching my arm away once we're in the empty hallway.

She glances around, then steps toward me. In a hushed tone, she says, "I'm your *mother*. You really thought I wouldn't notice you've been touching your stomach incessantly and haven't been sneaking merlot? Have you forgotten I've been in your shoes *twice*? I know exactly what it feels like, *looks* like, to be pregnant at your age."

"And look at you now," I say, tone dripping with sarcasm. "A teen pregnancy success story."

"You have no idea what I've had to do to get where I am," she grits out. "I raised you better. To *not* make the same mistakes."

"Is that what I was?" I snap, my voice getting louder. "A mistake?"

"That isn't what I meant," she says with a look that would usually hush me in a moment.

"Isn't it though?" I ask with a sigh, all the energy leaving my fight.

"Of course not."

"The only thing you care about is yourself, and your precious image, and this pointless election," I say, waving a hand toward the stupid party on the other side of the door.

"You're wrong," she says, and I *almost* see her crack. I *almost* feel a shred of caring from her.

"I'm keeping the baby."

"Okay." She swallows hard. "Given the way that man can't take his eyes off you, I'm assuming Noah already knows."

Her description of him pleases me. "He does."

"How far along are you?"

I take slow, steady breaths. "Five months."

Her lips part. "Charlotte."

Here it comes. "Yes?"

"Who is the father of this baby?"

A silence stretches between us. "Jonathan."

She sucks in a sharp breath. "And why is *Jonathan* not the one here by your side?"

"He's not in the picture."

"Not in the picture?" She laughs, but there's no humor in it. "So you're pretending Noah's the father?"

"No, I—"

"I'll speak to Jonathan." She waves a hand. "We'll sort this out."

She thinks I can't handle this myself?

"There's nothing to sort out." I shake my head. "He doesn't want to be involved."

"Well, he doesn't have a choice."

"If I listened to *his* choice, I'd be at Planned Parenthood," I say, and her furious eyes go wide.

"That still doesn't clear him of his responsibility. You're going to need child support."

"I don't want his money," I shriek. The last thing I need is another thing tying me to him. Giving him control over me. Would he use our baby—*my* baby—as a weapon?

After his reaction today, nothing would surprise me.

"So, what?" she scoffs, her eyes dropping to my stomach in disgust. "You expect me to give your trust fund back because you got pregnant?"

A pang of sadness hits in my chest. *Is this how she thinks of me?* "Don't worry. I don't want your money either."

"Then what the hell are you going to do? You can hardly afford tuition this semester. How will you afford a baby?"

"I'll figure it out."

"The only reason you're even still above water is because Noah's allowing you to live in his house." The corners of her mouth quirk upwards. "Oh." She nods. "Now I get it."

My skin crawls, her assuredness making me uneasy. "Get what?"

"You've manipulated Noah into paying for your mistake."

My lips part, chest aching. "You're wrong."

"Am I? Because as far as I can see, the only one benefitting from that relationship is you."

I fold my arms over my chest. "How do you figure?"

"You get an NFL football player with a seven-figure bank

account, and he gets a broke, aimless, has-been cheerleader knocked up with some other man's baby."

I seethe, tears stinging my eyes. "You're wrong."

"Noah's a fixer. I could tell from the moment I met him," she says, and it's true. He's the one our friends call when they need help. The one I call when I need help.

"Figure it out with Jonathan," she says, tone firm. "I won't let this ridiculous scandal cost me the campaign."

That's what she's thinking about right now? My veins buzz with anger. "No one cares about your stupid campaign!"

"Keep your voice down," she grinds out.

"Why?" I laugh hysterically. "Worried someone's going to find out your daughter's a raging whore with 'who's the daddy' problems?!" I cup my hands around my mouth like a megaphone. "Somebody call Jerry Springer!"

"Charlotte," she snaps, gripping my wrists and yanking them downwards. "You're making a mistake."

"What other choice do I have?" I say, exasperated, shaking her off.

"You can go on a little year abroad, we'll find a nice family for the baby, and then you can go back to your normal life."

My mouth falls open. "You want me to give the baby up for adoption?"

"It's what's best."

"For who?"

"You *and* this baby. You're not ready to be a mother," she says, her eyes softening.

"Because you're the expert on motherhood," I huff, pain encompassing my heart.

"I want what's best for you." She reaches for me, and I slap her away.

"You want what's best for me?" I fume, my fists curled at my sides. "You don't even know me."

"You have no idea how hard this will be."

"I've been taking care of the twins for years," I spout. "Given how busy *their* mother was."

"For what, an afternoon?" she scoffs. "If you think taking care of kids full time is so easy, then you should have no trouble taking the twins for their fall break next month."

I want to shout at her that she's using me for an excuse to pawn her remaining children off. That she's wrong about Noah and a raging, selfish bitch.

But all I find myself saying is "Okay."

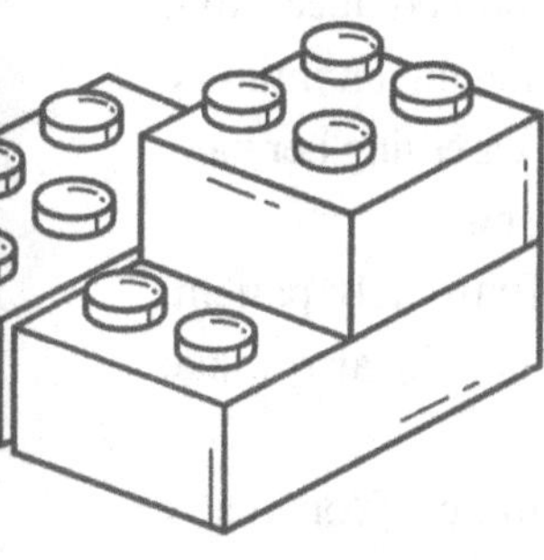

35

NOAH

My eyes scan the room. No Charlotte in sight. Bringing the mocktails to our table, I set them down, returning to my search. The dance floor is packed, and I roam the perimeter, wondering if maybe she got roped into another dance with a family friend.

It would be the third tonight.

The event has been stuffy and full of small talk, which I hate, but I can't deny it's a welcome distraction from the conversation with Mom and Tony today. The cherry on top is having Charlotte glued to my side, looking like mine.

Because she is.

"Hey," Charlotte says, and I spin to face her, sad, tired eyes boring into mine.

"What's wrong?"

She glances around. "Not here."

"Come on," I say, holding out a hand.

She slides her palm in mine, and I lead us to the middle of the dance floor, the crowd giving us privacy like at the Barracudas' gala all those months ago.

My free hand falls to her hip as we sway to the music, and I lean down to her ear. "Talk to me."

She rests her head against mine. "My mother took the news as expected."

I squeeze her hand. "I'm sorry to hear that."

"She doesn't think I'm ready to be a mom." Her voice cracks. "She thinks I can't do it."

I pull her head to my chest, covering her broken face from onlookers. To anyone watching, we're two lovers having an intimate moment. "You are going to be a *great* mom," I say, caressing her hair.

"You don't know that," she mumbles against me.

"Of course I do. You're fantastic with kids. Extremely patient. All the things that will make you a great teacher will also make you an incredible mom."

She pulls away, moist eyes looking up to mine. "You really think so?"

"I know so," I tell her with a soft smile.

She gnaws on her lower lip. "I may have also agreed to something stupid."

My muscles seize. "What?"

"I agreed to take the twins for their fall break next month."

My anxieties disappear, and I laugh. "What's so bad about that?"

"Well, I offered your house without even asking you."

"*Our* house," I remind her. "Or did you forget you live there too?" *Does she not want to anymore?*

She fights a smile. "Okay, but I still should have asked."

"You don't need my permission," I say, sliding my hand to the small of her back. "The twins are always welcome in *our* home."

"I will never be able to express how grateful I am for you." She rests her hand against my cheek, and my eyes flutter shut as I lean into it. "You make this all seem so easy."

Loving you is easy.

Like breathing.

Like gravity.

Like *home*.

"You're worth it." I bring her palm to my lips, kissing it.

"And I guess while we're at it, let's get the heavy stuff over with?" She smiles weakly, as we sway to the music. "So we can enjoy the rest of our *date night*?"

I nod, hooking a strand of hair behind her ear. "Only if you're ready."

"I am." She releases a heavy sigh. "Jonathan won't be a problem."

"What does that mean?" I ask, hand pausing against her face.

"He doesn't want to be involved."

Color me shocked. My lips flatten in a straight line. "He said that?"

"Actually, he threw money at me for an abortion," she says, and my mouth falls open, anger pulsating through me. "So that kinda got the point across."

"He did *what*?" My grip tightens on her hand.

"He"—she releases a shaky breath—"tried to pay me off so I'd get an abortion."

My jaw ticks, and I attempt to fight the firenado swirling in my chest.

I'm going to kill him.

"If I had slept with you over spring break, we could have at least tricked ourselves into thinking it wasn't his," I say, my tone lacking humor.

"Trust me," she deadpans, resting her head against my chest, "I think about that every day." We sway, and I shove down the anger. The song changes, and she looks up at me, our eyes connecting. "Ready to move on from the heavy stuff?"

"You lead, I follow, *soffione*."

She places a hand on my neck. "I've *really* missed you."

Guilt settles in my stomach. "I've missed you too."

"No." She shakes her head, the corners of her mouth quirking upwards. "I've missed *you.*" She rubs her thumb along the column of my throat. "And our *lessons.*"

I fight a smile. "You have?"

"Yeah." She nods. "Have you?"

"Of course," I say with a chuckle.

"Then why haven't you offered any classes, Professor?"

"Because I don't want to pressure you into anything." I've been so unsure where her head is, and the last thing I want to do is talk her into something she doesn't want. She mentioned Jonathan did that to her before, and I never, *ever* want to make her feel the way he did.

"You know what I want?" she asks, sliding her fingers into my hair and pulling me towards her. "To shut off my brain, pretend the world around us isn't imploding, and get fucked. Hard. Think you can help with that?"

That sounds incredible. And direct. "My office hours are open the rest of the evening, Ms. Benson."

"Wonderful." She grins up at me, dragging a fingernail along my neck. The entire room has faded away, once again, and all I see, feel, hear, is her. "And don't you dare treat me like I'm fragile. Tonight, I want to let go and have some fun." I nod, unable to speak. She stands on her tiptoes, lips to my ear. "Take me home, Noah."

Home.

The hum of the engine fills the cab, paired only with the shuffling satin of Charlotte's dress as she squirms in her seat. My left hand holds the steering wheel, the other is gripping her thigh, and I like to think I'm partly responsible for her restlessness.

It's eighty more minutes, give or take, to our house, and I am counting down the damn seconds. I'm dying to pull the truck over on this dark country highway, bend her over my tailgate, and fuck her senseless.

But I'm a patient man.

So I'll wait till we're at home, where I can watch her fall apart in the light.

Inching up the dress, I dip under her panties and coat my fingers in her arousal. She releases a breathy moan, and I bring my hand to my lips, sucking off her sweet taste.

"*Mmm.* I've missed you."

"Are you talking to me or my pussy?" she asks with a cheeky smile.

"Both."

In my peripheral, she shifts around the passenger seat, and ten seconds later, her panties land in my lap. I snatch them, side-eying her, and a lone streetlight briefly illuminates a dangerous, mischievous glint in her eyes. *I definitely like where this is heading.*

"Care to place a bet?" she asks as I shove them in my pocket.

"What do you have in mind?"

"If I can get you to pull over this truck and fuck me before we make it to the highway, then I get to be in charge when we get home."

As if she needs to win a bet to be in charge. "And if I'm able to make it?"

"I'll let you tie me up and blindfold me." My head whips to her, and she giggles. "Remember BDSM is part of the curriculum?"

My heart stops as visions of her bound and begging for me flash through my mind. "Are you sure?"

"Yes," she confirms. "I'm sure."

"Deal," I say without hesitation.

More shifting in the passenger seat, and a large clump of black silk is tossed my way.

"Holy shit. Are you naked?" My eyes dart to her briefly,

confirming my suspicions. I groan, forcing my eyes back to the road, and toss her dress in the backseat.

"Yes, Daddy, I am." My dick jumps.

"Don't you 'Daddy' me."

"But *Mommy* is *soooo* horny," she whines.

Yep. That's it. We're going to die here tonight because this woman gave me a heart attack by forcing all the blood to my dick.

"Charlotte," I warn, gripping the steering wheel. Sneaking another peek, I discover her hand is between her legs.

"Please, *baby*," she moans, and it's fake but it's still so goddamn hot.

Noah Caruso. You will not fuck this woman on the side of this highway. You will keep your dick in your pants and wait till you're home to tie her up and make her beg for being such a damn tease.

She gasps. "I wish you were inside of me."

Merda. I carefully but very quickly maneuver to the side of the highway, and Charlotte squeals with delight.

"That was easier than I thought." She beams as I put the truck in park and click on the hazards. While hopping out, I tug off my bow tie and then round to her side. Upon pulling open the door, she's illuminated by the cab's light, and I'm thankful there's no sign of life for miles. Her grin is wide and victorious, shoulders pushed back, tits begging for a taste.

Noah, focus!

Our eyes meet, and I grin, grabbing both her hands and bringing them before her.

"What are you…?" I wrap the bowtie around them, securing it with a tight knot. "Noah! You're only allowed to tie me up if you win."

"It's just your hands, *soffione*."

"I'm calling a flag on the play." She pouts, lifting her bonded wrists. "Holding."

"The penalty has been declined." I wink, slamming the door, and her protests are muffled as I round the truck.

"This isn't fair!" she insists as I get back in the driver's side. "How can I touch your dick with my hands tied?"

"Was that next on your itinerary of torture?" I ask, buckling myself back in.

"Honey, shouldn't you know better than anyone?" she says, the pet name making *me* squirm. "A quarterback doesn't share their playbook."

"If you're trying to get my dick hard with sports analogies," I say, pulling back onto the road, "it's working."

"Good, because I'm still on offense," she says smugly, and I shake my head. *Adorable.*

A symphony of sweet moans fills the cab, and every hair on my body stands.

"What are you doing?" I ask, readjusting my grip on the steering wheel.

"*Ohh yes*," she whines. "Yeah, baby. Fuck me harder!"

I pull her panties out of my pocket, reach over, and shove them in her mouth mid-squeal.

"There, that's better," I say, grin wide across my face as she shrieks through the fabric.

She spits them out. "Noah Gabriel Caruso! You are going to be in so much trouble when we get home."

"Didn't you say I'm not supposed to enjoy when you punish me? Because given your state of undress, I think I'll enjoy it very much."

"We'll see about that," she sasses, and I reach out, turning on the seat warmer so she won't get cold. "What are you doing?"

"Heating up my dinner."

She snorts. "You did not just say that!"

"If you don't stop talking, I'll shove the panties in your mouth again."

"Maybe I liked it."

I side-eye her. "I don't appreciate the reverse psychology."

Releasing a deep breath, I give myself a pep talk and remind myself of those rules I used to hate so much. Surely I can stick to them for another—I glance at the clock—sixty-two minutes.

One: don't touch Charlotte.

I tighten my grip on the steering wheel.

Two: don't think about Charlotte.

Well, that won't be possible. She's naked and desperate with desire on my passenger seat.

Three: don't text Charlotte.

Not relevant.

Four: don't kiss Charlotte.

I can definitely wait to break that rule till we're home.

One hundred percent positive I can do that.

Sixty-two minutes to home.

My jaw ticks as she rubs her tied-up hands along my thigh.

Forty-three minutes to home.

She's leaned back in the passenger seat, using her foot to stroke over my dick. Creative.

Seventeen minutes to home.

She's telling me about her most recent masturbation fantasy that included me, her, and a variety of sex toys I'll be ordering immediately.

I can't do it.

Our tongues tangle as the truck is parked in the corner of some gas station right off the exit in Crystal Bay. We're five fucking minutes from the house, but I need at the bare minimum to taste her lips. That's why my hands are in her hair, fingers arching inside her needy cunt, edging her till she hates me, and my dick is screaming at me to put the damn truck back in drive.

Gasping, I remove my hand, and she whimpers.

"*Noah*," she whines, squirming in her seat, her beautiful naked body quivering. "I fucking hate you right now."

"You think this is bad?" I say, forcing myself back in the driver's seat, a wide grin spread across my face. "Just wait till we get home."

Ten minutes later, she squeals as I toss her naked body on our bed and leave the room.

"Where are you going?" Charlotte calls after me, and I ignore her, rushing through the house to obtain a thin rope and a dining chair. When I return to the bedroom, her eyes widen, a huge grin spreading across her face. "What do you think you're doing?" she asks, hopping off the mattress and strolling over. My eyes trail her hungrily head to toes, elated to be back in a lit-up room where I can see the full masterpiece. *So much soft skin.*

"Preparing for your bondage lesson," I say, unravelling the cord, a rush of anticipation flowing through me. She snatches it from my hands with a smile so sinister I know I'll enjoy whatever comes next.

"Since you displayed poor sportsmanship"—she tsks—"I'm declaring myself the rightful winner."

"This is why players aren't allowed to double as referees," I say, feigning annoyance when in reality I'm more turned on than a rocket engine blasting to space.

"Sorry." Charlotte juts her lower lip out in a pout. "Maybe next time you'll play by the rules." *Unlikely.* She places a finger on my chest, dragging it against my skin as she circles me, eliciting full body shivers. I'm *really* going to enjoy this. "You've been a very naughty quarterback." Standing before me, she presses her hand against my chest and shoves me, forcing me to stumble onto the seat. The rope dangles from her fingertips. "Hands behind your back."

Oh, fuck.

The idea of tying her up and teasing her till she hates me is definitely appealing, but her doing it? I struggle to suppress my excitement. She can't know just *how* much I'm going to enjoy this.

"What are my crimes?" I ask in mock annoyance, bringing my hands behind the chair.

She wraps the cord around my wrists and then the back of the chair, tying it tightly in place. Yanking at them, I confirm she did a damn good job. I don't think I could even break this open with all my strength. *Fuck. This is so hot.*

"Well, your first offense is not giving me an orgasm in over two months," she says. "But since that was partially self-inflicted due to lack of communication on my part, I'll let you off with a warning."

I chuckle. "And my second offense?"

"Cancelling our FaceTime date when I was all dressed up—or rather, down—for phone sex."

My eyes snap to hers. "Excuse me, what?"

"When you were in New York and missed our FaceTime?" She purses her lips. "I had something special planned."

"Fuck, I'm sorry." Guilt racks through me. I'm trying to balance games and practices and press conferences, but Charlotte should never feel in last place.

"Save the apologies." She bites her lower lip to stifle a smile. "If you want me, you'll have to beg."

"Beg?" I repeat, hands secured behind my back, the chair digging into my biceps.

"Yep." Her smile is wicked as she places her hands on my clothed thighs. "Patience isn't always a virtue, Mr. Caruso." She slides them up slowly, and our eyes connect. *Have I died and gone to heaven?* "I was going to let you fuck me senseless in the back of your truck." My dick twitches, and her lips graze mine. "But now you'll have to beg."

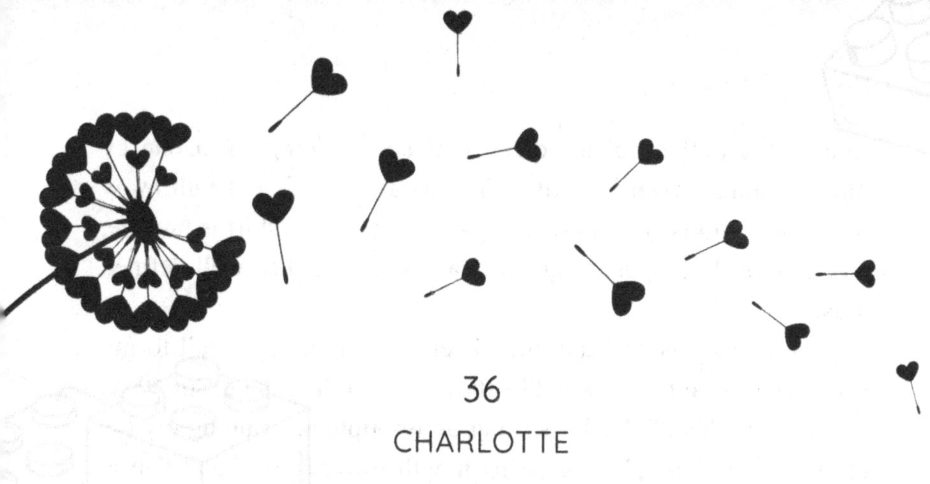

36

CHARLOTTE

Holy shit.

I'm doing it.

I'm really making Noah grovel for me. And from the glimmer of delight in his eyes, he's enjoying the hell out of it.

Seeing his excitement when he came in with the rope and chair drove me desperate to experience that rush for myself, and damn, it does not disappoint. Standing buck naked before Noah Caruso while he's tied up, his gaze following me like a lion stalks its prey, will forever be a core memory.

My eyes trail his body. His fully clothed body. *Shit, I didn't think this part through. We'll make it work.* I straddle his lap, grinding my sex against his very prominent erection, and he groans. "Bet you're regretting not going for the roadside fuck right about now, aren't you?" I ask, trying my hardest to exude confidence and sex appeal. Today was emotionally exhausting, but being able to forget about the heavy stuff going on and focus on my boyfriend is exactly what I need tonight.

"I know I'm supposed to say yes." His lust-filled eyes meet mine. "But you're unbelievably hot when you're bossy."

My soul leaves my body. *Down, praise kink.* I tsk, fingers

finding the buttons of his dress shirt and undoing them one by one. Leaning forward, I brush my lips against his but pull away before he can kiss me. *This is torture for two.* The shirt is undone, and I spread it open, fingers splaying across his well-defined muscles.

"Your body is so beautiful," I tell him as his eyes fall to my chest, analyzing my breasts like they'll be on the final exam. "You wanna taste them?" I ask, pushing on my tiptoes, bringing my tits closer to his face. He angles his mouth towards one, and I drop back to his lap with a soft thump. "Too bad."

His breathing intensifies. "*Mi fai impazzire.*"

I fight a smile, now knowing what the phrase means. His reassurance that my torment is working.

Sliding off him, I drop to my knees, fingers fumbling with his belt and pants. I tug them down, and his glorious hard cock is before me. Squirming, I squeeze my thighs together, the friction easing a minuscule amount of the ache Noah left between them in the truck. Our eyes meet, and I drop my focus to his shaft, hand gripping it. Pre-cum beads the tip, and I take him in my mouth and suck it off with a moan. *Fuck, I miss his hands in my hair.* His hips shift with need, thrusting into my mouth, and he releases a soft groan.

Popping off, I stand, spinning so my bare backside faces him. "It's been a long time since I did my stretches."

Folding over, ass to his face, I attempt to touch my toes, and he mutters an Italian curse. I spend a few minutes going through some teasing poses, many made difficult by the little bowling ball in my belly. Noah struggles against the ropes, the chair creaking.

"*Tesoro,* you're killing me."

"Then get to begging." He mutters another curse paired with a permanent wicked grin. I grip his shoulders, nails digging in, and lower my mouth to his ear. "How should I torture you next, *baby*?" Bringing my lips to his neck, I plant soft kisses, then bite, *hard*, and he releases a guttural moan.

"*Cazzo, soffione.* I'm going to come without you even touching my cock."

"Good." Pride fills me. "I recall you being very intrigued by the idea of sitting and watching."

"You wouldn't." His tone is sharp, solidifying my next plan of action.

I head to my bedside drawer for an extra teammate because as Andi would say, vibrators are a girl's best friend.

When I return to him, his gaze bounces between the elongated vibrator and my eyes, shoulders tense. "Charlotte," he warns once more.

"Yes, *Daddy*?" I say, tapping it against my hand like a ruler.

"If you don't let me be the one to make you come tonight, you're gonna be in so much trouble."

"Like I told you…" His gaze blazes across my skin, incinerating any insecurities. "All you have to do is beg."

He blows out a frustrated breath, and his lack of protest only proves how much he's enjoying this. He's curious how far I'll push this. Push *him.*

Well, class is in session, Noah Caruso, because this horny pregnant woman has got months of pent-up sexual frustration to release. My eyes drop to his cock, and fuck, do I want to impale myself on this man.

The point is to torture him, not yourself.

When I click on the vibrator, the buzz fills the room, and I place it against my nipple, the other instantly hardening. Noah's lips part, eyes hooded with lust as he watches me, unable to mutter a single word.

Stepping forward, I place my free hand on his shoulder and straddle my legs over his. I ease myself onto his lap, dragging the toy down my chest. My hand grazes his erection as I guide the silicone friend to my sex, and he shudders. Our eyes meet as it lands on my clit, and I whimper.

His shoulders struggle as he tries to free himself, with no

success of course. His eyes fall between us, and he groans. "You're incredible."

What's incredible is how he makes me feel.

I coat the toy with my arousal, my veins flushing with heat. Pushing to my tiptoes, I grip his shoulder, align my entrance with his cock, and lower myself, hissing as his tip stretches me open. *Focus. Mission. Torture.* His lips quiver, breathing shaky, and I fight for my own oxygen. When I sink all the way down, the breath is expelled from my lungs, and his mouth falls open, begging to be stuffed.

Grinning, I bring the vibrator between us. "Suck," I tell him, and his eyes flare with desire. This is the kinkiest shit I've ever done, and I think it may have changed my brain chemistry.

Noah opens his mouth wide, places it over the toy, and swirls his tongue around. *Fuck.* Why is this so hot?

He hums, eyes fluttering shut, and I rotate my hips, grinding against him needily while he sucks it clean. I remove it from his mouth, and he licks his lips, gaze meeting mine. He jerks his hips, thrusting deeper. "Now come for me, *soffione.*"

"Nah." I giggle, pulling off him, and his eyes widen.

"What the fuck do you mean… *nah?*" He groans as I slip off his lap. "Char, I can't take this much longer."

My stomach sinks. "Are you not enjoying it?"

He laughs, shaking his head. "The problem is I'm enjoying it *too* much."

"Oh." I beam, and a thrill runs through me. "Good. Because I have an experiment I'd like to perform."

His jaw ticks. "Care to share with the class?"

"Hypothesis: if Noah Caruso gets worked up enough, he'll come without me touching him."

"Don't. You. Fucking. Dare."

"It's in the name of science." I smirk, dropping to my knees before him and shuffling backwards. Leaning against the dresser, I spread my legs, giving him an unobstructed view.

With one hand I palm my tit, the other teasing my clit with the vibrator. I'm already so pent-up, a wave of pleasure racks through me, and I struggle to focus.

"Charlotte," he warns, jaw ticking, reminding me of the mission.

"Use your words, honey," I say, bringing the vibrator to my entrance. It's not as thick as he is, but it'll do the trick. Shoving it inside, I moan loudly, really making a show of it. "*Noah*," I whine, the same way I did in the truck, but he can't silence me with my panties this time. "*Yes!*" I cry, grinding against the vibrator exaggeratedly. "*So good.*" My eyes find his, and if looks could kill, his says he'd fuck me to my grave right now. "You look so pretty tied up for me." His face flushes, shoulders shaking as he struggles against the restraint. "I'm so proud of you for listening. Such a good boy."

"*Cazzo*," he groans with a shudder. "Fuck." He looks down, and I follow his line of sight, lips parting open in satisfaction. His cock twitches as white liquid shoots out.

"Oh my god!" I squeal, my arousal soaring, bringing me close to the edge myself.

His eyes meet mine, and I'm intoxicated. Knowing I have the power to make this man release without even touching him is euphoria.

I feel powerful. Incredible.

"Untie me," he demands, leaving no room for argument. "Now."

I remove the vibrator, clicking it off, and toss it to the side. "Only if you promise to continue being a good boy." He nods enthusiastically, holding my gaze as I stand and round the chair, grabbing the rope between his wrists. Yanking it softly, I bring my lips to his ear and whisper, "Are you gonna be a good boy?"

"Yes," he pants.

"Yes, what?"

"Woman," he growls.

"Yes, *what?*"

"I'm gonna be a good boy," he promises, and holy shit, is sub Noah hot.

"See, I knew you could listen," I tease, my heart pounding as I unknot the rope. The second it's undone, he yanks his hands free, jumps out of the chair, and spins to face me. "Wait." I point a finger his way, freezing him in place, our chests heaving in unison. "Take off your clothes." Within seconds he's buck naked in the center of the room, looking like one of those ancient statues of the gods. "Get on your knees." He drops to the ground, eyes holding mine. "Now beg."

"Please." His eyes glisten with lust.

"Please what?"

"Please, *soffione*." His voice is low. Husky. Seductively sinful. "Can I touch you?" My gaze falls to his shaky hands, and I clench my thighs together. This man is trembling with need, for *me*.

That's so hot. *He's* so hot.

"Are you sure you don't need a little intermission?" I ask, eyes homing in on his dick, which is *still* hard.

"Yes." His jaw ticks. "I'm sure."

I graze my thumb along his lip as he stares up at me. "You're so pretty when you beg."

A playful smile spreads across his face, and I release him, heading to the bathroom. "Where are you going?"

"What's it look like?" I say, reaching in the shower to turn on the water as he rushes after me. I step inside and turn to face him. "Are you just gonna stand there?"

"Wasn't sure if Mommy Dom was letting me join," he teases, hungry eyes raking over me.

"Hmm." I tap my fingers to my lips. "I'll allow it."

Noah's grin brightens, and he hurries inside the walk-in. The warm water streams down on us, our gazes locked. "Can I *please* touch you now?" he begs, and I step backwards, him following after till my back is flush against the cool tile. He places his hands on the wall behind me, caging me in, and our lips graze as he mumbles, "You made a mess of me, baby." He releases a shaky breath. "But I've missed you so damn much. Please. Please let me touch you."

My own body trembles with need, or maybe it's the freezing tile, but either way I find myself saying, "Yes."

Within seconds, his hands are in my hair, lips crashing against mine. Our tongues intertwine, and I whimper with need as we make up for lost time. He pins me against the wall, planting kisses along my jaw, down my neck, and rasps, "These last two months were torture. Sleeping beside you but not being able to touch you the way I want."

I place my hands around his waist, tugging his naked, wet body against mine. "Well, no more holding back. Touch me *any way* you want."

"Well, right now…" He drags a hand up my inner thigh. "I'm lacking the willpower to take it slow. Your little hypothesis made sure of that." He cocks a brow, and a satisfied smile spreads across my face. "So I think I'd like to kiss you senseless while fucking you against this wall, if that's alright?"

"More than."

He grips his length, swiping it between my center, and presses the tip against my entrance. "And I want to finish inside you."

"Noah. Stop telling me what you want to do and do it already." He's not the only one who's sick of taking it slow. I've been pent-up with need since we left the fundraiser.

Hell, since the Fourth of July.

His mouth slams against mine, tip stretching my entrance, and I melt. His tongue toys with the seam of my lips, coaxing out my own, and our kiss deepens. He thrusts inside, holding me against him.

"You okay?" he asks between kisses.

I chuckle. "It would be impossible for you to be a Dom for, like, five seconds, wouldn't it?"

"I don't want to get caught up and hurt you," he says, thrusting gently, looking between us. "Or the baby." *I adore this man.*

"I'm fine," I say, putting a finger under his chin, tipping his gaze to mine. "*We're* fine."

"You promise?"

"I promise," I assure him. "I'll let you know if something hurts. Now please ju—" *Thrust.* The air expels from my lungs, and a satisfied smile creeps across my face. "Thank you."

He continues his torture, and both of us are so worked up, it doesn't take but a minute till we're seeing stars, slumping against each other.

"I think that was my favorite lesson yet," I murmur into the crook of his neck.

He grins at me and steps away.

"Show me," he instructs, and I spread my legs, his cum trickling down my thighs. His face splits with a satisfied smile. "Mine."

37

NOAH

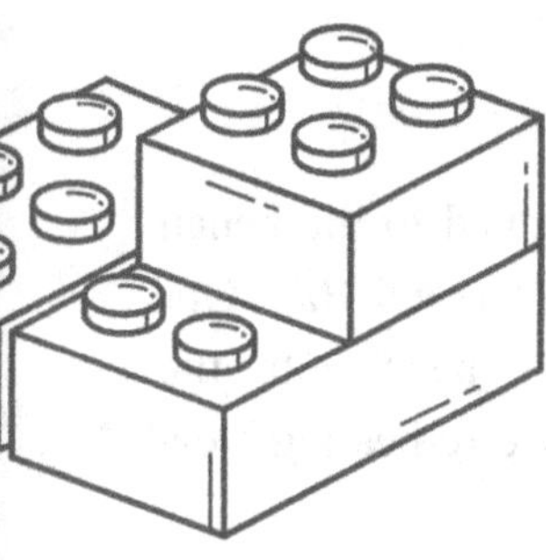

My veins buzz with adrenaline as my team and I jog out of the tunnel and onto the Tampa Barracudas' field. It's our first regular season game, and playing at home stadium is double the pressure. Although, my life's atmosphere lately could be compared to Neptune's. It's only a matter of time before diamond rain pours down on me from these extreme conditions.

Fortunately, Charlotte relieved some of that tension after the gala last night. In more ways than one. I've been so unsure where her head is at, and I know we still have a lot to figure out, but my god was it incredible to *be* with her and ignore all the chaos.

Making my way to the sideline, I scan the front row. As part of my contract, I get four season tickets to every home game. When I reach the bench, my eyes find Theo, Charlotte, Mom, and Tony. I know Mom and Tony aren't fully on board with Charlotte's and my situation, but I hope they won't do anything to make her feel uncomfortable.

Charlotte's wearing my new jersey, number thirteen, tight over her bump. *Mine.* Her attention turns toward the field, and when our eyes meet, vivid memories of last night come flooding through. *Fuck.* I shake them away, no desire for ninety thousand fans to see another premature ejaculation.

Part of me was embarrassed, but seeing the fire in Charlotte's eyes, how much it turned her on… yeah, she can tie me up and torture me any time. She picks up a sign and holds it above her head, and my mouth splits into a shit-eating grin.

The QB's going home with me!

Hell yeah, I am.

Three quarters pass, and my ass has been glued to the bench the entire time. A one-eighty from my time at Crystal Bay. Our first-string quarterback, Mike Lorraine, who's been with the Barracudas for years, is out there smashing it. We're beating New Orleans 21-7.

I want to be on a winning team as much as the next guy, but what I much prefer is actually *playing* on a winning team. Otherwise I might as well be in the bleachers. Glancing behind me, I see my fan club is still cheering excitedly. Mom and Charlotte are laughing together and seem to be getting along fine.

I force my gaze back to the field. *Focus.* I played in a few preseason games and even threw three touchdowns, but those don't count for anything. They're basically scrimmages with half a stadium of screaming onlookers.

"Caruso!" Coach Bexley calls, and I fly off the bench, helmet optimistically in hand.

"You're swapping in for Lorraine," he says.

I nod, throwing my helmet on and positioning the mouth guard. Lorraine runs towards us, and I sprint out, swapping places. Line of scrimmage is fifty yards from the end zone, and I set up behind the center.

Taking a deep breath, I shove all negative shit from my mind and do the one thing I can. Throw a fucking football.

"Seventy-two. Eighty-nine. Forty-four," I shout, veins buzzing, molars grinding on the mouth guard between calls. "Down." Glancing left and right, I ensure my running backs are in position.

"Set." My eyes focus on the ball below the center's fingertips. "Hike!"

It soars toward me, directly into my hands. I shuffle backwards, fingers gripping the leather laces, arm cocked back as I search the field. Trey Perez, our fastest running back, is sprinting down the field, a defender on his heels, but he's coming out ahead to the location the play instructed. I send the ball spiraling through the air and stumble to a pause.

The stadium falls to a hush, and as if in slow motion, it drops into Perez's arms.

"Yes!" I shout, jogging forward and watching as he continues outrunning the defender, gaining yardage.

He's at the thirty.

Twenty.

Ten.

Five yards.

And that's a motherfucking touchdown!

I yell, leaping up, a few of the Barracudas running over to me for high fives and a celebratory huddle.

I, Noah Caruso, Barracudas' quarterback, have thrown my very first touchdown in a pro game.

The huddle breaks, and I jog towards the sideline so special teams can plan for the extra point. Charlotte's eyes are following me, and I tap my hand to my helmet's chin mask, then throw it her way like a football, hoping she gets the point. She throws her hand in the air, "catching" it with a huge grin on her face, and surprises me by placing it on her stomach.

My smile is massive the rest of the game.

We win 28-14, and I may not know much right now, but playing the game I love with Charlotte screaming my name from the bleachers is all I'll ever need.

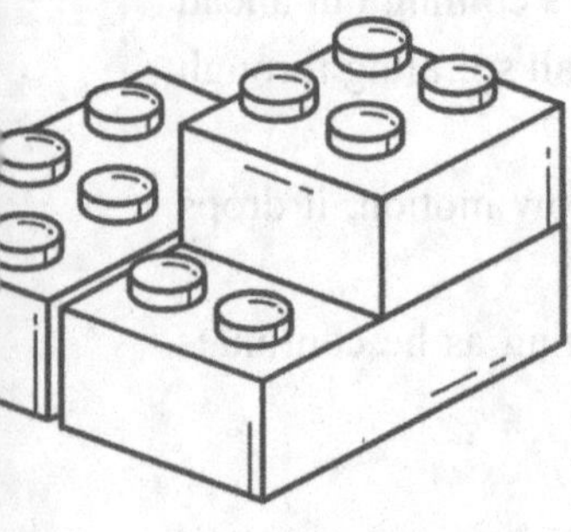

38

NOAH

Practice was tough, and I groan, grabbing my duffle from the passenger seat and hopping out of the truck. We've been in regular season for a month, and I'm trying to be extra conscious of that work/life balance despite my hectic schedule.

When I enter the front door, my senses are overwhelmed with a variety of sweet smells, which can only mean one thing.

Charlotte is stress baking.

After dropping the duffle by the door, I wander to the kitchen, my suspicions confirmed by dozens of muffins spread all over the island, kitchen table, and every square inch of countertop.

Charlotte closes the oven and turns towards me, wearing a cute little apron, mitt on her hand, holding *another* muffin tray. "Hey, honey."

"Whatcha doing there?" I ask, noting the dusty white powder all over her face.

"Baking muffins," she says, smiling wide, setting the tray on a cooling rack.

"For the entire neighborhood?" I ask with a smirk, and her narrowed eyes find mine.

"It's relaxing." She picks one up and hands it to me. "And tasty."

Our eyes lock, and I bite into it, adding a breathy moan for her benefit. "*Quasi meglio del sesso, soffione.*"

"Translate?"

I chuckle. "I said it's better than sex."

Her lips part. "Well, I would hope not!"

"It's a compliment," I assure her, finishing my muffin. "So what's got you all worked up?"

"Nothing." Her forced smile deepens as she returns to a mixing bowl and starts all over again. "Everything is fine. Perfect. Great. Wonderful."

I narrow my eyes. "*Tesoro,* your relaxing habit is stressing me out."

"Fine," she says, exasperated. "The twins are coming tomorrow for their fall break."

"And?"

"And what if my mother is right?" She cracks an egg in the bowl. "What if it's a disaster?"

Sadness surrounds me that Charlotte's own mother has her thinking she can't do this.

"You've been helping take care of them their whole lives," I remind her. "Next week will be fine. And I'll help as much as I can."

"But I don't want it to get in the way of your work stuff," she says after cleaning off her hands, now measuring vanilla extract.

"It won't." I stride across the kitchen to place a hand on her back because I know better than to stop her when she's panic baking. "Just relax."

She side-eyes me. "When in the history of history has a woman successfully relaxed after being told to relax?"

"Everything will be fine." I chuckle, kissing the side of her head, and back away towards our bedroom. "The only concern you should have is them suffering from muffin overdoses." She picks one up and chucks it at me, and I catch it, taking a big bite. "Looks like I'm your first victim."

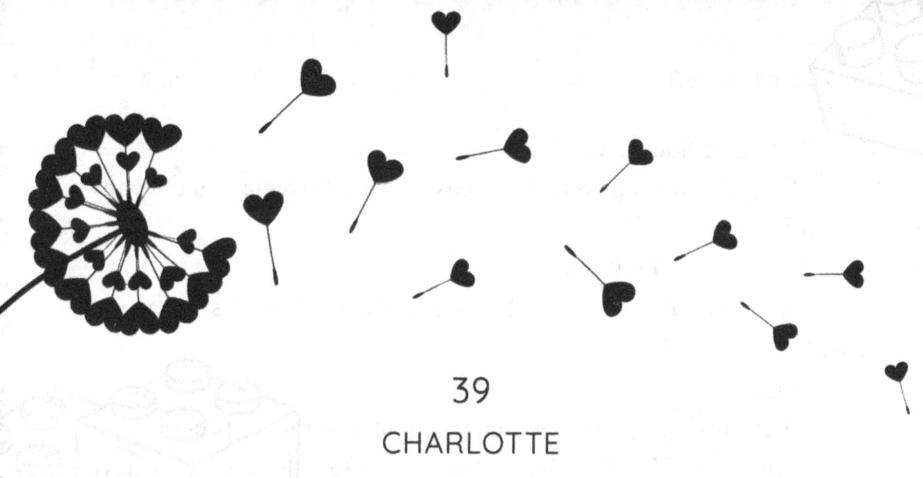

39

CHARLOTTE

"You feeling better?" I ask Denny as we walk through the aisles of the grocery store. Poor thing's had a queasy tummy since Patricia dropped them off yesterday. Okay, maybe it was after she ate nine chocolate chip muffins while ignoring my protests, but there's no way I'll admit that to Noah.

"I'm okay," she says paired with a little grumble.

"Bread is the last thing, and then we can go," I tell her and Nash.

"Oh, look, Lottie!" she says, grabbing a pink little baby teether off the end cap.

"No, this one's cooler," Nash says, grabbing one that looks like a key ring.

I smile down at them, appreciating their enthusiasm. "Baby won't need those for a while. Maybe next time."

"Fine," they huff, putting the items back.

My phone rings, and I pull it out to see Noah's name flash across the display.

"Hey," I say after accepting the call.

"Hey, *soffione*," he coos in his sweet tone. "You still at the store?"

"Yeah, be home soon."

"Can you pick up some little pasta stars? I wanna make Denny soup for dinner."

"You got it," I tell him.

"And actually, I need a few other things. Can I send you a list?"

"Sure."

After picking up the new items, we head to the register.

"That'll be $78.32," the cashier says after the groceries have been bagged and placed in the cart. I stick my card into the machine, and it makes a god-awful buzzing sound.

"Please remove your card, ma'am," the cashier says as a receipt spits out on her end. "It's been declined."

I stop breathing, glancing anxiously at the line of people waiting behind me.

"Can you try again?" I ask.

Another attempt, and the same result.

"Sorry," I tell the cashier, and the bystanders, as I pull up my banking app.

BALANCE: $22.06.

Shit. Tears well in my eyes as I stare at the cart full of groceries I can't afford.

Looks like the money from my grants and student loans has already run out. Shit.

"I… I have to put some items back," I say hesitantly, my resolve crumbling.

"Lottie, can we go?" Nash asks, tugging my shirt.

"One second, buddy."

The cashier huffs a breath. "I'll cancel the transaction. Just give me what you want."

Scanning quickly through the bags, I add up items in my head.

Noah asked for the pasta. *$2.31.*

I promised Denny the ice cream. *$4.99.*

We can make peanut butter sandwiches with the bread. *$3.49.*

Eggs. *$6.36.*

I'll tell Noah the rest of the stuff he asked for was out of stock. I hand the items to the cashier, and she scans them.

The tutoring job at CBU is sounding more and more appealing.

Holding my breath, I insert my card, and the little green check mark, paired with a beautiful ding, has me reclaiming oxygen.

I grab the lone bag of groceries and the kids' hands, and we rush out like we robbed the place.

Although, I'm pretty sure I'm the one who's been robbed. Where the hell did all my money go?

Tuition.

Textbooks.

Groceries.

Gas.

Insurance.

"Why couldn't we take the other stuff?" Nash asks, and a lump forms in my throat.

"My card was broken," I tell him.

"Can you fix it?"

"I hope so."

How the hell do you plan on doing that?

When we get to the Bronco, I secure the kids and round the back to put the single pitiful bag of groceries in the trunk. The trunk of the car my boyfriend bought me. Because I'm a broke ass bitch with no money and no direction and no damn plan. *Guess my mother was right about me.* If I weren't so dead set on following my passion instead of the "honorable" path she chose for me, maybe I wouldn't be four dollars away from penniless.

"Excuse me," I hear, glancing up to the sight of an older woman pushing a full cart my way. "You forgot these." She gestures to the groceries.

"Sorry, you have me mistaken."

"No." Her eyes bore into mine. "I don't."

Glancing at the cart and through the thin bags, I notice it's the items I left at the register. "I… didn't pay for those."

She hands me a receipt with a hesitant smile. "They're paid for."

My lips part open as my eyes flick from the receipt back to her. "I can't accept this."

"Well, it's here for the taking." She shrugs before removing one plastic bag that I assume is hers. She smiles and walks away, leaving me dumbstruck with the cart full of groceries from a stranger. Tears stream down my cheeks as I place each bag in the trunk, sending up a grateful prayer to whoever our guardian angel is today. I wipe my face dry before getting in the car. Settling in the driver's seat, I take a deep breath.

"Alright," I croak out and clear my throat. "Let's go."

Attempts to suppress my tears are useless, and I spend the entire ride home praying the two little angels in the back don't notice just how hard they fall.

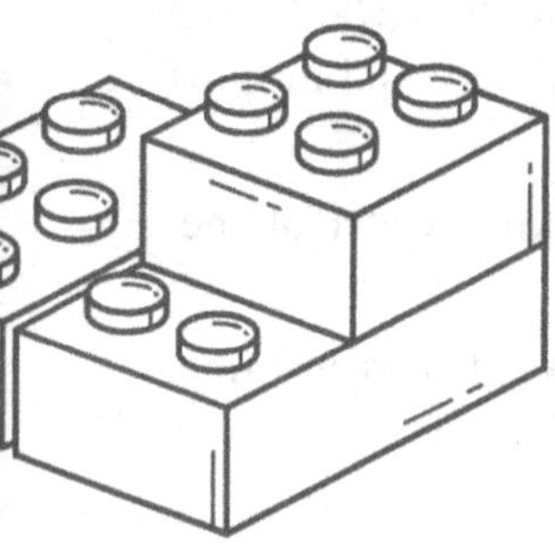

40

NOAH

"How's your stomach?" I ask Denny as she slurps another bite of the homemade *pastina* soup I made.

"Better," she says, relieving some of my concern.

"Good. But no more muffins for you, okay?"

"It wasn't the muffins," Charlotte argues.

I place my hand on hers. "Of course it wasn't."

Denny leans over, her voice a whisper. "It was totally the muffins."

I chuckle, turning my attention back to Charlotte. She's looked exhausted from the moment she walked through the door, and I worry she's pushing herself too hard. "How was your day?"

"Good," she clips.

"Do you want to talk about it?" I press.

"I'm fine." She plasters on the fake smile. "Just tired."

"Are you feeling okay? Everything okay with baby?"

"Yes, Noah," she says, exasperated. "Baby *and* I are fine."

We finish dinner and place our bowls in the sink. "Why don't you take a bath, and I'll clean up here?"

"I've got it." She turns on the water and squirts soap on a sponge. "You worked all day. You must be exhausted."

She's right. I'm exhausted. But not half as exhausted as I'll be if I stay up all night worrying about her instead of taking care of her.

Leaving the kitchen, I head to our bathroom and turn on the warm water. I throw in those Epsom salts she likes and make sure the temperature is pregnancy safe before heading back to the kitchen. I walk up behind her, snake my arms around, and turn off the faucet.

"Hey!" she says, spinning around and flicking water at me. "I'm doing dishes here."

"No, *I'm* doing dishes," I say, taking her wet hands in mine. "You're taking a bath."

"I told you I—"

"Water's already running." I press a quick kiss to her knuckles. "If you don't go check on it, we'll have a flood in our house."

"Fine, *Noah*," she says, cracking a smile. "No need to go building the ark."

"Take your time. I'll put the kids to bed."

"You don't have—"

I put a finger over her lips, silencing her. "I *want* to do these dishes, and I *want* to put the kids to bed. Denny and I are reading about a princess locked in a castle, and I've got to find out what happens next." That elicits a small laugh from her pretty lips.

"Fine," she huffs, slapping the wet sponge in my hand, and heads to our bedroom.

"You have fun at campus today?" I ask Nash as I tuck him in after a half hour of intense Lego building.

"Lottie took us to see the football stadium." He smiles, turning to face me and placing his hand under his head.

"Awesome," I say, and we bump fists. "Did you meet some of our friends?"

"Yeah, they played catch with me." He frowns. "But I wasn't very good."

"Wanna practice tomorrow? We can throw the ball around in the backyard."

"Yeah." He smiles wide. "I'd like that a lot."

"Good," I say, standing to leave.

"Noah," he says, sitting up.

"Yeah, buddy?"

"Can you help me with something?" My chest squeezes that he's comfortable asking me.

"What is it?"

He reaches under his pillow and pulls out a debit card. My brows furrow. "Lottie cried today because this card is broken," he says, handing it to me, and I glance down at the name: Charlotte Benson. "I don't think crying is good for the baby... and was hoping you can help me get her a new one."

"First of all," I say, cocking a brow, "don't ever take anything from *Lottie's* purse without asking. Understand?" He nods sheepishly. "Second of all, what happened?"

He fills me in on their entire trip to the store, including the "nice lady who brought out the groceries Lottie forgot," and my shoulders tense with each new piece of information.

After leaving his room, I pull out my phone and solve Charlotte's problem with the tap of a few buttons. And damn, does it feel good, alleviating all her stress with the simple swipe of my finger.

41

CHARLOTTE

"Ma'am, I can assure you, it's not a mistake," the bank teller from the 24/7 hotline repeats on the phone for the umpteenth time as I pace the floor of our bedroom.

"Well, it must be because I'm not sure where this money came from." I stare at my banking app, displaying the deposit of $25,000 from NGC Trust. I was having a very relaxing bath until I received a notification for a transfer that made my eyes bulge out of my skull.

"Are you sure there's no one who could have sent you this money?"

NGC Trust.

N "G" C Trust...

Noah Gabriel Caruso Trust.

"You've gotta be kidding me," I say, my mouth slack jawed. "Thanks, I gotta go."

"Is there anyt—"

I hang up the phone as Noah walks into the room, shutting the door behind him.

"Kids are down," he tells me, a glass of water in his hand.

"Did you just transfer me $25,000?" I ask, the cup pausing

halfway to his lips. His pleased eyes meet mine, and he sets the drink on the dresser.

"Instant transfer really does mean instant, doesn't it?" he says casually, as if he bought me flowers or a fucking cup of coffee.

My mind swirls in circles. "Why?"

"Nash told me about your 'card being broken.'" He shrugs. "You needed money, and I have plenty of it."

"Twenty-five *thousand* dollars?" I shriek. *This is too much.* "Have you lost your mind?"

"My mind is perfectly in place, thanks." He smirks a smug smile that makes it so damn hard to resist his charm. My heart pounds.

"I can't accept this," I say, holding my phone in his face. As if the gesture alone could transfer the money back to his account.

He grabs the phone, locks it, and puts it in his pocket. "I care about you. And I won't have you struggling with something I can solve with the tap of my finger."

Mom's words echo in my mind. *"You get an NFL football player with a seven-figure bank account, and he gets a broke, aimless, has-been cheerleader knocked up with some other man's baby."*

"I appreciate it, but it's not necessary," I say, holding his gaze, the black hole inside seconds away from swallowing me entirely. "There's a tutoring job open at CBU I'm applying for."

He scoffs. "You're not working some shit job paying twelve dollars an hour when I have plenty of money to support us. You need help. And I have the means to, so please accept it."

"How about *you* accept letting me pay my own way?" I say, poking his chest.

He wraps his fingers around mine. "We're having a baby, babies cost money, and, respectfully, you don't have any."

"*I'm* having a baby," I correct, and Noah tenses, pain flickering in his eyes. *Why did I say that?*

"Charlotte," he says, his tone concerningly calm. "I need to ask you something, and I need you to be honest."

"What?" I flatten my hand to his chest, and his heart pounds against it. His hand covers mine, relieving a minuscule fraction of my fear.

"And know that whatever you answer, it doesn't affect the money I gave you," he says, and my skin crawls with anxiety.

"Noah." My hand trembles against him. "Please spit it out."

"I've always said I'm not going anywhere, but..." He pauses, and my heart rate skyrockets. "I never considered asking you—to tell you that if you... if *you* want to leave, I would understand."

My mouth drops open. "You want me to leave?"

"What? No." He squeezes my hand. "I just don't want you to feel trapped."

"Do *you* feel trapped?" I ask.

"Of course not," he says, stepping away and dragging his hands through his hair. "Shit, this is coming out all wrong."

"Ya think?"

He releases a shaky breath, glistening eyes meeting mine. "All I'm trying to say is, I know legally you and this baby aren't mine. And I don't want you to feel like you're stuck here. And I want you to know, I support your decisions, even if they're not what I would want."

One look at his broken face, and the realization hits me.

My noble prince. The most selfless man I've ever met. He's accepted a woman who's pregnant with another man's baby, who he has no legal right to, and must be holding his breath she'll leave.

And yet... he's not pressuring me to stay.

He's not guilting me into submission.

He's terrified I'll go but still offers me an out.

Once again putting my feelings first. Putting *me* first.

"What do *you* want, Noah?" I ask, poking his chest.

His fingers wrap around mine again, and he flattens my palm against him like a tether. "It doesn't matter what I want," he murmurs, but the wild pounding of his heart tells me *just* how much it does.

"It matters to me." I slide my hand up and rest it against his neck. "Stop worrying about me, and what I want, and what you *think* I want or need or whatever. Just please, this once, I want you to be selfish. I *need* you to be honest. What do *you* want?"

"For you to stay!" he admits, tone laced with frustration.

"You do?"

"Of course I do."

"But why?" I put a hand on my stomach. "Why are you doing this to yourself? Don't let my mistake ruin your life."

"Ruin my life?" He laughs sarcastically. "Do you hear yourself?" He shakes his head. "You want to know why I'm doing this? Why I won't let you run away and deal with this on your own like you keep trying to? Because the idea of you not being in my arms, and this baby being anywhere other than this house, makes me sick to my stomach."

My heart aches at the pain he's enduring for me. For us. "You don't deserve that."

"I don't deserve love and a family?!" he shoots back, a tear rolling down his face.

"Of course you do. But you don't deserve to be sick to your stomach over a baby that's not even *yours!*"

He hooks an arm around my waist, tugging me to him, and splays his fingers over my stomach. "Do you wish she was mine?"

"Of course I do!" I say through a half-sob.

"Then let her be mine."

"Noah." Placing my hand on his, I stare into his eyes. "I'd wish on every dandelion in the world to make that happen. But nothing will change the fact she's *not.*"

"Let. Her. Be. Mine." His fingers cling to my stomach protectively. "Stop fighting this. Stop fighting us. Screw genetics. *She* is mine. *You* are mine. And if anyone doesn't agree, then fuck them."

I shake my head. "No one would *choose* this life."

"I would," he says, exasperated, then releases a shaky breath. "I am… if you'll let me."

"Just like that?" I ask hesitantly.

"Just like that," he says with a soft smile, brushing a strand of hair behind my ear.

For months we've been twin suns, dancing around one another in a celestial waltz. Noah has endlessly proven his devotion to me and this baby, desperately waiting for me to stop fighting his gravitational pull. I will never, ever be able to repay him for what he's done for us. What he continues to do. But I *can* stop saying shitty, hurtful things and letting my trauma get in the way of our happiness. Sliding a hand around his neck, I crash my lips to his.

"Everything's going to be alright," he murmurs as the cosmic kiss fuses us as one.

He's so steady. So sure. So absolutely in control that I almost believe him.

"See you in a few weeks," I tell Denny and Nash, giving them each a squeeze on our front porch. They head towards Mom's Porsche, and she stands before me, perfectly poised with pursed lips. Usually Patricia shuttles them, which means she wants something.

"It seems everything went well with the twins," she says the moment they're out of earshot.

"Does that mean you'll stop pushing me to give up the baby?" I ask, knowing it was never an option for me. After Noah's declaration this week, I'm more sure than ever of what our future looks like. Her judgmental gaze drops to my now noticeable bump.

"I can see you won't go for that," she says, cold eyes returning to mine. This look would usually have me caving in on myself. But I'm a mother now too. I'm not afraid of her threats. I have someone else to think about. "But let's discuss returning access to your trust fund."

"What?" That catches my attention. After my breakdown earlier this week, I wanted nothing more than to have that money. I'd never stress about a stupid grocery bill ever again. Baby and I would never have to worry Noah will come to his senses, realize how coo-coo bananas this all is, and kick us out.

Let. Her. Be. Mine.

But I have faith he won't.

"With conditions, of course," she adds.

Of course.

"Conditions?" I scoff. "What part of this"—I place my hand on my stomach—"makes you think we're having a negotiation?"

Baby kicks my hand, and it feels like she's saying, *High five, Mom!*

"Here's what's going to happen," she says. "You and Jonathan will make up. You'll move in together. Get married, because the press certainly can't know that I have a daughter who got pregnant out of wedlock. We don't need a Bristol Palin situation on our hands. That'll also ensure Jonathan can't up and abandon you. We'll tell them you had a private ceremony in the church earlier this year and only now officially legalized it with the state."

My jaw has hit the floor. The *audacity.* "You are out of your mind."

"Just think about it," she presses.

I consider what a life would be like with Jonathan.

Cold. Empty. Forced.

Noah's smiling face comes to mind, immediately filling me with a sense of security. Of divine bliss.

Being here, in this house with a man who *chooses* me, chooses *us*, day after day.

Yeah, I'm never giving that up.

No amount of money on god's green fucking Earth will buy my life from me.

My jaw clenches as we stand eye to eye. "Keep your hush money. I don't want it."

42
NOAH

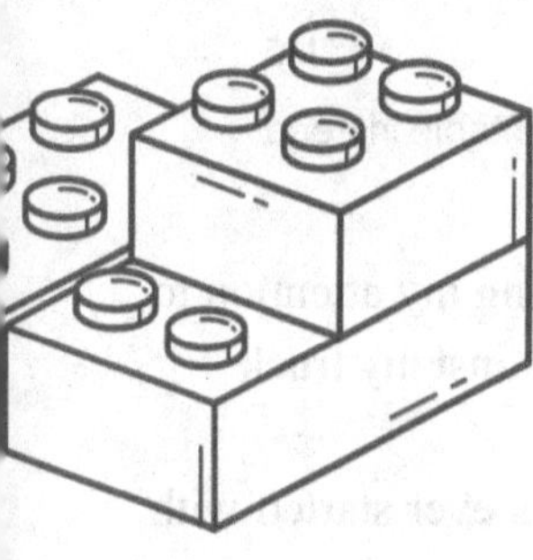

The sun beats down on me as I stroll across the training field parking lot toward my truck. My head is high, a stupid grin plastered on my face. It's been a few weeks since Charlotte finally accepted my role in her life. In *their* life, and everyday I'm grateful when practice ends so I can get home. Today is no exception.

Phone in hand, I pull up her contact.

ME

Fun Fact: Avocados are believed to be an aphrodisiac

CHARLOTTE

Adds to grocery list

What else?

ME

Oysters

CHARLOTTE

I would rather be celibate for the rest of my life than put an oyster in my mouth.

ME

removes oysters from grocery list

CHARLOTTE

Smart man

Sex is still on the table

ME

How about I put you on the table instead

"Noah," a familiar feminine voice says, pulling my attention to the last person I ever expected to find leaning against my truck.

"Georgia," I clip.

"We need to talk." No good conversation has ever started with those words.

"About?" An alarm is blaring in my head—DEFCON 1. Whatever reason she has for showing up here, and not my house where her daughter lives, cannot be good. I glance around the mostly empty, *secure* parking lot. "How did you get in here?"

"I have connections." She waves me off.

"What do you want?"

"You and Charlie need to stop this little thing you've got going on. It's time for her and Jonathan to make up."

My body flushes with anger, and I huff a laugh. "Are you crazy?"

"No. I just think things through."

Is she suggesting I don't?

"Charlie's using you," she says. "You must realize that."

Fury surges through me at the insinuation. "Bullshit."

"As soon as she gets her trust fund back, she'll leave you."

"You're giving it back?" I ask, shocked by the news. Georgia doesn't seem like the type to do anything without cause.

"When she agrees to my terms." *There it is.* Charlotte never mentioned anything about this. *Is she considering it?*

"She won't," I say with a scoff. I don't even need to hear the terms to know they're bullshit. And if they involve a life where Charlotte and I aren't together, then the chances of her accepting are null.

"You sure about that?" she replies with an icy smile, sending chills down my spine.

"Yeah," I say confidently. "I'm sure."

"Save yourself the drama and end things now."

I walk past her, opening the back door and throwing my duffle in. "Why the hell do you care anyways?" I ask, veins molten hot, slamming the back door shut. "Just leave Charlotte alone."

"Because the press will have a goddamn field day if they find out my twenty-year-old daughter got knocked up. Especially if it comes out she's living with a man who isn't the father. Even worse, a man like you."

I stand there slack-jawed, brushing aside the personal insult to focus on the most idiotic part. "You're telling me you want your daughter to live a pretend life, in a loveless relationship with a man who doesn't want his child, so that you can... what? Become governor?"

"Oh, sweetie," she says condescendingly. "That's step one. I've got my eye on a much *bigger* chair in a much *whiter* house."

"*You* want to be president?" The level of delusion is laughable. This woman should be in Oz under a house right about now.

"Yes, and that means my record needs to be squeaky clean. No mess. No slutty daughter." My veins buzz at how she speaks about her. "At least if Charlie's with Jonathan, it could appear planned. Honorable. A proper family."

A proper family.

Fuck. That.

"Thanks for your 'advice,'" I grit out. "But I'm not ending my relationship because you have a batshit dream to be president."

"I can make your life hell," she threatens, pointing a finger at me. "Ruin your reputation. Make sure you don't so much as coach a youth football team. Every news outlet in the country will be aware of exactly where Noah *Lewis* came from." Every muscle in my body tenses at her use of my father's last name. "Are we clear?"

Straightening my spine, I stare directly in Georgia's icy eyes. "Take my career. Take my name and drag it through the mud for all I care. Hell, take every single dollar I have. But let *me* make something crystal fucking clear. You will *never* take her."

"Don't underestimate me." She doubles down. "Jonathan and Charlie are getting back together. They will get married. Have this baby. And you're not going to do a damn thing about it."

I open my truck door, grinning ear to ear. "Watch me."

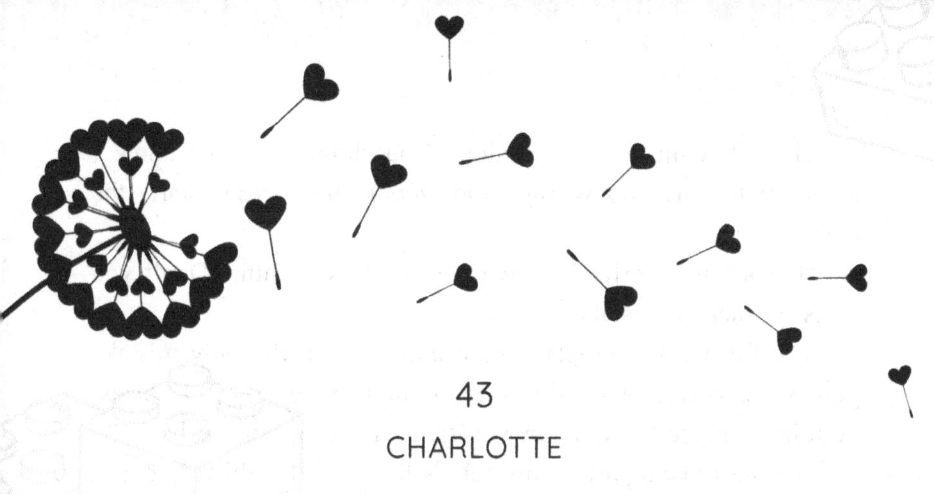

43

CHARLOTTE

I fold another burp cloth and place it in the dresser of the nursery. Nesting is in full swing, and at this rate, the baby's room should be completed next week. After pulling a pink sheet out of the basket, I hang it over the side of the crib to make the bed later.

A pounding knock comes from the front door, and I rush towards it. Throwing it open, I say, "Stop forgetting your house key! I really do—" The words fall off my tongue as a face I hoped I'd never see again stands on the porch. "What the hell are you doing here?"

Jonathan hurries inside, not waiting for an invitation, and I consider leaving the door open for a quick escape. Peeking outside, I check I'm not being punked or set up for some bullshit paparazzi blitz, and after deeming it's safe, I shut us inside.

How does he know where I live?

Jonathan turns toward me in the living room, scratching at his jaw. "We should get back together."

I blink at him. "What?"

"We should get back together," he repeats, tone void of emotion, reigniting the ember of anger I'd nearly reduced to ashes.

"You want..." My face scrunches, fingers pressed to my

temples. "Let me get this straight. You show up at the home I share with my boyfriend, and *that's* how you start the conversation?"

"Come on, Charlie." He releases a heavy breath. "Don't you think we made a mistake?"

The furious fire erupts. "According to you, the only mistake you made was fucking this cunt without a condom," I shriek, pointing at myself. "And now you're, what, asking for me back?"

"I want to be a part of this baby's life. I…" He shifts in place. "I need to be."

The fumes fog my mind, and my eyes narrow on him. "Why?"

"Because I do."

"What about all your big NFL dreams?" I ask mockingly.

"Charlie," he says with a sigh. "I'm trying to do the right thing here."

The *right thing*.

Red flags pop up like devil horns on Jonathan's stupid little head.

"Did my *mother* speak to you?" I roar, the flames scorching through me and decimating every shred of resolve in their path. He doesn't have to answer. I already know. *That meddling bitch.*

"It doesn't matter." He dismisses me with a flick of his wrist. The way he always did to say the conversation's over.

"Actually, it does."

His gaze holds mine. Crystal blue eyes that used to calm turbulent seas, now darker than the depths of the Mariana Trench. "We *need* to, Charlie."

"How much is she offering you?" The one thing about being mega uber rich is there is an endless supply of bribe money. And my mother *loves* using it.

"What?" he asks, brows pulled together.

"How much money did she pay you to come here?"

"None at all?"

"Then why would you—" I freeze in place, suddenly understanding. My mom loves bribery, but she's *addicted* to blackmail. "What does she have on you?"

"Nothing." His voice rises two octaves, and he clears his throat. "I just… I want this now."

He reaches toward me, and I swat him away. "Don't."

"Come on," he says, stepping forward, and I retreat, feet fumbling, and trip over the carpet. I shriek, bracing for the fall. Arms wrap around me, catching me before I hit the floor.

"Are you okay?" Jonathan asks, pulling me to stand, and I take a few deep breaths, placing my hand over the baby. Falling and hurting her is one of my biggest fears.

"I think so," I whisper, heart racing.

Jonathan rubs my stomach. "Come on, babe. Let's do this together."

His use of a pet name pulls me back to reality, and I wiggle out of his hold. "Just stop."

"Char—"

I fold my arms firmly over my chest. "The truth, or you leave."

He blows out a frustrated breath. "Fine. Your mom came to see me."

"Well, that makes a hell of a lot more sense than the Tin Man getting a heart."

His eyes connect with mine, full of hurt, but he doesn't deserve my sympathy. "Can't we at least pretend?"

I burst into laughter. "Fuck, no."

Panic sets in his eyes, and he bends over, taking deep breaths. The reaction I would have expected when I told him I was pregnant, not when he told me we should pretend to be together because…?

"Jonathan," I press, grinding my molars. "What does she have on you?"

"Nothing. It—"

"The *truth*," I repeat, pointing toward the door. "Or you leave."

He groans, dragging a hand down his face. "She has a picture of me doing coke at a party earlier this year."

My mouth falls open. "Why would you? How could you?" I shake my head, trying to bring myself back to the present situation. He's not my boyfriend. His drug usage is not my problem. But this is. "How does she even have that photo?"

"She was having me followed when we were dating," he says with a hardened jaw. "Said she wanted to make sure she knew the kind of person her daughter was with."

"So she saw cokehead party boy and thought, *Yeah, he's the one for Charlie?*" I mock.

"Actually, she told me to break up with you or she'd send it to my coach," Jonathan says, his tone lacking humor. "That it wouldn't be a good look if her daughter was *dating* a cokehead party boy."

My jaw drops to the center of the earth. I blink, unable to conjure up a single word. The last months of our relationship flash in my mind, trying to provide me with any signs I missed.

"That's why I had Eric run into you at Ken's Karaoke," he says, another slap to the face. My head spins, the blaze continuing to roar on my charred body.

"You…" My veins thrum. "You wanted me to catch you?"

Everything suddenly makes sense.

Why Jonathan's roommate insisted I go see him. Why Kendra didn't seem surprised by my arrival. Why he spewed every hurtful thing he could think of as I left. Why he didn't chase after me.

He nods.

"You wanted me to break up with you," I say, huffing a laugh, "because you were too much of a pussy to do it yourself."

"Charlie…"

"So you slept with me the day before as a farewell fuck?" I shriek. "I'm pregnant because you, what, wanted to fuck me over? Literally?"

"No, I just—"

"Save it." I shake my head and release a sigh. I'm so angry, but I'm also... glad? It's one more confirmation this is *not* the man I want in my life. *Not* the man I want raising my children. He could've just been a civilized human and dumped me. *What a piece of shit.*

"Is this why you don't want to be a part of her life?" I pause, placing a hand on my stomach, still needing clarification. Closure. "Because my mother blackmailed you?"

"When you showed up, I knew she must not have told you or you'd have used it to get me involved."

"I'm not my mother," I snap, the insinuation unwelcome.

"I know." He grits his teeth. "Just... We had already gone our separate ways. I've moved on, and it seems you have too," he says, glancing around. "I know I should say I want to be involved, but I—" He curses at himself under his breath before returning his gaze to mine. "I don't want to be a part of this. And I know that makes me selfish. But it's the truth."

"I believe you," I say, and somehow his admission lifts a weight off my shoulders. Because I don't want him to be a part of this either.

"But thanks to your mom, we don't really have a choice." He bites his cheek. 'We have to get back together."

A disgusted laugh leaves me. "There's always a choice."

"If you won't do it for me," Jonathan says, "you should at least do it for Noah."

"Noah?" I ask, guard flying up. "How could us faking a relationship possibly protect him?"

"Do you really think I'm the only one she has shit on?" he asks, and my heart sputters.

"You're lying."

"That's fine," he says, throwing up his hands. "Don't believe me."

"I don't." My tone is firm, but there's one thing the world

doesn't know about Noah. And I'm sure my mother has the whole goddamn file.

"What does she have on him?" I ask, curious if Jonathan has any inside knowledge.

"No clue," he says, and I narrow my eyes at him. "I swear." Something about his tone makes me believe him.

"Well, either way, my answer is still no. We're not getting back together. My mom's bluffing."

"You may be willing to take that risk, but I'm not."

"Well, it's not your choice! In the wise words of Taylor Swift, we are never getting back together. Like, ever."

"Please, Char—"

The front door flies open, and our heads swivel toward it.

Noah glances between the two of us, a furious expression on his face.

"Get the *fuck* out of our house," Noah says, his tone dripping with a venom I've never heard before. His face is red, chest heaving as his glare burns laser beams into Jonathan.

"It's not what you think," I say, wanting to laugh at how often that phrase seems to come up in my life.

"He's here trying to get you back?" Noah says, walking towards me. "Don't fall for it. It's all your mom's idea."

"She knows," Jonathan says at the same time I say, "I know."

"You know?" Noah says, brows furrowed.

"Yes," I say with a soft smile. "Don't worry. I didn't fall for it."

Noah glances between us, his forehead creased with worry lines. I take his hand in mine, and our eyes connect. He smiles softly, splaying his fingers protectively on my stomach.

Jonathan clears his throat. "This is cute and everything, but we still have a fucking problem."

I look to him. "I'll figure it out with the blackmail. Okay? Give me a few days to think about it. Maybe I can find the pictures and erase them."

"The blackmail?" Noah says.

"That's how Mom convinced Jonathan to come talk to me."

Noah nods. "Couldn't possibly be because he got you pregnant."

"Just let me know when you figure it out," Jonathan says, and he's out the door.

Noah takes my face in his hands and claims my lips with a searing kiss. Reminding me that while anger can feel like fire, passion also burns white hot. I slide my hands into his hair, and he picks me up, carries me to the kitchen, and sets my ass on the counter. Our hands explore, tongues tangling until we're both panting and coming up for air.

"What was that for?" I ask when he pulls away, green eyes boring into mine. While Jonathan's are the turbulence of the sea, Noah's are a calm, rolling meadow, keeping me grounded.

"Just needed to get lost in you for a few minutes," he says.

I brush my thumb against his cheek. "I'm sorry seeing Jonathan upset you so much."

"It wasn't him." He places his hands on both sides of me. "Your mom paid me a visit after practice."

"She what?" I shriek. *Could she get any crazier?*

"I'm not sure if she was trying to stall me so Jonathan had time here or what. But yeah, she threatened my career."

My stomach sinks. "And what did you say?"

His face scrunches up. "I told her to get fucked. That I'm never leaving."

Relief washes through me, dousing the raging inferno engulfing me just moments before.

"I don't want to be the reason your career tanks." My chest tightens. "The media would have a field day if they found out about your dad."

He shakes his head. "I don't care anymore. It was self-defense. The press can do what they want with it. And if the world finds out I was raised by an abusive prick, so be it."

"I'll find whatever she has and get rid of it," I promise. *My mother will not be the reason Noah's story is shared.* If it ever is, that should be *his* choice.

"You will not go to that house without me, do you understand?" His tone is firm.

"Noah," I say, tilting my head. "What do you think is going to happen?"

"I don't trust Georgia."

"She wouldn't hurt me." *I don't think.*

"She won't get the chance to. Because you are *not* going alone."

"It'll be harder to explain if you come," I say pointedly.

"So you admit there's a possibility you'll get caught." He places a hand on my thigh.

"A very *small* possibility," I assure him.

"I don't like the idea of you being there by yourself," he says, squeezing tight. "We don't know what she's capable of."

"It's my home. I'll be fine."

"No," he says sharply. "*This* is your home."

"You know what I mean."

"And what *I* mean is, home isn't a place you're uncomfortable, or afraid, or have to walk on eggshells." He taps his forehead to mine. "Home is a place you can be yourself. Be comfortable. Be safe."

Our eyes lock. "Wherever you are is where my home will be." I move his hand to my stomach. "Where *our* home will be." He smiles softly, and my curiosity gets the better of me. "What did my mom say to you?"

His jaw clenches. "That you and Jonathan were getting married and there wasn't a damn thing I could do about it."

"That will *never* happen," I promise, and he blows out a sigh of relief.

"She also said she offered you your inheritance back."

"And I told her to keep the fucking hush money." *Did he think I'd take it?*

"Why didn't you tell me about it?" he asks, a flicker of sadness in his eyes, and I curse myself for putting it there.

"Because I wasn't considering it." I take his face between my hands. "I swear."

He presses his lips together. "The thought of you marrying him makes me crazy."

He's not the only one.

I tilt my head. "She only suggested it so it'll look better to the press. She tried to pass it off as some ploy to trap Jonathan so I know he can't leave me alone with the baby. As if that's supposed to make me feel better."

"Well," Noah says, fighting a smile, "you can't marry him if you're already married to me."

My pulse stops. "What?"

"Think about it." His grin breaks free, and he runs a hand up my thigh, restarting my heart like a defibrillator. "Your mother is so focused on the fact you're unmarried." His eyes hold mine. "Let's get married." The storm of butterflies is once again released from their cage. "Jonathan would leave you alone, your mother couldn't keep threatening you, and, well, I'd get to call you *my wife.*"

My wife.

The last two words have my body trembling with nerves. The idea of being married to this man, of knowing he'll never leave my side, is the sweetest sound in the world. And I know it would ease his own worry of me running off with the baby. Although he'd never admit it. "I can't ask this of you."

"You're not." He squeezes my hands. "I am."

"Why would you give up so much for me?" *I'm so undeserving of him.*

"*Soffione.*" He shakes his head. "Haven't you realized I've given up absolutely nothing by being with you? I've only gained."

"I just feel like I came into your life and blew it all up, and you had no choice in the matter."

"Have I ever told you about the first time I saw you?"

"You know, you haven't."

"The first day of camp last summer." He drags his thumb across my jawline. "You were walking around with Andi. You laughed at something she said, and for the first time in my life, the entire world stopped."

"Noah…"

"I'm serious." His forest-green eyes glimmer with sincerity. "I heard that pretty sound matched with an even prettier face, and my first thought was, *Fuck, I'm done for*."

"Yeah, right." I look down at our interlocked fingers.

"Charlotte." He tilts my chin up, forcing my gaze to his. "I was mesmerized by you and the way you walked and talked and everything about you."

My heart is in my throat. "You never even spoke to me last summer."

"I know." He brushes a lock of hair behind my ear. "Because as I was standing there thinking how pretty our kids would look with your brown eyes… Jonathan showed up, making it clear exactly how off-limits you were."

"I didn't even think you noticed me," I whisper.

"I've always noticed you." His smile is soft. "Everything about you. The way your eyes light up when you're laughing with the girls. The little crinkle on your forehead when you're stressed. The shimmy of pride you do when someone compliments your baking. Your obsessive need to ensure everyone around you is taken care of regardless of what it does to you."

"I had no idea." I'm overwhelmed. Elated. Soaring through the clouds. "I thought Sophia's birthday was the first time you ever noticed me."

I mean, sure, we saw each other around at practices and games, but I didn't think he knew or cared I existed. He was head quarter-back, and I was a newbie cheerleader.

"How could anybody *not* notice you?" he asks with a look of such sincerity it brings tears to my eyes.

"I really am fucking up your five-year plan." I laugh hesitantly, internally freaking the hell out at where this conversation is heading.

"I updated it a few weeks ago anyways," Noah says, retrieving the list from the back of his phone case.

"You did?" I ask, snatching it from him.

Noah's Five Year Plan
Financial: Continue to support our family
Family: Be a good dad
Adventure: Take Char, baby girl, and the twins to Italy
Relationship: Marry Charlotte
Health: Stay fit enough to chase the kids around (and Charlotte)

"There's nothing about your career?" I say, full of surprise.

"Because I don't give a shit about it if this stuff doesn't happen." *Is he serious?*

I scan the list again.

Relationship: Marry Charlotte

"You want that?" My heart pounds frantically. "Why didn't you say anything?"

"Because I don't want you to feel trapped."

I laugh. "Trapped? There have been so many decisions taken away from me the past year. Or made for me. But you're the only one who ever stops to actually ask what *I* want. The one who makes me feel free." My heart soars, that same meadow of serenity filling me.

"And what do you want?" he asks, and for once, I'm one hundred percent certain.

"I want to have this baby. With you. To spend my life with the selfless man who *chooses* me out of love, not obligation." I pause, eyes dropping to my hands. "But I also don't want *you* to think I'm trapping you. Or forcing you into this or—"

"You should come to my game in Vegas this weekend," Noah suggests, cutting me off.

"I mean, I'd love to," I say, confused. "But that's a bit of a change of subject."

"There are a lot of *chapels* in Vegas," he emphasizes with a wicked grin.

"What?" I ask, eyes darting to his. "You're not serious."

Noah reaches behind his neck, removes his chain, and slides the pendants off. My lips part open as he holds his grandma's gold ring between his fingers.

"Noah, what the hell are you doing?"

He drops to one knee before me, looking into my eyes. "I meant it when I said I'm in this for the long haul. If you want reassurance, or confirmation, I'm not going anywhere. This is it," he says, holding the small ring between us, and I slap a hand over my chest to contain the happiness threatening to burst out of me. "Any day spent with you not being one million percent sure I'm in this forever is a day too long. And you being my wife would certainly solve that."

I stare down at the little ring. "Your grandma said you have to save that ring for a girl you—"

"Love," he cuts me off.

"Noah…" My hand covers my mouth, hiding a massive smile, tears welling in my eyes.

"Charlotte, I *love* you. I love everything about you. I love you so much it makes me crazy. *Mi fai impazzire.* I've loved you since I watched you wishing on dandelions, wildflowers in your hair, and every day since. I love you." He places a hand on my stomach. "And I love this little girl."

"*Our* little girl," I say, and his gaze locks with mine.

"Char," Noah says, eyes full of hope. Desperation. But saying it feels right. Because from the moment I saw those two little lines, I created an entire universe where Noah was the father. I never wanted that to change. And he's proven how much he doesn't either. In fact, his endless love for a baby that's not biologically his makes me love him all the more.

"Noah." I place my hand on his face. "Fuck blood or legality. You are the *father* to this baby. Because what the hell else am I supposed to call the man who loves and adores both myself and this little one growing in me? Who comes to every appointment? Ensures we're loved and cared for and want for absolutely nothing? Who spent five hours putting together a crib because you wanted to make sure it was perfectly safe?"

"*Soffione*, I don't want to pressure you. Titles aren't—they aren't important. I just want you to know I'm here for you. Both of you."

"And I want you to know that when she's born, and you're wondering what she should call you, the answer is Dad." I place my hand on his. "Or *papà,* if you prefer that."

"Charlotte." Tears well in his eyes, and it pulls them from

mine. Because having a six-foot-three man, the strongest person I know, dripping tears on me in the middle of *our* kitchen, while his hand rests on *our* baby—this is the most loved I've ever felt. "Please, marry me?"

"Noah." I release a steady breath, a grin breaking free as tears fall down my cheeks. "I love you too."

His eyes widen. "You do?"

"I mean, it would kinda be a requirement of me saying yes." My smile deepens, our hands shaking.

His voice trembles. "Are you?"

Of all the decisions I've made in my life, this is by far the easiest. "Yes."

44
NOAH

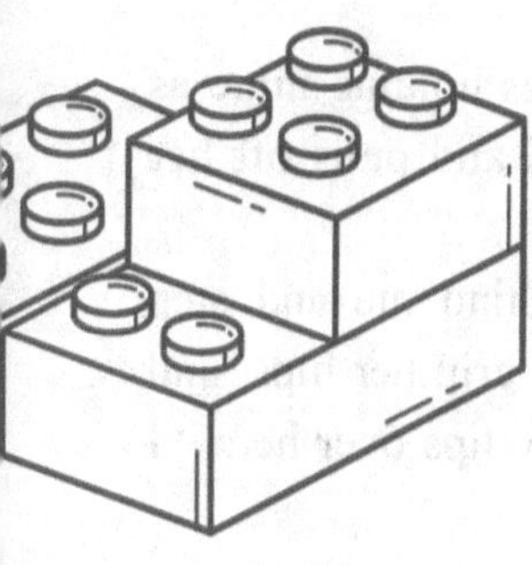

Scooping her in my arms, ring clutched in my hand, I blink back tears. *Charlotte is going to be my wife.* She squeezes me tight, and I slide my free hand in her hair, never wanting to let go. And now I never have to.

My body is overwhelmed with emotions. From the roaring rage I had driving home to the woman I love agreeing to be my wife. Every cell is firing off.

"I love you," I mumble into her hair.

"I love you," she says, kissing my neck.

When we pull back, I hold up the ring, and she presents her shaky hand. I steady it, sliding the band onto her ring finger. Her eyes bounce back to mine. "I love you," she says again, and I will never tire of hearing it.

"*Soffione.*" I hold her face in my hands. "I can't wait to be your husband."

Our lips crash, the stellar collision finally fusing two hearts as one. "Make love to me," she begs into my mouth, and I scoop her in my arms. *Don't have to tell me twice.* She peppers my neck with kisses as I carry her to our bedroom and set her gently atop the comforter. I tug my shirt off and toss it behind me, then drop my pants and boxer briefs to the floor.

A devilish smirk crosses her lips as her eyes roam me hungrily, the attention dancing across my skin. "My fiancé is so damn hot."

My smile widens, cheeks aching from how devastatingly happy I am in this moment. "So is mine."

Charlotte scoots off the bed and stands, eyes holding mine as she drops her shorts and panties to the ground and pulls off her shirt, tossing it at me.

I catch it with a laugh, then chuck it behind me and step towards her. Pretty brown eyes meet mine as I grip her hips, and she loops her arms around my neck. I brush my lips over hers. "I can't believe you love me."

"How could I not?" she says, and my heart squeezes. "You're an incredible partner. And you're going to be an even better father."

Her words surround me like a warm summer breeze. I press a gentle kiss to her lips, cheek, neck, and collarbone and drop to my knees, my face at her rounded belly. My eyes flutter shut, and I place soft kisses on the baby I'm finally allowed to call mine. That *always* felt like mine.

"I can't wait to meet you," I murmur against Charlotte's stomach.

"Hear that, little one?" she says, sliding her fingers into my hair. "That's your daddy. You're going to be really lucky to have him." My soul brightens, her words touching even the darkest parts.

Tears prick my eyes, and I tap my forehead to her hard stomach, the feelings overwhelming me. Kneeling with Charlotte before me, growing *our* baby, knowing she's mine. It's everything I never knew I needed.

After placing one last kiss, I stand. "Lie down," I tell her, and she grins, the gleam of mischief returning. She hurries onto the bed, resting her back against the pillows, and spreading her legs.

The mattress dips beneath me as I climb after her, and she trembles with anxious energy. I pause over her center and she bites her lower lip, well aware of my addiction to her taste. Hooking her legs with my arms, I grip her thighs, darting my tongue out while her gaze holds mine.

A needy whine escapes her, and I groan, eyelids fluttering shut as her sweetness dances over my tastebuds. I lap and suck and tease, face buried between her thighs while she grips my hair, holding on for dear life.

My excruciatingly hard cock is dripping, and I need to rein it in before I have another pre-ejaculation moment.

"Baby, this feels incredible," she pants. "But I really want you inside me right now."

Grinning, I kiss my way up her body, giving extra attention to her stomach, and continue the journey over her breasts and to her neck. Hovering above, I make sure not to put any weight on her. Taking in her radiant face, the only word that comes to mind is "mine."

I roll on my side beside her, placing a hand over her waist, and she shuffles so her back is to me. One of our favorite positions as of late.

"You're definitely wet enough," I tell her, bringing a hand between her legs and reconfirming what I already knew.

She lifts her leg, and I take my cock in my hand, swiping it between her till it's fully coated. Her soft breaths surround me as I press my tip against her. When I thrust in, she gasps.

"This okay?"

"Yes," she pants, and I grip her hip, rocking slowly.

"Soffione, ti amo tanto." I love you so damn much.

"Ti amo tanto,"[1] she repeats, placing her hand on mine, and I drop my head to her neck, my chest unable to take another surge of passion.

---

1. IT: *Ti amo tanto* - EN: I love you

Our bodies move in rhythm, panting filling the room as I plant kisses along her neck and back. Whispers of bilingual "I love you's" exchanged on repeat as the overwhelming emotions fill every corner of the room. It doesn't take long before we're both sweating, moaning, begging for release, my hand on her stomach holding her to me.

"Mine," I growl, and she reaches back, nails digging into my skin.

"Yours," she says with a moan. "I'm yours."

Ecstasy blasts through me, tingling down my spine. My balls tighten, and I groan, jerking inside her.

Her inner walls pulsate as she cries out in pleasure. We tumble through space and time, finally entering our galaxy together. That special place where only she and I exist in that beautiful celestial dance. The one where we'll now exist forever.

Our relationship may have been a cosmic collision, unexpected and chaotic.

But there's not a chance in the universe I'd change a thing if it led me to here, this moment, with my fiancée in my arms and our beautiful daughter growing inside of her.

BIG STING ENERGY

THEO SCHROEDER

Noah, why was a vase of roses with a football sticking out the top delivered to my house

ELIJAH ANDERSON

two vases, actually

ME

Did you read the note? Share it with the class

THEO SCHROEDER

Hold on

JULIAN LISCERO

i got one too, but no note

DESMOND BALL

i'm at the stadium, did you send your long lost
lover one?

ME

Yes, Des. Don't worry. You too have been
spoiled

THEO SCHROEDER

roses are red, footballs are brown, join me in
vegas for my final touchdown

DESMOND BALL

excuse me what

JULIAN LISCERO

are you quitting football?

ELIJAH ANDERSON

dude, there's no chance we're letting you quit

ME

I'm not quitting football dumbasses

Charlotte and I are getting married after the
Vegas game next week

ELIJAH ANDERSON

SHUT THE HELL UP

THEO SCHROEDER

the final extraction of your bro-hood is
scheduled

DESMOND BALL

FINALLY i get to see you guys again

JULIAN LISCERO

yooo so we're poppin bottles before you're popping bottles. tight

ME

Plane tickets are in your inbox. Coach Porter was informed & agreed since you have a bye week

See you boys in Vegas

And don't tell Char you're coming

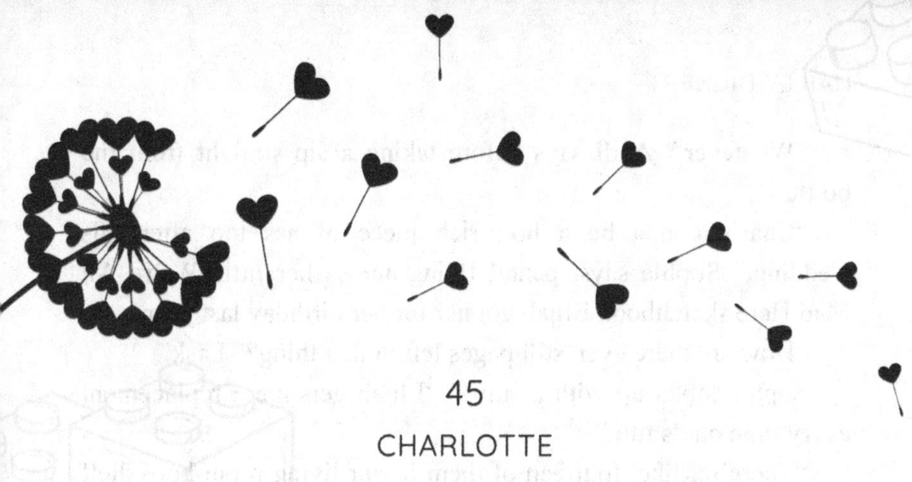

45

CHARLOTTE

"While I'm all for you nailing down that rich, hot piece of ass," Sage says, gazing out the floor-to-ceiling window of our Vegas hotel suite, "this is still insane."

"I'm totally down with insane if it means an all-expenses trip to Vegas," Andi says, plopping onto one of four couches with an open bottle of wine in her hand. Noah convinced me to come to his game with the promise of a simple elopement, but as I was about to leave for the airport, a party bus showed up with all our friends inside. "Thank your fiancé for me." A thrill runs through me. *Fiancé.*

"You sure it has nothing to do with a certain Tampa Bay defensive lineman being in the same city?" I tease.

"Would you give the Knox of it all a rest please?" she says with a warning glare that feels more chocolate lab than pitbull. "Besides, you're way off base."

"I'm just saying." I shrug. "He, too, is a hot, rich piece of ass."

"He's much more than that," Andi says, and I can't fight the grin that bursts free.

"Mm-hmm," Stella hums.

"Whatever," Andi says before taking a sip straight from the bottle.

"Char's gonna be a hot, rich piece of ass too after this wedding," Sophia says, pencil flying across her little We're All Mad Here sketchbook Elijah got her for her birthday last year.

"How are there even still pages left in that thing?" I ask.

Sophia looks up with a smirk. "Elijah gets me a replacement every time one's full."

"There're, like, fourteen of them in our living room bookshelf alone," Abbs says. "By the way, Char, Theo left a little gift for you in the bathroom. Something to wear for the game."

"Shouldn't I wear Noah's jersey?" I ask, standing, thinking of the one I stashed in my bag.

"Forget the jersey," Stella says, with the wave of her hand. "It's your bachelorette night! Get glam!"

I roll my eyes. "Fine!"

The girls and I rush to the large ensuite bathroom, and I discover a white fitted short glitter maternity dress with feathers at the bottom. After putting it on, especially with the bump, I look hot. *Noah's going to love this*.

"Now, are you ready for a little Married Mischief List?" Andi asks, winking at Stella.

My eyes light up. "I get to be involved this time?!"

"It's your list, baby cakes," Andi says, and I snatch it from her hands.

"No way." I laugh, handing it back to her. "Noah would kill me if I did half of these."

"Come on, it'll be fun!"

"Sorry, Andikins," I say. "That list will have to be all you and the others."

"Boo!"

"I'm sure you could find someone to join you on that fun," I say with a cocked brow.

"Don't start again." She narrows her eyes.

"We've gotta leave in twenty!" Sophia calls from the living room.

"I just have to freshen up a bit," I say, and Andi leaves me in the bathroom.

My phone buzzes.

NOAH

How's my (almost) wife?

ME

Fantastic

This hotel room is insane

NOAH

Only the best for my bride to be

ME

My god you're so cheesy

NOAH

Fun fact: There's over 1800 types of cheese

ME

And your Dad jokes are cheesier than all of them combined

NOAH

I've gotta get my practice in with little Brie coming soon.

ME

You did not name our baby after a type of cheese.

NOAH

Brie Caruso.

It has such a gouda vibe

ME

TRY AGAIN

NOAH

Fine, then little Ella

ME

Good. We're back to Gabriella

NOAH

What are you talking about?

Ella is short for Mozzarella of course

Although Gabriella does contain Brie and Ella.

I knew i liked that name

ME

And what would we have done if it was a boy?

NOAH

Cam(embert) Caruso

ME

If you keep naming this child after cheese, our marriage may not recover

NOAH

You gouda be kidding me??? We haven't even made it down the aisle

ME

the lactose intolerance is awakening

NOAH

Don't worry dairy free cheese is brie-licious

ME

You're making me curdle

NOAH

Hah! I've converted you! A cheese joke!

ME

It wasn't that grate

NOAH

I can die a happy man

ME

Well you can't die yet, but the girls think you might when you see what I'm wearing tonight.

NOAH

I'd rather see it off you.

Biting the inside of my cheek, I check the time. We still have fifteen minutes. I consider the perfect white lingerie set I'm wearing under this. It really would be a shame not to document it… Boudoir shoots *are* pretty common before your wedding.

A thrill runs through my veins, and I shimmy off the dress. In the mirror, my eyes fall to my large bump, and I absentmindedly place a hand over it. My back aches from the extra front weight, but when I think about what's inside there, I can't help but smile.

Another text pops in.

NOAH

I've gotta put my phone in my locker soon, so if you're busy, I love you, baby.

I snap a few photos, picking the best one out of urgency and hit send.

NOAH

Soffione mio, my god, what are you trying to do to me?

ME

That bad?

NOAH

You look downright fuckable.

Now all I'll think of when I see you at the game
is what you're wearing under my jersey

ME

I won't be wearing your jersey.

NOAH

Why the hell not?

ME

See you soon

NOAH

You're going to be in trouble later.

ME

Too bad we left the ropes back home. Love you
honey xox

"I think these are our seats?" I say as our rowdy group makes it to the front row. We met the boys—Theo, Elijah, and Julian—at the hotel and got delivered to the game on a party bus. *Noah really went all out, and he's not even able to enjoy it.*

The row is empty except for one seat, and the man stands up and turns, unsurprised to see us. My face must show the opposite because he laughs.

"I'm not here as CBU staff," Coach Porter says, hands up, addressing his football players more than me.

"Then why are you here?" Andi asks, tone sharp.

"It's fine," I whisper at her. "The more the merrier."

"I always come to Knox's away games when I can swing it," he says, addressing Andi.

"Of course you do," she says, with a tight smile.

My eyes bounce between them, and I lean over, whispering in her ear, "Looks like Coach Buzzkill might ruin those Knox shenanigans for you."

"Hmph," she huffs. "We'll see about that."

We all settle in our seats, Sophia on one side and Stella on the other. Somehow Andi ends up stuck next to Coach Buzzkill and I shoot her an apologetic look, which she doesn't even register because they're already in some heated debate.

Poor girl.

Music starts playing, pulling my attention to the field, and the players run out from the tunnel. My eyes scan the crowd of turquoise jerseys till they find number thirteen.

I can't help the dopey smile that comes across my face when my future husband, love of my absolute life, jogs onto the field. I can't see his eyes, but his helmet is pointed towards the crowd, surely searching. When he finally lands on our group, he taps his helmet's face mask and "throws it" toward me.

My heart swells as I "catch it," tapping my belly, then press my fingers to my lips and send a kiss his way.

That must have pleased him because he has an extra pep in his step as he files onto the sidelines with his teammates. A text pops in, and I try to ignore it. My phone goes off again, and I glare down at it.

JONATHAN
Your plan better work.

ME
It will.

Unfortunately, I had to unblock him so we could communicate about the blackmail of it all. I shove my phone back in my purse. Nothing from the situation at home will pop my happy bubble this weekend.

The reasons we're getting married might be complex, but I'm still going to enjoy the hell out of it.

The game goes by in a blur till we're down to the final two minutes in the fourth quarter. The score is 24-24, and all the excitement and screaming is beginning to overwhelm me. Noah got two sideline passes for the second half, so Theo and I are standing near his team's benches, and I have a hand on my belly, catching my breath. She's been kicking like crazy, and I wonder if she's clapping for Daddy too.

A warm feeling spreads across my chest. I've fought his role in our life for so long, and being here, his ring on my finger and just a day away from taking his last name, I feel so at peace.

The roaring stadium brings me back to the anxious present. We're on defense, and Noah's talking intently with the coaches. I'm grateful he can't see how worn out I am.

After all, *he's* the one on the field running his ass off and getting slammed by men four times my size.

Noah and the offensive line run back on the field, and I cheer like we're watching a championship game. *I can rest later.*

The teams set up on the line of scrimmage, and I anxiously toy with the gold band around my finger. The stadium grows eerily quiet.

A muffled "Down, set, hike!' is called, and within seconds, Noah's thrown the ball through the air, their running back catching it effortlessly and bolting into the end zone.

"Touchdownnnnnnnnnnnnnnn, Baracuddddassssss!" the announcer shouts, and I spring off the ground with a scream, exhaustion forgotten. Theo and I double high-five. Vegas fans throw their hats and boo, but we don't care. My eyes scan the field to see number thirteen heading my way, and excitement rushes through me as he rips off his helmet. Our matching grins meet, his eyes sparkling with pride, hair wet with sweat, and he rushes to me, sweeping me carefully in his arms.

He crashes his lips to mine in a searing, claiming kiss. If anyone was wondering his relationship status, it was made clear tonight.

We may not have won the Super Bowl, but I'm still getting a ring.

46
NOAH

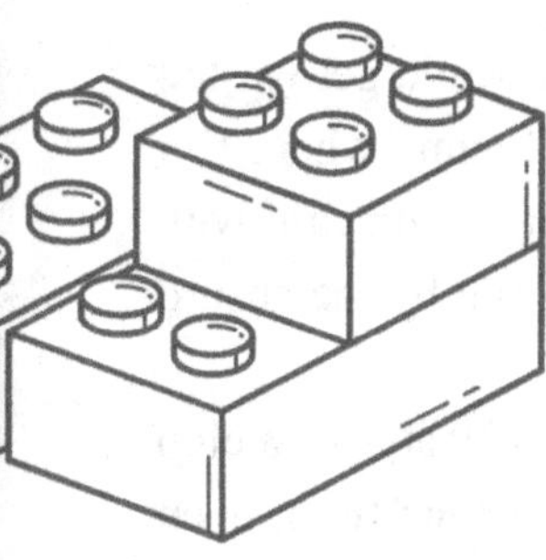

I can't shower fast enough. The team is set to fly back tomorrow morning, but with Coach Porter's help—who must have been mighty persuasive—Knox and I were able to get a few days off.

I pull the suit jacket over my shoulders, my typical post-game attire. "You ready?" Knox asks, duffle situated on his shoulder. "Porter said they're at the hotel."

"Hell yeah," I say, shaking off the nerves as we make our way out of the stadium. Knox booked a driver for us since it's definitely not safe to walk through the fans to take the party bus with everyone else. Desmond is joining us too, so we're meeting him at the pickup point.

"You *sure* you're ready for this?" Knox asks me.

"For Vegas?" I ask, brows pulled together.

"No," he says with a laugh. "The marriage. The baby. All of it?"

I think about my answer as we walk through the hallways under the stadium. I think about Charlotte and her laugh and how I never want to share it with anyone. And the look on her face right before she kisses me. Like I'm her whole world. And I think about that beautiful little life growing inside of her. "Yeah, I'm ready."

"Then let's go celebrate your last night as a single man."

I highly underestimated *how* quickly our friends would get wasted after having already been at a four-hour football game where I'm sure they drank their weight in beer. Elijah had my credit card with the instructions that drinks were on me, and judging by the absurd bill, they certainly took advantage of it.

My arm rests on the back of our booth in the VIP area of a club on the top floor of our hotel. Everyone's on the dance floor, even Charlotte, but my muscles are screaming at me after today's game. I'm trying to hang, I really am, but I'm utterly exhausted.

Charlotte's spinning around in a white sparkly dress that accentuates her baby bump in a way that shouldn't turn me on so damn much.

But honestly? Everything she does turns me on. And it's not because we weren't able to get out our pent-up energy in a few days between practices and me leaving early for the game.

Her eyes find mine, and she bites her lower lip. I laugh, shaking my head, and she arches a brow. Shimmying to the beat, she takes a finger and drags it down the side of her neck to her chest, pulling her top down slightly before it bounces back into place. I bolt to my feet, glancing around to make sure no one's seeing this performance that's just for me. That's *mine*.

I rush to the dance floor, grab her hand, twirl her, and pull her back flush against my front. "Should we continue the 'you're going to be in trouble' conversation?" I growl in her ear.

"I noticed a coat closet that was unattended when I came in," she says, and I drop my face into the crook of her neck and groan.

"Baby, that sounds so good." I release a heavy sigh. "But I'm an old-fashioned man, and we're getting married tomorrow."

She spins to face me, mischief dancing in her eyes. "Did you enjoy the photo earlier?"

More blood rushes south as I think about that sexy little picture. "Absolutely."

"Good," she says victoriously as we sway to the music. Her hips gyrate in a way that makes me unsure if I'll be able to fulfill my celibacy vow tonight. My eyes dart around the room for options. No, forget that. My fiancée deserves more than a closet fuck.

"Hey!" Sophia says, Elijah trailing behind her like always. Our eyes connect, and he must sense something because he tries to tug Sophia back, but it's no use.

"It's time for us to steal the bride-to-be," Sophia says, and before I even have the chance to protest, she's secured Charlotte in her arms and is dragging her away. "See you tomorrow." Sophia winks, and I can't help but smile because Charlotte has absolutely no idea what I've planned for us.

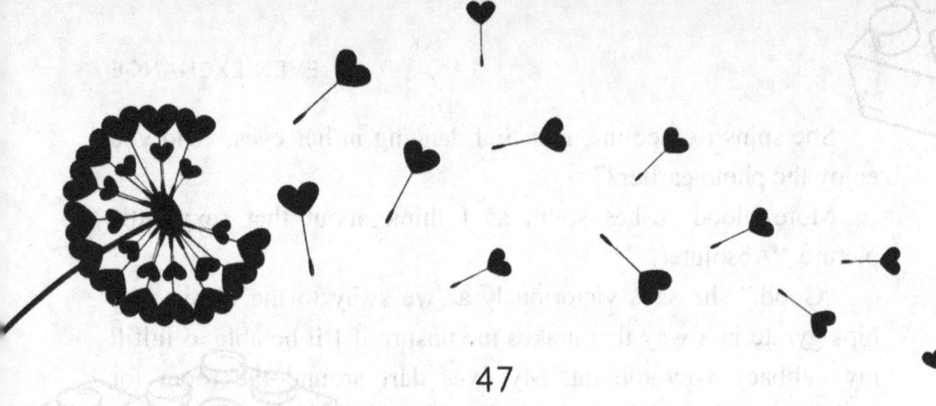

47

CHARLOTTE

"It's my wedding day, bitches!" The girls and I clink glasses in the middle of the glorious hotel room. It may only be ten in the morning, but their flutes are filled to the brim with champagne and mine with ginger ale.

We sip, and I return to my seat by the vanity so Andi can finish curling my hair. It reminds me of us getting ready for the gala at camp, and I can't help but smile at all that's changed since then.

"Is she almost done?" Sophia asks, dressed in jeans and a

cropped graphic tee that says The Camera Sutra with a bunch of funny poses of a photographer. Her own camera is flung over her shoulder.

"I'm right here?" I say. "You could just ask me."

Andi and Sophia share a mischievous look. "Yeah, she's almost ready."

"There are a few dress shops I found nearby," I say. "Hopefully I'll be able to find something there."

"I don't think you need to worry about that," Sophia says, fighting a smile, and I turn towards her, brows furrowed.

The door of the suite opens and closes, and Abbs walks inside holding a garment bag. "Theo sent this for you. He said he knew you were planning to go shopping, but he thought you might not mind the option." *I need to hire him as my personal stylist at this point.*

"So *that's* where you've been all morning?" Sage asks, and Abbs shoots her a glare.

"I was retrieving this for the *bride*," Abbs says.

"Gimme, gimme." I reach with grabby hands, hopping out of my chair. "If it's half as nice as the gala dress, Noah won't be able to breathe."

Abbs hangs it on a wall hook, and we crowd around. I unzip the bag, and a beam of angelic light streams out, displaying the most beautiful dress I've ever seen.

It's a white corset top covered in rhinestones, reflecting light around the entire room. A wink to the night Noah and I became friends officially while I was dressed as a drunk little disco ball. The bottom is a flowing satin that will leave plenty of room for my bump.

"It's perfect," I say with a breath.

"Put it on," Sophia suggests. "Make sure it fits."

"And put this on under it," Abbs says, tossing me a teeny tiny little lingerie set.

"Did Theo pick this out too?" I ask with a cocked brow. "Noah would not be very happy if his best friend knew what I was wearing underneath that dress."

"No," she says with a laugh. "That was all me."

"Pretty," I say, fingers dragging over the delicate lace. "But isn't it way too early for this? The wedding's not till…" My thoughts drift off. "Well, I guess I haven't been much in the loop of anything, but it's definitely later."

The only thing I was in charge of was picking out Noah's ring. And I am *positive* he's going to love it.

Sophia takes my hands and forces my gaze to meet hers. "Charlie."

"Sophia."

"Put. On. The. Dress. Before your fiancé kills me for making you late."

My veins buzz with excitement. "Damn, you don't have to go all *Mommy* on me."

"You're right," she says, placing a gentle hand on my belly. "That's your job."

Our town car flies through the Vegas streets, passing hotel after hotel. Every famous landmark I know from the movies zooms by. I've got the drop-dead gorgeous dress *and* the lingerie under it. Sophia is still in jeans and a tee, we left the rest of the wedding party back at the hotel, and I am utterly confused. *Maybe we're just taking photos?*

"Put this on," Sophia says, a white silk blindfold dangling from her fingertips.

"You can't be serious?" I ask with a laugh.

"Husband's orders," she says, and I narrow my eyes at her, eventually caving. Partly because I don't want to ruin anything

Noah's planned and partly because the thrill of the surprise really is exciting.

The blindfold is secured on my face, and it's another twenty minutes before I'm given a hand and taken from the car. Sophia leads me through—well, I have no clue where. All I know is a few minutes—and what feels like an elevator ride from the butterflies in my stomach—later, we're at the top of what I assume is a tall tower.

A door clicks open, and Sophia ushers me through it, warm, dry air hitting my skin.

"If you wanted to throw me off a roof, you didn't have to make it so mysterious," I tease.

"Don't worry," she says. "I would be way more creative than that."

"Good to know," I say, huffing a laugh. "Do I get *any* hints?"

"Patience, young grasshopper," she says. "We're almost there."

I swallow hard, and a little flutter in my belly has me placing my hand over her instinctively. It's like she can feel my excitement. She kicks again, getting my palm, and I imagine her giving me a little love tap of encouragement.

I'm happy you're here too, baby.

"Stay facing that way," Sophia says authoritatively.

"What do you—"

"Not you," she cuts me off. "Noah."

"Noah's here?" I ask, heart soaring, wiggling with anticipation.

"Of course he is," she says with a laugh. "Can't very well get married without the groom."

"Married?" I say, reaching up and ripping my blindfold off. My mouth falls open as I take in my surroundings. We're on the top of a building. A helicopter is parked in front of me with Noah facing it, bouncing on his feet. As anxious to see me as I am to see him. Sophia stands off to the side taking photos of us, and Elijah's behind her with a smug, happy grin on his face.

"You can turn around now," Sophia calls to Noah, and he

wastes no time turning to face me, his hand covering his mouth. I stand frozen, holding my breath as he takes me in. He glances to the sky for a moment, muttering something to himself, then strides towards me with glistening eyes.

Oxygen becomes more difficult with each step he nears until it's all but nonexistent as he stands before me, forest eyes locked on mine with a softness that tells me everything I need to know about this man.

My head becomes fuzzy as I drink him in. The blue fitted suit. The pure adoration on his face. The shiver that racks my body when he reaches out and tucks a curl behind my ear.

"Breathe, *tesoro*," he reminds me, and I gasp, sucking in deep breaths to replenish my oxygen.

I know this moment is supposed to be sweet and wholesome and lovely, but all that comes out of my mouth is "You look so fucking hot."

A sexy chuckle leaves his lips, and he leans in, breath fanning against my ear. "If I said what I was thinking"—he takes a deep breath, then releases it as if to steady himself—"neither of us would be able to think straight for the next several hours." He pulls away, nose brushing mine.

"I want to kiss you."

"Not yet." He smiles, taking my hands in his.

"Are we getting married here?"

"No." He gestures toward the helicopter. "I have something better planned."

I splay my fingers over my stomach. "Is it—"

"It's totally safe for baby. I even checked with Doctor Rigou."

"Aren't our friends gonna be mad?" I ask, shifting on my feet. "They came all this way to see us get married."

"They knew the plan," he says, waving me off. "Did you really think I was going to marry you in some cheesy wedding chapel with an Elvis impersonator as our officiant?"

I twisted my mouth. "Yes. And I would have. Happily."

"I know," he says, squeezing my hand. "But I wanted it to be about us. You and me, and the baby." He places a hand on my stomach. "When you remember us getting married, I want it to be perfect. Not smelling of old cigarettes and tequila."

"Anywhere would be perfect with you," I say. And I mean it.

"I appreciate that," he says with a wide smile, tugging me forward. "But could you get your beautiful self in this helicopter so I can make you my wife, please?"

"Who's gonna marry us?" I ask, glancing around.

"The pilot is an officiant," he says as Sophia and Elijah trail behind us.

"That's convenient."

"Well, it's kinda his business," Noah explains, helping me onto the helicopter, his hand protectively on my back.

"Alright, love birds," the pilot says once we're all buckled in. "Let's get you hitched."

Orange rock stretches as far as the eye can see, and the sun hits the canyon in a stunning scattered light. The only word I have to describe it? *Sensational.*

On a rocky platform, Noah and I face one another with the officiant between us. We're far enough from the edge we don't have to worry about falling but close enough to make my stomach drop.

Sophia circles us, snapping photos, while Elijah stands off to the side.

"Noah," the officiant says. "It's your turn."

Noah retrieves what I'm assuming is my ring from Elijah and returns his attention to me.

"Charlotte," he says, taking my hand, eyes boring into mine.

"*Soffione,* with this ring, I take you to be my wife. To have and to hold. To cherish and to make laugh. To love and to annoy."

"I don't think that's how it goes," I whisper, and he chuckles.

"I'm paraphrasing," he whispers back before continuing, "I know you're not used to people taking care of you. I know you want to be the strong one. The 'I can handle this on my own' one. But you don't have to do that anymore. I will hold you when you're weak. And stand behind you when you're strong. I will be your partner, lover, father to our children. Anything you need me to be. That's what I vow to you, today."

"Noah," I whisper, tears stinging my eyes.

"My *nonna* once told me when love knocks, answer it." He pauses, a soft smile coming to his lips. "I'm so glad it was *you* on the other side."

He squeezes my hand gently, the cool metal touching the tip of my ring finger, and I glance down, gasping. A gorgeous pear cut diamond ring on a gold band encrusted in more diamonds is slid on my finger, residing atop the band from Noah's *nonna*. My eyes bounce back to his, and he grins smugly.

"Charlotte," the officiant says, but I'm speechless. My eyes fall back to the ring.

"*Soffione*, you can stare at it all you want later," Noah says, pulling my gaze back to his.

"How am I supposed to follow those vows?" I ask, mouth agape, looking back down. "This ring? I didn't prepare anything. I..." My eyes dart to Noah's, panic setting in. *Why didn't I prepare anything?*

Noah squeezes my hand. "It's just you and me, baby."

"Right," I say, nodding, shaking my shoulders to hype myself. "I can do this." Noah bites his lip, shit-eating grin breaking through. "Are you *laughing* at me?"

"No," he promises, eyes soft. "I just love how flustered you are. It's cute."

"You know what?" I say, turning and retrieving Noah's ring

from Sophia. The one part of this ceremony that I was responsible for. The gorgeous gold band with a honeycomb design is pinched between my fingertips, and I'm reminded of my inspiration for it.

I return my attention to Noah, placing the band at the tip of his ring finger. "Noah Gabriel Caruso," I say, our eyes connecting, a wide shared smile between us. "With this ring, I will love you and be faithful to you. And…" I think hard. *It has to be good…* "I promise to never, *ever* break pasta again. To always build Legos when we're angry and make love when we're not. I promise to love your shitty Dad jokes, or at least to pretend I do. To appreciate every moment when you're home, and be understanding of all the times you can't be. I promise to be by your side always, loving you, appreciating you, and just being… yours." With a shaky hand, I slide the ring onto his finger. He glances down to it, eyes brightening at the realization, and they bounce back to mine. "And I *promise* our love will last like honey."

A breath sticks in my throat, and I nod at the officiant.

"I now pronounce you husband and wife," he declares. "You may kiss the bride."

Noah's hands are in my hair, pulling me to him. His mouth lands on mine, planting a kiss so deep, so searing, that even without the rings, I'm branded for life.

I am Noah Caruso's wife, and no one will ever take that away from me.

Especially not my mother.

48

CHARLOTTE

Tick. Tock. Tick. Tock.

Time is of the essence, and yet I'm chained to the driver's seat of the Bronco, down the street from the Benson estate, unable to drag myself inside.

How did we get here?

My own *mother* is blackmailing people over my love life.

What kind of psycho shit is this?

I know these elections are important to her, but for fuck's sake.

My phone buzzes, yanking me out of my spiral.

NOAH

Are you still at the library?

I blow out a shaky breath. The deal was Noah and I would come here together, but Denny let it slip they'd all be out of the house for an event today, and it seemed like the perfect opportunity. Given Noah has a game tonight, I knew there was no way I could bother him with it. He's already made it clear he'd tank his career for me, but I refuse to let him.

Being his wife is the safest I've ever felt, and I need to make sure he's protected too. Make sure whatever my mother has on

432

him is useless or we're fully prepared for it. The mere thought of him being hurt by something she does makes my blood boil.

In my head, I calculate how long until I can get to the Barracudas' stadium.

Ten minutes to find the documents.

Ninety minutes home to store them.

Thirty to the stadium.

Two hours and ten minutes… Let's say three to play it safe. A sinking feeling settles in my stomach as I type out a reply. But this has to be done. He'll forgive me later.

I hope.

ME

Yes. But I'm almost done

I'm going to take a quick nap at home then I'll be there

NOAH

Awh is my wife tired from growing little Brie

My wife. The guilt sinks further, but it's replaced by baby's movement, reminding me why I'm doing this in the first place.

I rest a hand on my stomach. "Wish Mommy luck, little one."

Releasing a shaky breath, I finally force myself out of the car. The driveway is empty, as expected, and I rush up to the entrance. If I'm caught, I'll just say I came to talk. *Figure something out.*

The front door creaks as I push it open, and the alarm sounds. I hurry to shut it off, grateful the code hasn't changed.

My footsteps echo through the quiet, empty halls.

The last time it was this still was after my grandma died. The estate was loud and chaotic for hours as they cleaned everything up, but once the coroners left and my parents went to the station to give their statements, it was just… silence.

A chill runs down my back. *I'm not here to reminisce.* I hurry to Mom's office, and once inside, my eyes bolt around for something, anything that could contain information on Jonathan—and possibly Noah.

Remembering the overheard conversation on the Fourth and the loud banging, I opt to start with her desk. As each drawer checked comes up empty, I begin to panic.

Where else could I look?

My hand grips the handle of the bottom drawer. The *last* one. I yank on it, and it rattles but doesn't budge. *Locked tight.*

"Bingo," I mutter to myself, scouring the desk for something to jimmy it. A letter opener is in a cup holder, and I pluck it, shove it in the lock, and decide I don't really care if I break the damn thing. I grab a book and bang the end of the letter opener, and it pops the lock.

"Yes!" I shout, then suck in a breath. *Shit. At least try to be stealthy, Mrs. Caruso.*

Sliding the drawer open, I buzz with relief and anticipation, finding a row of files. It appears to be organized by first name, and I flip through the tabs urgently.

There's one on pretty much every member of our family, and especially our friends.

Jesus, Mom.

My fingertips pause on a folder with Jonathan's name. I snatch it out and quickly flip through it.

Son of a bitch. She was having him—us—followed for *years*.

What kind of complete paranoia would someone possess to carry out this level of blackmail?

I find the picture of Jonathan snorting coke and notice Kendra behind him, a wicked grin on her face. My nose wrinkles in disgust. I'm sure his cheating tendencies far outlived the ultimatum from my mother. I slap the folder shut, set it to the side, and rifle through till my finger freezes on *his* name. My *husband's* name: Noah Caruso/Lewis.

My stomach sinks.

She knows about his father.

Does she know about the shooting?

Will she leak it to the press?

Did she already?

Sure, it was self-defense. But the tabloids can spin a story any way they want.

My hands shake, and a glance at the clock reminds me how long I've been here already.

I opt to take the folder with me and examine it at home.

Continuing my search, my finger pauses on another labeled Benson Autopsy.

My heart stops. *Why would this be in her archive of extortion?*

A car door slams, and I spring into action. Adding the folder to the other two, I slide the drawer with the rest of the files shut, although I probably should burn them all. As I stand, something falls onto the floor.

I glance down, finding a flash drive, and before I can think, I've swiped it up and shoved it in my pocket. Looking around, I ensure the room appears untouched and sprint out of the office, slip out the back door, and don't stop till I'm in my Bronco.

When I make it home, which took longer than expected thanks to an unwelcome panic attack, I'm still a fucking mess.

Rushing through the front door, I blow out a breath of relief when I lock it behind me. Noah's right. I do feel safe here. I check my watch, thankful I told Noah I'd be a while. There are two hours till the game starts, so even with a little research beforehand, I should make it.

I head to the couch, files in hand, and sink down, flipping them open.

My jaw drops.

Photos of Noah, me, and the twins from the camping trip are inside. But not the cute ones I took of us around the campfire. They look more… aerial. Like someone shot them from far away.

Anger courses through my veins.

Flipping through the photos, I discover one of me with my

head popped out of Noah's tent, him clad in shorts, no shirt, and a flashlight in hand.

Raccoon, my ass.

I shove down the anger, continuing through the folder.

It's all standard information. Medical records. Graduation certificate from CBU.

Damn, her private investigator is thorough.

My fingers flip to a page with the header Prisoner Release Form.

I gasp. She didn't.

My eyes widen, scanning the page.

She did.

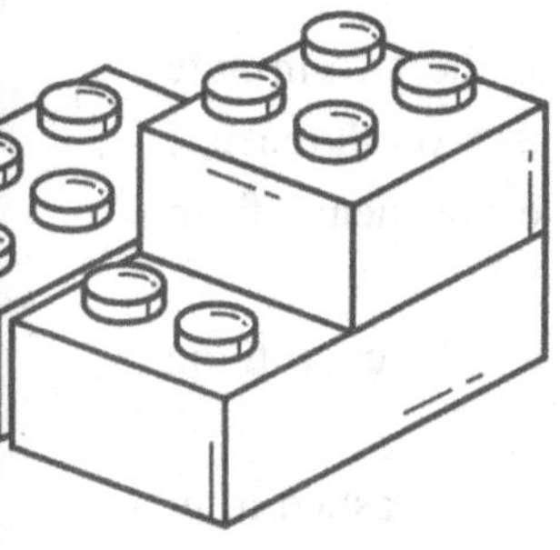

49
NOAH

Wife

I stare at the unread message. She hasn't replied in two hours, and I got the doorbell notification when she arrived home from the library, but damn, that must be some nap. I fight the disappointment that she might not make it to the first game she'd join as my *wife*.

She is growing a child, after all. *Our* child. My lips curl into a smile.

I type out another message.

"You coming?" Knox says, pulling my attention away from the phone.

I push down the anxiety and toss it in the locker.

The first quarter goes by, and if I'm not on the field, my eyes are scanning the crowd. Elijah, Sophia, and Theo are at my seats. Alone. No Charlotte in sight.

They're only twenty yards away, and during the two-minute break between quarters, given Barracudas will start on defense, I jog to the sideline and shout up to them. "Have you heard from Char?"

"No," Sophia calls back, brows furrowing. "Is everything okay?"

"Yeah," I say, waving them off. "She must have crashed after the library."

I rush back to my team and force myself to focus.

This job pays my bills.

This job takes care of my wife and child.

They're fine.

Just because she's not in your viewpoint every second of the day doesn't mean something is wrong. Maybe she went into labor? She's only a month away from her due date. I shake off the thought. If that were true, Sophia would at least know and be by her side instead of here.

Another quarter goes by, and she still hasn't arrived. Finally, halftime comes, and we jog through the tunnel and into the locker room. Now fully distracted, I fight to focus during Coach Bexley's briefing. When he's done, I excuse myself to the bathroom, sneaking to my locker instead to pull out my phone.

It's against league rules to do this, and I could very well be fined, but a simple reply back from her could totally change my headspace for the rest of the game.

There's one text notification and one from our doorbell cam.

I opt to check the text first.

WIFE

No cops or she dies.

My blood runs cold. *What the hell?*

I quickly swap to the doorbell cam for the most recent footage.

A man is banging on the door and looks toward the camera with a sinister smile. My lips part open, nausea creeping up my esophagus, and I struggle for air.

The face of my nightmares is right there on the small screen.

Don't answer the door, baby, I beg, glancing at the time stamp that shows this was an hour ago.

Shit.

My hands shake.

I'm desperate to call her, but I have to finish watching the feed first.

He pounds harder, and my breathing stutters.

No.

The door swings open.

Fuck.

"Can I..." Her voice falls off, and my father smiles, nudging her inside and off the camera. I tap furiously at the screen for more video, but we only have it set to record on motion. I check the live feed but only hear the normal street noises.

Panic courses through me. I can't call the police because I believe he'd do it, and I don't trust them to be discreet.

I fling my helmet in my locker and yank off my jersey, pads, and cleats. There's no way I can drive home wearing this.

"What the hell are you doing?" Coach Bexley's voice sends lightning through my veins.

"I have to go."

"Go?" he scoffs in disbelief, walking closer. "This isn't football at a Sunday cookout. We're in the middle of a pro game." I've stripped to my boxers, and I yank on shorts and a shirt, then slip into tennis shoes. "Noah." Coach Bexley grabs my shoulder. "Stop!"

"I don't have a choice," I repeat, rushing towards the exit.

"Excuse me?" he scoffs as I grip the metal handle. "If you walk out that door, you're done. You'll never play pro again."

My eyes meet his. Never in my life has a decision been so easy. "Then consider this my resignation."

My heart pounds in my chest. This can't be happening. He's supposed to have at least a few more years. A few more years for me to prepare for his release. Figure out a game plan.

He's not supposed to be in my home, with my pregnant wife, doing god knows what.

A chill scatters down my spine.

Don't let your mind go there, Caruso.

My fingers itch to call Mom. She'll wonder why I'm not playing since I was on the field plenty in the first half, but she'll explain it away with me being benched or injured. The last thing I want is her showing up when we have no idea what's going on.

He has the upper hand once again.

There haven't been any other doorbell notifications, so I suspect they're still inside.

How many times have I screamed at the TV screen to call the damn cops, and here I am, being an absolute idiot.

This is stupid. This is so stupid.

Snatching my phone from the cupholder, I call Elijah. His dad and brother are cops from Longwood. I trust him and he trusts them, so it's the best I've got.

It rings once.

"Where the hell are you?" Elijah asks, voice panicked, the loud noise of the crowd almost overpowering his voice. "Why are you calling me? Why—"

"My father's out of jail," I tell him.

"What?"

Realization hits me he has no fucking clue what I'm talking about.

"I don't have time to explain," I say, passing cars at a speed that could put *me* in jail next. "CliffsNotes version. He's psychotic. He went to jail. Now he somehow got out of jail."

"I'll ruin your life" rings in my head, and I shudder.

"What?" he says, background noise getting quieter, as I assume they've left the stands. "I don't understand."

"My father's dangerous. He's at my house." I swallow hard. "And he has Charlotte."

"Don't worry about her," Elijah tells me as if that's an option. "Go back to the game, and we'll call you when it's handled."

"You think I'm leaving the fate of my wife to someone else?" I huff a sarcastic laugh. "I'm already on the way. I called for reinforcements."

"What do you need?"

After filling Elijah in on my very shitty plan and a panicked drive, I pull onto our street. Charlotte's Bronco is the only vehicle in the driveway, and I'm hoping they're still inside and didn't sneak out the back. I pass the house, trying to peek for signs of movement but seeing none, and park down the street.

Elijah instructed me to wait till they arrive before going inside, but if he thinks I'm letting Charlotte and our baby be in danger for a single second longer, he's delusional.

I stumble out of the truck, rush up the street and around to our backyard, and quietly unlatch the gate. It closes with a click, and I crouch down, circling the perimeter of the house.

Peering in the kitchen window, I see someone walk by, and I duck. Taking a steady breath, I look again, albeit slower. My father is pacing in the kitchen, and Charlotte is nowhere in sight.

Where is she?

Is she okay?

I need to get to my bedroom and retrieve my gun from the safe.

How can I get inside without him noticing? Or maybe I *should* go inside. Distract him, and Charlotte can run and get the gun.

Thank god I showed her where it was. A fucked-up sense of relief fills me. What if this happened when I was at an away game?

A high-pitched scream comes from inside, and I sprint around to the front door, finding it unlocked. I throw it open and rush in, finding my father's hand on Charlotte's shoulder as she holds her stomach. A blinding rage courses through me.

"Stop!" I shout, rushing towards them. "Get your hands off my wife."

My father spins, arm flying up, a gun pointed straight at me, and I freeze in place.

"No!" Charlotte screams before another shriek racks her body as he grips her wrist. My blood boils.

Slowly raising my hands, I remain in place even though I'm desperate to grab Charlotte, take her in my arms, and never let her go.

My father stands before me. Our matching green eyes meet for the first time in almost a decade.

His gaze wanders over my body, a sickening smile on his face, and my skin crawls.

"You've grown, son," he says.

My lips snarl. "*Don't* call me that."

He laughs calmly, lowering the pistol. "I'll call you whatever I damn well please."

"What did you do to her?" I snap, feeling braver since there's not a barrel pointed at my face.

"Me?" he says, placing a hand on his chest. "Nothing." He

waves her way. "I simply told her to stop trying to escape or I would blow her brains out."

My lips part, nerves buzzing.

After I shot him, the emotions came in waves.

Guilt for pulling the trigger.

Anger he put me in that position in the first place.

But now, more than any moment ever, I'm enraged I let him live. *Should have finished him off when I had the chance*

My eyes fall to his gun. There's no way I can take him unarmed.

"She's going into labor, you asshole," I say. I'm not sure she is but it could be a good excuse since she's so close to her due date, and she definitely looks the part.

He shrugs. "Not my problem."

"This is between me and you," I urge. *Beg.* "She doesn't need to be involved."

"But doesn't she?" he says, his smile sinister, tightening his grip, and she flinches, knees buckling in pain. Her eyes meet mine. *I'm so sorry, baby.* She smiles weakly, telling me it's okay. This is anything *but* okay. "She is your *wife*, after all."

"Just let her lie in our bed." *So she can get a gun...* "Unless you know how to deliver a baby?"

"No." He shakes his head. "She's fine right here."

My eyes find Charlotte's again, a single tear rolling down her cheek. "What do you want?" I ask him.

"Isn't it obvious?" he says, digging the gun into Charlotte's side, and my body seizes. Heat courses through my veins. Every single moment of the last six months flashes through my mind. Our first kiss. Her naked in my arms. Early morning runs and fancy galas. The baby. Coming to terms with being a father. The cliff of the canyon where I made her my wife. All of it. "I'm here to balance the scales. A bullet for a bullet."

"To *what*?" I shriek.

"Did you forget you *shot* me?" he asks.

"You almost killed Mom!"

"And she would have deserved it," he snarls.

My body trembles with rage. The gun pressed into Charlotte's rib is the only thing keeping me from ripping him apart with my bare hands. If he shoots me, so be it. If he shoots her? We might as well both go because there's no way I could live a life without her.

"You'd really shoot your own grandchild?" I say, grasping for something, anything to bring humanity back to the monster before me.

"Of course not," he says, tone full of humor. "But it's not your baby."

"Yes. She is." *How does he know that?* Sure, our friends and immediate family are aware, but it's not common knowledge.

"That's not what Tabitha said," he replies.

Charlotte and I share a look. The only reason his lawyer would know that information specifically is if a certain politician informed her. I assumed Georgia helped him get released, but hearing it confirmed?

Fuck.

Seeing Charlotte in danger, whimpering in pain, triggers a panic in me I've never felt. I should have listened to Georgia. If she blew up my career, so be it. But this?

"Then let them go!" I plead.

"*Tsk. Tsk. Tsk.*" He pulls the gun away, waving it towards me, and I let out a silent sigh of relief. *That's right. Keep it on me. My life for theirs. An even exchange.* "You still have *such* a temper."

I'm fourteen again. Useless. Helpless. Even the self-defense classes won't help for shit if I can't get Charlotte out of here. Risking a bullet going off and hitting her is not an option.

Something crashes outside. *Shit. I hope the guys didn't give themselves away.* My father drags Charlotte with him as he looks out the window, gun in his right hand. She turns, eyes finding mine.

Run, I mouth to her, pointing towards our bedroom and making a gun hand gesture hoping she gets the message.

He turns, dragging her back towards me, pistol pointed towards the floor. I sidestep so I'm on the same side. If I do this correctly, I should be able to knock it out of his hand and she can get to the bedroom.

"I kept waiting for you to visit me in jail," he says. "To apologize."

"Apologize for what?" I say, squaring my shoulders and stepping towards him to reduce our distance. He takes a step too, dragging Charlotte. I force a smile on my face. "You deserved it."

His jaw ticks, and he lifts the gun my way. Charlotte swings, knocking it out of his grasp, and it slides across the floor. She bolts from him and scrambles for it as I tackle my father to the ground. I don't have time to be furious she didn't listen as she snatches up the gun, pointing it at us.

"Put your hands on the ground," she shouts, and my father laughs, flipping us and pressing a knee to my chest. *Shit.* "Get off of him!" she shrieks, gesturing again with the gun, her hands shaking.

"Come on," he says, and I jerk beneath him, unable to get free. Useless. Powerless. I'm fourteen again, watching Mom take another beating I couldn't stop. "Put it down, *sweetheart.*"

"Don't call her that," I growl.

He smiles at her. "Guns are not for pretty little things like you." He tugs me up, and my muscles tense as he uses my body like a shield. With both hands, I grip his arm around my neck. He extends his opposite hand towards Charlotte. "Give it to me before you hurt someone."

Charlotte's eyes meet mine, and I bring a finger up, tapping his arm near my shoulder, trying to signal her to aim there and praying she's a good shot.

Bang.

She's not.

"*Fuck*!" I gasp, pain radiating throughout my shoulder.

"Oh my god," she gasps. "I'm so sorry."

My father releases me, charging at her, and I ignore the blinding pain, jumping to my feet. Her eyes are wide, and she bends, sliding the gun across the floor towards me.

And misses me by a mile.

Soffione, I love you so much, but what the fuck?

She's married to a quarterback, and her aim is worse than a drunk idiot at a urinal.

Spinning away, I fight for mental clarity, rushing after the gun. It lands next to the fridge, and I snatch it up, turning to face them with a wince, veins going cold. He's straddling Charlotte on the ground, hands around her neck, her face beet red as he squeezes the oxygen from her lungs.

"Let her go!" I shout, pointing the gun at him, my arms bloodied. Luckily she shot my left shoulder, and my shooting hand is functional. Although the blinding pain I'm experiencing makes focusing incredibly difficult.

"Drop the gun or I break her neck!" he shouts back as she slaps at his hands.

My body flickers with indecision. She needs oxygen urgently, and if he doesn't release his grasp, she could die. Baby could die. I would die.

"You have one more chance!" he sneers, tightening his grasp.

I grip the cold metal in my hand.

Finger on the trigger.

Take a deep breath.

Bang.

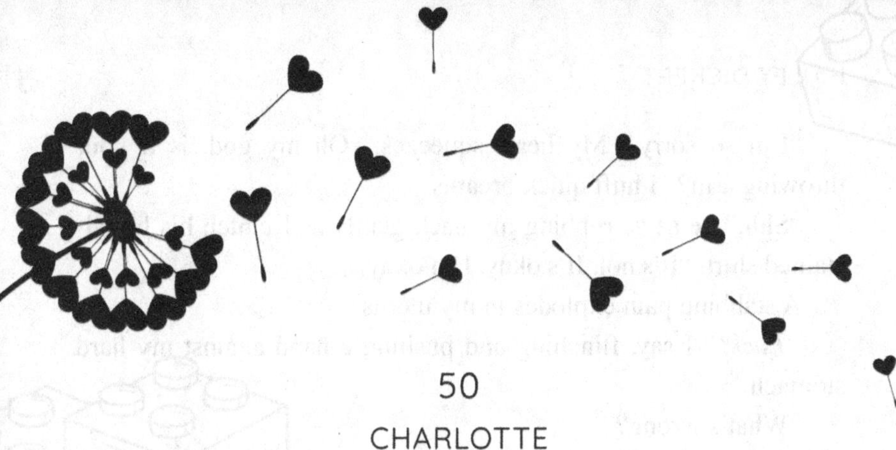

50

CHARLOTTE

Air floods my lungs at a speed I've never experienced as I wheeze, gulping, gasping. Noah's father is slumped on top of me, and I sob, trying to shove him away, but I'm too weak from lack of oxygen. The body flies off of me as Noah tosses it to the side, his panicked face coming into view.

"Are you okay?" he asks, eyes trailing my body, widening at the sight of blood.

So much blood.

I pat myself down and glance at his father, limp on the floor.

"No," Noah chokes out, hands frantically flying over every inch of me as he winces in pain. "No."

"It's not mine!" Our eyes meet as his hands continue their desperate search. "It's not my blood. I'm okay."

"Are you sure?" he asks, unable to let go of me while he gasps for air himself.

"Yes." My eyes fall to his shoulder, which *is* soaked with *his* blood. Tears burst free. "I shot you, oh my god, I'm so sorry." He pulls us to standing, and I flop against him, body entirely drained from the adrenaline.

"*Oww!*" He flinches, gripping me with his free hand.

"I'm so sorry." My heart squeezes. "Oh my god, is it your throwing arm?" I huff quick breaths.

"Shh," he says, rubbing my back gently as I clutch his blood-stained shirt. "It's not. It's okay. I'm okay."

A stabbing pain explodes in my uterus.

"Fuck!" I say, flinching and pushing a hand against my hard stomach.

"What's wrong?"

I take short quick breaths till the pain subsides. "Nothing," I rush out.

"Is baby coming?" I shake my head. "Are you sure?" I shake my head again. "We need to get you to a hospital."

"Um…" I gesture to his arm. "I think *you* need a hospital."

His pained eyes find mine. "You and our baby are first priority."

I glance to the lifeless body on the floor, unable to conjure up any feeling of empathy.

"Is he—"

"Yes, he's dead," Noah assures me. "I didn't miss this time."

Sadness surrounds my soul at everything Noah's been through.

The front door bursts open, and two men run in, guns at the ready. My pulse skyrockets, and I grip Noah with a squeal. My body shakes as I dig my face into his chest. *Please, don't hurt us.*

"They're cops," Noah tells me.

"What?" My eyes widen, darting to the crimson floor. *Will they believe it was self-defense?*

"I called them," he adds, calming my anxiety. Of course he did.

Pain racks through me again, and I fold over.

"We need to get her to a hospital," Noah tells them, and I glance up noting that I do in fact recognize the men. It's Elijah's father, the Longwood Sheriff, and his son, Cole Danvers, a deputy.

"Looks like you need one too," Sheriff Danvers says as Noah cradles his arm.

"See?" I cry through what I'm assuming is another contraction.

"*Soffione*," Noah grits through his teeth. "Now is not the time for I told you so's."

"Go," Sheriff Danvers says, ushering us out. "We'll call this in."

"It was self-defense," I tell him through the pain.

"We know," he assures us.

Noah releases me, using his good arm to grab the hospital bag, and we rush outside. Elijah, Theo, and Sophia are in the driveway, and I don't have time to ask questions.

"Oh my god," Sophia shrieks, noting the blood on us.

Our eyes connect, both slick with moisture. "It's not mine," I assure her, shaking my head as the tears burst free. "It's not mine," I repeat, quieter.

"We need a hospital," Noah tells them, gripping me tight, and Theo grabs the bag from his hand.

"Get in the truck," Elijah says, and we rush towards it.

My due date isn't for another month, but it's no surprise she's coming early given the—

Oh, fuck. It's happening again.

Seventeen hours and an epidural later, I'm holding our little one in my arms. Ten fingers. Ten toes. And air in her lungs. We were terrified her oxygen levels would be low, but the staff assured us they're in perfectly healthy range.

The emotions we've endured the past twenty-four hours are nothing short of horrific, but this remains the most incredible moment of my life.

Noah smiles, pulling me back to the present. His gaze is adoring as he brushes my hair back with his good arm, his opposite shoulder wrapped and in a sling. Fortunately he only needed stitches as the shot was through and through. He's banned us from discussing his injury until I'm recovered. "You did so good, *tesoro*."

"I still can't believe I shot you on her *birthday*," I say with a shaky laugh now that we're hopefully moving forward from the darkness.

He grins. "She wanted to come into this world with a bang."

"Aww," I say, grinning up at him. "Your first official dad joke." Even in the darkest of days, he's my light. Now I understand why Luna calls him *sole mio*.

"Do we have a name?" the nurse asks.

Noah's adoring eyes meet mine. "Gabriella Sole."

My chest warms. "I love you, Noah *Gabriel* Caruso."

"I love you, Charlotte *Caruso*," he says, and a wide smile fills my face.

Because I thought I loved it when he said my name, but I love Charlotte Caruso even more.

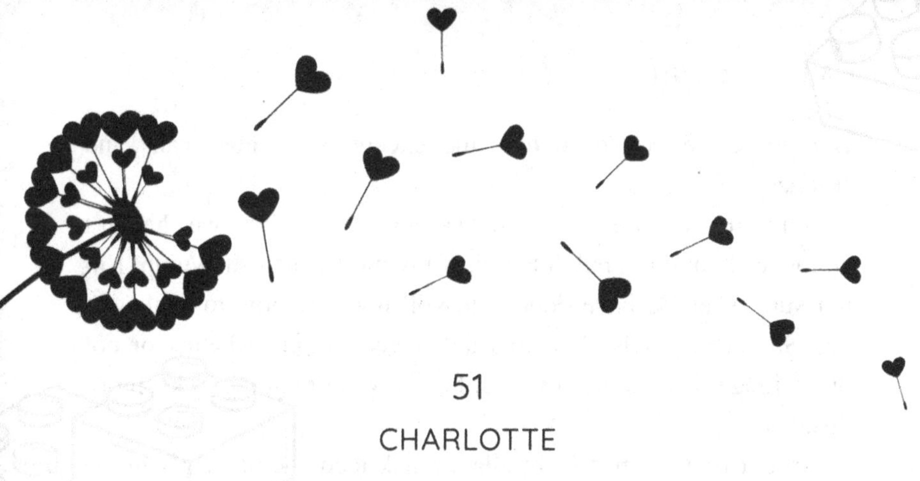

51

CHARLOTTE

The only thing hotter than a man wearing a backwards ball cap is a man carrying a car seat one-handed with a baby sleeping soundly inside.

I slowly trail Noah up our driveway, and he sets Gabriella down to unlock the door, given his other arm is in a sling. We make our way inside, the overpowering smell of bleach assaulting my senses.

Our eyes meet.

"Want to stay somewhere else tonight?" Noah suggests.

I shake my head. "This is our home. We can't let what happened here take that from us."

He smiles softly. "Scars and all?"

I nod. "Scars and all."

We can think about moving some other time. Right now I need to lie down, rest, and snuggle my little Ella. I'm sore as hell, my boobs are throbbing, and walking is a bitch, but I did it. She burst out of me, and I survived.

Noah won't admit it, but he's exhausted too. After all, *he's* the one who was shot. By me. His wife. *Never gonna live that down.*

But he refused to leave my side except for a few scans and stitches.

Our friends were in the waiting room, but we haven't announced anything publicly yet. If my mother had shown up, I'm not sure what I'd have done. I'm still not sure how to deal with her. She clearly helped Noah's father get out, but whether or not that's illegal is to be determined. For now we're going to keep our distance.

In our room, I give Gabriella a quick feed and place her in the bassinet next to the bed. In the closet I grab comfier clothes and spot the dress I wore to break into the Benson estate on the floor. I pick it up to toss in the hamper, and the little flash drive I stole clicks against the floor.

In all the craziness, I completely forgot about it.

I bend down, wincing, and pick it up. After changing and putting on that god-awful postpartum underwear, I grab the baby monitor and wobble to the living room.

"Can you get a laptop?" I ask Noah.

"Shouldn't you be resting?" he asks, using his one good hand to wash a dish at the sink.

"Shouldn't you?" I counter, with a cocked brow.

"Touché."

"I found a flash drive with the files," I tell him, sinking onto the couch.

"Can't checking it wait?"

"Given the amount of info my mother had on you, I'm sure she's heard about your father's death and Gabriella's birth by now. I want to know every detail before she tries to contact me."

"What's on it?"

"I have no clue. But it was in a locked drawer, so it seemed important."

"Do you *want* to look?" Noah asks timidly.

I spin the little thumb drive between my fingers. "It would

probably be more dangerous not to," I point out. Knowing her affinity for blackmail, it could quite literally be on anyone.

We pull out Noah's laptop and a USB to USB-C converter and plug it in. He gestures for me to go ahead, and I suppose since it's my mother's collection of chaos, I should do the honors.

Only one file is on the device. A video that's password protected, but after a few tries—she's so damn predictable—I've cracked it.

An uneasy feeling settles in my stomach.

Clicking the video, it opens wide on the computer screen, and I turn up the sound. There's a full view of the study at my parents' house.

Grandma sits in her chair, working as usual, a glass of wine to her right.

A door creaks open, and her attention turns towards it.

"Georgia?" Grandma says. "What are you doing here?"

"I need the money."

"And I'm not giving it to you."

"If I don't secure a donation from the Benson name you always drone has so much weight, how is that going to look?" my mother asks.

"That's not my problem."

"Don't you realize how good it will be for you when I'm in office?" Mom presses.

"The fact you think you can win president, let alone governor, is embarrassing."

"I'm so sick of you underestimating me," Mom says, tone sharp.

"I'm not. I don't place bets on dead horses."

"Transfer the fucking money."

"No," Grandma says.

"Don't make me do this." Mom's tone is indecipherable as she reaches into her handbag.

I gasp.

She points a gun at my grandma. At her own mother.

"Make the transfer," Mom shouts.

"What are you going to do?" Grandma laughs. "Shoot me?"

"If I have to."

Mom rounds the desk, clicks around on the computer, and aims the gun at Grandma's head.

"Make. The. Transfer."

"Over. My. Dead. Body," Grandma seethes, and Mom pulls the gun back, then whacks her in the head with it. She slumps to the floor, no longer visible due to the camera angle.

Mom returns to the computer, and a satisfied smile spreads across her face. After a few minutes, she looks to the floor, bends down, and curses.

"Shit." She stands, setting the gun on the table, and drags her hands through her hair. "Fuck!" she shouts.

"What just happened?" Noah asks, voice at a whisper.

"I think we witnessed my grandmother's murder," I say as the footage keeps rolling. "But I don't understand why my mother would keep this. It only incriminates *her*."

"Maybe she—"

"What's wrong?" my dad shrieks, running in the room, and he stalls in place upon seeing Grandma's body. "What did you do?"

"What had to be done," Mom grits out.

"Don't you think this has gone far enough?" Dad exclaims, running to the body and assumedly checking for a pulse. "She's not breathing."

"Help me clean it up."

We watch silently as Dad helps rearrange Grandma's body on the floor. Wipes off the blood on the edge of the desk. Makes it look like an accident. And I realize why my mother kept this video. Why my parents' marriage has been strained since my grandma died. Why Dad can barely stand to be in the same room as her. Why he's never home.

She's blackmailing her own husband.

Well, screw that.

Once upon a time, I made the mistake of holding on to a video. I won't be doing that again.

"I didn't want to help her cover it up, I swear," Dad promises, eyes full of pain.

"I believe you," I say because hell, I saw the video. He pleaded with her to call an ambulance, but she refused. "We need to bring this to the police."

"I know." Dad nods. "It's time." He shifts in his seat at Noah's and my kitchen table. Noah is beside me, a protective arm resting on my leg.

"Did you know she had this video?" I ask.

"I didn't at first. Not until I requested a divorce a few months after the incident."

My lips part in surprise. "You wanted a divorce?"

"My wife murdered her own mother in cold blood," he deadpans. "Yeah, I wanted a divorce."

"But she was worried about the optics?" I pressed.

"God forbid the real world interrupt her political aspirations," Dad scoffs.

My brows pull together, sadness consuming me. "If you knew she was dangerous, how could you leave her alone with us? Especially the kids."

"I'm not proud of that." He shakes his head. "But I hoped her violent streak started and ended with her mother. She'd always hated her."

"But you weren't worried about me?" I ask, chest aching. My whole life he was my protector—the one I could count on. I didn't realize he was knowingly leaving me in danger.

Dad reaches across the table and places his hand on mine. "I always worry about you. But I know you can take care of yourself." His eyes flick to Noah. "Although, it seems that won't be necessary anymore."

Noah's grip on my thigh tightens. It's nice Dad thought I could handle myself, but it doesn't take away the sting of him choosing apathy over protection.

"So how is this going to work?" I ask.

"Well," Dad says, "you are staying out of this completely."

"What?" I scoff, annoyance filling me. "But I found the—"

"There is absolutely no reason for you to be dragged into the depositions and hundreds of hours of legal prep this case is going to take. Besides…" Dad's eyes fall to the nursery door behind me. "You're new parents. Noah's going to be busy with physical therapy for his arm. This is the last kind of stress you need."

Guilt fills me again at the reminder of the injury I caused. And when my mind travels to Gabriella, I know I would do anything to protect her.

"Dad," I say, tilting my head, "I can handle plenty." And while I think I can trust him, I'm still not fully comfortable handing this over to him.

"I'm your father," he says, tone firm but soft. "Let me take care of this. It's too dangerous for your mom to know you're the one gunning after her."

Noah's protective husband senses must be tingling because before I can argue, he says, "That's fine. Under one condition." This is the first time Noah's spoken since we began, and my father eyes him curiously. "We choose the lawyer."

"Isn't Tony more used to family court law?" I ask Noah, although it is the best way for us to be uninvolved but still aware of everything.

"He worked as a high-profile defense lawyer for years before that," Noah states. "And besides, this definitely sounds like *family* law."

"Fine by me," I say, returning my attention to my father. "We'll stay out of the way. But you have to use Noah's stepdad for your lawyer."

"Deal," Dad says immediately. Relief trembles under the surface. If we play this right, my mother will go away for a long, long time and Dad should be able to plead forced coercion.

"Are you okay?" Noah asks as we're snuggled up on the couch hours after Dad left. Gabriella is in my arms, sleeping peacefully, and Noah's uninjured arm is around me as I lean against his chest.

"I will be," I tell him, eyes finding his. "Are you?"

"I'm fine," he says, swallowing hard.

"Have you heard from Coach Bexley?" I ask hesitantly. I'd like to say I'm shocked Noah left a professional game to save me, but after all he's done for us... I know he didn't hesitate for a single moment.

Noah nods. "I talked to him when we were in the hospital."

"Really?" I ask, a rock in my stomach. "What did he say?"

"I explained everything. Porter helped too..." He sighs, and my anxiety heightens. "They're going to help me in my recovery, and if I'm cleared to play, I'm back on the team on a probationary basis."

"Oh my god," I squeal, and my eyes widen, darting to Gabriella, who *just* fell asleep. She squirms. I brush a finger over her soft brown hair, and she dozes right back off. *Sweet little thing.* "That's great," I murmur.

"Yeah." He shifts in place, jaw clenching.

"What's wrong?"

"I was thinking maybe I should just take this as a sign to stay home with you and Ella," he says, reaching out and lightly rubbing her head. The tenderness in his eyes is so strong I can feel it to my core. *Absolutely not.*

"Noah." His gaze returns to mine. "There is no way in hell I'm allowing you to do that."

"It's my choice," he says, but I can see the flicker of indecision.

"No." I shake my head. "You've worked so hard your entire life. You were *made* for that job. I appreciate you're willing to give it up for me, for us." He runs his fingers along my arms, my sense of security overwhelming. "But I wouldn't be a good wife if I allowed you to."

"You're a great wife," he says, with a teasing smile.

"Thank you," I say, returning the gesture. "And this great wife is telling you there's no way in hell you're quitting."

"What if—"

"No," I say firmly. "I forbid it."

He chuckles. "So bossy."

"Damn right." I grin up at him. "My husband *is* an NFL quarterback, and it's going to stay that way."

"The doctor said recovery's going to be hard," Noah says, masking the concern in his eyes.

"And I'll be here for you every step of the way," I assure him, placing a hand on his cheek.

He presses a soft kiss to my lips, and my eyes flutter shut. My arms are filled with love, my heart filled by him.

Basil. Cedarwood. *Home*.

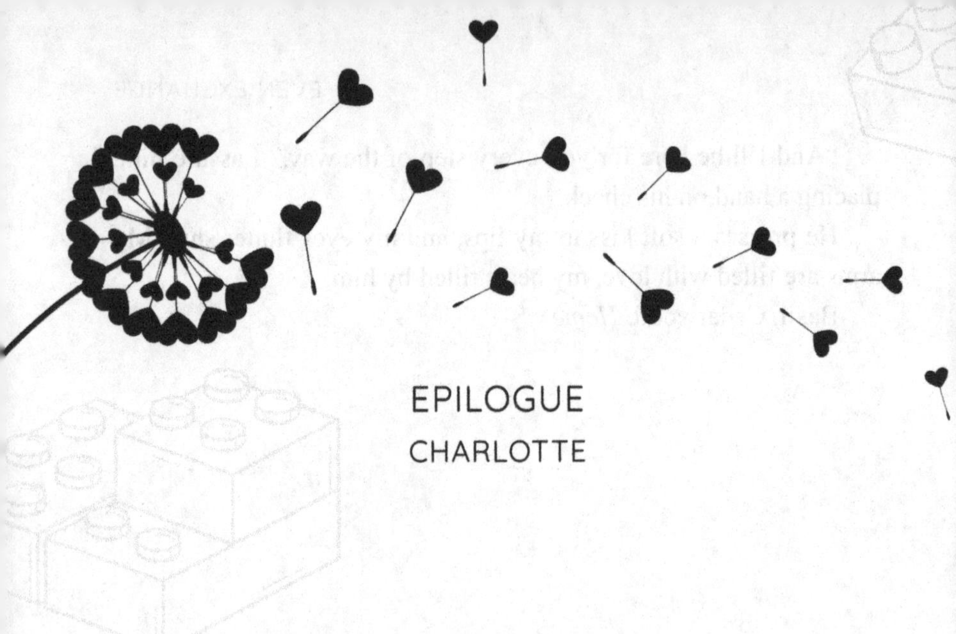

EPILOGUE
CHARLOTTE

Ten Months Later

My eyes fixate on the clear partition as an uncomfortable plastic chair makes my back ache. Given the wide array of my mother's crimes—murder, blackmail, bribery, political espionage, the list goes on—she was sentenced to life with the *possibility* of parole. *Hopefully it's a minuscule possibility.* Her parental rights to the twins were also, thankfully, terminated.

It was a justified punishment, but I can't deny the pain I felt trying to explain all of this to them. My mother was far from perfect, but in their seven-year-old brains, it didn't matter—she was *theirs*. And now, she's gone.

Given my dad's involvement, we gained guardianship of the twins during the trial.

Do I forgive him? Depends on the day.

Do I trust him with the other two humans I love most in the world to always look out for and protect them? Unfortunately not.

But that's why they're in our home now. It really didn't take much convincing for Dad to let us adopt them. He knows we're the best option for them.

Thankfully Tony and Luna help as often as they can, too, which made it possible for me to attend some classes this semester. It may take me longer than anticipated to graduate, but I'm still trying.

I've avoided seeing my mother, but we're coming up on Gabriella's first birthday, and I'm ready to close this chapter of my life so I can enjoy my family. Noah thankfully had a full recovery and is back to being one of the NFL's best rookie quarterbacks.

The sound of screeching metal brings me back to the present.

Every nerve in my body fires off warning signs to leave, but I need to do this.

I need closure.

My mother's tired eyes meet mine as she takes a seat on the other side of the partition. The polished politician is long gone, replaced by a worn, wary woman. Not even a faux smile for my benefit.

She picks up the corded phone, and I follow suit.

"It's nice to see you, Charlie."

Wish I could say the same.

"Hey."

"How is Gabriella?" The idea of her even knowing my daughter's name makes my veins buzz, but I ignore it.

"Good."

"And the twins?" she asks. *As if she actually cares.*

"They're fine," I say.

"How's school?"

I purse my lips. "Is this really what we're doing? Bullshit small talk?"

"I don't know what you want from me," she says, exasperated. "You came to see me."

Swallowing my anxieties, I ask, "Do you regret it?"

Her brows pull together. "Regret what?"

"The things you did."

She tilts her head. "Of course I do."

"Because you were caught, or because you know it was wrong?" My heart pounds as I await her response. I don't even know why I want these answers, but my therapist seems to think a conversation with her will help my healing process.

She waves a hand. "Does it matter?"

"Of course it matters," I scoff, anger rolling through me. "Noah's father almost shot me thanks to you!"

"I told him the baby wasn't Noah's because I thought he'd leave you out of it," she says, lips tight.

"Well, all it did was make him more eager to jam a gun in my side," I say, a shiver racking through me. "So thanks for that."

"Someday you'll realize being a parent is not an easy task." She shakes her head. "The decisions you make might blur the lines of morality." Her eyes bore into mine. "But you'll do it because it's for your family." I huff a laugh. *Even jailed for life, she's still lying through her teeth.* "What's so funny?"

"You're sitting here, using your family as a cop-out for the decisions *you* made." I purse my lips. "You're using us as an excuse."

"Everything I was working towards was for our family," she says, jaw tight. "I was making sure none of us would have to worry about anything ever again." I don't have the energy to argue with her delusional logic. It's as if she forgot she cut me off financially when I needed her the most. I did *plenty* of worrying. "I brought us money, power, and security."

"We didn't want any of it," I say, no fight left in me. "We just wanted a *mom*."

"You were more than happy to accept access to your trust fund again," she says condescendingly. "You must care about the money a *little* bit."

"Honestly? When I got the call from the estate lawyer, I almost told them to shove the blood money. Because we both know that's what it is."

"Charlie," she warns.

"But I quickly realized there's a lot of good that can be done with it." Pride fills my chest. *So* much good can be done. "In fact, I'm headed to a charity event right after this."

A smile quirks the corner of her mouth. "Following in your mother's footsteps after all."

It's clear she's not remorseful. She still doesn't view the things she did as wrong. She's unapologetic. Hell, maybe she should be in a psych ward instead of a prison.

"Goodbye, Mother," I say, and it feels final.

Her gaze holds mine, and I *almost* see a crack in her resolve. *Almost* see a hint of moisture in her eyes. "Goodbye, Charlie," she says, hanging up the phone, standing, and walking away without a second glance.

As I leave the prison, a single tear rolls down my cheek. My mother did a lot of fucked-up things in her life. But if there's one thing she taught me, it's what *not* to do with my family. Because of her, I will be the most loving, understanding, present parent to our children. I'll never take my husband for granted or forget to tell my friends how much I appreciate them.

My mother set fire to my life, like Noah's father did to his, but they didn't realize it would ignite a raging inferno *within* us. A burning desire to share that light with the world.

Thanks for dropping the match.

NOAH

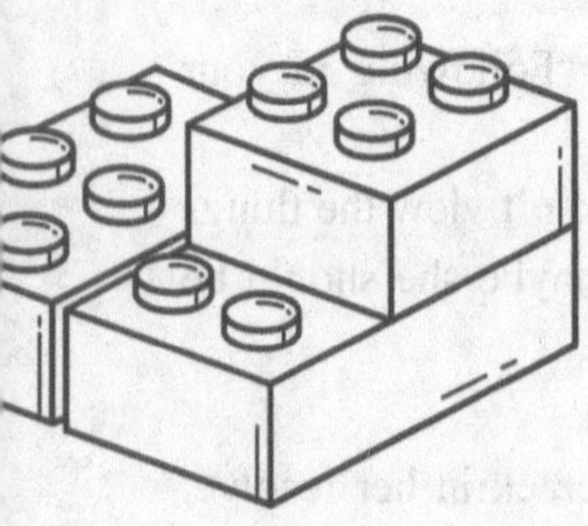

"Sorry I'm late," Charlotte tells me, leaning in, and I kiss her on the cheek.

"It's okay. We haven't started yet," I assure her as we stand backstage, preparing for the opening speech of the inaugural Caruso Safe Haven charity event. A weekend filled with relays, NFL player/fan meet and greets, a silent auction, and a formal gala, all raising funds to benefit the Hope House, a shelter for those impacted by domestic violence in our community.

After Charlotte received her trust fund, she came to me with the idea. Since my father was gone, *for real this time*, Mom and I agreed to share our story and utilize my platform and connections to bring awareness to the cause. With Charlotte's money, we created a safe haven, a house of hope, where victims can come when they feel there's no way out.

Mom walks up, and passes our sweet little Gabriella to Charlotte. A small smile graces my lips as my daughter's beautiful brown eyes meet mine. She looks just like her mother, and my chest squeezes.

"Ready, *sole mio?*" Mom asks, pulling my attention to her.

"Yes." Anxiety squeezes my chest. *I can do this.* "I'm ready," I say, and Charlotte's eyes meet mine. *"Ti amo."*

"Ti amo," she repeats, with an encouraging smile, and I press a kiss to her lips.

I plant another in Gabriella's dark hair, turning to follow Mom to the stage for the opening speech. We climb the stairs, her hand in mine, and the crowd of at least a thousand people wearing various shades of purple comes into view.

I'm handed a microphone, and Mom squeezes my hand, stepping off to the side. *"Sono orgogliosa di te,"* she tells me.

'I'm so proud of you.'

"Welcome, everyone," I say, the volume of the microphone silencing the crowd. "Thank you for being here today. For those of you that don't know me, my name is Noah Caruso—" The crowd shouts, and I wave a hand to simmer them down. "Thank you." I fight a smile. "Thank you, I appreciate that, but I'm actually not here today as Tampa Bay's best quarterback—"

"Hey!" Mike Lorraine calls from the crowd.

"Sorry, Mike," I say, shooting him a smile and garnering some laughter. I take a deep breath. *Here it goes.* "Tragic fact: in the United States alone, there are over five *million* cases of domestic violence. Every. Single. Year." I shake my head, disgusted by the number. "Throughout most of my childhood, I was one of those cases." A hush falls over the crowd. "For years, my mother and I were physically and mentally abused by my father until he was finally arrested when I was fourteen." I bring a hand to the back of my head, dragging my thumb along the raised skin. "My scars always felt like reminders of all those moments of weakness. Of the times I didn't have the strength to fight back… It took years to come to terms with everything that happened in my life." Pulling the microphone away, I release a shaky breath. "But now I view each scar not as a moment I was weak, but as a moment of darkness I *survived.*" I jab a finger at my chest. *"I'm. Still. Here."* The crowd applauds, and my eyes find our friends in the front row cheering me on. Elijah gives me a nod of encouragement, and I swallow hard.

"All my life, I considered myself a *victim* of domestic violence," I say, pausing, trying to find the right words. "Today I stand before you a *survivor*." My gaze finds Mom's, and she nods in encouragement. "*We* are survivors." I walk across the stage and take her palm in mine. "But we almost weren't." She squeezes my hand. "Mom's family was in Italy, and we were alone. We had no one to notice the signs. No one to call for help. No one to give us refuge. No one to care."

I pause, gathering my thoughts. "My wife, Charlotte, and I started this charity to make sure our community knows there's always someone who cares. You will always find safe refuge and help and guidance at Hope House. There will be mental health counseling, safe living quarters with security while residents figure out their next steps, and assistance in relocation, working in partnership with local law enforcement."

"Our goal," I continue, "is for every victim who comes to Hope House to leave a *survivor*."

The crowd roars, and my eyes blur as I scan their faces. "As you spend the weekend playing games, meeting your favorite players, and *hopefully* opening your wallets," I say, garnering a laugh from the crowd, "please take a moment to remember what we're all doing this for." I pause, the emotions overwhelming me. "And we want to say a huge thank you in advance for helping provide the safe space, the house of hope, my *mamma* and I never had," I say, choking up on the last words. "Thank you!"

The crowd thunders once more as I walk off the stage, wiping away tears, a sense of pride filling me with all the people Hope House will help. Charlotte awaits me, Gabriella tucked on her side, and I loop my arms around them.

"You did great," Charlotte says, pressing a gentle kiss to my lips and wiping a tear off my cheek. "I'm so proud of you."

My eyes meet hers, and I shake my head in disbelief. "This

was all your idea. And mainly your money." *Turns out a fifty-million-dollar trust fund goes a long way.*

"Dadadada," Gabriella coos, reaching for me, and I grin, scooping her into my arms, readjusting her dress with tiny lemons dancing across it.

"I know," Charlotte says as Gabriella situates herself, resting her head on my chest, and I rub my hand along her back. *Daddy's here.* "But it's *your* story. *Your* platform is getting the cause out there."

Leaning over, I kiss her softly on the lips. "And I couldn't have done any of this without you."

Charlotte's woven in my heart like the fabric of the cosmos. She's the gravity keeping me in orbit, and without her I'd drift away, lost to the vastness of the universe. After my shoulder was injured, I suggested quitting so I'd be around more, but Charlotte said she'd shoot me a second time if I even considered giving up my dream.

But I'd give up football and touchdowns for honey and lemons anytime.

Maybe someday she'll realize my dream—my wish since the very first dandelion—is her.

A perfect even exchange.

FOR A SPICY BONUS CHAPTER
SUBSCRIBE TO MY NEWSLETTER

Trust me, you don't want to miss this.

CRYSTAL BAY UNIVERSITY BOOK 4
COMING SOON

Did someone say, "best friend's sister"?
And they're roommates?

Also by Hailey Dickert

The Sister Between Us

Dickert's debut novel that started it all is a second-chance soccer romance. This friends-to-lovers, best friend's brother, love story includes shared grief, and is guaranteed to make you ugly cry and put you back together.

Return Policy is the first novel in the Crystal Bay University series by Hailey Dickert. It can be read as a standalone; however, since Sophia is a side character from Dickert's first novel *The Sister Between Us*, it is suggested to read that first for the best experience.

Merry Mischief List is the second installment in the Crystal Bay University Series. It's a light-hearted age-gap holiday novella about cheerleader Andi Lyons and CBU football coach James Porter. (And sometimes his best friend Kensington Knox.)

Acknowledgments

I hardly know where to start.

My heart is overwhelmed that I've even made it this far again after almost two years. There were truly days, many days, when I thought I'd never publish another book. I began writing this book specifically in February 2023, and I wondered if it would ever make it into the world. So first, I think I'd like to acknowledge to myself that I did it. Even through all the heartache, cross-ocean moves, craziness of life, I did it. I published again.

To my readers, it's been a long journey getting to this point. I was worried some of you may not still care about my stories when I took so long to write this book, but if you got to this page, that means you did. Thank you so much for believing in me and sticking by my side.

Firstly, I have to recognize the incredible support system I have and thank my parents for raising me to follow my passions—*no risk, no reward*—and for endlessly supporting me and my family as I pursue a career that I love. (I think the boys prefer being at Grandma and Papa's house anyways.)

Thank you to my husband. *Ich liebe dich für immer und ewig.* You've shown me a love that lasts like honey, and I am so grateful to have you by my side. You are the one person I sincerely couldn't do this without. Thank you for supporting me endlessly, being a loving father, and most importantly, my best friend.

When I started my journey as an author, I felt so *alone*. It took time to find friends that feel like family. The friends that I know are my shoulder to cry on, wall for bouncing ideas, and hype squad when the imposter syndrome has returned once again.

Meg Jones, I will never be able to express the gratitude I have for our friendship. One day you came into my life, and I am never, ever letting you go. I don't think you realized how much I needed you. I always do. Thank you for letting me sprinkle little bits and pieces of you into my books. My heart squeezes, and I know you'll be a part of me forever. Love you xx.

Maria Rigou, I'm not sure if you believe in fate, but I do. The fact that we even met is kismet, and I'm so blessed to have you in my life. You have shown me a friendship that loves without wanting anything in return. I can always count on you. I hope you know you can count on me too. Good luck ever getting rid of me. *Te amo.*

Ambar Cordova, you are sunshine. On the darkest days, you bring a light to this community like no other. Your kindness, grace, and support does not go unnoticed. You're a cheerleader, trend setter, and a literal icon. I am so honored to call you friend.

After being in this industry a few years, I am so fortunate to no longer be alone. On a day to day basis, I have the most incredible women by my side, and I'm so grateful for you—Caroline Frank, Katie VanBrunt, Ronnie Mathews, Dany Crooks, Ruth Stilling, and so many others.

Elena, thank you for helping me to make Noah into a beautiful image of Italian culture. You have been such a pleasure to work with, and I'm so proud of the character we've created. I hope the readers fall in love with him and his culture as much as we have.

Alli Morgan, you are superhuman. I'm amazed by you every day, and I'm so grateful for your continued help with my books. You + Me = Magic.

To my alpha and beta readers, each one of you helped shape this book into the story it's become, and I can't thank you enough for your contribution: Rebekah D., Mary Kate, Kayla M., Anna A., Bella P., Bry, Jess R., Tracey K., Paola A., and Kaylee B. An additional huge thank you to my early ARC readers for helping me find the final little typos! I'm so grateful.

Jordana Blake, thank you for helping me ensure a proper and respectful portrayal regarding the domestic violence aspects in this novel. I am grateful for your assistance and friendship!

Katherine Bitner, you are my rock right now. You are the best PA a girl could ask for, and you make it possible for me to focus my efforts where needed. I am so glad I found you, and please don't ever leave me.

Katie Pridige, thank you for creating the beautiful illustrated cover of my dreams!

Cassie Rottink, thank you so much for kicking ass at marketing and keeping me in check. I am so grateful for you!

Katie W., my incredible editor, I can't imagine going through this process without you. You always instill a sense of pride into me that is unmatched, and you make sure my manuscripts are polished perfectly before they head out into the world.

Thank you to everyone who read this far. I can't wait for you to see whose story I bring to life next!

Italian Glossary

Incorporating the Italian language and culture was a highlight of writing this book. Here you'll find some of my most used words and phrases.

Italian - English

Cazzo - Fuck

tesoro - Sweetheart

soffione - Dandelion

Grazie - Thank you

Porca troia - Holy shit

Santo cielo - Holy sky

Che stress - How stressful

Stai bene - You're okay

Ti amo tanto - I love you

Mi fai eccitare - You make me horny

Non posso vivere senza di te - I can't live without you

Facciamo l'amore - Let's make love

Ti voglio scopare - I want to fuck you

Chi non risica non rosica - No risk, no reward

Quasi meglio del sesso - Almost better than sex

Mi fai impazzire - You make me crazy

Mi piaci da impazzire - I like you like crazy

É normale avere paura - It's okay to be afraid

Dicktionary

For those of you who'd like to find (or avoid) the smut quickly, it can be found in the following chapters:

- Chapter Sixteen
- Chapter Seventeen
- Chapter Twenty-One
- Chapter Twenty-Three
- Chapter Thirty-Five
- Chapter Thirty-Six
- Chapter Forty-Four

Spread those pages.

Content Warnings

Please be aware, *Even Exchange* contains topics that could be uncomfortable for some readers. These include but are not limited to a cheating ex, alcohol consumption, vulgar language, consensual sexually explicit content, pregnancy, male main character is not the father, discussions of abortion, light bondage, death, murder on page, blood, graphic physical violence, domestic violence, domestic abuse from a parent, guns, and gun violence on page.

Should you need to speak to someone regarding domestic violence, please reach out to 1-800-799-SAFE (7233), the National Domestic Abuse Hotline. Your voice matters.

Should you be having a mental health crisis, please reach out to 9-8-8, The National Suicide and Crisis Lifeline. Your mental health is important. Your life is important.

Should you need to speak to someone regarding sexual assault, please reach out to 800-656-HOPE (4673), The National Sexual Assault Hotline. Your voice matters.

About the Author

Hailey Dickert is a contemporary romance author born in a small coastal Florida town who grew up writing songs in her bedroom.

When she's not writing at her kitchen table or in her favorite local brewery, Dickert spends most of her time reading, making memories with her husband and two sons, and running an online book store (Scribbles Book Shop) focused on selling signed books by 150+ authors. An admitted sports fanatic, she feeds her addiction to football by watching the Miami Dolphins games on Sunday afternoons.

Keep in touch with Hailey Dickert via the web:
Website: haileydickert.com
Book Shop: scribblesbookshop.com
Facebook: https://www.facebook.com/haileydickert/
Instagram: https://www.instagram.com/haileydickertauthor/
TikTok: https://tiktok.com/@haileydickertauthor/

www.ingramcontent.com/pod-product-compliance
Lightning Source LLC
Chambersburg PA
CBHW010603310726
48969CB00010B/2544